THE
STAR
FAMILY

a mystery

Theresa Crater

For Ralph Jacob Crater

"And the end of all our exploring
Will be to arrive where we started
And know the place for the first time."

~ T.S. Eliot

PROLOGUE

Philip Martin parked his Porsche in a strip mall in Alexandria several blocks away from his destination and started walking up the hill. He preferred the anonymity of a public parking lot. No little old ladies peeking out through their curtains and calling the police to report strange cars in the neighborhood. He passed neat brick houses with tidy postage-stamp yards. Up the hill a few blocks, the houses grew larger—eighties split-levels with deeper yards and more shrubbery. Piece of cake to break into. Farther up, the lots expanded to half-acres and the houses vied for attention. He passed a stone and glass beauty set in trees, an English Tudor, a Frank Lloyd Wright wannabe.

He jogged ahead and waited until a Lincoln Town car arrived at the gate of the Queen Anne he was headed for. He paused in front of the neighboring house. The driver leaned out to identify himself to the security man, and Philip took advantage of this distraction to slip behind a large box hedge next to the drive. Unnoticed by the man at the gate, he jumped a small fence and made his way to the side of the house. He paused and straightened his jacket, wiped his damp shoes on the mat and tried the kitchen door. It opened and he slipped in.

He grabbed a couple of crab puffs off a tray and popped them in his mouth. Then stepped into a hall bathroom, washed his hands and patted down his hair. He cleaned some mud off his shoes with a hand towel and tossed it into the cabinet beneath the sink, then slipped into the front room.

Their host, Henry Coche, stood in the foyer greeting one of the last guests, Valentin Knight. Philip stood with his hands behind his back, not drawing attention to himself by craning his neck and looking around like some rube. A group milled around the formal living room. A few were seated, receiving homage from those standing around them. No hors d'oeuvres had been served yet. Those were for later. Philip ran his tongue over his teeth to clean off any tell-tale bits of food, then took up a position just to the side of a cluster of people so that he looked as if he were part of the group. From this vantage point, he surveyed the room.

The head of the Grand Lodge of D.C. sat in a high-backed Wedgewood blue chair near the window, his clipped grey hair neat above a white shirt and blue tie discreetly decorated with the compass and square. Beside him stood a senator, the head of an important lobbying group and the assistant director of an intelligence organization. Across the room seated on chintz sofas on either side of a marble fireplace, Philip recognized two other heads of different lodges, each attended by equally powerful men. No women were present.

The front door closed and Henry Coche followed his last guest into the room. Coche stood an easy six feet, his brown hair graying at the temple. Dressed in a blue, boardroom suit, he was unremarkable in appearance. But, it would be a serious mistake to underestimate him. Coche owned the most powerful conglomerate in the world, aside from the Saudi family, of course.

His guest, however, did stand out. Elegant and cultured, Valentin Knight gathered the attention of the room. He wore a designer suit and a silk ascot decorated with a small winged Isis pattern. His neatly trimmed hair was a venerable silver. The most revered mystic in America.

Conversation stopped and those standing turned to face their host. Coche waited until every eye was on him, then said, "I am so pleased to have you all here for this very special evening. I'm sure you have heard about the recent prophecy." A few heads nodded. Coche paused and looked around the room, acknowledging a few of the more eminent guests.

"Ordinarily, we would conduct such an event in one of our temples, but discretion is of the utmost importance, especially if there is any veracity to these predictions. Our prophet—" he placed a slight emphasis on the word to suggest this was a question still to be decided "—awaits us in my private sanctuary." He stepped aside and extended his arm toward two young men who turned and began to lead the group through a corridor and down a flight of steps of polished wood. Lapis blue carpet runners softened their steps.

On the bottom floor, Philip followed the group down a long hall of Italian tile, avoiding notice for now. Nooks held marble statues of various Egyptian and Greek deities. Philip didn't know all their names. They were ushered into a long room, this one tiled in black and white squares. More statues dotted the sides at intervals. Simple wooden chairs lined the spaces in between. A flat wooden table stood in the middle surrounded by three candelabras. At the far end of the room, steps led up to a raised platform flanked by a black and white marble pillar on either side. A row of what Philip would describe as thrones lined the dais. He found a seat near a statue of Venus—this one he recognized—between two inset lights so his face was in shadow while the group sorted itself out according to their notions of who was more important. The heads of the various lodges took their places on the platform on either side of an elaborately carved chair. Knight entered last and took this seat. No one wore robes or regalia.

After a few minutes, Coche came in accompanied by two people, a paunchy middle-aged man and a young wisp of a fellow, his hair like spun gold. This man carried something wrapped in dark blue velvet. Coche called over the two attendants who'd led them to this room, whispered to one, then gestured for the two guests to join him at the altar. The paunchy man produced a three-legged silver holder and placed it on the gleaming wood. The younger one, who Philip had surmised was the alleged prophet, unwrapped his burden. It turned out to be a large, perfectly clear crystal ball.

Philip hid a smile behind his hand. Could they be more stereotypical? But the others in the room watched these proceedings with serious faces. Philip turned his attention back to the altar in the middle. The attendants brought a chair for each of the guests and they settled near the crystal that reflected the light from the candelabras surrounding the table.

Coche walked to the dais, taking the throne next to Knight's. Valentin Knight surprised Philip by leading the group in a brief meditation. He supposed Coche was softening the old man up. Knight asked them first to relax their muscles, then breathe rhythmically. Philip had always found these exercises practical, clearing the mind of clutter while in the field. He'd grown accustomed to doing them regularly. After a series of energy flows which Philip found rather fanciful, Knight spoke, his voice soft, but easy to hear with the well-designed acoustics of the room. "Our guest will go deeper into trance and tell us what he finds."

The young man had scooted his chair up to the altar and now sat with a hand on either side of the crystal. He peered into the sphere, occasionally humming vowel sounds. After about two minutes, his eyes seemed to lose focus. Then, as if an invisible string were attached to his shirt, his back straightened. The air around him seemed to glow. He raised his head and looked around. His energy had shifted, become somehow imperial, commanding, even haughty. Entirely different from the soft young man who'd started this ritual.

"I bring you greetings from the White Brotherhood."

Philip bit his lip to keep himself from laughing, almost drawing blood.

The young man frowned at him, even though Phillip knew he'd made no outward sign. The prophet turned his focus back on Knight. "The time of the great shift is upon us now, and so it will be in each power center on the Earth, for the time spoken of has arrived."

A shudder passed through the man's frame. "In the center of the grid laid down by your ancestors lies an eight-petaled figure, just as there is another where the lost treasure is kept. There are those who would control it to stop the feeding of the grid. This will block your leadership from the new guidance."

The young man paused and cocked his head as if listening, but said no more.

What the fuck does that mean? Philip thought. *Weird syntax and vague generalizations anyone could interpret to fit their preconceived ideas.*

The young man slumped as if he'd run a long race. The paunchy assistant leaned over to steady him so he wouldn't slip out of his chair. A stir rustled through the group. They glanced around at each other, some perplexed, some obviously in awe, but no one broke protocol. They remained silent. Eventually all eyes returned to Knight, who made a curious gesture in the air, then said, "We thank you for your message, Lodge of the White Brotherhood." He seemed perfectly serious. "Is this all?"

The young man remained slumped in his chair. His assistant leaned over and whispered something in his ear. The prophet shook his head and his assistant stood and intoned in a sanctimonious voice, "The White Brotherhood has concluded its message."

They might as well have said nothing in Philip's opinion, but he wasn't paid for that. He was paid for action. He'd receive his instructions later. At least he'd enjoyed some excellent crab puffs.

The assistant wrapped an arm around the prophet, tucking a hand under the other's arm pit, and lifted him from the chair with an audible grunt. Philip drew back at the sound. The paunchy man led the prophet from the room, leaving behind his crystal ball, silver stand and a length of blue velvet. So they weren't departing yet.

Philip waited for the buzz of conversation that usually followed group events so he could slip out and wait in an empty room, but it never came. Instead they all rose, allowing their dignitaries to walk out first, then followed in single file. Philip blended in as best he could. Each man seemed absorbed in his own thoughts about the display they'd just witnessed. Halfway down the hallway, the group began to break into clusters, talking amongst themselves.

Philip slipped into a dark bedroom farther down and waited for the group to move on. After a few minutes, the hallway grew silent. Now he could sneak out. Just as he reached for the door, it opened inward. He stepped back into the relative darkness deeper in the room. The light switched on and two table lamps on either side of the bed illumined his hiding place.

One of the young attendants who'd led them into the temple stood facing him. "Mr. Coche asked that you wait for him in the library."

The attendant stepped aside and gestured toward the door, then walked beside Philip up the steps. The buzz of conversation and clink of dishes grew louder. To his relief, the assistant turned a sharp left and they climbed another flight, leaving the group behind to speculate about what the White Brotherhood's message meant.

The assistant opened one of a set of double doors and stood aside. Philip entered a large library filled with leather bound volumes, the classics, English and American literature, gleaming and untouched by the look of them.

"May I get you some refreshment?"

Philip started to say no, but then thought he'd like some time alone here—to pick the lock in the desk across the room. "Please. I missed dinner."

The attendant stepped to the door and pushed a button in a panel on the wall, spoke into it, then stood back. "Your food will be up shortly."

"Thank you." Philip hid his disappointment. "How long have you worked for Mr. Coche?"

The man paused a moment, then said, "My orders are to wait with you. I'm afraid I'm not to answer any questions." He inclined his head apologetically.

"I see." Philip studied him a moment. "Mind if I look around?"

His guardian extended a hand in invitation. "Please."

On the wall across from the bookshelves hung a painting that depicted a winding stair with elegant, rather Art Deco looking women who carried pitchers and platters upwards. Two angels descended with books, their heads bent in conversation. Higher up more women walked hand in hand. The blue stars at the bottom gave way to gold, then a round disc with rays. He leaned forward and found a plaque—*Jacob's Ladder* by William Blake.

Philip moved to the first shelf and started reading titles. Biographies of political leaders, political commentary—these spines seemed to have been bent at least once. He took one down at random and found a signature on the title page. "Thanks for everything, George W."

Before he could scan another shelf, his food arrived and he sat in one of the chairs and made a show of eating with relish. "Eat when you can," his father had told him many times during his spare childhood. "You never know where your next meal is coming from." Philip worked out enough that he didn't need to worry about occasional rich food, so he downed more crab puffs, spicy tuna sushi, beef sandwich wedges, vegetables and cheese on fancy crackers. He washed it all down with an excellent red wine. He'd have to ask the vintage. Just as he sat back and the assistant took his tray, the door opened and Henry Coche walked in.

"I was finally able to get away."

Philip stood.

Coche nodded at the assistant, who left, closing the door behind him. Philip didn't hear any more footsteps, so he assumed the man had taken up his station just outside. Coche sat in the chair across from Philip and gestured for him to sit back down. "I wanted you to observe the event tonight and see who was involved."

Philip sat up a little straighter. "I noted the more important guests. Would you be willing to give me the full roster?"

Coche hesitated a second before agreeing. "We need to figure out what this prophet means by the eight-sided figure, but what I want you to focus on first is finding the painting."

"You think the treasure he mentioned is a lost painting?"

"We think there's a connection."

Philip stopped himself from shifting in his chair. He didn't want to telegraph his attitude. "The comments were quite vague. Do you have any more details?"

"We have reason to believe that the lost painting is one by William Blake."

Philip glanced at the one hanging above the mantel.

Coche smiled. "Yes, another Blake."

"How did you reach this conclusion? Are you sure you aren't letting your own taste affect your judgment?"

"From other sessions, plus historical records. A few groups in North America had contact with William Blake and his family."

"And you think the message is referring to this continent?"

"Nobody's certain, but the plan is to investigate possibilities close to home before extending the search."

"And the grid? Any thoughts on that?"

Coche pointed to the bookshelves farther along the wall. "Lots of people have written about energy grids being laid down before buildings were started. More grids are supposed to exist around the world, but we think these messages are aimed at the U.S."

Coche reached into his pocket and took out a piece of paper. "About the painting. The occupant of this house has family ties back to Blake. She might have originals. We—I want you to start here. Then we'll focus on the grid problem."

Philip wondered briefly the identity of this 'we'. He'd find out. He took the slip of paper and glanced at it. He kept his expression neutral, concealing his surprise. Definitely not a place he'd been expecting.

CHAPTER ONE

The sharp ring of the house phone cut through the night, startling Jane from a deep sleep. The green numbers on the alarm read 4:33 a.m. She listened for the machine downstairs to announce the caller. The mechanized voice droned something, but she couldn't make it out. Was a deal falling apart somewhere in the world where it was afternoon and she was expected to be available? She ran through the list in her mind. England, Germany, Saudi Arabia. Nothing in South America, not this month. They'd just have to wait. She closed her eyes and snuggled into the pillow.

Maybe somebody died.

She fumbled for the phone, but the answering machine beat her to it. She lifted her head and listened. The thread of a frail voice drifted up the stairs like smoke from a cigarette, triggering something from long ago. She couldn't put her finger on it exactly. Not a family member. Who?

Jane grabbed the phone from under the bed, but the machine downstairs clicked off. She poked the button to see the readout, but it said "Private Caller."

"Later," she mumbled, pulling the covers over her head, but sleep would not come. After a while, Jane heaved a sigh and checked the time again. She'd had six hours. More than usual.

The needle spray of the shower finished waking her. Jane threw on some sweats and made her way down the stairs of her townhouse. She pushed the play button on the answering machine. The tape whirred as it rewound—quaint technology she supposed, but remembered when these were a marvel. She still hadn't given up her land line. The lawyers preferred them.

"Jane Catherine, is that you? Hello?" The woman's voice had thinned with age, so much so that Jane still didn't recognize it. But it plucked at her memory like wind on an Aeolian harp. "This is Emma. Emma Essig."

She hit the pause button, finally remembering.

The tick tock of the metronome that had sat on the window sill in Miss Essig's living room sounded in her ear. The forefinger tapped on the side of the grand piano, the nail smooth, the polish clear, followed by that voice.

"*Adagio*, please Jane. The piece slows here," Miss Essig said, her eyes closed above the lace collar of her china blue sweater. "We have soared to the heights—" she lifted her arms like a ballerina "—and now we allow ourselves space—" her arms lowered to form a circle in front of her chest, if one used the word 'chest' in association with Miss Essig "—and time for the listener to regain her balance. To feel the change the music has wrought in us." She opened her eyes and fixed them on Jane's mouth, busily chewing gum.

"Oh." Jane hunched her shoulders. "Excuse me."

Without a word, Miss Essig plucked a tissue from a box in a crocheted cover that picked up the russets and browns in the drapes. Jane stuck her gum inside, wrapping it carefully before handing it over to Miss Essig, who put it into a small waste can tucked neatly in the corner, then dried her fingers on a second tissue. Jane's cheeks flamed.

"Now again."

The memory cleared, and Jane hit the play button on the answering machine.

"The letter I wrote to you was returned yesterday." Miss Essig paused to catch her breath. "George found your number for me on the computer."

Jane wondered who George was. As far as she knew, Miss Essig had never married and certainly had no children. A former student or nephew?

"I'm sorry to call you unannounced, but I really must speak with you." Miss Essig tried to catch her breath again. "You see, dear, the lot has gone to you." The message ended here, and the machine recited the time of the call in its tinny, vaguely female voice.

'The lot'. What in the world did she mean by that? Sounded like a piece of property, but somehow she didn't think so. Jane moved over to her computer and Googled the phrase. The search results indicated a short lived TV show and the name of a restaurant. No help there.

Jane dialed Miss Essig's number, but got a busy signal. She touched the star pendant she still wore, a confirmation gift from her old music teacher. Hanging up, she switched on her bank of work computers. Her firm had sold their building and were in the process of moving, so she'd set up here temporarily. Temporarily had stretched into two weeks. She'd been able to handle most of her work from home and toyed with the idea of making the arrangement permanent. Except she'd miss out on all the office gossip and jockeying for position that anyone who wanted to keep their edge had to stay on top of. She checked her emails. Nothing important.

Jane pulled her favorite dark roast beans from the freezer and put them in the grinder, inhaling the rich aroma as the machine chewed them into the right consistency. Better than the taste, really. She emptied them into the coffee maker. When the hot liquid poured out, she shoved her mug under it, then added half and half, her guilty secret. Mug in hand, she drifted over to the market charts on the monitors, all arrayed on her desk, looking like scales climbing high into the treble range, dropping down to the bass, rising again. Sometimes she felt like a conductor, the Asian markets the flute and wind instruments, Europe the strings, and America percussion and big horns. Maybe a bit stereotypical, but it served.

Back to Miss Essig. Just as she reached for the phone, one of the computers gave off a warning ping. It turned out to be the Asian markets—dropping precipitously during the last few minutes. She clicked on a few stock symbols. Something to do with a new Chinese company and problems with oil contracts between them and one of her company's major investments in Saudi Arabia. No big surprise, really. She'd thought China was going to get serious about solar and wind, and urged her firm to invest in several new companies making solar panels, plug-in cars and hydrogen cell technology. Her presentation had been politely received, but Mr. Davis and his staff seemed more interested in the startlingly long legs of their latest hire than her idea. These girls didn't realize how much work it had taken to get women into the hallowed halls of business as anything other than secretaries. Women her age had endured a lot of butt pinching, rude jokes and propositions before the harassment laws had grown any teeth. And now the young ones laughed and played along, dressed like sluts, maybe even slept their way to the top. "Why not use all the weapons in my arsenal," the colt-legged Tami had asked.

So women can move beyond the oldest profession, Jane had thought, but kept it to herself. Maybe bumping their heads against that infamous glass ceiling would wake them up. She reached for her old outrage. It used to warm her, but she couldn't stir up a flame from those ashes. Let the next generation figure it out for themselves.

The other markets were responding to the Chinese dip, and she watched the ripple effects. When she figured out the trend, she started issuing orders about moving money. By the time she'd finally gotten most things squared away, the bottom of her computer screen read 8:57 a.m.

She stretched her back and reached for the phone. Maybe she could reach Miss Essig now, but the phone rang before she could pick it up. The display listed her firm's name. She answered.

"Jane? Mr. Davis has been trying to get a hold of you," his assistant said, her voice just shy of scolding.

Honestly, the nerve of these neophytes.

"Thank you, Crissy," Jane answered evenly.

Her boss came on the line. "Haven't checked your email yet, Frey?" He called all his managers by their last name.

"Of course, Mr. Davis. I've been working since five this morning. Got ahead of that dip in China." She opened her work account and found the message. Just a brief note asking her to make an appointment sent only half an hour ago. Something was up if he was calling about this already.

"China? Oh yes, good work." Then he spat it out. "Thing is, I need to see you this afternoon. How about two?"

"Certainly, sir. Are there any projects you'd like to discuss in particular?"

"Talk to you then." He hung up before she could say anything else.

Odd. She poked around the company website, sniffing out hints. All her reports had been approved, her division's numbers were higher than most, the clients happy, and the company had recovered well from the recession—well enough, although her private accounts still needed some attention. Maybe the company was finally ready to let her into the boy's club and promote her to director. Maybe hell was freezing over, too.

Jane spent another hour on client accounts, then ate a light lunch and took her time dressing in her pin-striped suit. She was glad they were back in style. Nobody would guess this skirt and jacket was over twenty years old. A few minutes before two o'clock, she pulled her BMW into the parking garage and rode the elevator up to the nineteenth floor. She walked to the main office, the heels of her pumps sinking into the deep carpet.

Crissy greeted her coolly. "He'll be with you soon." She nodded toward the waiting area and did not offer any water or coffee.

Jane sat on the edge of a grey leather chair, the nervous zinging in her limbs giving way to a tight knot in her stomach. This was not the way the new Director of Global Investment Management would be treated. Maybe Crissy had another favorite and was disappointed. That one was a political animal inside and out. They all were, this new generation. Sell their first born for the key to the executive washroom.

Oh, stop it, she chided herself. *You sound like an old lady*

Jane watched the play of light and shadow on the mountains. Such a commanding view. It still might be hers soon. Crissy answered yet another call, then hung up and looked over. "He'll see you now."

Jane nodded and stood up, pulling down the back of her jacket. Her hands were cold. Crissy opened the door, and Jane stepped inside. She kept her gaze on Mr. Davis, his grey hair matching his charcoal suit, and not the panoramic view of the mountains. Out of the corner of her eye, she caught a glimpse of long, graceful legs.

Mr. Davis nodded at Jane, then turned to the other woman. "That will be all, Tami."

The statuesque blond stood, her blue pin-striped skirt falling to mid-thigh, longer than usual. Her four-inch heels made her almost as tall as Davis and showed off her well-toned calves.

"Thank you, sir." Her voice suggested an intimacy Jane hadn't been aware of. Davis cleared his throat and pushed a few papers around on his desk. Tami turned to Jane and nodded, her eyes predatory. She strutted past and let herself out. Cheery babble between Tami and Crissy rose up before the door closed.

"Thank you for coming, Frey. Please have a seat."

So I'm Frey, but the new one is Tami.

The knot in Jane's stomach hardened to stone, but she schooled her face to polite interest. She settled in a wooden chair with rounded arms, which she resisted gripping. "How can I help you, sir?"

Davis rustled a stack of papers with his forefinger, his eyes turned down. Then he shook his head. "Ah hell, I'll come straight to the point. With our recent money problems, we've decided to combine Global Investment and Global Research into one department. We only need one director. Upper management has decided to give it to Tami."

Jane blinked. "Tami, sir?"

He grimaced. "I'm afraid so."

She opened her mouth, but finding nothing acceptable to say, closed it again. Tami had only worked here a couple of years. She must have family connections—or she'd slept with the entire board of directors. Those were the only two possibilities. CEOs usually didn't hire on the basis of sexual favors. At least she hoped they didn't, but it might explain some of the ridiculous decisions that had led to the financial collapse a few years back. Tami probably looked good behind a desk—or bending over one.

Tami. Crissy. Didn't they have real names? She forced herself to take a slow breath to stop her train of thought.

Davis watched her like a man trapped in a cage with a cougar.

"And you have confidence in her?" Jane asked in an even voice, trying to indicate that he wouldn't be dealing with any hysteria from her.

"Oh, she'll do well enough." Davis waved his hand dismissively.

When he didn't say anything else, she asked, "What does the firm have in mind for me, sir?" She was going to make him spell it out.

Davis stared at her, eyes wide with disbelief, before catching himself. He shifted his gaze to his desk, his neck reddening. Why was he so uncomfortable? Surely a man at his level had experience reorganizing departments, even hiring and firing, only they wouldn't call it that. Did Tami have something on him?

"I've orders to downsize my area," he said. "We have an excellent severance package in mind."

Now Jane did grip the arms of the chair. So it was over—her career here. And everywhere else, most likely. No one would hire a fifty-something female financial manager. Not in this market. She looked back up to find an expression of sorrow on Davis's face.

"I'm sorry about this. I really am. If it's any consolation, I voted for you."

"Thank you, sir." She nodded, widening her eyes to keep tears away. "If it's all the same to you, I'd like to study the offer in private. Consult with my attorneys." She only had one, but plural sounded better.

"Of course." He stood eagerly, his relief at being spared a longer scene obvious.

Who does he take me for? she wondered.

"And you'll be sending someone around to collect the company's computers from my apartment?" She'd taken all her things out of the old office before the move and hadn't brought back anything personal. Jane wondered if somewhere in the recesses of her brain she'd known. She pushed the thought down. She'd dissect it all later.

"Of course. We'll be in touch." He laid what he must imagine was a comforting hand on her arm, but it only forced her to be sure she wasn't shaking. They walked to the door. "We appreciate your service. I think you'll be pleased with our offer."

She almost thanked him, but caught herself in time and simply nodded. Jane walked out of the office, eyes forward. A quiet laugh came from Crissy's desk just as the door closed.

Why do they hate us so? she wondered. *If it wasn't for us, they wouldn't even be here.*

Once Jane reached home, she turned off the bank of work computers, resisting the childish urge to reformat the hard drives. She took a loop around her apartment, aimlessly picking things up, then putting them down again. She returned to her personal computer and punched up her financial portfolio. She'd hoped for a couple more years to rebuild it. The severance package would have to make up the difference. She'd insist on that. But what would she do with the rest of her life? She'd traveled the world on her job, worked eighteen-hour days for years.

A hot bath. A safe next step. Jane climbed the stairs and found some rose bubble bath from a Christmas gift basket she'd gotten at some company function and dumped it in, watching the white suds rise like clouds in her voluminous Jacuzzi. She sank into the water and covered any exposed flesh with hot wash cloths as if she were treating strained muscles. After a minute, she sank beneath the foam. Her pulse beat steady in her ear. Surfacing, she took a breath, then submerged again. She lay under the surface, only her nostrils above the water level like a hippopotamus, soaking in the heat. She shifted her position, creating waves. Inhaled some water and came up sputtering.

The phone rang. She let it go to the answering machine.

"I'm calling for Mrs. Jane Frey."

Not Mrs., Jane thought. She didn't recognize the voice.

"My name is Anna Szeges. I believe Emma Essig left you a message earlier. She needs to speak with you urgently, Mrs.

Frey. Emma is not well. I believe she told you that the lot fell to you. Please call back." Then she gave her number.

"What the fuck does that mean?" Jane yelled.

She stood up, suds sluicing down her body, then dried off. She slipped into her morning sweats and went down the stairs. Listening with her musically trained ear to the voices, she replayed both messages again. Miss Essig—she could never call her Emma—sounded weak but peaceful. Anna's voice carried the overtones of irritation beneath that polite veneer, and something else—worry was it? Not quite that simple.

Something tickled her memory. She turned to her computer again and this time typed in the word 'Moravian' before 'lot' and came up with a list of scholarly articles. One sentence caught her eye. "In contrast, all of the supernatural elements of the *Moravian lot* drawings appeared mundanely; no voice of God or revelatory vision descended . . ."

Jane stared at the screen. What could this have to do with Miss Essig? More to the point, what did it have to do with her? She clicked the first link and it led to an article describing this decision-making process. Three pieces of paper were put into a box. One had the word 'yes' written on it, the second the word 'no' and the third was left blank. The petitioners prayed before drawing one piece of paper. When the answer to a question could not be found by reason alone, her ancestors had resorted to this technique. They felt that the hand of God guided the choice, so this was a way to discover his will. At first they had used it sparingly, then more frequently during the mid-eighteenth century. After that, a bishop had warned against excessive reliance on the lot, so its use was curtailed and it was consulted only for dilemmas or when there was deep disagreement even after extensive discussion.

Superstitious nonsense, she thought.

Jane tapped her finger against her chin. Surely the contemporary Moravians weren't still using the lot, but the message suggested otherwise. She felt certain that Miss Essig still attended church. Her house stood right next to one. She'd directed the choir forever.

Jane wondered for the first time in years if she still considered herself a Moravian. She'd spent her childhood going to Sunday school, then to service when she was old enough, been confirmed at thirteen, sang in the choir. She still had fond memories of Christmas Eve—the Candlelight Lovefeast, when the lights were dimmed except for the Advent Star that hung above the sanctuary and the *dieners* came out, handing the beeswax candles trimmed with red crepe paper down the pews. Then the person sitting next to the aisle lit their candle, and the light was passed down until the whole church glowed and they sang—what had that hymn been? On the last verse they'd lifted their candles high.

Tears filled her eyes. She wiped at them half-heartedly. Surely she was just upset about the job. Being fired was a new experience, but not enough to make her have a sudden conversion. Yet the childhood memories kept flooding back.

On Easter the brass band played at the street light on the corner, way before dawn, to call them to the sunrise service. The day before, her father and his siblings met at God's Acre, the graveyard in Old Salem, and washed the identical white marble headstones of relatives, then put out flowers. Some graves had two arrangements, but her aunt hadn't liked that. "It makes it look like the family couldn't get together," she'd said. Jane still sent a check every year to her cousin Frank to cover the expense of flowers for her own parents' graves. She missed the rows of neat white headstones and blooms atop green grass, the trees and rows of jonquils in full bloom. That was spring for her, not the tentative green braving the heavy, wet snow of Colorado.

Yet the church was still small. If anyone ever asked her what religion she'd grown up in, their response to her one word answer, "Moravian," was usually a blank look sometimes followed by, "Oh, I used to know someone who was a Mennonite. Did you have electricity when you were growing up?"

"Different group," she'd answer. "We're modern."

As an adult, Jane had come to think that being Moravian was a bit like being Jewish. It was a cultural identity, even ethnic for the settlers of Salem and Bethlehem, and you were still Moravian whether you were observant—the Jewish expression—or not. Jane had ceased to be observant a long time ago.

She picked up the phone and dialed the number on the calls-received display. It rang through to an answering machine. Just as she took a breath to leave a message, someone answered. Jane gave her name, then added, "I'm returning Miss Essig's call."

The woman who'd answered introduced herself as Anna. "We believe Sister Emma has been waiting for you before she passes."

Sister? Jane thought. *Has she joined a cult*? Then the word 'passes' hit her.

"Miss Essig is dying?"

"She is in her nineties, dear. The Lord is calling her home."

This last phrase brought Jane up short. Just how fundamentalist was this woman? But Jane didn't know any Moravian fundamentalists. That had been the other side of the family. Finally she said, "I have to admit I was a bit confused by the message. Miss Essig and I haven't been in touch for years."

A soft chuckle, then, "I can well imagine. But if you have some free time, I hope you can come and say goodbye. Hear what she has to say."

Now it was Jane's turn to laugh. "Free time is one thing I have in abundance at the moment."

"How serendipitous."

Jane was reassured. Fundamentalists did not use words like 'serendipitous'. At least, she didn't think so.

"But I'd hurry. She could go at any time."

CHAPTER TWO

Jane drove through the brilliant fall colors of North Carolina in early November, enjoying the vivid reds, incandescent oranges and even the browns. More than just the yellows of Colorado. Once she'd decided to come to Winston-Salem, the arrangements had fallen into place easily. She'd booked an early flight to Greensboro from Denver. As for work, she really didn't care when they got their computers back.

She angled off the interstate and headed down Main Street with its rows of white wood-framed houses. She slowed at the one her parents had lived in when she'd been born. No white flowers bordered the walk now. Anna Szeges had urged her to get to Miss Essig's as quickly as possible, so she passed the turn that led to her grandfather's old farmhouse. His fields had sprouted houses since then, instead of the harvest of vegetables her grandmother and aunts had canned in that hot kitchen over a wood stove. She'd have to save the full-blown nostalgia tour for later.

Yet when she turned down toward the Washington Park neighborhood and slowed a bit, the memories flew at her like bugs hitting a windshield. There was the house where her brother had mowed the lawn, next the large brick ranch house where she'd first eaten pizza, and the small white one where she'd learned about sex from the book her friend's mother had bought. She shook her head against the swarm. On the next block she steeled herself, then pulled in front of the English

Tudor belonging to Miss Essig, the house that still appeared in her dreams after all these years, the one that as a child she'd secretly pretended belonged to her family.

The front looked much the same with the tall, spreading evergreens sheltering the horse-shoe drive that disappeared behind the house, the neat rows of trimmed hedges lining the front walk, the golden and brown house itself rising majestic and unexpected in this mixed-up neighborhood. The lands surrounding these colonial mansions had been sold off, leaving only the four surrounding the old church. The buyers had cut the trees and built first the large, respectable brick houses of lawyers, doctors and dentists, then the smaller white cottages of factory workers, each with the same floor plan. Her grandfather's farm had sold them vegetables and eggs.

She wondered if Miss Essig had kept the full acre her house occupied, surrounded then by boxwoods and containing the most wondrous gardens, at least the most wondrous a six-year-old could imagine. Jane parked and made her way up the walk, past the ginkgo tree with its green fans for leaves, the first tree to turn a bright yellow in fall. This late in the year it was bare. She stepped up to the covered porch and paused, gathering herself, then knocked.

For a few minutes, no one answered and she admired the ivy in the beds next to the house, the flagstone path that led to the screened-in porch on the side. A sound interrupted the nostalgia she'd promised not to indulge in. The dark oak door opened to reveal a tall woman, her grey hair caught up in a bun. She wore a navy dress that buttoned down the front covered by a white apron. Steel-rimmed glasses finished the look. Cool blue eyes assessed Jane. "May I help you?"

Jane recognized the voice of Anna Szeges. "I'm Jane Frey."

The cool veneer melted and Anna pushed open the screen door. "Thank God. You've made it just in the nick of time. I was beginning to doubt." She said this as if chiding herself. "Please come in."

Jane stepped into the familiar foyer, the cool soothing her. A coat rack still stood to the right accompanied by the umbrella stand. Her eyes strayed to the left to catch the gleam of a mahogany dining table and the small crystal chandelier. Everything was the same.

Anna grasped her forearm and said in a low voice, "Let's go right up." She stepped forward, but Jane didn't move with her. Anna frowned. "Don't worry. I'll stay with you."

Now that the moment was upon her, Jane was unprepared to meet her dying mentor, but she'd flown here to do just that, so she followed Anna up the stairs and down the hall, past the laundry chute she'd longed to jump down as a child—she'd never found the nerve—into the master bedroom. Several women about the same age as Anna clustered around the four-poster bed. The room smelled of medicine and sickness. A hint of lavender almost masked the unpleasantness. At the head of the bed, a man with dark hair and matching intense brown eyes read from a bible open in his hands. A white sash decorated with a lamb carrying a cross was tucked under the lapels of his suit coat. He looked up at Anna and paused.

Anna nodded and turned toward the bed. "Jane is here, dear."

A fragile hand, the veins large and blue, reached up and a frail voice asked, "Jane? Where is she?"

Anna turned and reached for Jane, pulling her close. Miss Essig's emaciated body barely raised the covers. Her arms were the sticks of birch trees, and her cheeks almost transparent. But those eyes, the blue of a pale winter sky, were the same. "Here I am," Jane said.

Sibilant whispers rose like a gentle wind from the chorus of women behind her. Miss Essig reached her bony hands out for Jane, who sat on the edge of the bed, capturing them in her own. They were cold and spoke of the grave, but Jane remembered them fleshed out, with her one pearl and ruby ring flashing as they danced over white and black keys, calling forth the most beautiful music she had ever heard.

"I'm happy to be going home, Jane. Remember this is a time to rejoice." Her voice was as thin as an onion skin.

"Yes, Miss Essig," Jane said, as she had said so many times before, "I remember."

Someone started to play the grand piano in the living room on the floor just below them. A violin joined in, then a woodwind. Miss Essig closed her eyes. Her breathing slowed. Anna settled on the opposite side of the bed, and the minister watched from a comfortable distance behind Jane's shoulder. The women started to hum the tune, faint and soft, their complex harmonies twining like the ivy outside. Peace filled the room.

"Just think, Anna." Miss Essig strained to speak. They all leaned forward to hear her. "Soon I'll see Him—and all our old friends."

"Yes, dear." Anna patted her shoulder. They listened to the music for another minute, then she said, "Perhaps you should tell Jane why you've called for her."

"Oh, yes." Miss Essig opened her eyes, which shone with an almost childlike joy. "You see, Jane, I must find just the right woman." Everyone in the room nodded as if this were plain as day. Miss Essig caught her breath and said, "The lot went to you, my dear."

"So you said, Miss Essig," Jane said, "but I don't really know what that means."

"Oh, don't worry, dear. Anna will explain it all." She closed her eyes for a moment, then opened them again, her brow furrowing. "But will you accept it?"

Jane hesitated, not wanting to vex a dying woman. "Accept what?"

Miss Essig looked surprised. "Why, my house, of course."

Jane shook her head to clear it. Surely she'd heard wrong. "Your house?" she repeated.

Miss Essig nodded.

"But you must have family or someone close." She glanced around the room, but all eyes were on the dying woman.

Miss Essig shook her head slightly, then struggled to catch her breath. "No, you," was all she could manage.

What in the world was happening? Jane looked around at the group, the women humming, their eyes moist but at peace. Anna sat waiting, collected, offering no pressure to decide one way or another. They were losing their close friend, but showed no agitation or fear.

Jane realized she still loved this frail bird of a woman, whose elegance and manners camouflaged a steel will, an uncompromising moral compass that she never forced on anyone, but that had left Jane yearning for that kind of certainty within herself. And her talent. Her music had soared and whispered, flirted and comforted, finally leading Jane and all who could accompany her to a silent, secret place inside that answered all questions and soothed all aches.

Anna's voice broke her reverie. She repeated the question that Miss Essig, who lay on the bed struggling for breath, could not ask again. "Will you accept this house and all that it entails?"

Jane looked up at her, hearing something more in the question. "Entails?"

Miss Essig's breath took on an ominous rattle and her eyes lost focus, yet her hands clung to Jane's.

"I don't—" Jane began.

"I'll explain everything later," Anna interrupted, "but she needs to hear your answer."

It was all happening too quickly. Jane shook her head.

"No?" Anna asked. "Are you refusing this offer?"

Miss Essig struggled and caught one breath. "Please, Jane."

A sharp pain tore Jane's heart, as if a dagger had cut open some covering and exposed her rawest emotion. Her left hand flew to her chest, pressing against her breast bone to ease the ache. Her right still cradled Miss Essig's feather-light hands. Jane nodded her head, hot tears splashing onto the cold fingers. "All right."

"You accept?" the relentless Anna asked.

But Jane's answer was for Miss Essig. "Yes. I'll take care of things for you." How much trouble could it be, after all, to see to her meager belongings, sell the house and distribute the proceeds properly? Then her old childhood passion for the place and all that it had meant to her swelled up like a chorus of violins. "I'll cherish your home for you. I always have. I'll always love you."

"Thank you, Jane." The cold hand reached up and touched Jane's star pendant that had slipped out from under her blouse. "You still have it. And the ribbon?"

Jane had forgotten about that. Miss Essig had given her a pink ribbon—"For your cap," she'd said—at the special ceremony her family held after her confirmation. She'd been thirteen and rolled her eyes. Moravian girls didn't wear caps in the twentieth century, but she'd accepted it gracefully and tucked it in a special box for keepsakes.

"Yes, I still have it."

"You were always such—" Miss Essig struggled for a breath. Caught it. "—a good girl."

This last cracked the dam and Jane broke down. Arms lifted her, guided her out of the room and down the stairs to a chair in the living room, where a wind quartet played softly, the piano now silent. Listening to them, Jane remembered her deeper childhood dream, not that she wanted to live in a fancy house, but to lead others with her own music to the silence Miss Essig had shown her. These people were doing just that—ushering a beloved friend through her death, spreading balm on the pain and fear of loss.

Jane squeezed her eyes shut, tears cascading down her cheeks. She'd never had the discipline or the passion to accomplish her goal. Certainly not the patience to teach children, to sit through their fumbling scales, the delicacy and surety to embarrass a gum-chewing neophyte and usher her little by little into graceful womanhood and mastery of music. Instead, she had settled for money. Jane got up and tiptoed into the library where she closed the door, threw herself on the chintz sofa and wept. The music swelled, soothing her battered heart.

The sound of a door opening reached into Jane's dream. She'd been conducting a symphony in some gilded hall. The last strains of the music still filled her head. Startled, she sat up and looked around. For a few seconds, she couldn't remember where she was. Then the shapes of the familiar room, the rows of books around the windows, the desk in the corner, the stone fireplace, the silhouettes of chairs in the dusk brought it all back.

Someone flicked on a floor lamp in the corner. The light shone amber through a Tiffany shade, revealing one of the women she'd seen upstairs. "I'm sorry to wake you," she said.

"No, it's all right." Jane sat up and rubbed her eyes. "I apologize for falling asleep on Miss Essig's sofa."

The woman lowered her rotund body to the edge of an armchair and leaned forward. "Emma passed into the more immediate presence of our Lord about an hour ago."

Jane flinched, her hand reaching out for—something.

"She went peacefully. There was no pain or struggle." The woman's tone was soothing.

Jane absorbed this. No tears came. Her fit of weeping had left her stripped clean like a tree after the first violent winter storm. She felt like herself again for the first time since sitting down in Mr. Davis's office.

"Anna said to bring you some tea." She held out a plain, white mug like they used in lovefeasts.

"Thank you, but—"

"It's chamomile."

Jane accepted the mug with another word of thanks. Then she noticed a tan and white English bulldog sitting by the door. His head drooped and his eyes expressed a soulful sadness.

"Oh, that's Winston. He's—was Miss Essig's dog." She patted the side of her leg. "Come here, boy."

The dog ignored her.

"I wanted a bulldog when I was little." Jane took a sip of tea, then squared her shoulders. "What can I do to help?"

The woman's brow soothed a bit, but her hands still twisted in her lap. "The funeral home took her not half an hour ago."

"I'm very sorry for your loss . . ." Jane paused, hoping the woman would supply her name, but she didn't notice. She just shook her head, trying not to cry, but silver tears traced a path down her weathered cheeks. She took out a white handkerchief and wiped them.

"I will miss our dear Emma, but she led a rich and blessed life."

Jane murmured her agreement.

"Oh, it might not have seemed that way from the outside." She lifted an eyebrow. Jane blushed, wondering if this woman guessed how out of place she felt with all the 'Lords' and 'blesseds' being dropped.

"Miss Essig taught me much more than music," Jane said.

The woman nodded and sat back in the armchair and gazed out the window at the deepening dark. Then she straightened her back. "Well, we have work to do. Sister Anna asked me to invite you to eat with us if you'd like. Or you could stay here. There's food in the kitchen."

A chilly wave ran up Jane's spine, a combination of Miss Essig's recent death and being left on her own to face the blank page of her life. "I think I'd like the company."

"Good. In about an hour. Anna will show you the way. She's still tidying up Emma's room." She hopped up, nimble for her size.

"Thank you . . ." She let the sentence hang in the air and this time the woman did supply her name.

"Dorothea," she answered. "Come on, boy."

Winston looked up at Dorothea, then trotted over to Jane. He circled around and laid down, his rump on her feet.

Dorothea nodded. "Good," she said.

Jane sat alone for a few more minutes trying to gather her thoughts. She should call her family, tell her aunts and uncles and assorted cousins she was here—at least until she could sort out the house. She pulled her Blackberry out of her pocket and checked for missed calls, but it had been uncharacteristically silent since her dismissal from her job. Tami had probably contacted her clients and reassigned them. She pulled up her family list and scrolled through the names, but couldn't decide who to call first. And what would she say?

I just got fired and I don't have enough money, but don't worry. Miss Essig died and left me her house, so I'm moving back and fulfilling my childhood dream of being a musician.

Was it an adult's dream, she wondered. Uncle Pat would be sure to tell her she was headed for hell fire mixing with those Moravians who weren't Pentecostal and therefore not real Christians. That's what he'd told his own sister after she'd married one, but Jane would have to pay him a visit anyway. How that stiff necked old codger had survived all his siblings was a mystery to her. She closed the list without calling anyone, switched the phone to vibrate and stuck it back in her pocket. She didn't know where all this would lead. Best to do the work that was immediately at hand.

Jane walked outside and drove her rental around the curved driveway into one of the stalls of the three-car garage. She parked next to an ancient blue Buick that sat at the end, at least forty years old but still gleaming. She retrieved her small suitcase and climbed the back steps. The door to the screen porch was open and she stepped into the hallway, paused to listen. Someone was coming down the steps, so she walked toward the front foyer she'd entered as a guest just a few hours ago.

"Oh, there you are." Anna's voice was subdued, but still the essence of competence. She took in the overnight bag. "Shall we put you in the room at the top of the stairs?"

"That sounds fine."

"I've given you fresh sheets and laid out towels. You should find everything you need."

"You shouldn't have gone to any trouble," Jane murmured the prescribed Southernism, true this time, and followed Anna up the stairs, trying not to slip into her childhood again. "You have so much to do. Please let me help."

Anna turned at the door of the room, relief flitting across her face. She acknowledged the offer with a nod. With a flick of her wrist, light flooded the room revealing a single bed with a star-burst quilt, pine night table and chest of drawers, both the color of dark honey. An old fashioned lady's dressing table with its three-paneled mirror took up one wall. Only a bottle of scent and hand mirror remained. A few dresses still hung in the closet. She glanced at Anna. "I don't want to turn anyone out."

"Dorothea's already moving back into our other house. She was here to take care of Emma." Anna dried her eyes with the back of her hand. "We all took turns, but Dorothea trained as a nurse." She looked around, twitched the quilt straighter, then said, "I'll let you freshen up, then we'll walk over in say fifteen minutes?"

Jane nodded, still wondering what she meant by 'our other house'. She'd figure it all out later. Anna shut the door and Jane sat in the rocker by the window, released from the competent ministrations of these German women who had kept her childhood running smoothly —but Szeges was a Czech or Polish name probably. When she'd stayed here as a child, another twin bed had taken up the wall where the dressing table now stood. Miss Essig had babysat for many families in the neighborhood. She and her old friend Shirley had loved this room because when the old ladies went to bed, they could slip out onto the balcony and then up the narrow stairs into the gloomy attic stuffed with old furniture, clothes, boxes of books and games—all kinds of treasures. The house had been full of beautiful things, old ladies and music—always music.

Jane went into the bathroom and washed her face, then changed into slacks and a nice shirt. She'd just finished running a brush through her hair when Anna knocked on her door. Jane followed her outside and into the back yard, where they walked through a tunnel of Chinese cherry trees, a few leaves still clinging to their branches—she'd have to stay a year to see them bloom again. Anna ducked through the opening in the hedge next to the old pear tree. Jane followed, shaking her head against the swarm of memories rising like the yellow jackets had from a fallen pear she picked up from the ground. But she'd have time for all this later. Nothing but time.

They walked east a block in the dusk, passing three small, white cottages like the ones on Broad Street, then the New Marienborn Moravian Church in its own circle of land. The roads ran off from it like spokes on a wheel. On the next block, they turned up the back drive of the brick Colonial mansion across from Washington Park. So this was the mysterious other house Anna had mentioned. She'd drooled over this one as a child too, but never gotten inside. She wondered who owned it.

Once inside, they made their way down a white hallway with a polished wood floor, then entered a long dining room where about a dozen women of varying ages sat along a rectangular table that ran the length of the room. Chatter stopped, all heads turned, and a dozen sets of eyes studied her, many kind, some frankly curious. Anna went to the head of the table, stood in front of her chair, and motioned for Jane to take a seat about half way down one side of the table. Anna sat, and everyone followed suit. They bowed their heads and recited the Moravian Blessing. Jane remembered the words from her childhood—short and simple: "Come Lord Jesus our guest to be, and bless these gifts bestowed by thee." She intoned

"Amen" and reached for a piece of bread, but the others added another verse she'd never learned. "And bless our loved ones everywhere." She snatched her hand back. "And keep them in Your loving care." Around the table a few lips twitched in amusement.

After the prayer, all eyes turned to Anna. "You are all aware that our sister Emma passed away this afternoon. It was a peaceful death and we'll have prayers for her after supper. Jane Frey has agreed to take on her house."

Nods of approval and murmurs of welcome came from around the table. Jane had to admit she was pleased not to hear any "Thank the Lords."

Two women carried in large white tureens of soup, set them down at either end of the table and lifted the tops with a bit of flourish. The aroma of earthy vegetables and green herbs filled the room, and Jane's stomach woke up for the first time in two days. She accepted two ladles when her turn came—potato soup, thick and creamy, with a faint hint of dill served with plenty of vegetables. Crusty bread fresh from the oven sat in baskets around the table. She spread butter thick on a slice. They ate mostly in silence at first, all needing this comfort food that filled the hollow places left by loss and grief. The root vegetable whispered to them of saving the spark of life through the cold of winter and waiting for spring rain and warm sun to grow once more.

After a few minutes, her immediate neighbor introduced herself as Roxanne and asked where she had been living. Jane filled her in briefly on her return to business school and her financial career that had taken her to New York, then Chicago and finally Denver.

"I'm surprised you didn't stay in music. You sang the best 'Morning Star' I've ever heard."

"Oh, you're that Roxanne." Jane's hand covered her face for a second. "I'm so sorry. I didn't recognize you."

Roxanne just shook her head. "We were in children's choir together, but I didn't expect you to remember after all these years."

"And you? What have you been doing?"

"I married. Those are my teenagers." Two gorgeous blonds who could give Tami a run for her money sat toward the end of the long table, their heads bent over cell phones, fingers flying. "My husband is in the mission field now. We often spend time with the sisters when he's gone a long time."

Jane looked around. There were certainly no men here. Before she could ask who were her sisters, Anna's chair scraped back and all eyes turned to her. She announced a Bible reading in the library, then looked at Jane. "You're welcome to attend, of course."

"Thank you, but I think I'll be getting back."

Dorothea scooted her chair back. "Let me just get you a key."

Jane followed her into the kitchen, a surprisingly modern affair with a bank of ovens and a huge stove with six burners and a grill top. Copper pots gleamed above it. An industrial size refrigerator took up part of a wall. Dorothea waddled to the end of the room and rummaged through a drawer. She pulled out a keychain with a single key dangling from it, then scribbled a phone number on a notepad by the wall phone. She tore off the sheet and handed it to Jane. "In case you need anything during the night. The first night in a new place can sometimes be difficult, especially under the circumstances."

"I'm sorry to take your room," Jane began, but Dorothea waved her hands.

"I used to stay here—" she used the African American expression "—before Sister Emma took ill. I'm returning home, just as you are."

Jane's eyes filled with tears, but she blinked them back. It was true. She was coming home.

☆ ☆ ☆

The next three days ran together in a blur. Miss Essig's funeral was first and foremost a musical extravaganza. Crowds clogged the viewing at the colonial brick funeral home on Main Street. Jane paid her respects to Miss Essig from a distance, preferring not to view the corpse. Her memories of seeing her parents laid out, their bodies stiff and cold in their Sunday best, one death following so closely on the other, still haunted her. In a separate room, musicians took turns playing tributes to their teacher. Clusters of people stood or sat, listening to the music or reminiscing quietly. Most played familiar Moravian hymns, muted for the occasion. A violist offered Bach's *Air on a G String*, a pianist performed Bach's *Gymnopedies #3*, then a brass band stood outside and played more hymns.

Someone touched her elbow and Jane turned to find Anna Szeges standing beside her. "Emma's family would like to meet you."

"Certainly." Jane's shoulders tightened. She'd come to think Miss Essig hadn't had any family left. Anna led her to a small room where a middle-age couple waited. Two children sat in the corner, bored and fidgety. The girl swung legs encased in white stockings and ending in black patent leather shoes. The boy pulled at his bowtie and his father kept telling him to leave it alone. Some things never changed.

The woman had Miss Essig's eyes, but not her gift for peace. She twisted a handkerchief between her fingers and dabbed her red and swollen eyes, trying to keep her mascara from streaking down her face. She'd been successful for the most part. When Anna introduced Jane, she burst out with fresh tears, shaking her head. Jane's stomach twisted, anticipating a family feud.

"I can't tell you how grateful I am that you've taken my great aunt's house."

Jane tried not to let the relief show on her face. "We had no idea what to do when Aunt Emma called to say she was so ill."

"I see." Jane had to say something. Then she caught herself. "I'm sorry for your loss."

Fresh tears streaked down the niece's face. Her husband took over. "I have a large medical practice in California and we just couldn't move back. Of course, the house can't be sold, so . . ." He trailed off when his wife blew her nose.

Jane didn't feel this was the time to ask why not. She frowned at Anna, who was watching the niece and didn't notice.

The niece recovered enough to ask, "You were her student?"

"Yes, she taught me piano as a child, then was one of my faculty at Salem College." Jane leaned forward. "Your aunt woke my love of music."

She nodded. "I'm glad you have the house, then. There's so much happening over there. Our family would be in the way."

"Of course not," the ever-composed Anna said.

The niece smiled, "That's nice of you to say, but I know what goes on—"

"Will you be staying long after the funeral?" Anna interrupted.

Jane frowned at the discourtesy. The strain must be reaching even Anna.

The husband looked back and forth between Jane and Anna, then answered in a stiff voice, "I have to get back right after the funeral, but my wife and children will be staying in town for a few days."

Jane intervened. "Please feel free to come over and spend some time in the house. Look through Miss Essig's things and take what you like."

Anna shifted in her chair. The niece looked at the two women, then angled her body toward Jane. "That is very kind of you."

Jane jotted down her cell number on an old business card and handed it to the niece, who stuffed it into her purse and stood up. "I think I'm ready to go," she said to her husband.

He gave Anna a curt nod, but smiled at Jane. "Aunt Emma made a good choice."

"Thank you," Jane answered. The couple gathered their children and left.

"What was that about?" Jane asked after the door had closed.

Anna slumped in the chair.

Jane reached out her hand, alarmed at this sudden show of weakness.

"It's a long story. Can we talk in a few days?"

"Yes, you've been working nonstop. Have you slept or had a minute to yourself?"

A single tear ran down Anna's cheek. She wiped it away impatiently, then took a deep breath and stood. "I'm needed elsewhere."

"Of course. What can I do?"

But Anna just shook her head and left the room.

☆ ☆ ☆

The next morning Miss Essig's students—old, young and in-between—gave a concert in her honor. The funeral services followed in the afternoon. Both were held in the old church just across from Miss Essig's property. Many of her former students, her friends, and people in the church from around the Carolinas, Pennsylvania and even Germany and the Czech Republic came for what they now called a celebration of her life. With only three days' notice, Jane wondered how the Europeans had made it. She hadn't realized her old mentor had enjoyed an international reputation—at least amongst the *Unitas Fratrum*, the official name of the Moravian Church.

Jane attended with her favorite cousin, Frank, who seemed to have already heard about the inheritance. "I'm glad I'll be seeing more of you," he whispered to her in the pew before the funeral began. After the church service, they drove together down to God's Acre, leaving their car in the visitor's lot for Old Salem since the funeral was so crowded. They walked past Home Church, Jane's square-heeled shoes doing well on the cobble stones. Frank told her how one of the big hurricanes had knocked down several of the old trees in the square years back. The band started playing and the two fell silent, listening, Jane remembering the other services she'd attended here. They followed the music. Miss Essig would be interred in the Single Sister's section, an area with a few spots still left in the original part of the cemetery.

In the early eighteenth century, Jane's ancestors had lived communally, dividing themselves by choirs. As far as she knew, the practice had started when they'd founded their village, Herrnhut, in Saxony. Count Zinzendorf had taken in the religious refugees. In the choir system, infants lived with their mother, but moved to the nursery around eighteen months, where they stayed in the Little Boys' or Little Girls' Choirs. At twelve, they graduated to the Older Boys' or Girls'

Choir, and at eighteen joined the Single Brethren or Sisters'
Choir, as the case might be. Each group lived, ate and attended
daily worship together, sleeping in dormitories in their choir
house. When people married, they joined the Married Brethren
or Married Sisters' Choir. At the death of a spouse, they moved
to the Widows' or Widowers' Choir. As the frontier turned into
towns, married couples started living more and more in their
own homes as nuclear families.

The choirs had been an excellent support system. People
who shared a certain station in life understood each other. Each
member was surrounded by choir and family members. There
was always someone to talk to. People worked for their choirs
and were cared for in turn. And women had been freed from
doing only domestic work. Jane had always been proud of this
innovative lifestyle. Of course, choir supervisors had poked
their noses into how people were living and doled out
discipline. They'd been strict. She'd read reports on her own
ancestors from the archives. But for the most part, the choir
system had made for tight, supportive communities. These days
the only remnant of the system was being buried with your
choir.

Jane and Frank walked up the slope of the cemetery toward
the large crowd gathered around the grave with the family
sitting in a row of chairs at the front. She and Frank stood
toward the back, making the proper responses in the liturgy.
Jane chided herself for not feeling grief now. After all, this
woman had meant so much to her. But she remembered
holding Miss Essig's cold hand on her last day, how her pale
blue eyes seemed to look through the film of this world into the
next as if it were the real one and not this solid earth. Perhaps
she was listening now to that great circle of archangels whose
only job was to sing at the throne of God, ready to suggest
improvements. Jane wished her a good concert.

When the final words were spoken, Frank turned to her.
"Shall we go and visit our relatives?"

"Sure," Jane said.

First they found their aunt who had died in the 1918
influenza epidemic in the Single Sisters' section, then their
grandparents' graves, one across the cemetery under a big tree,

the other all the way down the hill. After that, they strolled down the paved sidewalks to the newer section, which stretched up a hill to the east, women on the left, men on the right. Burials were by date, which made finding a relative tricky until someone had posted an electronic map. Frank steered her through the rows of white headstones, all the identical size and shape since all were equal in death, and pointed out the family graves, catching her up on deaths, marriages and births, even some gossip. By the time he dropped her off at Miss Essig's house, they'd reestablished their easy childhood friendship.

The next evening brought yet another concert. The local symphony performed Mozart's *Requiem* in Miss Essig's honor. Jane imagined it was a piece they kept honed if they could perform it on such short notice. Local singers added selections from Puccini and Bach. A young monk in orange robes offered overtone chanting in the Tibetan style. His deep tones opened Jane completely, allowing all the knots to loosen. It was now that the grief rose up—the loss of Miss Essig, of childhood innocence. The waste of all that time advising companies to invest in a better world, only to have them pursue money with no regard to the trail of carnage left behind. Suggesting to her new female colleagues that bringing a woman's perspective to business would make for more justice, only to find them as greedy and unscrupulous as the current CEOs.

The conductor picked up his baton again, and the symphony began to play Barber's *Adagio for Strings*, a piece dedicated to love, but expressing the unutterable sadness of loss of all that is beautiful, a piece grieving for the heroism of humanity reaching again and again for perfection, and the inevitability of those efforts to somehow fall short or even become corrupt. Silent tears flowed down Jane's cheeks. She wiped them, unashamed, and once the tears were spent, the piece lifted her into serenity, into the inexpressible beauty of the world she dreamed of, the world the piece somehow promised was real— a place of harmony and peace and light.

The conductor, eyes closed, a beatific look on his face, closed his fingers, and the music faded into the silence that now ruled Jane's heart. After the cellos had sounded their last deep note and the bows were lifted from the violins, the sound hung in the air, pure and light and vibrating with all the yearning of humanity for that golden dream. The audience waited and she wished fervently that they would rise and leave in that silence, but of course respect was due the musicians, so the clapping began. It swelled and the audience stood, an offering for music and for her music teacher.

Jane slipped out of the auditorium, thoroughly marinated in sound, her heart tranquil, certain that her decision was right. She would go back to her childhood dream of making music. She would practice again so she could play with this kind of power and help people believe in beauty again. Maybe she'd believe again, too.

CHAPTER THREE

David Spach slowly lowered his trombone and watched Jane slip out of the concert hall. He bowed with his section of the orchestra, barely noticing the thunderous applause. He'd hoped to find her after the concert, speak with her about Miss Essig, catch up. Now she was gone, would leave Winston-Salem and fly away to her glamorous life in the city. Somebody had said it was Denver now, but last he'd heard she'd been in New York. Wherever it was, it was far from him. The audience started to stand, gather their belongings, greet their neighbors, and soon their noise filled the hall. He took his trombone apart and methodically cleaned each piece with a cloth, then packed it up and headed back stage.

"Great concert," the conductor said, extending his hand.

David shifted his case and shook the man's hand. "That last piece worked well, especially the violins." The conductor nodded and moved on to congratulate more musicians. David made his way outside and found a group standing around a couple of smokers. Nobody who played a wind instrument indulged in the old habit, he noted. They nodded to him and his friend Brian made space in the circle.

"So they've got her on some new medication," Vernon continued, "and she's feeling better."

"That's good," someone said.

"Expensive as hell, though. Glad to have this gig at least."

Vernon was talking about his wife's cancer again. David hunched his shoulders against his own memories. It had been two years, but that was nothing compared to thirty-five years of marriage. He didn't know Vernon well and had never met his wife, so he let the conversation fall over him like a symphony passage for other instruments.

After a while, Argus picked up his viola case. "Hey, I'm hungry," he said. "Anyone else up for a bite?"

The group settled on a local brew pub, and David decided to tag along. Nobody waited for him at home. The kids had flown the coop well before Marlene had gotten sick. Maybe he should get a dog. It seemed weird, though, replacing people with animals, but hell, he was lonely. People made their goodbyes and the group pared itself down to five. Their instruments didn't fit in Brian's sedan, so they followed him in their own cars. David switched off his old cassette player and drove the few blocks in silence, thoughts of his lessons with Miss Essig filling his mind. And Jane.

He found the group toward the back of the restaurant. Just as he sat, a waitress put down a pitcher each of Salem Gold and People's Porter, two of Foothill's favorites. He ordered nachos and poured himself a mug. He took a long swallow, then said, "It went well."

Argus raised his mug and everyone did the same, James hurrying to pour one for himself, raising a dangerously high head of foam in the process. "To the old lady."

"To Miss Essig," David said as the others repeated Argus' toast.

Brian swiped his moustache with the back of his hand. "Did you know her?"

"She was my first music teacher," David said.

"Really?"

"Yeah, Mom used to take me over to that big ole house. She had a grand piano in her living room. A real stickler, she was, but nice. Visited Marlene regular." David took another gulp.

Brian didn't say anything for a minute. The nachos arrived, some onion rings, French fries and BBQ wings. David picked up a ring and dipped it in ketchup. Brian wrinkled his nose. "What?" David challenged him. "You got a problem?"

"Ketchup does not belong on onion rings. It belongs on French fries," Brian declared.

"Absolutely not." James's Scottish accent somehow enunciated every possible sound in those two words. "Vinegar. That's what you put on chips."

"Chips? Why do they call them that?" Brian asked.

David ate another onion ring, then started in on the nachos, while Brian and James debated the proper names for food and the correct condiments to accompany them. The talk turned to a new jazz singer who'd been featured at a local club. "Best scat I've heard in a while. We got to open for her," Brian said.

James nodded. "So we've heard."

Brian punched his arm. They worked their way through the array of appetizers. The others made their excuses after the platters were empty and headed off. Brian's burger arrived. The waitress placed a salad in front of David.

"You a rabbit now?" Brian jutted his chin toward David's plate.

"Doctor's orders," David joked.

"I ignore them."

They ate for a while, old friends comfortable with silence. Halfway through his meal, David found Brian's eyes on him. "So you going to call her?"

"Who?"

"Don't give me 'who'. You know."

David picked up his mug, but found it empty. So was the pitcher.

Brian grinned. "You want some of the Salem Gold?"

"Sure." Brian poured out the rest of the beer, looked around for the waitress, then shrugged. "I guess we've had enough."

David took a long swallow. "You going to improv tomorrow night?"

"Oh now, you're not getting out of this question."

"What question?"Brian sighed like a long-suffering mother. "Jane. Are you going to call her?"

"She left."

"That's not what I heard."

"She snuck out of the concert right after the Barber piece. Probably had to catch a plane. She's gone." He waved his hand as if to dismiss her.

"No, she's staying in Miss Essig's old house."

"But—" David blinked. "Where'd you hear that?"

"Reverend Fischel over at Friedberg told me."

"How do you know him?"

"I'm choir director out there."

"No way."

"Way. A man's gotta eat." Brian devoured the last bite of his burger as if to demonstrate. "Besides, I've been a Moravian all my life. My family goes way back. Just like yours."

"So she's staying at Miss Essig's house?"

"Who?"

David reached over and punched Brian's shoulder. "Jane, you moron. You brought her up in the first place."

"Like I didn't see you drooling all over your trombone tonight. And at the cemetery."

"Was not."

"You couldn't keep your eyes off her."

"Could so."

Brian regarded him. His expression softened. "It's been two years. Marlene would want you to be happy."

"Happy? With Jane. She wouldn't . . ." he sputtered to a stop.

"Wouldn't what?"

"You know."

"How do you know? You dated, didn't you?"

"In high school. Three centuries ago."

Brian chuckled. "Feels like that sometimes, doesn't it?"

David relaxed his shoulders. "Definitely. You're an old man now."

"Yeah, you just keep telling yourself that."

CHAPTER FOUR

Jane flew back to Denver to tie up loose ends. It took nearly a week to pack up most of her belongings and make arrangements for movers. She put the townhouse on the market with a good realtor, then spent her last night in Colorado with friends, telling them about her new house and thoughts about returning to music. They predicted she'd go stir crazy within two months—one claimed two weeks. But her calm certainty remained.

The next morning Jane sold her BMW. She really couldn't afford it anymore. The dealership gave her a ride to the airport where she said her goodbyes to the white peaks of the Rocky Mountains, thinking it a fair exchange for the soft round hills of the Piedmont and the blues and greys of the Smokies.

Once her plane landed in Greensboro, she rented a car and drove to her new home. She carried in her suitcases and dropped them at the foot of the stairs. It was early evening. A glass of merlot in hand, she walked out to the back yard, where she found Winston lying in the middle of the dormant rose garden, gazing up at the trees, sniffing the air.

"Did Dorothea let you out?"

He licked her hand. She plopped down beside him. Together they watched the stars come out. A bat flew overhead, swerving this way and that, picking off the last of the insects.

Something soft nudged Jane's back. Turning, she found a calico cat. A second cat announced his presence with one loud meow from the nearby tangle of honeysuckle, forsythia and barberry bushes.

Jane looked down at the bulldog. "There are cats, too?"

He wagged his stub of a tail in answer.

The calico settled in her lap, kneading her jeans, warm and purring. Jane picked up her tag and angled it toward a streetlight. It read 'Suzie B'. She laughed. So Miss Essig had been a feminist.

After a long while, the night chill penetrated Jane's light jacket. She stood, dislodging the cat, who grunted her protest. She strolled back to the house, the animals following. Winston trudged up the wooden steps to the back porch and waited at the closed door, his great tongue lolling.

"You and I need some exercise," she told him.

Jane looked around just in time to see the cats duck into the greenhouse that jutted off the side of the basement. She walked back down the steps and found one of the window panes missing. A cat door of sorts.

Inside, she found the two felines already sitting beside their bowls, looking up at her expectantly. The cat hiding in the bushes turned out to be an enormous black long-hair complete with ear tufts. His tag read 'Marvin'.

Okay, Marvin Gaye and Susan B. Anthony. Miss Essig was turning out to be more than a proper music teacher.

Jane inspected the pantry and found a bag of kibble. Some fancy kind that claimed to be organic. Chalk another one up for her old music teacher. Jane sprinkled food in each bowl and was rewarded by purring and chomping.

Instant family.

Life settled down to a regular pace. In the mornings, Jane and Winston went for a run in Washington Park, under old trees and past covered picnic shelters, down to the creek. The route took her through what was now a series of baseball diamonds and soccer fields, across the bridge spanning Salem Creek to the dog run, and up to the elementary school she'd attended, then back again, her calves burning on the ascent. Winston panted heavily the first week, but soon kept up nicely.

One day she stooped at the edge of the water and lifted a few round, grey stones, but no Crayfish scurried for cover and no minnows swam in the shallows. The creek seemed empty of life; too much concrete for her taste. She remembered the gang of girls splashing in the creek on the endless hot days of summer, watching the crustaceans scuttle around. Or just lolling in the water, their assorted dogs lying in the shade watching as if their young charges were a flock of sheep.

The rest of her mornings she spent getting the house in order, but Jane dedicated her afternoons to music, starting with the grand piano in the living room. Nimble from the computer, her fingers soon remembered their way amongst the black and white keys. A stack of Miss Essig's workbooks for students were in the piano bench, and she played her way through them in one sitting. The next afternoon she leafed through stacks of sheet music, deciding to start with Beethoven's *Moonlight Sonata*. Once she felt proficient again, she'd audition for a group in town, work her way up to the symphony. Maybe offer private lessons. Continue the tradition of this being a musical house.

In the evenings, Jane went over to Dorothea's, as she now thought of the big, brick mansion she'd been invited to the night of Miss Essig's death, and ate with whoever turned up. It seemed like a gathering place—but only women came, sometimes with children, but usually for the evening meal like she did. Some seemed to come for counseling with Anna and stayed for supper. After the meal, Jane joined the cleanup crew, a fair exchange she hoped. Soon she'd have her own kitchen in order, but she had to admit she found this odd assortment of women good company. At night, she read or watched a film. She'd start her family visits soon.

One morning Jane came back from her run, ducking back through the hedge next to the pear tree, and was greeted by the sound of a leaf blower. A gardening crew swarmed over the yard, trimming, raking, even turning over the compost. She asked around until she found the supervisor and introduced herself as the new owner.

"Sí," he said, "Mr. Dreher, he tell me about you."

Jane didn't recognize the name, but asked the gardener his.

"Julio Rodriguez."

"The place looks great. I'd like to hire your crew."

"We already hired, Miss. Trabajo por la firma."

Jane wasn't sure what firm he was referring to. "Yes, but now that I'm here, you'll be working for me."

He squinted at her in the sun. "But Miss Essig, she no pay."

"If she owed you money, I can take care of it." He shook his head, but she continued, "Can I get your number?"

Julio reached into his pocket with grass stained fingers and handed her a business card.

"Just let me know how much I owe you."

"But Mr. Dreher, he pay. We do todos los jardens por el."

Jane could follow most of his Spanish inserts, wishing her grasp of the language had survived since junior high so she could answer him. She'd ask Anna about this money arrangement later. For now, she and Winston followed Julio around the acre, Jane asking question after question, Julio answering readily, proud of his work. She asked how the daffodils and tulips were. Years ago, their blossoming had assured her spring had arrived. He admitted they could use some work and agreed to have a crew dig up the beds so she could replenish them. Retirement was turning out to be busy. How had she ever had time to work?

After talking with Julio, Jane entered the house through the kitchen where she grabbed a towel and blotted her face, grabbed a bottle of water from the fridge and headed into the living room. After downing the water, she decided it was time to unpack the cardboard boxes of books that had arrived a few days ago. She dusted off even the cheap paperbacks as she pulled them out of the boxes, stuffing the shelves in various rooms to their limit and piling the rest on the floor for future homes.

Miss Essig's collection included the classics and a surprising assortment of contemporary fiction. But her music books were the real treasures. Jane lost herself amongst them until her stomach demanded attention. After lunch, she finished up, discovering a section on Moravian church history that intrigued her.

What puzzled her was the wall of metaphysical titles. It seemed Miss Essig had a sweet tooth for the mystical, everything from kabbala and western metaphysics to astrology, paganism—which really surprised her—and something called sacred geometry. "Math and music are kissing cousins," the introduction to one declared. She thumbed through another. Platonic solids, Fibonacci spirals and other beautiful shapes, a discussion of the effect of shapes on human consciousness. Jane wondered if Anna knew Miss Essig's little secret. She hadn't tried to hide the books, though. They were in the library, although tucked in a corner that was squarely blocked by an overstuffed armchair. Dorothea would be scandalized, Jane was sure. Uncle Pat would damn them all to hell, his favorite pastime.

The next day, Jane decided to work on the two small bedrooms above the library. Maybe she'd remodel, put in a spiral staircase and join the two floors together. She recognized that she was avoiding the master suite where Miss Essig had lived and died. It wasn't superstition, really. She just felt like she'd let the room sit for a full month. Let Miss Essig get used to her new home before changing her old one, although there was no sense of a lingering spirit. The animals never stared at empty space as if they could see someone she couldn't. Such a peaceful death should leave no unfinished business. Miss Essig was likely with those old friends she'd mentioned or still listening to the celestial choir.

The first room overlooked the garage and the crab apple tree. A single bed with another star burst quilt stretched against the wall. A wicker basket in the corner overflowed with toys for boys. Trucks, guns, a cigar box full of plastic soldiers. She thought of the child fidgeting with his bowtie at the funeral. She'd write and ask if he wanted any of these. She hadn't heard from the family. The niece had never called. She'd ask Anna for their address. The room just needed dusting. She let it sit for now.

The next room turned out to be another matter. It was filled with art. And not just any art. William Blake reproductions covered the walls and more were stacked in the corner. Heavy drapes of Jamestown toile blue with a thick lining blocked the light from windows that would have admitted the morning sun. Jane switched on the overhead light. She'd loved Blake in college. In the first painting, an old man emerged from a circle of brilliant gold and orange, leaning down to measure the universe. She couldn't remember the figure's name, but thought it was from the poem *Jerusalem*. Next to this, a youth stood in front of another sunburst of color, his arms spread with palms out as if he were holding back the dark edges of the painting.

Jane sat on a stool next to the small closet. The cats arrived, eager to explore behind a previously closed door. There might be mice, after all. More reproductions that she recognized from *The Songs of Innocence and Experience* covered the north wall of the room. She looked through a stack leaning in the corner. A heavily muscled man with mangy, long hair and beard crawled on all fours. A dragon hung over a woman dressed in red, her arms mirroring its wings.

Then she found pencil sketches. One contained what looked for all the world like an Advent star in the middle. On the edges the star had been unfolded and thirteen points lined up. At the top and bottom sat an eight-pointed star with an equal-armed cross. The next one looked more like the Blake she knew. A man hovered over a woman, both nude, his hand reaching between her legs. In the next drawing, a nude male figure reclined below a block of texts, but on the side a woman stood, her vagina and uterus drawn as the inside of a cathedral. Another showed a fully erect phallus.

"Miss Essig," Jane exclaimed. Again, she imagined Dorothea's face if she saw these. She flipped to the next sketch, but these were miniatures of domestic life drawn inside borders shaped like eyes or mouths. On the edges, phrases were written in German. Little blessings for the house, she imagined. Tame compared to Blake's erotica.

Jane restacked the art carefully, then stood up and moved closer to the wall covered with paintings. She switched on the light over one. It looked like oil. She ran her finger gingerly over one corner of the painting and found ridges. Someone must have copied bits of Blake's work as part of her art studies.

Perhaps she'd want them back. But who? Another question for
Anna. Jane called the cats and shut the door.

☆ ☆ ☆

That night at Dorothea's, after the dishes were washed and
the leftovers tucked away in their various containers, Jane
made her way down the hall to the front of the house and
knocked on the door of Anna's office.

"Come in," Anna called out.

Jane pushed the paneled oak door open but stopped
abruptly. Anna had company. Male company. Something she'd
never seen in this house before. Jane shook off her surprise. If
she wasn't careful, this place would turn her into a prudish old
maid.

Anna greeted her with a nod. "I believe you two have met."

This was the man who'd been reading to Miss Essig when
she'd first arrived. He'd also officiated at her funeral. "I've
seen you, but never caught your name," Jane said.

"John." She inclined her head toward the man. "Meet Jane
Frey."

Jane stepped forward, hand out. "It's nice to meet you."

"Likewise." He shook her hand. "I hope we'll be seeing you
at church. We could use a voice like yours in the choir."

Flustered, Jane wondered how he knew she could carry a
tune. She hoped they weren't going to start pressuring her.

After an awkward silence, Anna asked, "Did you need
something?"

"I do have some questions—" she gestured at Anna's
overflowing desk "—when you have the time."

"I can always find time for you, Jane. What were you
wondering about?"

"Well, the gardener for one. He didn't seem to think I
needed to pay him. And I wondered if Miss Essig's family
would like to have any personal items."

"Just odds and ends, then," Anna said.

"And I'd like to get the title switched to my name. Take care
of the insurance."

Anna's forehead wrinkled in confusion. "Title?"

"To the house. I'd like to get the legalities taken care of."

Anna set down the pen in her hand and looked at John. He put his finger up to his mouth, his brown eyes studying Jane. The ticking of the grandfather clock in the hallway filled the silence.

After a minute, Jane asked, "Is there a problem?"

John cleared his throat. "No, I was just thinking through my schedule."

"*Your* schedule?"

Anna intervened. "Why don't you email me your schedule, Jane, and I'll let you know when we've figured out a time when all the parties can meet."

"This sounds a bit complicated." Jane said. "I'm completely free, so just let me know when you've coordinated with the others."

"Not complicated, really. I just need to get a few folks together," Anna said.

Jane walked back down the hallway, avoiding the kitchen, and continued down the drive. Once she was out of sight of the house, she stopped and took a few deep breaths.

Clearly, there was a problem.

What have I done? She'd just turned her whole life upside down because on her deathbed, her mentor and second mother had given Jane what in her secret heart she'd always wanted. And now it was clear there were strings attached. To be fair, Mr. Davis had turned her life upside down first. But then she'd gone and jumped on the next opportunity. Mindlessly. Without a thorough investigation. How many clients had lost their bacon because they'd done just that? "Never follow your heart until your head has gone first," she'd told them. But did she take her own advice? Apparently not.

She walked home—yes, she thought of it that way already—through her tunnel of cherry trees, wondering what kinds of strings these would turn out to be. No mortgage to pay and the proceeds of her townhouse helped with her tight finances, but how could she have been so hasty?

Then she remembered those last words, "Please, Jane." How she'd thought at the time that she'd just take care of things for Miss Essig, then figure out what came next for herself. She hadn't followed up with her attorney either. Uncharacteristic.

She shook her head at her own foolishness. But now as it turned out, it was a good thing she'd spent some time in the cutthroat world of high finance. She bet these men were used to dealing with pliable, naïve women. Except for Anna, of course.

The smell of overturned earth drew her to one of the flower gardens. Piles of bulbs lay on the side. The earth lay rust red and smooth, ready to be replanted. She might as well finish this project. Someone would enjoy the flowers in the spring.

Inside Winston waited, his stub tail wagging. She bent and buried her face in his side. The two cats appeared and twinned around her ankles. She fed them a late dinner, then poured herself a big glass of her favorite red and took a few sips before heading to the library. She checked her email and found Anna had scheduled a meeting for the very next morning.

Too exhausted to sit up all night combing the internet, she had no time for research on the property. She finished her wine, and then climbed into the single bed she was still sleeping in. The animals jumped up and arranged themselves around her. In the morning, she'd listen to Anna and John's presentation, and then take her time to respond. Tell them she had to consult with her attorneys. Always use the plural.

CHAPTER FIVE

Jane rode the elevator up to the ninth floor of the Reynolds Building in downtown Winston-Salem, the one that had inspired the more famous Empire State Building in New York City. This property was for sale, as were many of the old mills just north of downtown. Just how many new, spiffy lofts did the town really need? Outsourcing had taken its toll on this once prosperous manufacturing center. She realized for the first time that those factory owners had been lucky to employ her ancestors, used to hard work and frugal living, dedicated to honesty and a good life. The elevator door opened and Jane pulled down the jacket of her pin-striped suit, the one she wore for bad news, she thought wryly when she put it on this morning.

Just listen, she reminded herself, then opened the door to the offices of Heren and Holler, Attorneys at Law. The receptionist ushered her into a large conference room where Anna Szeges sat with John and three other men, attorneys and assistants Jane supposed. The door opened again and her cousin Frank rushed in, a bit out of breath. He sat next to her, but before he could say anything to explain his presence, Anna began introducing her. "You've already met John."

Jane nodded to him. The two men next to John turned out to be Mr. Heren and Mr. Holler, whose names graced the firm, the first in his sixties, the other younger by a generation, both with affable smiles useful for putting people at ease. Jane resisted.

"This is Mr. Boehme," Anna continued, nodding to a round, blond man around Jane's age who seemed a bit too serene for this time of the morning, "and you already know Frank, of course."

"Indeed I do." Jane smiled at him.

"Gentlemen, this is Jane Frey, who has taken on Miss Essig's house."

Everyone murmured greetings.

"Coffee?" Mr. Heren asked.

"I'll take a cup," Frank said and turned to Jane. "Would you like one?" He poured one before she could answer.

"Donuts?" Mr. Heren pointed to a long, white and green box of Krispy Kremes, which Jane had intended to resist—eating at meetings was not exactly professional—but when he lifted the lid, the aroma filled the room. She took one—they were still warm—and pushed the box back along the long conference table out of reach. "Thank you."

With everyone provisioned, Anna took control. "Yesterday, Jane—"

"Ms. Frey," Jane interrupted. If these three men got called by their surnames, then she had to insist on equal treatment.

"Y-Yes, of course."

Good, she'd interrupted Anna's rehearsed speech.

"Ms. Frey asked about having the title to the house put in her name." Nods all around. No surprises here. Anna was teeing up. "I was pleased we could meet so quickly to settle this matter."

That sounded promising.

"Mr. Frey?" Anna emphasized the appellation with the arch of one trimmed eyebrow.

Frank's smile was sheepish. "As you may already know," he addressed himself mainly to Jane, "in 1727 our ancestor Jacob Frey emigrated from Upper Alsace to Pennsylvania, and then moved south to the banks of Muddy Creek where he settled."

"Yes, Frank, but what does our family history have to do with this?"

Frank held up a finger, asking her forbearance. "His son, Hans Jacob, bought a large tract of land south of Salem Creek, on the other side of town, where he built a farmhouse."

"Where our grandmother took care of us," she finished for him. She pushed down an incongruous memory of the two of them around the age of three playing in an enormous mud puddle and their grandmother finding them smeared and wet. She picked up her coffee cup to keep herself from laughing.

Frank smiled, his eyes warm. "I remember it fondly. But before that, Hans' son, named after his grandfather, so another Jacob—" he held up fingers to keep them straight "—gave part of his estate to an organization of mostly Moravians that he was a member of. They built three more houses and allowed a church to be built there."

"Oh," Jane said, "Miss Essig's house and yours." She looked at Anna. "So that big white antebellum must be the other one. I don't know who owns it."

"That's the thing," Frank said. "No one person owns any of them. The organization still holds those houses and the land the church is on in trust. Jacob Frey put in his will that the organization was to keep the title to those properties in perpetuity."

So those estates in her old neighborhood had not sold off their land as she'd previously thought. It had belonged to her own kin.

Frank continued, "In a way, our family already owns the house you're living in. And we've always honored our great, great, great grandfather's wishes."

"I never knew this before," Jane said. "Thanks for the explanation."

He nodded and took a sip of his coffee, then frowned at the cup. It had probably grown cold.

"So, may I know what this organization is?" Jane asked while an assistant freshened everyone's coffee.

Mr. Boehme leaned forward. "That's why I'm here, Ms. Frey," he said, his voice resonant and rich. She wondered if he was a singer. "I am the current head of the OGMS."

"OGMS?" she repeated.

Mr. Boehme smiled. "Omega Grant Management Systems."

"So this company manages real estate? Writes software?"

"We do property management, among other things," Boehme answered.

She mulled this over, then said, "I'd like to see all the relevant documents."

Mr. Holler slid a large manila envelope down the polished table toward her. "I believe you'll find copies of everything here. Study them at your leisure. Let us know if you have any concerns."

"May I have access to the originals if necessary?"

"Yes," Mr. Holler said, "but the papers establishing the trust are kept down at the archives. You'd have to consult with them to see it."

The Moravian Archives were housed in a brick building kitty-corner to God's Acre. Jane had always thought it looked like an old-fashioned school. She'd never been inside, but knew it held some of the oldest documents in the country, many of them still not translated from eighteenth-century German.

Mr. Boehme leaned forward. "I'm sure that wouldn't be a problem, as long as you follow their procedures for handling antique papers. I could set it up for you if you'd like."

"I'll let you know if that will be necessary," Jane said. She slipped the envelope into her briefcase and stood. Mr. Holler's eyes rounded in surprise. "Thank you, gentlemen. Ms. Szeges. I'll look these over with my attorneys and let you know if they are to our satisfaction."

☆ ☆ ☆

As soon as she got home, Jane spread the documents out on the table in the breakfast nook, then called Lois Williams. She'd first started using Lois's legal services when she worked in New York and had kept her on retainer through her various moves.

"Jane—" Lois's voice worked like a shot of espresso "—have you finally come to your senses and decided to sue those bastards for age discrimination?"

Jane laughed. "It's nice to hear your voice."

"What's up? I've got two minutes before I've got to run off to another meeting."

Jane caught her up quickly. "I'm sick of being jerked around. First the job, now this house situation. I just want to be sure I'll be safe living here as long as I want."

"Sure," Lois said, "just fax me everything."

"You do realize I don't have a secretary anymore," Jane quipped.

"Think you can remember how to work a fax machine?"

Jane chuckled. "I can figure it out."

"I'll look them over in the next few days, then get back to you. You know you should have told me about this before you moved in."

"I know. I don't know what's gotten into me."

"Getting senile already?"

They laughed.

"Come visit," Lois said. "We'll go out on the town, see a show."

"Sounds great."

"Later." Lois hung up.

Maybe I should take a trip up there, Jane thought. The roar of the city might be just the thing to break her nostalgia or whatever it was that had taken hold of her.

Jane hooked up the fax to her laptop and did a test run. It worked on the first try. She skimmed the documents as she sent them out. The attorneys had included what amounted to a rental agreement explaining that she could live in the property indefinitely, but couldn't make changes without the agreement of the board of OGMS and that the house could not become part of her estate. She had a friend who'd built a cabin in a national forest and the situation there had been similar. One of the signatories to this agreement was a John Szeges. She wondered how he and Anna were related. Maybe brother and sister. They certainly didn't live together.

Her great, great, great grandfather's will appeared to be about a fifth-generation copy. She wasn't sure it would come out clearly on the other side. Maybe she'd have to go down to the archives after all. It might be fun to see. She could get a family history done. She'd lost the one her father had given her years ago. Maybe they'd discovered something new. She ran her finger over the old signature. At least they couldn't take away those roots.

She gave herself a shake. What had come over her? She'd spent a good forty years happily away from here. Now she was pursuing her childhood musical dreams, owned the dog she'd wanted as a ten-year-old, was getting to know family again, tracking down her ancestral records, and had a date with her high school sweetheart, who had called yesterday. Next she'd get married, put up a white picket fence and pop out 2.5 children. Just like Uncle Pat wanted. Except it was too late for that.

A seal at the top of the next document caught her eye. A tree with something written beneath it, too fuzzy to make out. The initials OGMS stood out at the bottom. The border was scribed with what looked like Greek, but she couldn't read it. A trip to the archives was definitely in order. But first she got ready for another visit she'd been putting off for too long.

☆ ☆ ☆

As Jane's faxed documents printed out in her attorney's New York office, a man pulled duplicate copies from a third machine in a separate location. The halogen desk lamp sharpened the angles of his face. He read each page as it was received, his eyes avid. His plan was working perfectly so far. When the machine beeped to indicate the transmission was complete, he stacked the pages carefully. Two vital documents had been blurred. Surely the attorney would tell Jane to resend them. Or he'd get into the archives himself. His contact there believed his cover story.

☆ ☆ ☆

Uncle Pat still lived out in the country. Suburban sprawl had not reached his land, tucked in a hollow between two old homesteads that had become prosperous horse farms. After a long stretch of white picket fence, Jane turned down his dirt drive. Only a few feet in, the trees thickened overhead, the underbrush scraping against her car. Across the creek, kudzu had choked the hill and taken over a stand of trees. That stuff could eat a house in one summer.

Jane parked under a spreading maple and checked to be sure her star pendant was tucked safely under her blouse. The beagles set up a loud baying as soon as she took a step toward the moss-roofed house, its paint peeling off all along one side. She glanced over at the caged animals, remembering how as a child she'd urged her uncle to let his dogs run free. "It's not fair, keeping them locked up," she'd said.

"They're huntin' dogs, not pets." He'd spat a long stream of brown liquid and moved his chewing tobacco to the other cheek. "I take 'em out plenty."

She'd always brought them treats, escaping the family visits and going out to the dogs, feeding them and letting them lick her hands. Until her uncle caught her at it. Now she walked toward the house, steeling herself against the hope in the dogs' voices.

The screen door opened and a young woman appeared. She wore a flowered housedress, faded and loose, her wispy red hair caught up in a quick twist. She straightened her dress, tucked a stray strand behind her ear, then nodded when Jane stopped in front of her. "Granddaddy told me you was coming," she said.

Jane introduced herself and extended her hand. The young woman frowned for a minute, then put her limp hand in Jane's. "Misty."

"Uncle Pat was my mother's brother."

Misty's eyes shifted toward the door.

"So, we're second cousins?" Jane asked.

"I reckon. My dad's Elmer."

Jane tried to remember him, but failed. She nodded like she did.

"Don't just stand there jawin'," a voice bellowed from inside the house. "Let her in."

Misty rolled her eyes, the first sign of any spunk, and moved aside. "We'd best git inside afore he tries to get up."

Jane nodded again like she understood, but was even more confused. Inside, a well-worn sofa took up one wall and a frayed arm chair stood at an angle. The pot-bellied stove still dominated the room. Newspapers and logs were stacked near it, none too neatly, along with a box of kindling.

"So where is she?" The voice emanated from the back.

Jane turned to Misty, her eyes asking the question.

"I been takin' care of him since the operation."

"Operation?"

"Cancer," she whispered.

Misty led the way through the hall and stopped at the bedroom door. "Here he is."

Jane peered around her, feeling again like the child she'd been the last time she'd been here. Uncle Pat sat propped against several pillows, their cases now grey rather than white, a pile of magazines next to him. The top one sported a man with a rifle and spiffy hunting clothes. She looked back at her uncle, still clean shaven, searching for bandages, any sign of where the surgery had been, but saw only flannel pajamas with a long brown stain on the front.

Her uncle reached out his hand. "Come here and let me look at you. Just like your mother, you are." He gripped her wrist tight and she winced, trying not to pull back.

"Well, thank you, Uncle Pat. How you doing?"

Misty shifted at the door. "Can I git you anything?"

"Nothing for me," Jane said.

"Bring her a chair, girl. And some tea."

"Oh, don't go to any trouble—"

"Ain't no trouble," he spat out. "Do like I say," he shouted. The last word came out as a gasp and he started to cough. Misty rolled her eyes and handed him a dirty handkerchief. He hawked and spit. Jane took a step back. He wiped his mouth and handed the hankie to Misty, who took it and left.

"I didn't know you'd been sick, Uncle Pat. You should have said something when I called." Jane sat in the chair from the kitchen table Misty brought her, draping her coat over the torn upholstery. "What do the doctors say?"

"It's them chem trails that's got me." He peered at her through watery eyes. "You know 'bout them, don't cha?"

"Can't say as I do." She caught herself falling into their vernacular. Her mother had struggled to stop speaking this way all her life.

"Figures," he mumbled.

Misty appeared and handed Uncle Pat a fresh handkerchief and set a Mason jar full of sweet tea on the bedside table. She handed a second jar to Jane. "Call if you need anything," she threw over her shoulder. The door to the bedroom next door closed and the muffled sound of the television came through the wall.

Jane picked up her tea and took a tiny sip, then a gulp. Misty had added some kind of fruit juice and lemon. Delicious. She looked up to find Uncle Pat studying her. "Chem trails?" she said, trying to get back to their conversation.

"You don't need to pretend like you believe me. Got that big college degree, but ain't got no common sense. Just like your mother." His eyes took on a far-away look.

"I could help with the doctor bills."

He looked back at her and frowned. "They done passed that socialist medicine now. Whole country's goin' to hell."

"Just let me know."

"I got my Medicare. I don't need no charity." He took a long swallow of his tea.

Jane suppressed a smile, not bothering to point out that his Medicare came from the government and some people would call that socialist. These holes in her relatives' arguments used to drive her crazy when she was younger.

"So, you come home now?" he asked, his tone suddenly mild.

"My company downsized," she began.

"Got fired, did ya?" He chuckled with glee.

Jane sat back in her chair, wondering why he was so pleased. Then she decided to just tell him. What difference would it make anyway? "They gave my job to a younger, prettier woman," she began.

"Whore."

She couldn't disagree with him there. "And my old music teacher passed away."

"She's doomed to hell fire, just like the rest of them Papists."

"She was a Moravian, Uncle Pat, not a Catholic." Jane didn't bother to explain that the Hussites had been one of the first groups to rebel against Catholic rule. Her mother had told him at least a hundred times. He didn't know the history of the religion he preached so vehemently.

He scowled at her. "Just like your mamma. Her own family not good enough for her. Married into those Moravian heathens."

Jane forced herself to stay still. Anyone who didn't belong to Uncle Pat's gospel church was a Papist or a heathen in his eyes, sometimes both, depending on his mood. Then she said, "She asked me to take care of her house."

Her uncle frowned. "Who did?"

"My music teacher." Jane waited for him to nod. "You remember the one near Daddy's house where I grew up? The English Tudor?"

He blinked. "That was always a pretty place." He picked up the tea again, then set it down without drinking. "Guess I won't see your mamma again when I pass into glory. Some of the family'll be there, though."

"Are you in much pain?" she asked.

He ignored her question. "We was the closest in age, your mamma and me. We used to run around in them woods, climb trees. She was as good a climber as any boy." His eyes glowed. "But she turned on us. Went and got all highfalutin'." He shook his head.

"I'd love to hear more stories about those times," Jane said, meaning it.

"You wanna hear 'bout the depression, do you? Eatin' beans for weeks on end. Couldn't get no work. You with your fancy job. Took you all over the world."

"I thought you'd be pleased if family did well, Uncle Pat."

"This world's a vale of tears. Says so in the good book. Anyone who trucks with sinners is damned sooner or later. That's what you did, girlie."

Before she could think of a response, a mischievous look came over Uncle Pat's face. "Now you done got fired and you're all alone, right?"

"I still have plenty of family here."

"You never got married, did ya?"

Here we go. Jane sighed.

"No, sir. I guess I was too busy at my job."

"You're one of them bull-dykes, most likely."

Jane's eyes went wide. This was new. "Excuse me?"

"Just like the rest of them bitches over to Salem College."
Jane opened her mouth to say something, but he marched on.
"Got that Single Sisters' House. Dykes, every last one of 'em.
Whores."

"How can they be both dykes and whores, Uncle Pat? Isn't
that a contradiction?"

"Don't you sass me." He pointed a finger at her.

Jane stood up. It was worse than she remembered. "Let me
know if you need anything, Uncle Pat. A ride to the doctor,
someone to take care of your dogs."

"You always cared more about those damn dogs than your
own kin," he spat.

She turned to leave and found Misty standing in the hall
watching. Jane pulled an old business card out of her pocket,
wrote her cell phone number on it. "Call me if you need
anything."

"We'll be all right, I reckon. Have been all these years you
been away."

Jane nodded. *Fine, if that's the way you want it.*

"Nice to meet you," she said aloud.

"You leaving already?" Uncle Pat's voice was querulous,
aggrieved. "You just got here."

Jane turned halfway, exasperated.

"He's just that way," Misty whispered. "Getting worse, too.
Doctors give him two months at the most."

"God will damn those quacks," he shouted. Apparently
there was nothing wrong with his hearing.

"Take care, Uncle Pat. I'll come see you again." She knew
she was lying.

"Watch out for those adulterers you've taken up with," he
said, eyes narrowed, his face full of venom.

Jane turned and walked toward the front door.

"Whore," he shouted after her, "Heretic."

Outside, Jane marched over to the row of dog pens and
started opening the tiny cages. The beagles swarmed out, tails a
blur, licking her hands. They ran to the bushes, lifting their legs
or squatting as the case may be, then circled back and turned
their noses to the ground, milling around. One lifted his head

and bayed. The rest of the pack sniffed around him, then they took off into the woods as one.

CHAPTER SIX

I should have brought flowers, David thought for the hundredth time. Then the one that followed. *But that would make me look desperate.*

He'd called Jane a few days after the memorial concert, discovering to his surprise that she was indeed staying at the house. "I promised Miss Essig to take care of things," she'd told him. He'd invited her to dinner and been flabbergasted when she accepted.

David got out of the car, looked in the back seat and on the floorboards to see if he'd missed any trash. Looked clean enough to him. She wasn't going to sit back there anyway. It wasn't like they were teenagers and he was taking her to the drive-in. Had he ever taken her to the drive-in? He couldn't remember. He locked the car, pulled down his corduroy jacket and walked between the trimmed, box hedges to Miss Essig's English Tudor. He stuffed his hands in his pockets.

No, that makes me look stupid.

Pulled them out again. Tugged at his jacket. If he'd brought flowers, he'd have something to do with his hands. He was usually carrying an instrument case. Ringing the doorbell saved him from further worry. About that, at least.

He heard rapid footsteps, snuffling near the door sill, then a bark. She had a dog? Slower footsteps approached, a low voice, and then the door opened. There she stood, her blond hair now silvered, her eyes still that lapis blue, accentuated with laugh lines on the sides where he used to kiss, the right height to fit under his arm perfectly. He shook his head. Felt a nudge and looked down. An English bulldog squatted at his feet, slobbering all over his shoes. "You have a dog."

"Winston." The name held a command. The dog looked up at her adoringly. "Behave yourself." She patted the side of her thigh. The dog sat back up and studied David, one crooked tooth protruding past his jowls.

David bent and scratched the dog behind his ear. Winston leaned his head into David's touch and his back leg thumped as if to scratch, only it was too much trouble to really do it when you could have a human oblige. "I had boxers when I was a kid."

"I remember." David looked up to find Jane smiling down at them. "I'm glad you like him," she said.

"I love dogs," David said. "Did you drive out with him? Denver, right?"

"Yeah, I was in Denver." She turned and gestured for him to follow her into the living room. Winston padded beside him. "But the animals all belonged to Miss Essig."

"Animals, as in more than one?" David looked around.

"Two cats." She sat on one of the loveseats framing the fireplace.

David's gaze traveled around the familiar room and lit on the grand piano taking up most of the back corner. "Oh, my." He walked to it, turned up the key guard and played a few notes. "This brings back memories."

"You studied piano with Miss Essig?"

"Yeah." He smiled, played the first few bars of *Ode to Joy*. "But she always said the only way to stop me from talking all the time was to give me a horn."

Jane burst out laughing, like the clear ring of a bell. "Miss Essig said that? I can't imagine. She was such a lady."

"Maybe with you."

"I've learned a few things about her living here. She had some interesting tastes."

"Yeah?" David sat across from her. "Like what?" And just that easily they slipped into their friendship again.

Jane told him about the metaphysical books she'd discovered. "She was wild about Blake, too. There's a small room upstairs with replicas of his paintings, colored prints, and stacks of sketches."

"Blake?"

"The poet, painter and print maker. Said his poems were dictated by angels." She raised an elegant eyebrow.

"Oh—something about the doors of perception?"

"Yeah," and she quoted, "'If the doors of perception were cleansed, everything would appear to man as it is, infinite'. A few of the sketches were a little racy."

"Really? Miss Essig thinking about sex? I can't imagine that," he said, then realized who he was talking to and blushed.

Jane smiled. "So, what have you been doing since college?"

"You want my whole life story?"

"Absolutely." She sat back on the loveseat, a look of expectation on her face.

"I'm kind of hungry. How about over dinner?"

"Sure." She stood up and walked back to the foyer. Grabbed some kind of fancy microfiber parka that looked like it was made for hiking the Rocky Mountains. "Where should we go? I don't know the restaurants anymore."

"What do you like?"

"Is Sam's Gourmet still around?"

"They closed."

"Then you decide."

He'd been afraid she'd say that. He'd asked Brian where to take her. "Go to Foothill Brewery. You know you like their food."

"Naw, not somewhere we like to hang. What if it doesn't work out?"

"The K&W Cafeteria. You can afford that."

"Brian, it's a date."

"So?"

In the end he'd decided on a little place in the Arts District. "Let's go to Sweet Potatoes," he said. "Soul food New Orleans style."

"Sounds great." Over grits and shrimp, catfish, drunken duck, okra and, yes, sweet potatoes, they talked. Or he talked.

She kept asking him questions—about college in Chapel Hill, his marriage, his two kids, his long stretch working at Hanes. An excellent bottle of *Viognier* finished loosening David's tongue, and the whole story of Marley's battle with cancer spilled out of him.

He looked up to find her watching him, her eyes moist, a wistful look on her face. "I'm sorry," he blurted, "I've been going on and on."

She reached over and squeezed his hand. "Don't apologize. You've led such a rich life."

"Rich? Me? You're the one's been gallivanting all over the world, making scads of money." He kept his hand very still, hoping to prolong the touch. "I suppose."

Their eyes caught and held. The old fire stirred—just as one of the servers came and asked if she could clear their plates. Jane pulled back her hand, looked at her watch and sat up straighter. "I hadn't realized how late it is. We should let these people close up."

"But I haven't heard anything about your gallivanting," he said.

"I guess we'll have to go out again," she said, a coy look on her face. "Or I could ask you over to look at my sketches."

☆ ☆ ☆

During her morning run, Jane pushed herself hard, trying to drive away the images of David's face, his hands picking up a wine glass, the sound of his laugh. Then her mind would switch to worrying about what to do if it turned out she couldn't keep the house. Where would she move to? What would she do? She pushed herself harder, panting up the hill. Winston finally laid down in the middle of the path in protest. She doubled back, jogging in place. "Lazy dog."

He rolled over and offered his belly.

"Oh, all right." They walked the rest of the way home. They passed the newly tilled garden and Jane decided it would be a shame to let it go to waste, even if she was unsure about her future. She drove around to various nurseries, Winston hanging his head out the window in delirious delight. She bought a few sacks of bulbs—daffodils, tulips and jonquils, deciding to add irises because nothing was more depressing than a one-season flowerbed.

But when she got home, she headed for the piano. She'd let two days slip by without practicing. She'd just worked her way through a difficult passage in one of Bach's Concertos when the doorbell rang. She stopped mid-phrase and pulled the cover down over the keys as if to hide something precious. She tiptoed to the front door, avoiding the windows, and put her eye to the peep hole. Two people stood on the front stoop. The man wore a well-cut navy suit, the woman an aqua dress with a linen jacket. They both carried black bibles.

Just what I need.

She backed away, hoping they hadn't heard her, but ran smack into the umbrella stand. It fell, scattering its contents on the hardwood floor with a loud clatter. The doorbell rang again.

Damn it.

Jane plastered the smile of a Southern belle on her face and opened the door. "May I help you?"

"Ms. Frey?" the man asked.

She closed the door part way. "May I tell her who's calling?"

The man handed her a Victorian-style calling card of heavy ivory stock. "My name is Philip LeBelle." His accent was unremarkable, but his well-toned physique and hooded eyes suggested more than some garden-variety Christian out to save a few souls.

The name was printed on the card in an elegant font in dark sepia. A French name, perhaps from New Orleans? Beneath was a phone number. Jane didn't recognize the area code, but it included the country code of the United States. An international traveler.

The woman stepped forward, extending her hand. "I'm Margaret Burgundy." Her accent dripped deep South— magnolia trees and Spanish moss. "We wondered if we might have a bit of your time." Her hand came to rest on the bible she carried, suggesting the topic of their conversation.

Jane didn't believe her for a minute. "I'll tell her you called." She started to close the door.

"Please." Philip put his hand out to stop the door. "We knew Miss Essig and wanted to meet the new occupant."

Jane didn't believe that either, but didn't force the issue by slamming the door in his face. Maybe she'd learn something new. "Would you like some coffee on the porch?" she asked. Better to keep them out of the house. It was warm for November.

"That sounds just delightful," Margaret said.

"Since you knew Miss Essig, I'm sure you can find your way to the side porch. The door's unlatched. I'll just fetch the coffee." She smiled as she shut the front door.

In the kitchen, Jane used up the rest of the grocery store coffee Miss Essig seemed to have preferred, and while it perked, found some Moravian lemon cookies and spread them on a plate, grabbed mugs, cream and sugar. She poured the coffee in a carafe and headed to her guests.

Margaret had settled herself on a wicker chair in the corner of the screened-in porch. Philip stood by the door gazing off toward the line of bushes shielding the back yard. When Jane stepped onto the porch, he offered to take the tray.

"Thanks, but I've got it." She set the tray on a low table beside a rocking chair and poured mugs for everyone, then offered cookies. Margaret accepted, but Philip shook his head.

"I guess you've figured out that I'm Jane Frey."

Philip nodded, but Margaret feigned surprise. "How nice to meet you."

"I'm sorry I can't offer you anything stronger, but I haven't gotten around to creating a liquor cabinet." Jane watched to see if they'd be shocked by this suggestion. Uncle Pat would go apoplectic at the idea of drinking hard liquor, but these two simply nodded. The bibles were definitely props, she decided.

"Miss Essig didn't have anything alcoholic, of course."

"Coffee is just perfect," Margaret said. "And I just love these Moravian cookies. They're a weakness of mine." She must imagine her little girl imitation was fetching.

Just as Jane poured herself a cup and sat down, Winston ambled up from the backyard and scratched on the door. Philip opened it, but Winston studied him before coming in.

"What an adorable dog," Margaret effused. Winston walked over to her and snuffled over her shoes. The woman tucked her feet under the chair to avoid his jowls. The bulldog waddled over and sat in front of Jane, his eyes on Philip who finally took a seat. Once Philip seemed settled, Winston let out a sigh and laid down, his haunches on Jane's foot. He didn't trust this guy either.

Philip looked over at Margaret, who gave him an almost imperceptible nod. The man turned to Jane. "I suppose we should be direct with you about the purpose of our visit."

Jane put on her game face. "That would be best."

Margaret leaned forward, which surprised her. She'd thought Philip was the brains of this operation. Maybe he was the muscle. "You see, Miss Essig was my old piano teacher. I just adored her."

Jane nodded.

"About six months ago, Miss Essig called me. She was concerned about some strange goings on around here." She paused.

"Strange?" Jane prompted.

"Well, yes." Margaret crossed her ankles and took a sip of coffee. "You see, she knew about my cousin Philip."

"So, you two are cousins," Jane said.

"Right. Philip once worked in military intelligence."

Jane sat forward. "That sounds serious."

"She didn't want to hire a detective in town or get the police involved." Margaret wrinkled up her nose at the word 'police'. "You know what a small town this is. Of course, it's grown, but still."

"You both grew up here?"

That accent didn't come from the Carolinas, Jane thought. *But I don't sound like I grew up here either after living in the north for so long.*

"Well, I did, but Philip's family is from—"

"We don't want to waste Ms. Frey's time." Philip's voice had an edge.

Winston lifted his head and growled.

"Miss Essig," he continued in a softer tone "told me she'd heard voices in the night and one day she discovered that some of her things had been gone through."

"I see." Jane soothed Winston, leaning down to get control of her expression.

Philip cleared his throat. "I wanted to alert you to the situation. Offer my services if anything unusual happens. I have connections that the local authorities can't access."

"Well, I have your card." Jane shifted in her chair.

But he didn't take her hint. "You probably know she has quite a Blake collection. A few originals. She was concerned."

"Is that right?" Jane looked from one of her guests to the other. "Now that she has passed, what is your interest?"

"We just wanted to be sure you were safe," Margaret said, all wide-eyed innocence.

"I suggested that Miss Essig put in a new security system," Phillip said. "I hope she took my advice."

Jane smiled. "One must take care of such valuable art. Originals, you say?" It had never crossed her mind any those paintings and sketches she'd discovered could be originals. She doubted it.

"I'd be happy to recommend someone."

"If you could send me your resume, I'd appreciate it." Jane glanced at his card. "I'll email you."

The muscles in Philip's jaw tightened. "Of course."

Jane allowed the silence that followed to lengthen to the point of becoming uncomfortable. Someone started up a leaf blower across the street.

"I hope you'll forgive me for saying so," Phillip finally said, "but we're concerned that you've been pulled into something you don't fully understand."

Margaret leaned forward. "You see, Miss Essig suspected that someone in the neighborhood was involved in pagan rituals. Perhaps even devil worship."

Jane blinked. "Excuse me?"

"Miss Essig didn't just hear voices at night. She heard chanting," Margaret explained.

Jane pushed down a spike of anger. "In this day and age, I'd hope that people would understand the difference between the indigenous rituals of old Europe and devil worship."

Phillip took his turn. "The Moravians have been involved in questionable practices in the past."

"Such as?" Jane's voice rose. This was getting to be a trend.

"They were run out of one town in Germany because of their—" he paused to consider his next word "—parties, let's say."

"Parties?" Jane's face burned. "I'm sure I don't know what you mean. And I can assure you, Ms. Burgundy, that if the Moravians went in for paganism, I would know it." She stood up, dislodging Winston from her foot. "Good day to you."

Margaret gaped at her. Phillip stood up and held the door open for his cousin, who fluttered a bit, then said, "I'm sorry if we offended you."

Margaret walked out the door, followed by Phillip, who turned and said, "My offer of assistance still stands."

Jane nodded, not trusting herself to speak. She watched the two walk along the edge of the graveled driveway to their car. Just what had she gotten herself into? Did these people know something she didn't? But devil worship? That was ridiculous. The Moravians had never gone in much for dire warnings about the devil, not like her mother's side of the family. Surely these two could do better than that. One of her secretaries had called herself a pagan. She'd told Jane that they were resurrecting the Goddess, returning to the old ways—whatever that meant. It had all sounded harmless enough. But these two knew about the Blake collection. What was their interest in it? And what else did they know?

The next morning Jane woke from an intense dream and tried to carry the music she'd been hearing out with her. She'd been walking down a hallway, some urgency pushing her onward. The music swelled around her. Glorious music. The kind she fantasized writing as a child. Before she'd given up music for money.

She stumbled down to the grand piano in the living room, trying not to wake up fully, but by the time she reached it, the music had fled, replaced by the jubilant song of birds.

Back upstairs, she showered. After her usual breakfast of toast and French roast, she went out to plant the bulbs. She really should talk to Anna about her two visitors from yesterday. She'd seen a security panel next to the front door, but it wasn't connected. Nobody had mentioned it or shown her how to use it. Maybe it was time to get it working.

Thoughts of her first date in years distracted her from actually making the call. David was a good man, handsome, kind, worth cultivating a friendship with at the very least.

Friendship, right. Then why did you flirt with him?

She walked away from this thought toward the old tool shed. An examination turned up a good set of rakes and hand spades along with a wide-brimmed straw hat. Winston found some shade in the clump of bushes that separated the gardens from the driveway, burrowing deep into the red earth. The cats stalked birds and insects—there'd still been no hard frost—then found their own hidden spots to doze.

Jane took her time, first sorting through the bulbs the gardening crew had piled at the sides of the beds. She took out the bulbs she'd bought, comparing them to match species, then made piles. Then she stood back and planned a design, putting irises next to early bloomers, taller plants in the back, then started planting.

Around one o'clock, Dorothea dropped by and watched from the shade of an apple tree. Late bees droned amongst the brown spotted apples that lay half hidden in the grass beneath the tree. After a few minutes, she broke their companionable silence, "We decided not to cook tonight. Everyone's busy, so I thought I'd take a break."

Jane looked up and wiped sweat from her eyes. "Good idea. Should we go out?"

Dorothea shook her head. "I'm planning a quiet evening."

"I could make some spanakopita. It's one of my specialties."

"What?"

"Greek. Spinach and feta in filo dough." Jane stood up and stretched her back.

Dorothea made a face. "Feta is too tart."

"You'd like it the way I make it."

"Maybe some other time." Dorothea smoothed her ever-present apron. "Will you go anywhere tonight?"

She started to ask Dorothea if she knew anything about her two mysterious visitors from yesterday, but decided to wait. She'd talk to Anna instead. Anna seemed more worldly than the motherly Dorothea. Instead she answered the question. "No, not after all this bending and squatting. I think I'll need a hot bath."

"Well, have a nice evening." Dorothea walked down the length of the garden.

"You, too," Jane called after her.

Dorothea ducked through yet another gap in the hedge that Jane remembered from hide and seek games with her friends. Her father had built his own house only blocks away from his family home, the one he and all his siblings had been born in, the one her multiple-great grandfather had built. She had sold her father's house after he died, thinking she'd never come back.

The civil rights movement had punctuated her childhood and by her junior year, all the schools were integrated. Jane's friends came from both sides of the racial divide, but were united in their views. They'd marched and partied together. She still remembered coming out of a restaurant and some old man spitting on her shoes because she'd sat at a booth with two black kids. They got their share of threats, nasty comments spit through the telephone. Men following her in their cars. Being pulled over by the cops and told where she'd been all day long. No tickets, just letting her know they were keeping an eye on her. Later, she figured it had steeled her nerves for business with bankers and oil executives.

Women's liberation didn't really get going until college, and she'd jumped in with both feet, throwing off the admonitions of her mother and aunts to act like a lady with the same glee she'd experienced during the lunch counter protests. The condemnations and judgments of her small town had threatened to constrain her like a plant whose roots had already filled its tiny pot, prompting it to stop stretching for the sky and start working on the next generation. She'd gone where she could stretch and continue to grow. Not like David, who settled down when Marley had found herself pregnant.

But now Jane found new restrictions on returning to her hometown. The house she'd thought was a gift turned out to be a loan. A life-long loan, yes, but what other conditions would she discover? Maybe she'd been right back then. Maybe she should just pack up and leave. Again.

But then there was David.

Jane sat in the dirt, looking at her new garden in the slanting rays of the afternoon sun. Her life had been rich and varied, that much was true, but she'd found as many restrictions out in that big world. In the early days, male executives were treated to lavish parties with cocaine and bought women while their female counterparts were expected to go to their hotel rooms and pretend they didn't know anything. The men had their families who were invited over to the CEOs house for barbeques, but if the women married and took the time a baby demanded, they found their careers derailed.

Now some of the new professional women took it all for granted—professional careers and families. These employed a small army to care for their enormous houses and small families, like the royalty of old Europe. And the women warriors who'd fought for their access were now an embarrassment to some. Too strident. No sense of humor. Too many younger women didn't have a clue they were repeating the very words used to condemn the feminist movement twenty years earlier, the movement that had made their current lives possible. Not all, of course. She'd mentored some excellent assistants. Just not enough.

Jane dusted off this familiar round of thoughts along with the garden soil on her jeans, gathered her tools and put them away in the shed. She walked back through the lengthening shadows, her animals trailing after her. In the kitchen she found a thermos with a note. "I heard you have some sore muscles. These herbs should help you sleep." There was no signature. She'd heard Anna knew some folk remedies, although this fit more with her image of Dorothea.

Jane didn't think she'd need this kind of help. Instead she ran a bath with Epson salts and found a good bottle of Chardonnay—much tastier than an herbal drink and just as effective. She drank half of it in the tub. Later, wrapped in a thick terry-cloth robe, she finished off the wine with some chilled shrimp and cocktail sauce. She washed her one dish and one glass, then went up to the single bed in the bedroom just up the stairs. Only her animals crowded in with her.

CHAPTER SEVEN

Philip slipped into the back door of Jane Frey's house onto a screened-in porch. The lock on the kitchen door took about two seconds to pick. He paused and listened. Silence. He took a step inside and shined his penlight around. Light bounced off copper pots hanging above an island cook top. He pushed through a swinging door into a breakfast nook. The dining room next to this was filled with unopened boxes. Books sprawled in the corner.

Coming to the house yesterday had been a risk, but worth it. He'd hoped to do a bit of reconnoiter, figure out where to look. Also to win her over, convince her there might be some risk of burglars. Older women who lived in small towns were usually easy to manipulate, but her background in big business had made her more sophisticated than he'd anticipated. Not that much, though. She knew about the Blake prints. He could tell by her response, but nothing more.

In the long living room he looked for a safe behind pictures and books. Nothing. Then he moved to a library, pushed all around the fireplace, but nothing moved to reveal a hidden nook. He checked behind pictures and more books, then made his way up the stairs, listening for any movement. The house remained silent.

Behind the door at the top he heard snoring—two sets of snores, in fact. Good. That little night cap always did the trick.

He moved down the hall, heard something. He turned back. A gleam of light reflected back at him. He moved the penlight and found a cat watching him. The cat remained still. Philip pushed open a door to a room directly above the library. A small bed, a box of toys.

In the next one he hit the jackpot. Paintings covered the walls. He moved closer. Looked like Blake to him. He'd done a crash course on the plane. He closed the door behind him and switched on the light. The door rattled. He looked down and saw a paw groping underneath. He opened the door before it could make any noise and the cat ran in, rubbed its chin on the corner of the room and sat to watch him.

Philip started snapping photos. He carefully set each sketch against a blank wall and took a picture. The cat pushed at the door, asking to leave. Philip opened it quickly before the calico's request was verbalized, then shut it as the mottled haunches and straight tail vanished down the hallway. He heard singing in the distance. Probably a radio from a neighbor. He finished up the pictures, turned off the light, then heard the bedroom door down the hall open.

A woman's voice said, "You're supposed to protect me, you know."

He stood stock still.

★ ★ ★

Late in the night, something woke Jane. She lifted her head from the pillow and listened. Faint singing floated up from somewhere. A radio probably. She pulled a pillow over her ear and burrowed deeper, but sleep did not return. Wrapping up in her robe, she moved toward the sound, thinking maybe she'd left a window open, but the windows in the front bedroom that adjoined the one she was using were all closed tight.

She called Winston. "You're supposed to protect me, you know." He licked her hand as if in apology and walked down the hall in front of her. The sound grew more distinct. Was someone parked in her driveway listening to music? The door to Miss Essig's room stood ajar. She pushed it open and the singing grew louder so that she could almost make out words. Maybe some drunk sat outside singing to the moon.

She walked over to the windows that faced the front of the house, but they were closed also. The other set looked out on the backyard. Closed. A half-moon lit the new garden. The rose bushes looked like a pencil sketch in the muted light. Suddenly Marvin burst from the walk-in closet.

Jane screamed.

Winston barked.

Suzie B ran in from the hallway to join him.

A tiny, dark shape dove under the bed. The cats followed in hot pursuit.

"You scared the crap out of me!" she scolded.

The mouse made a dash across the floor and squeezed behind the chest of drawers. The cats took up positions on each end, tails twitching, ears perked, ignoring her. Then she realized the singing had stopped. The car must have driven away.

How had a mouse gotten up here? Steeling herself for more rodents, she walked to the closet and nudged the door open the rest of the way. She'd expected it to be stuffed with Miss Essig's old clothes, decade after decade of fashion, but instead she found bare wood. Except for a shadow in the corner.

Her hand groped for a light switch, but slide down a smooth wall.

"Winston," she called.

Loud breathing announced his presence.

She swung her hand over her head. A string brushed her fingers. She tried to grab it, but missed. On the second attempt, she captured it and pulled. Harsh light from the bare bulb flooded the closet. She closed her eyes against the glare for a second, then squinted.

The dark shadow in the corner remained. A panel stood partly open. She'd thought the wall was just that—a solid wall. But there was an opening. Winston sat in the doorway, his head cocked. The singing had started again, softer this time. It was coming from behind the open panel.

Jane forced herself to move. She walked to the wall, pushed the panel all the way open and carefully looked inside. A narrow set of steps descended at a steep angle into darkness. The singing was even louder inside the stairwell. She didn't know if she would fit inside. It was too steep for the dog, that was for sure, but the cats would have no trouble with it. At least the mystery of how the mouse had gotten in had been solved.

Jane ran back into her room and threw on sweats, laced up her running shoes, then rushed down to the kitchen and rummaged through a drawer. She finally found a flashlight in the corner of the pantry. She ran back upstairs with it and shined a beam of light down the steps. No cobwebs. It had been used recently. Or cleaned. And not by a rodent, but someone tall enough to clear the cobwebs. Steeling herself, she stepped into the narrow passage.

But what if she ran into an intruder? Thieves usually didn't sing, but still. Jane backed out again and surveyed the room. A set of antique irons, heavy black metal, sat on a table next to the chaise lounge, serving as bookends. She picked one up and swung it in an arch. It would work. Jane made her way back to the closet, squeezed into the steps and started down. Her shoulders were too broad, so she angled her body and kept descending. Winston stuck his head through the opening and whined.

"Hush," she whispered, then listened. The singing continued. It sounded like a rhythmic chant now.

What had Philip and Margaret said? That Miss Essig heard chanting? A shiver chilled Jane. She steeled herself and moved forward.

A few more steps and the flashlight faded. She hit it against her hand. A flicker, then nothing. "Damn," she muttered. Wouldn't you know the batteries would go dead? She tucked the useless plastic cylinder in her pocket.

Encased in the deep dark of the narrow staircase, Jane forced herself to keep descending. Her upper thighs, already aching from an afternoon of squatting in the garden, started to shake. A dank, moldy smell wafted up from below, making her appreciate the clean, dry scent of old wood. She kept going.

A few more steps and the dark greyed. On the next, her foot hit dirt. Mildew filled her nostrils. She lifted her face but no breeze touched her cheek. She must still be inside. She held up her hand and could just make out its shape.

Then she heard someone breathing. She froze. Her heart pounded. Damn, it was a burglar. Or worse. Lifting the iron in front of her, she took a step toward the sound. Then another. Her knee bumped into something dense and warm.

She screamed.

Winston barked.

"Oh, my God." She reached out and found the solid shoulder of the bulldog. "You guys are going to scare me to death."

Winston licked her hand.

"How did you get down here, anyway?"

As if in answer, Winston turned away from the secret stairway and headed into the darkness. She grabbed his collar and followed, slowing him down so she didn't scrap her shins. He made his way through a lighter grey patch in the darkness. The texture of the floor changed from compacted dirt to concrete. Square shapes hunkered in the corner. She reached up and found another string. Flicked it. The washer and dryer gleamed stark white under the light from another bare bulb. She stood in the basement right next to where the laundry chute dumped out. Just beyond that, a set of stairs went up to the hallway near the small library.

Now that she could see, Jane walked back where she'd come from. Winston had led her through an opening between two overlapping walls. No wonder she hadn't noticed it before. She went back through, the bulldog at her heels, and found Suzie B sitting at the bottom of the steps busily cleaning her face. It would seem the mouse had been dispatched.

Jane looked around for another light switch or a string hanging from an overhead bulb. Finding none, she moved so the light from the laundry room fell on the far wall. Only a thin beam of light made it through the opening, revealing paneled walls just like the ones in the closet upstairs. Did one of them pop open to provide access to yet another set of stairs or a passageway? Jane ran her hand over the wood, pressing at the joints. Nothing.

A cat rubbed against her leg. She reached down and found long fur. Marvin. She scratched behind his ear, grateful for another warm body. Then she leaned her head against the wood and listened. She thought she heard a scrape, then a murmur of what could be voices. She pushed against the panels more firmly. Nothing budged.

"Damn," she whispered. It was too dark to really see anything. This would have to wait until morning.

Jane made her way back to the laundry room, then down the hallway that led to the greenhouse to the right. She lugged two large flower pots back and put them in front of the opening. Any intruder coming out from a secret panel in that wall would trip over the pots, making a clatter. She climbed up into the house and locked the door behind her. Then walked into the kitchen, put the flashlight on the counter and grabbed a pile of dishes which she propped against the door to the basement, then locked the new pet door she had installed. She'd hear if anyone tried to come in.

The clock on the stove read 3:33. Too early to stay up, but could she sleep after this? She thought about the herbal tea in the kitchen, but if she drank it, she'd sleep too late. Winston headed up to the bedroom and the cats bounded up behind him. Jane picked up the antique iron and followed. She went into Miss Essig's room and closed the panel in the closet, locked the door to the room, then walked back to her bedroom, locking that door behind her as well. All three animals lounged on the bed watching, eyes shining. To them it was all a grand adventure.

Philip waited until Jane was in the master bedroom and slipped down the stairs silently. He walked carefully through the long living room and out through the side porch, then jogged to his vehicle, watching for lights or cars. Once there, he emailed all his pictures to Coche, then headed to his hotel. He probably could grab a couple hours sleep before he got a response.

CHAPTER EIGHT

Jane woke to a riot of grackles in the tall fir outside her window. Marvin was tearing at the rug in front of the locked door. She opened it, ran down the stairs behind him, and let him out. Then she unlocked the pet door to the basement. After a shower, she brewed up some French roast and took it to her computer where she checked the Asian and Middle Eastern markets. Oil and gas prices were mimicking a roller coaster. On Monday, she might move some money if the conditions were right.

She wandered outside, quite aware that she was avoiding the dank basement for the moment. She strolled through the yard sipping her coffee, enjoying the tepid sunlight of a November morning.

Bells rang in the steeple of the New Marienborn Moravian Church announcing the beginning of Sunday school. She walked over to the hedge and glanced through a small gap in the boxwood hedge. Cars filled the parking lot. People walked in, greeting each other, some dressed in jeans, others in nice dresses and suits.

She briefly considered calling David, but decided against it. She could face the dark basement on her own. Jane veered off to the shed. She was going to find out if that wall was solid even if she had to do some damage. She picked a strong hammer from the pegboard on the wall, then a larger one just in case. A crow bar leaned against a corner. Grabbing it, she made her way into the basement, taking two flashlights and new batteries with her. The cats followed, hoping for more mice. Winston stretched out on the concrete floor and was soon snoring. Some watchdog.

Rummaging around, she found two milk crates and set one flashlight on each, illuminating the wall as best she could. The old, knotty pine paneling, expensive for a basement and even a closet wall, had darkened over time to a deep honey. Starting at one end, Jane walked the ten feet or so of wall, pushing against the paneling as she went. Nothing gave way. She tried higher on the wall with no results. With her ear to the paneling, she tapped, listening for any change in the sound. About half way, the tap hollowed out, changing key. She kept going and after about three feet the echo from the panel deepened again. About the width of a door.

Containing her excitement, Jane went back to the hollow sound and tapped higher up. Her knuckles produced the same empty echo. She continued along the panel until the echo changed back to a solid sound. She grabbed a flashlight and turned the beam to high. Sure enough, just where the sound changed one panel ended and another began. Working her way along the edge, she pushed against it, hoping to spring a lock. About a third of the way down the wall, the panel moved inward and with a click, swung open.

Marvin ran inside.

"Wait," she called after him.

Suzie B followed.

"Damn," she muttered. Grabbing the flashlight again, she pulled the panel fully open, took a deep breath and stepped inside. She'd expected a continuation of the concrete walls of the basement, maybe even a packed dirt floor, but instead she found smooth walls painted a soft ivory. Beneath her feet ran a maroon carpet, as dark as spilled blood. There was something familiar about it.

She listened but heard nothing. A couple of feet inside the corridor, a sconce with an amber glass covering hung on the wall. Better not switch on a light and give away her presence, although it might be too late for that since she'd been tapping and banging.

Jane followed the well-appointed hallway until she came to a set of stairs that led down. She stepped onto old wood, worn into a dip in the middle from the passage of many feet over more than a century. The next step groaned beneath her weight. She paused, but heard only silence. She crept down the old staircase, testing each step to see if it would hold her, hoping to avoid more creaks. The structure was sturdy. At the bottom, two corridors stretched off at a right angle. Picking the left one at random, Jane walked about five feet before coming to another door. Leaning her ear against it, she listened. Silence. She tried the handle and it turned. She pushed the door open and stuck her head around the door, then stepped inside. Out of habit, her hand reached for a light switch. She found one and after a moment's hesitation, flipped it on.

Dappled light yellowed the ivory walls to papyrus. Two large metal stars with tiny flower cutouts suspended from the ceiling created this effect. Paintings hung at intervals, separated by curtained alcoves. The room was redolent of rose incense. At the other end of the room hung an enormous painting in vivid reds and oranges. Jane walked toward it. The piece had the look of William Blake, which didn't surprise her given Miss Essig's collection upstairs. She wondered if this was what her visitors had been after.

The colors resolved into forms, and they stopped her dead in her tracks. A man sat on a stool of some kind. Great golden wings rose from his back. The halo around his head erupted into gold and scarlet, a look of ecstasy on his face. And he might well be ecstatic. A woman straddled him, her long, luxurious curls entwining with her own wings, her limbs wrapped around her mate, her head surrounded by a vivid aura, her face tilted upward. One of her arms stretched up toward a figure of Christ standing in a garden, a beatific look on his soft, androgynous face, graceful hands held out as if offering comfort. His side dripped blood. Bees flew around his wound as if it were a flower.

"Oh, my God," Jane whispered.

On the low table in front of the painting sat a small version of a standing stone, its surface rough, rising to a rounded point. Balancing this piece on the opposite side sat a chalice cut from alabaster. A gutted candle in a glass holder gave off a strong scent of beeswax. It reminded her of Christmas Eve.

Jane turned and looked at some of the other paintings. Their subjects met her expectations—Christ meeting with his disciples, a close-up of Jesus with his crown of thorns and hands folded in front of him, a third of Count Zinzendorf preaching to a crowd of early Moravians, rays of light falling on his heart and around the room. She pulled one of the blue curtains aside and found a door painted the same shade of blue. It opened into a small chamber, the same color blue, only slightly larger than a closet, furnished with a simple ladder back chair and a side table. On the wall hung a print just like the ones she'd found in Miss Essig's Blake room featuring a bed in a simple bedroom enclosed in an elaborate scrolled border.

In a larger alcove sat a double bed neatly made up with white sheets and covered by a quilt with the same star pattern as the one she now slept under. Jane touched her star pendant. Two white robes hung on a hook on the back side of the door. A white cap with a blue ribbon. Hadn't married women worn blue, unmarried pink?

Jane shifted uneasily, then opened a drawer in the small wooden bedside table, painted blue to match the walls, and found a pamphlet with the seal of the OGMS on it. She opened it and leafed through the pages, finding hymns and some liturgy. Moravian hymns were catalogued by tune name, and the name for the first one caught her eye: *Seelenbrautigam.*

Soul bridegroom. Jane whispered the translation.

All the implications coalesced in her mind. Overwhelmed, she slammed the book shut. Ran out to the main room, found a bench and sank onto it. After a minute, she looked back down the length of the room to the painting and the altar—there was no other word for it.

Bells clanged somewhere above her head and echoed down the hallway. She jumped up, startled by the sudden noise, and wrapped her arms around herself. Time for church.

Time for church indeed, she thought. She wondered how many of the people settling into their pews right now, opening their hymn books, shushing their children, had any inkling of what lay beneath them. She imagined her grandmother's reaction.

But why was she scandalized? She'd been to feminist workshops reclaiming the goddess or exploring sexuality. Hell, there'd even been a seminar where they looked at their genitals in mirrors, trying to challenge cultural conditioning that told them the vagina was dirty and disgusting. She'd gotten tickets to the opening of the artist Judy Chicago's *The Dinner Party*. Plates around a dinner table, painted with labial folds as flowers, each one for an important feminist figure.

But this? She was not prepared for this. Jane shivered, trying to accept what she was seeing. These were rooms for sacred, ritualized sex. What else could they be? Right under a Moravian church? She hugged herself tighter.

After a minute, Jane gave herself a shake and walked back to the room with the bed. She checked to see if the drawer in the bedside table was completely closed and pulled the star quilt taut. She didn't think she'd touched anything in the main chamber, but checked to be sure, then walked back to the door, turned off the lights and made her way back down the hallway. She paused where the corridor branched off and listened. Footsteps sounded from the direction she hadn't explored. Growing louder.

She ran to the basement opening and ducked through, closed the panel quietly behind her, raced up the stairs to the kitchen and stood at the sink, heart racing. No sound came from the basement steps behind her. After a few minutes, she figured no one was following her. Jane turned around, wondering what to do next and noticed the thermos from Anna sitting on the counter.

"No, they couldn't possibly . . ."

She picked it up, screwed off the top and took a whiff. It smelled like chamomile with honey. But she'd found it in the kitchen last night. If it had more than chamomile in it, then that faint singing would never have awakened her.

Jane rummaged in the pantry. Toward the back of the top shelf, she found clean mason jars. She took one down and poured the herbal concoction into the jar, washed out the thermos and set it in the drainer. But where could she take the liquid to be tested? She reached into her pocket for her cell phone, but it wasn't there. Had it fallen out while she was in that room? She'd checked everything carefully. She picked up the house phone to dial her number, then imagined whoever belonged to the footsteps finding her mobile. She hung up the house phone and ran up to her bedroom. The cell sat on the dressing table.

She called Lois Williams. The call rang through to her voice mail, but just as Jane took a breath to leave a message, Lois answered. "Jane. What's up?"

"I'm sorry to bother you on a Sunday, but—"

Lois's hearty laugh interrupted her. "Oh girl, we've got to get you out of the South."

This warmed the chill in Jane's belly a little. "Maybe so. Listen, some weird things are going on. I found a secret stairway behind the closet—"

"A what?"

"Stairway. It leads to the basement."

"Maybe it was built during the Civil War. You know, to hide from us Yankees."

Jane wondered how many martinis Lois had drunk already. "I need to have some tea analyzed to see if there's a sedative in it."

Silence.

"Lois?"

"What did you say?"

Jane repeated herself.

"That's what I thought you said."

"I want to get it tested. Does your firm have any contacts down here?"

"What the fuck is going on?"

"That's what I'm trying to find out." She told Lois about the two visitors, the sounds she'd heard last night and the room. But she couldn't bring herself to tell her what she'd found there. Not yet. "This Anna, she's probably the one who left me the tea. I want to know if she was trying to knock me out last night so I wouldn't hear anything."

"Jane, this is serious."

"Why do you think I called you?"

"Okay—" Lois seemed out of breath "—I'm heading up to my computer. We have a contract with a national lab. I'll see if they have an office in Greensboro."

"Winston-Salem," she corrected.

"Whatever. I've got the address in my computer. Call you back."

Jane sat in the rocker in the corner of the bedroom looking out at the tall evergreen just outside. A robin sat on a branch looking back at her. And if the tea had something else in it besides chamomile? What then?

She jumped when the phone finally rang. "Yeah?"

"Got the address," Lois said. "I called and said we had an emergency. Do you know where Baptist Hospital is?"

"Of course." Jane's tight shoulders relaxed a little.

"What's with you guys down there? Is everything religious?"

Jane laughed. "Not really."

"The lab is just down the street from the hospital." Lois gave her the name and address. "They'll be expecting you."

"Thanks."

"Will you be safe tonight?""I've got things locked up."

"Yeah, right. Sounds like that place has more holes in it than a round of Swiss cheese. I'm going to ask the local police to drive by and keep an eye out."

"Don't."

"Why ever not?"

"It'll get back to Anna. This is a small town."

"Jesus," Lois said. "You'd better take care of yourself.""I will. I've got Miss Essig's bulldog with me."

Lois snorted at this, then said, "Listen, I'm doing a little checking on this OGMS. I'll call when I get the report. Can you get me some clear copies of those old documents? They were just too blurred."

"Yeah, I'll go by the archives tomorrow."

"In the meantime, the lab will send me a copy of their findings. I told them to give you one, too."

"Talk to you later."

Jane grabbed her purse and keys, and went down to the kitchen. She wrapped the mason jar of tea in a dish towel to cushion it and placed it in a cloth grocery bag. Then she called Winston. He ambled into the kitchen and sat down, head cocked. "Want to go for a ride?"

The bulldog barked in the affirmative.

"Come on, then." They jumped into her car and drove across town.

Baptist Hospital had grown since she'd been born in it. The glass-front structure dominated the hill above the freeway. The receptionist at the lab just half a block away told her it would take an hour for the results and asked for her fax number.

"I'll come back to get my copy." She didn't want anything going to the house, so she gave them her cell number, then drove down Hawthorne Road to the park where she ambled around with Winston, to his great delight. She'd always liked this neighborhood, with its big hill rounding up from the creek in terraced streets dotted with old Queen Anne homes. During her senior year in high school, she'd worked in an Italian restaurant just across the road and bugged the owner to let her sing once in a while. That same year, she and her best friend had driven in the little Peugeot her uncle had bought her to Reynolds High School to take an advanced placement course. Every inch of this town brought back memories. Jane realized she was trying not to think about the present. Better to wait for facts than let her mind run through various scenarios. But run through scenarios was just what it did. She walked faster, but her thoughts kept pace.

True to their word, the lab called in just over an hour, rescuing her from her imagination, and she drove over to pick up the results. The receptionist handed her an envelope through a slot in her little glass cage. Jane sat in the one chair in the alcove that passed for a waiting room, opened it and scanned the list of chemicals, which turned out to be all in Latin. She went back to the desk. "Excuse me."

The round-faced woman looked up.

"Would it be possible to get a little help interpreting this?"

The receptionist rolled her brown eyes and with a sigh picked up the phone. Jane couldn't hear what she said. Then the woman turned back. "Someone will be right with you, ma'am."

After a minute, a lanky man with thin blond hair and bulging eyes opened the door and led her to an office with a small round table and two chairs. They sat. "I'm sorry to inconvenience you, but I need some assistance reading this." She slid the report over to him.

He pulled a pair of silver reading glasses from the pocket of his white lab coat and hunched over the paper. "These ingredients here—alphabisabolol and bisabolol oxide derivatives, farnesene, matricine, chamazulene, apigenin and luteolin—suggest this is some kind of herbal concoction."

"What do those chemicals do?"

"They're anti-inflammatory and anti-spasmodic mainly."

"Would this add up to chamomile tea?"

"Could be." He shrugged.

She let out a long sigh of relief. "Anything else?"

He peered back at the sheet of paper, running his thin forefinger down the list, stopping toward the bottom. "Barbiturates."

A jolt of adrenaline straightened Jane's spine. "How much?"

"Let's see." He chewed on his lip.

"Is the dosage lethal?" she asked.

"For an adult? No. But there's enough in there to knock someone out for the night. It would depend on the weight of the subject."

Jane jumped up and refolded the report. "Thank you for your time."

He blinked, startled. "Glad I could be of—"

The door closed, swallowing his last word. Jane hurried outside, jumped in the car and pointed it down the hill, then found her way onto the interstate. She drove. She had to think. Anna had tried to drug her, which meant she was involved in the tantric room, as she'd come to think of it.

Winston whined, then turned and licked the closed window. Jane grimaced, but opened it for him. He hung his head out. They reached Clemmons. She took the closest exit and headed toward Tanglewood Park.

Jane guessed she wouldn't want to be interrupted if she had a sex party planned. But she wouldn't drug someone to hide it. She'd invite them to join in. She guessed. Actually, she'd never been to an orgy. Had a three-way in college once, but that had been during the sexual revolution. What she'd heard last night hadn't sounded like wild debauchery. There'd been singing—then a chant. Maybe it had been some sort of sexual ritual. There seemed to be small rooms along each side for privacy. Had she heard more than two voices?

Weren't these people some of the leaders of the church? It had seemed that way during Miss Essig's funeral. If that's where the sound had come from. She hadn't explored the whole underground structure yet. And how had Philip and Margaret known about chanting? If those were their real names.

What if Miss Essig had been involved when she was alive? The rooms hadn't looked new. Those steps were worn. They'd definitely been there a while. She must have known. The thought made her cringe.

Jane pulled to a stop behind the last car in a long line to get into Tanglewood Park. It was Sunday afternoon, after all. She didn't want to sit and wait. To face the possibility that her beloved music teacher—the most proper and self-contained woman she'd ever known, the woman she'd modeled herself after as a budding adolescent, the woman who'd shepherded her through college, who'd been a second mother, her mentor in female independence and grace—had either been involved in group sex or been drugged so she wouldn't know it was happening. A cold shiver ran the length of Jane's body.

She pulled the car out of line and headed back to I-40. She drove toward Mocksville. If she moved fast enough, maybe she could outrun the logical, but completely unacceptable, inferences arriving in her mind. Her Blackberry rang.

It was Lois. "Barbiturates."

"They told me," Jane said.

"I want you out of there. Somebody tried to kill you."

"But it wasn't a lethal dose."

"Maybe they're just incompetent. Maybe they'll get the dose right next time."

"Next time?" Jane shook her head. "I'm not going to let them do this to Miss Essig." A tear rolled down her cheek.

"What are you talking about? She's dead. You're the one they're after now."

"But that doesn't make sense. If they didn't want me in the house, why call me at all? Why tell me about the lot?"

Jane pulled the car over and more tears rolled down her cheeks. Winston whined and tried to lick her face. She pushed him away.

"The lot? There's an empty lot next to the house?"

Jane explained how the lot was used to make decisions. Then she told Lois about the tantric room, tears seeping from her eyes. Winston kept trying to climb into her lap to comfort her. She scratched his chest to appease him.

"Jesus, Jane, these people are some kind of cult."

"We're just ordinary—" She stopped when she heard herself.

"You're lucky you didn't drink that tea," Lois continued. "Then you'd have been the star in *Rosemary's Baby*."

The image pulled a sputtering laugh from her. She wiped her face with a paper napkin she found in the glove compartment. "I'm not convinced they're dangerous. Decadent, yes."

"The first sign—denial."

"Come on, Lois."

"I could arrange for private security, but it's expensive."

"Not yet."

"I'm going to deepen our investigation of this Anna. And all the people who were at that meeting. I'll let you know what we find out. In the meantime, you be careful."

"Will do."

Jane hung up, turned the car around and drove back to Miss Essig's house. It didn't feel like home anymore. When she arrived, everything looked quiet. It was past two o'clock and the church parking lot stood empty. When she opened the car door, Winston headed for the garden and she decided to let him be. She went inside. Still quiet. She opened the door to the basement and listened. Nothing.

Jane meandered through the bottom floor from the kitchen to the breakfast nook to the formal dining room, now full of boxes—each area setting off new memories. She settled at the piano in the long living room. Her fingers moved through a few scales, some chords, then she found herself playing Debussy's *Clair de Lune*. Her heart swelled with the music. She'd learned the piece on this very piano with Miss Essig at her side, whose eyes had been fixed just above the mantle, staring out at her own private dreams, her elegant hands moving in the air counting time. She'd stood and applauded when Jane had finished the piece for the first time without making any mistakes. "Beautiful. Doesn't Debussy speak straight to our hearts?"

Jane played for an hour, moving through piece after piece that evoked memories of Miss Essig, college and her amateur concerts, sinking into a trance. She found herself playing the opening of the music in her dream, but ran up against a blank. No sound rose to guide her forward. She played the beginning again, but the next phrase eluded her. Peace eluded her also.

That evening, Jane decided to face the enemy. She walked to Dorothea's house in the early evening to see what she could find out about last night. She hadn't thought she could hide her emotional turmoil through a whole meal, but for a short visit, she could behave normally.

Dorothea greeted her with a big hug. "You didn't come for supper."

"I ate at home."

"Missing anything?" Dorothea asked, a look of mischief on her face.

A chill ran through Jane. "Not that I know of."

Dorothea pointed to a corner of the kitchen where a black cat lay curled up on top of a multicolored throw rug.

"Marvin," Jane exclaimed.

He greeted her with a 'meep', then tucked his nose under his tail and closed his eyes.

"How did he get here?" Jane asked.

"Found him in the root cellar when I went down for onions."

"How in the world?" Then Jane remembered him running into the hallway when she'd opened the panel in the basement wall. With everything else, she'd completely forgotten about the cats.

"Guess he was out wandering and found a way to get in. I thought it was locked up tight." Dorothea shrugged. "He's good company, though. Been watching me cook."

"Where's the root cellar, anyway?"

Dorothea gestured toward a door just off the back. "Just off the basement."

Which meant the hallway and rooms somehow connected to this house. Unless there were other exits to the outdoors and he had found a way into the root cellar as Dorothea thought. Suzie B had followed him when he'd run into the hallway. If she turned up in a locked room, somebody might realize they'd come through the underground passage. And that Jane might know about it.

"Don't worry," Dorothea said. "He hasn't bothered me."

"I just don't want him in the street is all." The door to the dining room opened and one of the regulars came in, arms loaded with dishes. "Is Anna in her office?" Jane asked.

"No, she's helping John at the church tonight," Dorothea said.

Jane was disappointed and relieved all at once. She excused herself from cleanup and scooped Marvin up. She carried him across the street and into her yard, where she put him down. He sauntered over to the compost pile and crouched, ready for unsuspecting rodents. Inside, she found Suzie B curled up on a couch in the living room. The cat lifted her head and yawned, innocent of all wrongdoing. Jane was just glad she'd come back without causing more questions.

CHAPTER NINE

Jane started her day with the usual toast and French roast while checking the markets, which were climbing a bit. She decided to wait a day before making any trades. Then she called Roxanne for an impromptu lunch. She wasn't going to tell her about the tantric room, but maybe she could find out something useful while Lois did the heavy lifting. They decided to meet at Old Salem Tavern, a place that had not been a feature of Jane's childhood.

Years ago when a grocer had announced his plans to build a store in an empty lot next to the oldest house in the original settlement of Old Salem, people had realized that the village needed protecting. A drug store and one of the first Krispy Kreme donut shops were already located on that street. Citizens and members of the church community had founded an association to protect the historic site, and over the years it had grown into a tourist attraction complete with guides dressed in period costumes, artisans practicing the old trades, and shops.

Now the group was returning the settlement to its original condition, at least as close as possible, adding gardens, restoring old homes, using the records from the archives. They advertised it as a living museum, but the place had always been living to Jane. Home Moravian was an active church, and Salem Academy and College still women's schools. Most of her family was buried in God's Acre. But she was grateful the settlement was being preserved.

She parked in a spot across from the town square near the Market Fire House where a young boy worked the water pump and other children ran screaming around the spurting, cold liquid. The weather continued to be unseasonably warm. The children's mothers watched with arms folded or heads together talking, occasionally telling them not to get wet.

Good luck with that, Jane thought. She remembered doing the same with her cousins. She wondered when children had started playing here or if it had been all work in the early days. In college she'd read Comenius, the early educator who encouraged play and liberty, not just rote memorization. He'd been a Moravian bishop, so she bet Salem children had played as much as they'd worked or studied.

Jane crossed the street and walked down the cobble stone sidewalk, past the Buehler House, then the Schultz House and Shoemaker Shop. Several private residences dotted the block. What would it be like to have tourists peering through your antique glass panes at all hours? Yet she understood the attraction of this neighborhood.

The restaurant had taken over the Old Salem Tavern annex in 1969. Jane had come to eat shortly after it opened and been surprised that pumpkins could be turned into soup and were not just for pies. She hoped the food was as good now as it had been then. She climbed the wide steps and entered the eighteenth century. A woman garbed in period dress with a white apron welcomed her. Jane gave Roxanne's name and the hostess led her to a table in the front room where her friend waited.

Roxanne scrambled up and gave her a hug. "Thanks for the invitation."

"I appreciate you coming," Jane said. "I've been wanting to catch up and thought it would be fun to come down here."

"I hate eating alone, too," Roxanne said with an understanding smile. "That's why I go to the Sisters' House so often."

The waitress arrived with a basket of bread and filled their water glasses. "I took the liberty of ordering some pumpkin rolls. I can't get enough of them," Roxanne confessed.

Jane glanced over the wine list and asked for a bottle of the reserve chardonnay, then looked through the menu. "When did chicken pot pie become Moravian?"

Roxanne stifled a laugh. "They found someone's old recipe, I guess. Something about double crust and no vegetables."

"I hear all the pubs near Rosslyn Chapel suddenly changed their names to something with 'Grail' in it after Dan Brown made the place famous."

"It must be good for business." Roxanne shrugged.

Jane ordered Moravian Chicken Pie and Roxanne, joining in the spirit, asked for Moravian Meatloaf. They joked that they'd never had either one before. "Oh, try the onion soup. It's wonderful," Roxanne said in a contrite voice, perhaps feeling guilty for teasing in front of the waitress.

Roxanne talked about a few of the changes in Old Salem, how they'd turned the old Coca Cola bottling plant into offices, moved a bridge and put it over the road so the tourist wouldn't stand in the middle gawking and get run over, and remodeled the old Zinzendorf Laundry into a visitor's center. There had been a Zinzendorf Hotel as well, both named after the Count who had allowed the *Unitas Fratrum* refugees to settle in Saxony and begin their church again after the Thirty Years War.

"There's St. Philip's, too. I never knew that African-Americans had their own church here."

"Really? Where?"

"At the end of Main."

"You mean behind that old white house at the end of the road?" Jane asked.

"Oh, that's been torn down."

"That beautiful house?" She brushed crumbs off the white tablecloth.

"Well, it wasn't really part of the old settlement, and the African American graveyard was back there."

Jane had known the people who'd rented that place just after college. They'd found graves in their backyard, which hadn't made any sense to her at the time, so she'd called her minister to come take a look. Apparently it had panned out.

Their food arrived and between bites, Roxanne explained how the African slaves had worshipped with the whites in the same church and been buried in the same cemetery—until segregation laws had come into effect.

"In the early 1800s, they started being buried in the Stranger's Graveyard. Then they built their own church and had their own." She paused. "At least we kept teaching the slaves to read and write even when that became illegal."

"I never knew that." Jane let the other part go—that the Moravians had still held slaves even if they did educate them. She didn't need to climb on her soap box today, even though Roxanne would probably agree. She let Roxanne ramble on, waiting for a natural turn in the conversation to bring up her subject.

"They know so much more about church history these days than when we were kids. You should read up on it."

Jane frowned.

"No, really. It doesn't matter if you're religious. Moravian history is fascinating." Roxanne picked up her glass and swirled her wine before taking a sip. "Not always what you'd expect, either. One of the associate ministers had a Sunday school class at Home that went through all of it. And there are new books that came out for the five hundred and fiftieth anniversary."

"There's a big collection in Miss Essig's library," Jane commented.

"You'd be amazed." Roxanne polished off the last bite of meatloaf.

"Dessert?"

"I shouldn't."

"Speaking of church history and all, I've been wanting to ask you. You keep calling Dorothea's house 'The Sisters' House'. I wondered about that."

"Oh, you don't know?"

"Know what?"

Roxanne looked around. "Let's go for a stroll. I should walk off those pumpkin rolls."

"If I can move." Jane paid the bill and followed Roxanne up a side street past more private homes.

They walked down Church Street past the oldest dormitory of Salem College. "Now that building was the original Single Sisters' House," Roxanne said.

"Right, I remember that." Jane glanced at the brick structure with its white framed windows. "And now?"

Instead of answering, Roxanne turned between the red brick buildings of the college, Jane following, until they made their way down into the natural amphitheater called the May Dell. Only then did Roxanne break her silence. "They used to crown the May Queen down here."

"Did they dance around the May pole and fertilize the fields afterwards?" Jane teased.

Roxanne's laugh was bawdy. "I don't think they did that last part. Not before they married, anyway."

The two settled on the lowest bench of the round rows of seats and enjoyed the bower, a few leaves the color of a full moon. The tiny creek winked silver light. Roxanne finally spoke again, "You know about the choir system, of course."

"Yes, it started in Herrnhut. We're still buried in choirs. That's the only remnant of the system left," Jane recited.

"That's what most people think." Roxanne pulled her scarf close around her neck. "Some people think the system developed from Philipp Spener. He thought that small groups encouraged spiritual growth."

"Spener? Never heard of him."

"Really, Jane, you're shamefully uninformed."

Jane's head snapped around to find a playful smile on Roxanne's face. "So, enlighten me."

"Spener founded the Pietist movement." At Jane's blank look, Roxanne continued, "He thought personal religious experience and devotion more important than dogma. Zinzendorf's family were Pietists, Spener his godfather."

"I never knew—" Jane stopped herself from confessing more of her ignorance.

"Choirs lasted until the settlements were well established, when people started living in nuclear families for the most part." Roxanne waved her hand to indicate the exact date wasn't important. "But the system was popular and some decided to continue it. The numbers have dwindled now, so we combined the single and married divisions, and now women live in the Sisters' House and men in the Brethren's'."

Jane thought of the collective households of the sixties and beyond, women living together, but under the guiding light of feminism instead of Christ. They'd turned out to be challenging—everyone bringing their unresolved issues along with their idealism.

Roxanne studied Jane's face for a minute, then continued. "Since the church's mission work has picked up, it's come in handy for me, at least. We don't live there, but it helps to be able to eat with the sisters and drop the kids off if I need someone to keep an eye on them."

"If Dorothea's house—"

"But Jane, surely you know now that she doesn't own the house." Roxanne's tone held just a touch of impatience. "It's held in trust. From your own great—" she waved her hand again, meaning she didn't know how many generations it had been, "—grandfather, I might add."

"So I've discovered." Jane's tone was wry. "Does that make the antebellum house on the north side of the church—"

"The Brethren's' House, yes."

Jane looked up at the interwoven branches above her head. "I don't want to make you uncomfortable, but what about Anna and John? How are they related?"

A rich laugh rose from Roxanne, merry as the babbling brook in front of them. "They're married."

"What? But they don't live together—oh."

"Right." Roxanne nodded approvingly. "Each is head of their respective house."

"But—" Jane really didn't know how to ask this next question. She was relieved when Roxanne anticipated it.

"Where do they have marital relations?" She whispered the last two words, but it was the question that had been in Jane's mind, although she would have used a different term. Jane nodded, blushing like the old maid she supposed some people thought she was.

Roxanne chuckled, then took pity on her. "You'd have to ask them yourself. You never married, did you?"

"No, I guess I was just too busy. Did have a couple serious relationships, though."

"If you married in the church, you'd have a pleasant surprise."

Jane looked at Roxanne, intrigued. "What?"

"You know how our ancestors thought women should be educated as well as men, even back in 1772 when this school was founded?"

"Yes." Jane smiled. Roxanne was sounding like a tour guide now, but really, she was right.

"Turns out they had some liberated attitudes about sex, too."

"Like what?" Jane asked.

Roxanne studied her face. "I think you should ask the head of the Sisters about that."

"That would be Anna, right?"

"Correct."

☆ ☆ ☆

Jane left Roxanne, thinking that maybe the room she found had a less lurid purpose than she first imagined. But she still had trouble picturing herself talking about it to Anna. She headed up the hill to the archives. To her surprise, once she arrived she discovered they'd moved to a new brick colonial behind Cedarhyrst, the stone mansion at the top of Church Street in Old Salem. Once inside the new building, she walked down a long hallway hung with replica antique lanterns. A young man at the reception desk greeted her and she told him what she needed.

"We'll see if we have a pdf of that. If so, you can download it off the website, or we can print one out for you, if you'd like. The general public doesn't handle the actual documents."

"I'm family," Jane said.

"Oh," he sat up a touch straighter. "I'm sure you understand that antique papers must be protected."

Jane smiled. "Your group does excellent work. Would it be possible just to see the original?"

"I'll let an archivist know you're here."

He escorted her to a reading room where she sat at one of the polished tables. The arched windows and the regularly spaced columns gave the space a soothing feeling of symmetry and balance. The walls glowed under the candelabras and sconces giving the feel of sitting inside a glowing eggshell.

"Miss Frey?" The quiet voice whispered almost in her ear.

Jane turned to find a woman wearing a plain skirt and oxford shirt standing beside her. "My name is Barbara. I understand you'd like to see some documents?"

Jane told her about her ancestor's will and the document with the fuzzy seal. "I'm just following up on Miss Essig's estate."

"Yes, we all miss her. I'm sorry to have to ask, but may I see your driver's license? It's procedure."

Jane pulled her wallet out and opened it.

"Colorado," she said. "You've been far from home."

"I've moved back. Guess I need to get a new license." Jane wondered if she'd be here long enough.

"We've had a lot of interest in these documents."

"Oh?" Jane asked.

"Well, with her death and all."

Jane accepted this rather cryptic response, imagining archivists were like librarians who protected the identities and reading habits of their patrons.

"Wait here, please," Barbara said. "I'll bring them up to you."

Jane barely had time to look around before Barbara reappeared carrying two white boxes. She opened them both, put on white cotton gloves and carefully looked through the contents of the first box, then pulled out a few yellowed pages. "Here we go." She laid them out on a protective pad in front of Jane and handed her an instrument to use to turn the pages. "I must ask that you not touch the paper. Oil from our hands can cause damage."

Jane leaned over and read the will. After some brief flourishes in the way of introduction, it left the farm to her great grandfather, Reuben John, and the rest in trust to the OGMS. Jane leaned back and nodded. "Can I get a copy?"

"We don't photocopy documents older than 1900," she said.

"But—" Jane started to object.

"The light and heat damages the originals. You may take a non-flash photo."

Jane pulled out her cell phone. The picture would be better than the grainy blur the attorneys had provided.

"The OGMS paperwork is in here." Barbara picked through the second box like a hen turning her precious eggs.

Jane snapped pictures of each page, then leaned over the documents. She pointed toward the seal on the first page. "Do you recognize this?"

"That's the seal for the Order of the Grain of Mustard Seed."

Jane looked up, startled. "The what?"

"A group that Count Zinzendorf founded in his youth. He wanted to bring people together based on the underlying spiritual truths and stop the hair-splitting arguments that divided so many Protestants in those days. They even mentioned reconciling with the Jews and Catholics, which was unusual then."

"Does this group still exist?"

"Oh, I don't think so. He did revive the group as an adult and there's a list of the members somewhere." An abstracted look came over the archivist's face. She seemed lost in thought. After a moment, she said, "I can't recall the names, but I'm sure we could find them for you."

Jane shook her head. "I don't want to put you to any trouble. I could probably look that up myself. Why would a group use this emblem now?"

Barbara shook her head. "Maybe nostalgia?"

Jane had her doubts about that.

"You'd enjoy reading up on the history of the church. It's part of your family tradition, after all." Barbara pointed to the will.

Jane chuckled. "I keep hearing that."

"I'll just put these back," Barbara said.

Jane thanked the archivist and paused at the window. Outside God's Acre stretched to the north, a deep green with rows of white marble, the reds and oranges of late fall leaves under the bright sun. Her eyes strayed from her grandfather's grave nearby to the trees at the top of the hill where her grandmother lay, and finally over toward Miss Essig's area.

She could never have imagined these stern guardians of her youth had kept so many secrets.

She drove home, her mind buzzing with questions. Was it just coincidence that the property management firm had the same initials as some obscure group Zinzendorf had founded? That was the most likely explanation, but she didn't believe it for a second. Maybe she should read some of Miss Essig's books on the church. She might find some answers there.

Once at the house, Jane let Winston out. She checked her voice messages, but found nothing. Lois would use the land line for sensitive information and might not even leave a message, but the calls received list didn't show that she'd even called.

She dialed Lois' number, but it rang through to the answering machine. She left a message about the documents and Zinzendorf's OGMS group, then added, "I'm going to do some reading and see if I can find out more about the history involved." She told herself that Lois would call as soon as her detectives came up with anything.

Before settling down, Jane grabbed her camera and headed upstairs to the Blake room. The cats followed. She took the paintings stacked together and leaned each one against the wall, then switched on the lights above the oils. Jane snapped pictures of each, then went to her computer in the library and downloaded the file. She sent emails to two New York art dealers she knew, asking who was the best expert on Blake's art. They'd probably answer her tomorrow.

After the pictures were sent, Jane took her laptop into the library with a bottle of Merlot from a local winery. It was late afternoon. She promised herself she'd practice the piano tomorrow. The cats arrived and settled in their favorite spots—Suzie B on the overstuffed chair by the fireplace, Marvin next to her on the sofa. Winston worked on his favorite chewy in the middle of the room. Jane poured a glass of wine and let it sit for a minute while she searched the phrase 'Order of the Grain of Mustard Seed'.

It seemed Zinzendorf had started the group with some other sons of the nobility at the Halle Academy, naming his group after the bible story about faith. They'd wanted to spread the gospel, which was a typically vague teenage goal, but as an adult the Count had revived the group. Kings, archbishops and even a man named Tomochichi, reported to be Chief of the Creek nation, had been members.

Jane took a sip of wine and her mouth puckered. Too many tannins. Oh well, you never knew unless you tried. She walked back into the kitchen and put the bottle in the refrigerator. It would be fine for cooking. She chose an organic Frey—not a relative unfortunately—pulled the cork, and went back to the library with a fresh glass.

She clicked the next link, which took her to a contemporary group with the same name as Zinzendorf's that dedicated itself to 24-hour prayer. Again the famous members were listed. This organization said that Zinzendorf had been revolutionary because he swore his loyalty to Christ alone, leaving aside the fealties due his king and the aristocratic order he'd been born to. Revolutionary, yes. And downright risky considering the time period.

Then she saw something that seemed familiar, a phrase in Greek. But this was legible. *Κανένας από μας ζωές για τον.* She printed the webpage, put the pages one behind the other, the webpage over the fuzzy phrase on the OSMG trust document, and held them under the light. They seemed to match. Same length. The accent marks appeared in the same places. If that's what those fuzzy marks were. She decided it was close enough. The translation given by the website was, 'None of us lives for himself'.

She went back to the search list and clicked the next link. This guy claimed that the OGMS was a group of contemplative, Gnostic Christians. Apparently this was a bad thing, at least in this guy's opinion. This didn't match her own memory of confirmation class, though.

Oh, how I love conspiracy nuts. Jane had heard some doozies working in oil and gas finance. She took a sip of wine and kept reading.

The article jumped from here into Arthurian connections, comparing the ring worn by group members of the OMGS to the ring carried by Frodo in—she paused in delighted anticipation, guessing where the writer would turn—*The Lord of the Rings*. Jane laughed out loud. Winston looked up, a question in his eyes, and wagged his stub. Jane reached down and scratched his ears.

"This guy probably doesn't even know about Tolkien's books," Jane informed the dog, who turned back to his chewy with a snort of derision.

The diatribe ended by declaring that the OGMS was trying to take over the world through establishing a new global community in Christ. A few comments defended the Moravians, but wasn't that a bit like casting pearls before swine, Jane wondered. Maybe they'd been added to soothe the unsuspecting Moravian reader.

That had been a bit of fun. She sent a few of the links to Lois, who still hadn't called, and polished off the wine. So she was living in a house with a room for sacred sex run by people whose goal was world dominion. Started by her own ancestors. What next?

CHAPTER TEN

Valentin Knight sat beside financial mastermind Richard Brandon, who'd put the new portfolio together, and watched him explain their plan, this time to a company based in the Arab Emirates. They had put together a list of major oil companies who seemed open to new technologies. They'd worked their way through a third of the companies with some success. Knight felt cautiously optimistic.

"Gentlemen, there's one natural resource that your region has even more of than oil—" Brandon clicked to the next image, which delineated desert lands, "—and that is sunlight. The areas I've shaded golden are uninhabited and not in private hands. Those in yellow are under title, but could easily be purchased for insignificant sums. They all get 365 days of sunlight per year." He smiled. "Okay, maybe 364."

He clicked to another slide. "The lands are flat and the winds have been measured up to 100 miles per hour—or 106.93 kilometers per hour." He gave a little bow producing a few grudging laughs. "In your more mountainous regions, well placed turbines on ridge lines will double your production.

"Of course, you're not restricted to land within your own country." He clicked to a map of the region. "If the other companies do not decide to take advantage of this resource, here are other areas close to you."

"In the Americas, these lands are suitable." He showed another map. "And the vast plains of Central Europe and Asia provide equal opportunities." He moved through two more slides. "The wind turbines can also be placed in the sea, just off particularly windy coastlines." He put up a picture of a line of towers with huge propellers in the North Sea.

Paper rustled as people checked their packets to read the small print on investment and maintenance costs vs. estimated income.

"Knight Incorporated has purchased many manufacturing facilities and retooled them to produce top-of-the-line solar panels and wind turbines." He showed a couple of images of these products. "Most importantly, we have developed a very efficient way to store the energy you generate in easily transported hydrogen cells." He clicked to a close-up of the cell.

"This has been the stumbling block to switching to world-wide solar and wind technology. Connecting to grids. Batteries demand rare earth minerals, which presents other environmental problems. But now with these hydrogen cells, direct connection to electronic grids is no longer necessary."

The group focused closely on the presentation, obviously intrigued.

Brandon continued. "Our factories are ready to go into production immediately. Your new energy fields will produce enough to replace your oil income in five years." He paused to gather their attention. "That's correct, gentlemen. Five years."

"That's quite a claim, my friend," the CFO of the company said.

"It is. And I stand by it. You have the figures in your packets." He dropped his voice slightly as if this next part was a secret. The group leaned toward him. "We all know that even the richest oil fields are running low."

Knight resisted smiling. Brandon was a natural salesman and he believed in this product.

"The costs of extracting oil are growing exponentially." He clicked his mouse and a chart with spiking columns running into more billions each year came on the screen. "And the environmental price is becoming unacceptable to many of us." He moved through several images of oil streaked ocean water, oil soaked birds, black shores surrounding huge ice fields in the Arctic.

"This is painful evidence, but even more painful to some is the amount of money our colleague shelled out after the recent two spills." He flashed to a screen that reproduced that figure with all its zeros. He left it for a moment, then continued. "With the increasing difficulty of accessing oil in remote areas, these costs will continue to increase dramatically."

He caught each man's eye. "With our plan, you can replace your income and maintain the lifestyles you have grown accustomed to, while preventing further ecological degradation."

Brandon gave another slight bow, indicating his respect for his audience, then turned and inclined his head to Knight.

Knight stood, letting his height reinforce the dominance that his portfolio already demonstrated. "Thank you, Mr. Brandon. I know I am impressed by your presentation," Knight turned to the men who sat around the table, "which is why I have made the investments Mr. Brandon spoke of. We at Knight Corporation are ready to help you retool for the next energy economy."

He lowered his voice and spoke more confidentially. "Gentlemen, there is no need for desperation now. We all know the extremes some are going to in order to maintain the status quo, but I ask you to consider a simple fact. Change is the only constant in the world. What child does not grow up? What building does not begin to crumble? What empire rules for millennia?"

He looked around. "Rome fell. Even the Moorish empire receded. But if we adapt, if we become the masters of change rather than its victims, then we can continue to enjoy the benefits and profits we have begun to take for granted."

A few quiet comments and the rustling of paper followed.

Knight extended his hand toward the door. "Refreshments are available in the next room. Our representatives will be standing by to discuss specifics. Please let me know how we can assist you."

A tilt of the head from the Sheikh's advisor brought Knight to his side. Abdul-Aziz's stance and movements displayed the unconscious arrogance bred from oil wealth and a life-long association with power. Knight had to admit he had impeccable manners as well. He steered the man away from the conference room.

Aziz's white thobe stirred in the light breeze of the small lobby. "The Prince sends his regrets that he could not attend your presentation himself," he said.

"But of course. His Highness has many responsibilities and you are a most capable advisor."

Aziz inclined his head, accepting the comment as no more than his due. The elevator doors whisked closed and the car began a swift ascent. They rode in silence, which remained until they stepped into Knight's private office and he closed the door. "Would you like juice or water? Something else?" He pointed toward the bar in the corner of the room.

"No, thank you."

They sat across from each other in luxurious armchairs that afforded a view of the White House, the Washington Monument rising behind and the Capitol off to the left.

"You do have the Prince's ear," Aziz said, raising his index finger. "However, the Consortium has his other ear, and they say you have gone soft." Aziz spread his hands apologetically.

Knight smiled a bit like Lewis Carroll's Cheshire cat. "Soft because I believe in global climate change or in some other way?"

Aziz allowed himself a soft chuckle. "Both, my friend. The Prince must listen to all who have the power to reach him, even if what they say is not worthy, but he asked me to warn you that your enemies spread tales."

"What tales might those be?"

"Nothing we believe, of course." Aziz made a deprecating gesture.

Used to this Arabian dance to the point, Knight leaned back in his chair slightly and glanced out at the view, subtly reminding his guest of his connections.

"One source claims your research is flawed, that the hydrogen is unstable, even in the solid form used in the cells. Mr. Davis, who represents the Consortium, is adamant on this point."

"Mr. Davis is a financier, is he not?"

Aziz nodded to concede this point.

Knight continued. "We will, of course, provide any demonstrations that would set the Prince's mind at ease," Knight said. "The Hindenburg explosion did make everyone cautious of hydrogen, but as you rightly pointed out, the solid form is stable."

Knight made himself sit perfectly still, waiting for Aziz to reveal his true message. But still he didn't speak.

"Please rest assured that my office has the most advanced security systems. Nothing can be overheard," Knight remarked casually.

The relaxing of Aziz's shoulders was almost imperceptible, but Knight felt it nonetheless. "We assume your company is equally well guarded against industrial espionage."

Knight allowed himself a somewhat sardonic expression. "Cowboy boots make more noise than those wearing them realize."

Aziz laughed, then gestured toward the bar.

Knight rose and asked, "What can I get you?"

"But I cannot ask you to serve me."

"Please. We cannot allow anyone else to overhear us."

"Then I'll have some of that fine California vintage you served me last time."

Knight searched his memory, then pulled out a bottle of shiraz. He poured two glasses and carried them back to their seats.

Aziz took a sip and settled back in his chair. "There are stories of a prophecy. We recognize the one, true prophet, but lesser predictions do occur."

"I've heard something along these lines," Knight said.

Aziz's forehead furrowed. "The Prince must listen to the Imam, but the Sufi Master Rafiq speaks to his inner heart."

"That is good news, my friend."

"Rafiq tells the Prince that the light is growing in the world. He suggests that you are standing in the doorway of this light."

"I hope I am not blocking it," Knight said.

"To the contrary. He says you usher it in."

Knight's eyes filled. He bowed his head slightly as much to hide his tears as his surprise. "If I am called to serve in this way, I am honored."

"Rafiq will put his group in your service and the Prince will order our company to invest in your—" he waved his hand "—collectors of the sun and wind."

Knight sat forward. "I am deeply honored, Aziz. Please convey to the Prince my sincere thanks."

Aziz polished off his wine and held his glass up. "An occasional lapse is forgivable for such a delightful taste, is it not?"

"I'm sure Rafiq would agree, my friend." The Arabs said 'my friend' almost as often as they said '*Inshallah*'. Over the years, Knight had grown to appreciate the nuances of their culture.

Aziz stood. "I will convey your appreciation to Rafiq. He will be in touch."

☆ ☆ ☆

"You did find a couple of originals, but not the one we were hoping for," Coche said.

Philip sat in a Starbucks in one of the shopping malls where he blended in, listening through his ear buds. He cupped his hand around the dangling microphone. "What do you want me to do?"

"There's one painting we're looking for in particular. We think it was commissioned by the Fetter Lane congregation, but no one's seen it for years."

Philip didn't know what congregation he was talking about. He probably didn't need the details to do his job, but he'd check anyway.

"I'll send you a mock-up of what we think it looks like so you can have some idea. Check the other houses, even the church."

"Other houses?"

"The ones owned by the OGMS."

"Will do." He should be able to slip in and check these places easily enough. He went online and searched for blueprints. If he was lucky, he could do the surveillance tonight, get in the next night, and then fly back to D.C. Small towns made him twitchy.

Henry Coche ended his conversation with Philip and turned to the video monitor, watching his assistant prep their stable of lobbyist on the president's latest energy bill. His people in the White House had kept him abreast of the progress, and although he'd tried hard to waylay and subvert the language, this commie bastard was really going to send it over to the Hill. It was a fucking waste of time, not that the whole pile of brown-nosers and yes-men in the House shouldn't all be lined up and shot, but the people needed to believe they had some influence in how the world was run. Delusion worked so much better than outright repression. He'd tried to explain it to many world leaders. He thought Orlov in Russia was finally getting it. Just ride that motorcycle and shoot a few elk or reindeer or whatever the fuck they had over there in that God-forsaken wasteland and the people would cheer their guts out, then go mind their own goddamn business.

His entrance cue was coming up. "Okay, Okay." He hurried the two young women who tended to his hair, brushed off his suit jacket, and made sure he looked like the picture of health and savoir-faire. "Let's get this show on the road."

He walked to the door of the large conference room and heard, "And here is Mr. Coche himself."

He pulled in his stomach and charged through, a look of fierce determination on his face. "So you see what we're up against. After that little accident in the Gulf and then the unfortunate spill in the Arctic, it looks like they're going to try to get serious about switching us to what they call green energy." He put venom into these two words.

"But we can still stop it. You've seen your budget. You've got the talking points. You each have your list of who to see and a full dossier on each one. You will find links to our database containing video files when available. That's if you need to remind these cowardly—uh, honorable representatives what information we've collected on them."

His audience laughed appreciatively.

"These videos are view only. In other words they cannot be copied, sent as attachments or deleted. All that goes through me." He took his time catching the eye of each man in the room. "Do you understand?"

After he'd gathered nods, he continued. "With this amount of money, the bill should be dead in two weeks. Any questions?" He paused for two seconds. "If so, talk to your team leader."

He extended his arms wide in invitation. "Afterwards, I expect to see you enjoying yourselves. The bar and buffet are downstairs. The ladies are waiting there also. If you want to swim or get into the hot tub, suits are available, but not mandatory." He gave them his go-be-a-bad-boy smile. He hoped they would. He had cameras standing by. He didn't just keep files on politicians.

But he didn't have time to linger. He'd grown jaded, he supposed. Preferred to take his pleasure in private. Besides, he had business to attend to. That was his real pleasure.

★ ★ ★

Coche usually slept on his flights to Riyadh—and drank extra water. The punishing desert sun sucked him dry in an hour, leaving him parched and withered in his western clothes. He'd be damned if he was going to walk around in one of those long dresses they called 'thobes' or put on a pansy-ass Panama hat and light khaki shirt like those fucking Brits. Which reminded him. The captain of his tanker fleet had sent him several urgent messages while he'd been on his way to the airport. After take-off, he returned the call.

"Mr. Coche, I'm sorry to bother you, sir," the man shouted into the phone.

Coche could barely make him out against the howl of something—was that an engine whining? "What's the problem, Clive? I can barely hear you." He heard a door being hauled closed and the line cleared.

"Rather bad bit of weather, I'm afraid. Bit of a hurricane blowing off the coast."

"This time of year?"

"Afraid so, sir."

"Can't you outrun the damn thing?"

"It's rather large."

Fucking Brits. You could never tell how serious anything really was with them, with their stiff upper lip and all, but they were still the best seamen. "What do you recommend?"

"I'm requesting permission to bring the tankers in. We're taking heavy waves. I know you wanted to wait another few days, but the damage to our ships might just take away—" he hesitated, searching for the most diplomatic word.

"Profits?" Coche supplied.

"Err—yes, sir."

Coche jerked his head in irritation. He could buy five new ships with what he'd make if he could wait only two more days. The price of oil had risen steadily over the last week and would continue to rise, but if there was another spill . . . "Permission granted. Bring them in, then."

"Aye, aye, sir." The relief in the man's voice was palpable.

This would lose him a few million, but it couldn't be helped. Coche drank glass after glass of water while reviewing financial documents from Davis and his new tart, what was her name? Tami, maybe. He was glad they'd gotten rid of that stick-up-the-butt feminist, Jane Frey. He'd dropped enough hints. At least this new one was easy on the eyes. He finished up the last report, then fell asleep.

His assistant woke him in time to freshen up and eat a bite. Once they landed, he glanced out the plane window and saw a black limo waiting on the sweltering asphalt. The cabin door opened and the heat reached in, searching out any drops of humidity and sucking it up. He'd consumed almost a gallon of water, but it would sweat out of him quickly.

Oh, stop whining. He gave himself a shake, pointed to all his paperwork and brief case for his assistant to gather, and walked down the steps into the blistering desert.

Coche relaxed as soon as the gates to Mishari's grounds closed behind them and he was ushered down cool, tiled hallways, through a garden green with flowers and a splashing fountain, to a guest suite. "Dinner is at eight. Mr. Mishari will meet with you afterwards."

Damn Arabs never do anything in the afternoon, Coche thought. His hopes to spend the night on his plane returning to the U.S. vanished.

A knock sounded on the door. "Yes?"

The rustle of long skirts made him turn his head. Two beautiful women entered, both blonde and blue-eyed, probably from the American Midwest or Eastern Europe. "How may we serve you, sir?"

He was getting too old for all this nonsense. "Run me a bath. Lukewarm. Then bring me a snack and some tea an hour before dinner. Where's the bottled water?"

One girl opened the refrigerator in the bar and brought out a bottle. "There are six more there," she said. "The climate is dry. It took me—"

Coche snatched the bottle from her hand, cutting off her ramblings. The other girl ran his bath, then they both left without another word.

After his soak, Coche made a few more calls, checked the markets, then slept. The girls returned a few hours later with tea and mango slices. They stayed to help him dress for dinner.

That evening, Coche ate lightly while the others stuffed themselves. He needed to keep his wits about him. He finally met alone with Mishari under the deep blue of the evening sky on a pleasant terrace overlooking yet another garden. Nightjars called to each other from the trees beyond, hunting in the dark. Gardenias perfumed the air. Mishari offered him an aperitif, but Coche refused. Best to match the customs of his hosts. He was served mango juice.

"From my own trees," Mishari said.

Coche held his glass up and waited for his host to drink before he took a sip.

Mishari made the first move. "The company is willing to renew our contracts, but the price will have to go up." He named a figure.

Coche's body tightened like a panther hearing the rustle of prey nearby. At last the hunt was on. "Mishari, I would hate to see our long friendship interrupted after these long and profitable years." They began to haggle over costs, both enjoying themselves.

When Mishari refused to budge anymore, Coche threatened. "The Brits are anxious to recoup their losses after my government cheated them out of a few billion for the oil spill. I'm sure they will be more reasonable." He made to get up.

"My friend, please." Mishari touched his arm. "You cut my heart."

Coche had heard the very same expression in the suks bargaining with the merchants. It meant they were close to a deal.

After they settled on a figure, Mishari changed the subject. "Your Mr. Davis assures us that Knight's new scheme is nothing but a—how do you say it—pipe dream?"

"That is exactly how we say it. He imagines we are running out of oil. That the sun can replace the black gold." He snorted. "Our geologists assure us the world's oil reserves are plentiful. We need to get our engineers working on better extraction methods for the oceans."

"And your president? What of his new bill?"

"We'll chop it off before it gets going." Coche cut his hand across the space in front of him. "Our people are taking care of it as we speak."

"So it will die in your House?"

"Rest assured, Mishari. We are still in control."

They shared another glass of mango juice, then Coche stood up. A servant appeared to escort him to his suite.

At the door, he asked, "Is there anything else, sir?"

"Bring me someone younger than those other two. Untested."

The servant bowed his head slightly. "Right away, sir."

CHAPTER ELEVEN

"I agree she's a wild card," Anna tempered her voice when she realized she was close to shouting, "but what can we do? We've always chosen the keeper of that house by lot, old fashioned as the method is."

This was Anna's fifth meeting of the day. Usually she switched hats effortlessly, becoming the chair of the Women's Mission at one meeting, then treasurer of the Moravian Music Foundation at the next, and so on. But this meeting was the most important. They were closing in on vital information and it wouldn't do to let her fatigue get the upper hand.

"Jane is from the original family," John offered in a mild voice.

They both looked at Dreher who seethed at the head of the table, his blue suit crisp, his buzz cut neat, his neck thick as a bull inside his collar. "Then perhaps you can explain what we found on our surveillance cameras?" Dreher pushed a button and the flat screen on the opposite wall came to life. Jane walked down the temple hallway, then the view switched to her just outside the Blue Room.

Anna stifled an oath, then asked, "Did she go in?"

"The board has never allowed us to have cameras in the Blue Room or the main temple." Dreher's voice suggested disapproval.

"But you do realize the electronics would disturb the energies," John reminded him.

Anna cut off this familiar dispute. "How did she find it so fast?" She addressed herself to Frank as if he were his cousin's keeper.

Frank shrugged his shoulders. "She's always been smart," he offered.

"But has she ever expressed any interest in spiritual matters?" Boehme's voice was a balm on troubled waters, even when he expressed doubt.

Frank frowned in thought. "Not really. The closest would be her music. She once told me listening to Miss Essig play made her very quiet inside, like she was connected to everything."

"A good sign," Boehme offered.

"I think that's why she majored in music at Salem," Frank continued. "She may have tried one of the eastern meditations back when they were popular for a little while."

"That could prove useful." Boehme looked around for agreement.

"But then she turned to the worldly market, hoping to pile up riches—and not the spiritual kind." Dreher's tone was derisive. "How could she possibly understand what she saw in that room?"

"If she went in," Anna added, although she knew in her heart that Jane had. She suppressed a shudder, feeling as if the newcomer had gone through her personal belongings, broken into her bedroom and handled her intimate lingerie, even though Anna didn't own anything she couldn't hang in the backyard to dry.

"The point is we cannot allow this woman to interfere with the work we need to do." Dreher tapped the table with his forefinger. "We've waited too long for the conditions to be right."

"To think it might happen in my lifetime." John's eyes shone. "Our true purpose fulfilled."

Salali Waterdown, who'd only been listening to the exchange so far, leaned forward, her hair a river of black on both sides of her face. She fixed the reverend with a pointed look. "But do we know for sure? How can we be certain we're interpreting the signs correctly? The prophet may be inaccurate."

Dreher sat forward eagerly, but Boehme spoke first. "There is a worldwide sense that change is eminent. The masses are responding with fear, fed by our old enemy, but more voices are raised every day to question whether disaster is the inevitable outcome."

"Please excuse me for asking," Salali continued, "but your culture is prone to predictions of Armageddon. There's hardly been a time in your history for the last thousand years that some group or other is not proclaiming that the end times are near."

Boehme nodded. "Granted, but we're not talking about the end. Rather a new beginning."

"My elders still don't put much stock in written evidence," Salali added.

Frank spoke up. "But do you think this is just hysteria? Indigenous leaders worldwide are bringing out secrets held for centuries. And your ancestors have been a part of this group for as long as the Order has been in the Carolinas. Don't they agree that a shift is upon us?"

"We think it likely, but—" Salali turned her palms up "—I just want to be sure. We have to be careful not to succumb to these huge surges of group emotion."

"Agreed," Boehme said. "I have attended several of the prophet's sessions. He seems accurate."

Salali sat back, apparently satisfied for now.

"Which leaves us with the problem of what to do with Jane," Dreher said.

All eyes shifted to Anna, who sighed, then squared her shoulders. "I had hoped her awakening would come gradually, so we could broach these subjects as they naturally arose."

"Except that we don't have much time," Boehme said. "It would seem the Cosmic is in rather a hurry."

Anna smiled at this apparent contradiction. "I'll take care of it."

"I'd like to be at the meeting as well," Dreher said.

"Absolutely not." Anna held a hand up. "It is my responsibility as head of the Sisters' House. This is a delicate matter."

"But—" Dreher began.

"Anna is right." Boehme cut him off, his voice soft but firm.

"As you say, *Jünger*." Dreher inclined his head, taking a moment to recover from this rebuke. He looked up after a moment, the red in his cheeks subsiding. "We should hear more about the timing from Prague any day. I'll keep you all informed as usual."

"Excellent," John said.

"Let us know how your meeting works out, Sister Anna," Boehme said.

Anna acknowledged this last statement with a nod. After a prayer, the group adjourned.

Jane glided down the red carpeted hallway, following the sound. She opened door after door, but still couldn't find the musicians. She traced her steps back to where the hallway met up with another at right angles and turned down the other side. The floor slanted down at a gentle angle and the complex harmony grew stronger. The music swelled, filling her senses. Her heart ached to join the musicians, to add her note, the essential last note to complete the piece, to connect the circuit. Filled with urgency, she ran toward a dark archway, but the floor opened beneath her and she fell, arms flailing, reaching for something to grab. She screamed.

And woke up on the sofa in the library. She jumped up, books flying, and looked around. A dream, but she could still just hear the music. She scrambled over to the desk where she rummaged through the drawers, looking for paper and pen, anything to capture the fading music. Finding nothing to write on, she rushed to the piano in the living room, but as soon as she'd pulled the keyboard cover up, the melody had vanished. She tried a few tentative chords, but nothing sounded right. Resting her head on the piano, Jane closed her eyes and listened.

Silence. The piece was gone.

As a child, Jane had dreamed of being a composer, but the first theory class in college had dissuaded her. The urge had returned soon after she'd moved into Miss Essig's house, and now she'd dreamed a symphony. Or something like that. A complex harmony that reached down into the sinews of earth to her fiery center, then climbed back up through the slow and patient rocks, into the rhythmic, surging waters of the ocean and then leapt up into the air and blew with the wind, knitting the elements together. Finally, it reached up into the stars, to a particular star.

Okay, maybe that's a bit grandiose, she thought.

But she knew that if she waited, silent and alert like an ibis poised on one long stalk of a leg, head cocked, the music would flash silver in the water like a fish, and she could capture it.

Chuckling at herself, Jane closed the piano. She walked back into the library and switched on the floor lamp. Amber light mellowed the room. She'd fallen asleep reading. She fished her Blackberry from between the sofa cushions.

One of the art dealers had already sent her a message. "Please call me on my private line."

Jane checked the time and decided it was not too late for a New Yorker. The phone rang only once before an excited voice answered. "Hello? Ms. Frey?"

"This is Jane Frey."

"I sent your jpg's on to a professor at New York University. I hope you don't mind. He says a couple of these are new."

"How so?"

"They've never been seen before. The Blake experts don't know anything about them, but they look authentic."

"As in originals?" Jane flashed on Philip and Margaret's visit. That's what he had said.

"This professor is eager to see them, do some tests. Would you be willing to bring the pieces to New York?"

"Uh, I suppose I could bring the sketches, but I don't know how to pack them safely. Some of the colored prints aren't that big—" she hadn't mentioned the large painting in the tantric room "—but I'd need help."

"I'll send you directions for the sketches and get some assistants over tomorrow to take care of the prints. If you don't mind, that is. We have top notch security." The man paused for her answer. When none came, he added. "The art world would be indebted to you. It's a big find—if we can authenticate it."

"Why not?" Jane thought she should probably clear this with the OGMS, but they had hidden things from her. Better to know what she was dealing with before approaching them. She wasn't selling the pieces, just furthering her research.

"We'd like to see them as soon as possible. Could you come day after tomorrow?"

"Oddly enough, my schedule is clear." She could drop by and see Lois. Find out what she'd discovered. Try some of those cocktails her favorite news commentator kept making on TV.

"We'll cover your expenses. I'll send you an itinerary as soon as my secretary finishes the booking. I can't tell you how grateful we are for your cooperation."

"See you then."

Next morning with her cup of French roast in hand, Jane went back to the pile of books she'd been reading in the library and spent the rest of the morning trying to educate herself about her own heritage. Hours later, Winston's exaggerated sighs made her realize she'd skipped their morning run. She changed into her running clothes and called him. He scrambled up and followed her outside, where after a few stretches, they ran through the park.

She still wasn't sure what to think about what she'd been reading. Apparently the Moravians had scandalized some people in the eighteenth century with their ideas on sexuality. Zinzendorf had taught there was no shame in the human body, that all parts of it were sacred, redeemed by Christ's death on the cross. He'd described human salvation in erotic terms, a mystical marriage with God. Not only that, but sex itself was considered sacred, a reenactment in the flesh of the spiritual marriage of salvation. In the colonies, where Moravians lived in single-sex choirs, these rituals had been scheduled, a special place set aside for couples.

Having a mate and independence, both at once—Jane had to admit the arrangement did have its appeal. Anna and John seemed free to pursue their careers full force. One partner did not have to sacrifice their life's work for the other. And not every woman's life work was to make a home, although

Dorothea seemed happy to do it, and ironically, she was single. At least, Jane thought she was.

A surge of pride filled her, giving her a burst to run full clip up the final hill. Leave it to her ancestors to come up with a solution to women's unequal share of work sooner than the rest of the world. It certainly wasn't the first time they'd figured out a sticky social problem in a simple, practical way. Except then everyone's work and life was dedicated to God, and the church had pretty much told people what to do and whom to marry. Bethlehem and Salem had been a theocracy. Things were different now. Jane mused that she would want both a separate space and a commons where she and her mate could watch movies or listen to music together. She snorted. Like that was going to happen at her age. For the first time, she thought of the room below her house with a smile.

Jane forced herself to run all the way to the back porch. Once inside, Winston lapped up water, then stretched out on the kitchen floor and was soon deep in doggy dreams, his paws twitching. Jane cut a slice of olive bread and put it in the toaster. When it popped up, she took a bite and walked into the pantry, searching for something quick. Just as she reached for a can of lentil soup, the doorbell rang.

"Damn," she whispered.

She took another bite of the olive bread, then peeked through the dining room window. Anna Szeges stood there, tall and straight, silver grey hair pulled back in her ubiquitous bun, hands folded in front of her. Like a nun.

Jane snorted and dismissed that image. More like a competent administrator. She realized for the first time that Anna had not compromised, not like she had. But there was the thermos—and the lab report. Time for the show down.

She opened the door. "What a surprise," she said.

"Sorry to drop by unannounced." Anna's smile was hesitant, "but I wondered if you had time to talk. We really haven't had a chance to get to know each other since you moved in."

"Come in." Jane stood back for Anna to enter, then led her into the library. "Would you like some tea or water?"

"Nothing for me."

Jane gestured toward the overstuffed chair next to the fireplace, then sat back down where she'd been reading. The cats arrived and arranged themselves on the back of the sofa.

Anna made small talk about settling into the house, how the animals were adapting, then she started on what Jane imagined was the real agenda. "We both grew up in the church. You here, me in Bethlehem, but you stopped attending soon after college, isn't that right?"

"I did." Jane couldn't attest to the rest of Anna's statement. She tucked one leg beneath her and settled back, curious to see how Anna would work her way around to the subject.

Anna looked down as if in thought and saw the books strewn across the floor. Three titles were easily visible— *William Blake's Sexual Path to Spiritual Vision*, *Community of the Cross*, and *Jesus is Female*. Her mouth formed an 'oh'. She looked back up at Jane. "I see this talk is well overdue."

Jane couldn't help but enjoy this moment. "I've been advised to study church history," she said, not quite succeeding at keeping the spite out of her voice.

Anna flushed crimson.

"I have to admit, at first I was shocked," Jane said.

Anna squared her shoulders, gathering herself. "How much have you read?"

"A bit of each book, plus some online sources."

"Do you have questions?"

"Let's see if I have it straight. Our ancestors created the choir system in order to deal with building a new village, first in Herrnhut. The structure was particularly suited to wilderness and missionary conditions, so they continued." Jane glanced at Anna, who nodded her agreement. "They never went in for celibacy, so—"

"In the early days, some did," Anna said. "It took a while for clergy to be allowed to marry."

Lucky for you, Jane thought, but stopped herself from saying it. Instead, she continued her narrative, "So, they made arrangements for couples to have a place for intimate relations. Children were important. They even had a schedule—" she raised an eyebrow "—such orderly Germans."

"My ancestors are Czech," Anna said primly, "as are John's."

Jane ignored this comment. "When the choirs were disbanded, a few decided to keep them going. In secret."

"Not secret exactly," Anna objected. "We just don't advertise the fact."

"So you have this place—" Jane lifted her arms, palms up "—and the other houses. At least, that's what Roxanne says."

"Roxanne?" Anna exclaimed. "My, you have been busy. Why not come to me?"

"You weren't there the night I came to see you," Jane said, "so I asked Roxanne out to lunch. But she told me I needed to get the details from you."

"I'm glad to hear that, at least," Anna said. "What else have you learned?"

"It seems that Zinzendorf scandalized the other Protestants by preaching that the Holy Spirit was our Mother, a balance to God the Father and the son Jesus. Although—" she pointed to the pile of books "—Fogelman seems to think it was Jesus who was female."

"A radical interpretation, but do you understand why he says that?"

"Something about the side wound. That Christ gave us new birth through his suffering on the cross."

"Close enough," Anna said, "although Zinzendorf preached that Jesus was the one true male. What about the spiritual teachings about sexuality?"

"I just thumbed through the book on Blake. His mother attended the church in Fetter Lane." She looked up at Anna, her hostility slipping into curiosity for a moment. "I never knew the Moravians were in England."

Anna nodded. "Zinzendorf sent missionaries many places. Miss Essig's family came from that congregation."

"That explains the paintings."

Anna's eyes widened, but she remained silent.

Jane was beginning to feel like a student in confirmation class, but she decided to play a while longer. "The sexual teachings explain that we are brides of Christ. I didn't read much more than that."

"I see." Anna sat for a moment, head down, her focus inward. Then she looked up at Jane. "When Miss Essig insisted we put your name in the lot, I resisted. Usually the keeper of this house comes from someone who's done . . ." she seemed to be searching for the right word, "advanced study."

Jane snickered.

"I'm perfectly serious," Anna snapped.

"I can see that you are." Jane pushed images of entwined, naked bodies firmly out of her mind. Anna would never indulge in such things, she was sure.

"I'd wondered how to approach you about the more spiritual practices of our group."

"Umm," Jane murmured, letting Anna run with the line like a hooked fish.

"My new class is in its third week, but considering your reading—" Anna cocked her head "—perhaps you could join us and catch up. Learn the deeper spiritual teachings of your tradition."

Jane pounced. "So now you're offering to teach me instead of drug me?"

"What?" Anna sat forward in her chair. "What did you say?"

"Drug me." Jane pronounced each word distinctly. "Are you trying to deny it?"

"I have no idea what you're talking about." Anna's face flushed and her voice held an edge of anger.

"The thermos of tea with the little note? Pretending to be so solicitous of my health," Jane spat out.

Anna shook her head.

"On the night of the chanting?"

"What thermos?"

Jane jumped up and stormed into the kitchen. She grabbed the red plaid cylinder from the counter, then rushed back into the library. She shoved it at Anna. "This one."

Anna looked at the thermos, then shook her head. "That's not mine."

"It's certainly not Dorothea's. She would never do such a thing."

Anna opened her mouth to say something, her face bright red, then seemed to think better of it. She took a deep breath, then spoke in a calmer voice, "You keep saying someone tried to drug you. Please tell me what happened."

"I didn't drink it, thank heavens. But the next day I took it to a lab that my lawyer has an account with."

"Your lawyer?" Anna's voice rose an octave.

The cats jumped down and hid behind the couch.

"That's right. I'm not defenseless, you know."

"And the lab test?"

"The results showed barbiturates."

The color drained from Anna's face. She pulled her cell phone out of her skirt pocket and pushed a button. Jane heard a male voice answer. "John, call Dreher," Anna said. "We've been breached."

Jane stared at Anna, who folded her phone back up and put it into her pocket. "Do you have a copy of the lab results?"

"What?" Jane blinked at her.

"The lab results? Can I see them?"

Jane started to get up, then sat back down. How had she lost control of the situation so quickly? "Who did you call?"

"My husband, of course."

"And why did you ask him to call the property manager?"

Anna shook her head in confusion. "The what?"

"The property manager," Jane repeated through clenched teeth.

"Oh." A look of comprehension came over Anna's face. "Dreher is our head of security."

"Security? What do you need security for?" Jane's voice grew louder. Then she heard what she'd just said and laughed. The unasked question finally burst out of her mouth. "Why would somebody want to drug me?"

Anna leaned toward her and put her hand on Jane's knee. "That is what we're going to find out. And we're going to protect you."

"Lois is already investigating this." Jane fought back sudden and surprising tears.

"And who is Lois?" Anna asked.

"My attorney."

"Just how many people have you told about this?"

"Only her," Jane said. "The lab, of course, but I didn't explain the circumstances." Anger rushed through her again. "Why? What are you trying to hide?"

Anna opened her mouth to reply, but the front door burst open. Jane was sure she'd locked it.

"Anna?" Jane recognized John Szeges's voice.

"In here," Anna replied.

John rushed in followed by a well-muscled man—blond buzz cut and sharp blue eyes. He was squat and powerful like a linebacker. He looked her up and down, then turned to Anna. "What happened?"

"Apparently someone left a thermos of tea for Jane here." She pointed at her. "Jane, meet Dreher."

Jane nodded at the man. "How did you two get here so fast?"

They all ignored her question. "The tea was laced with barbiturates," Anna continued.

"How much?"

"I haven't seen the report yet."

"When did this happen?"

"The night of our ceremony."

"So they hoped to knock her out and sneak in through this house." Dreher addressed this statement to John. He pointed at the coffee table where the thermos stood. "This is it?"

"Yes," Jane said.

"Has anyone handled it?"

"Uh, I did," Jane confessed.

He favored her with a look that suggested she had no sense whatsoever.

"And I washed it out." She winced having to admit this.

"Great. There go the fingerprints." He shook his head in disgust.

Why didn't I think of that? Jane wondered. She'd been so sure the thermos belonged to Anna.

"If there were any," John said.

Dreher snorted. "You're right. They'd be careful."

"Who?" Jane asked.

But Dreher ignored her question again. "What made you have the contents analyzed?"

"Oh, let's see." Jane rolled her eyes. "I'm awakened by chanting in the middle of the night. Then I discover a secret staircase. Then I find a secret hallway off the basement. And then—"

"Yes, we know what you found after that." Dreher's voice dripped venom.

"How did you know?" she asked. At that point, Winston arrived at the library door, panting. He made a beeline for Jane and pushed himself between his mistress and this ominous human.

"Get control of that dog," Dreher shouted.

Winston growled.

"He lives here," Jane said. "You do not."

"Oh, great," Dreher said, "and why didn't you stop the intruder, Mr. Bulldog?"

Winston showed his teeth.

"Enough." John's low voice silenced everyone.

Winston sat on Jane's foot, apparently satisfied that someone else had taken charge besides the man yelling at his human.

"Look," Jane said, trying to keep her voice even, "I thought the tea came from Anna. We were out in the garden all day. I told Dorothea I'd have sore muscles—" she stroked Winston's back, soothing herself more than the dog "—and the thermos was sitting in the kitchen when I came inside. After I woke up in the middle of the night, then found that room the next morning, well, I just assumed she'd tried to put me out so I'd sleep through whatever you guys were doing."

Anna put her head in her hands.

John flushed bright red.

"Besides, there was the note."

"Note?" This came from all three of her visitors at once.

"Don't tell me. You threw it away," Dreher said.

"I most certainly did not," Jane flashed out at him. Then her business training surfaced. She had to stop reacting to this man, letting him dominate. Clearly that's what he was used to. "I'd be happy to show you the lab results and the note, but you need to explain a few things to me first."

He frowned. "I'm not so sure—"

"Tell me," Jane rolled over him, "is the OGMS really the Order of the Grain of the Mustard Seed?"

Dreher glared at Anna. "I thought you were going to take care of all this."

"Answer my question," Jane said.

Dreher put his hands on his hips. "I am not accustomed to being spoken to in that tone of voice."

Jane matched his stance. "And I am not accustomed to living on top of some sort of a . . ." she flourished her hands in the air, searching for a word.

Anna stretched her hands out to placate Jane. "I promise I will answer all your questions, but I am the proper one to ask."

"Was Miss Essig a member of your group?"

Anna chewed her lip before answering. "Yes, as is Dorothea. We all are."

"Did she take part in your," Jane's lip curled, "rituals."

"No, the *hieros gamos* is for married couples only."

"And what else do you do besides this *hieros* . . ." Blast, she couldn't remember the second word.

"Our purpose is to continue Zinzendorf's work, of course. To spread the teachings of Christ."

Jane considered them all for a moment. Somehow she doubted it was this simple, but Dreher looked like he'd been put in his place for now. "Okay, I'll give you a copy of the test results. I suppose you can take the thermos, although I don't think it will help you much. I'm sorry I washed it. I wasn't thinking," she said, trying to meet them part way.

Jane walked over to the desk and fished around in the top drawer. She pulled out the lab report. She'd scanned it already. The file was still in her computer, so she handed the original over to Dreher.

He took the lab results and the thermos and marched out the door. John nodded more politely, then followed him.

"We'll talk soon, but your safety is paramount," Anna said. "Dreher will most likely post a guard around our complex for a while."

"I'm going out of town for business tomorrow."

"When will you be back?"

"I'll only be gone a day or two."

"Check with me when you return. We have a lot to catch up on." Anna smoothed down her hair, waiting for an answer.

"Fine," Jane said reluctantly.

CHAPTER TWELVE

Jane sat in the back seat of the black Lincoln Town Car the museum had sent to pick her up from her early morning flight to Newark. A security guard sat next to the chauffeur. The portfolio case containing the Blake sketches lay on the leather seat beside her, packed exactly to specifications. She'd brought only three of the seven that were new to the art world.

About an hour after the OGMS people had left, an art team had descended on her house complete with two armed security guards. She didn't think Dreher had beefed up security that quickly. The team crated up two paintings from the Blake room. She didn't let them take all the ones they claimed were originals. These had been shipped overnight under heavy guard. She'd followed very early the next morning.

The car rolled by blocks of restaurants, coffeehouses, dress shops, drug stores, the sidewalks full of people jostling, gossiping, gawking. Jane rested her head against the window, feeling the invisible social restraints of the South relax. She checked the markets on her Blackberry. Still climbing, slow and steady. She looked at a few specific stocks. Not so good. Still not time to trade.

She took a deep breath and sat back, still grappling with all she had learned yesterday. It would take her some time to readjust her attitudes about her childhood church. Guilt nagged at her for taking the paintings without asking, but she pushed it away, telling herself she was looking out for her own interests, that she wasn't stealing anything, only borrowing. Besides, they'd hidden things from her. The paintings would be back before anyone knew they'd been on this little excursion. She closed her eyes a moment, and the music from her dream played softly in the background. Good, it was still there.

They pulled into a loading zone in front of Mr. Weststone's gallery on West 24th and the driver came around to open her door. "I'll carry the case for you, madam."

Jane allowed him to take the awkward portfolio and then slid across the seat. The crisp air warned of snow. She pulled her coat tighter, following the chauffer and guard into the building. They skipped the gallery proper, taking a side hallway to a back elevator, the guard gliding like a mountain lion, scanning every innocuous corner.

The chauffer pushed the button for an upper floor, then stood almost at attention on the ride up. The old elevator clanged to a stop. He pushed the metal cage door open, then ushered her down the hall. The security man took up a position outside the door.

The office they entered was punctuated by various work areas, all lit by an expanse of windows. Mr. Weststone jumped up from his desk toward the back when they entered, hurrying to greet them. He wore a peacock blue shirt topped by a darker blue silk jacket. His tie was the exact green of a peacock feather.

"Ms. Frey, it was good of you to come on such short notice." He held out his hand, which she shook. "Can I get you something? A cappuccino? Mineral water?" He glanced at a clock on the wall. "I suppose it's a bit early for wine, but if you'd care for some . . ."

"I would appreciate some coffee," Jane said.

Weststone flapped a hand at his young assistant, who disappeared into a back room. "These are the sketches?"

The chauffer handed over the portfolio case to his boss and, with a nod, left.

"May I?" Weststone asked, inclining his well-coiffed head slightly.

"Of course." Jane followed him through the greeting area, past his desk to a conference table toward the back, lit not only by the large windows, but also skylights. Jane glanced up. All the windows were tinted, filtering the sunlight. A tall Norfolk pine stood in the corner absorbing the rays. The paintings and colored prints that had been shipped yesterday stood on easels against one wall.

"Don't you just love this room?" Weststone held out his hands, turning slightly to show off the space like a lovely woman presenting merchandise on a game show. "Good art demands the right illumination."

The harried assistant arrived with two coffees on a tray and placed it on the end of the table, his eyes darting to the portfolio case as he poured the coffee. Sliding the case well away from the liquid, Weststone opened it and then donned white gloves. He took out the sketches, handling them like delicate Ming vases, then placed them on a clear lectern, brushed them off with what looked like a feather boa, and covered them with sheets of Plexiglas. He stood back and held out his hand without looking at his assistant, who carefully gave him coffee. Jane accepted her cup with a bit more grace.

"Come, stand with me," Weststone said to her. "I find it best to look at a new piece from a distance first. To see it whole, as the artist conceived it."

Jane walked to the end of the table and stood beside him. The two of them studied the sketches, sipping a mellow blend. In one, a male and female stood together in a garden, a snake twining up a tree. In this light Jane made out details she'd missed before. The spherical apples were named in tiny Greek letters. In another a couple seemed joined in sexual congress, the woman reaching her hand up toward a golden sphere of light. It reminded Jane of the larger painting. Perhaps the sketch was a study for it.

Mr. Weststone couldn't restrain himself any longer. He set down his coffee and moved close, leaning back, then forward, cocking his head from side to side. "Excellent," he murmured, "Really excellent."

Footsteps approached and Jane turned to find the assistant escorting two people into the room, one in a tweed jacket, the other dressed in a black skirt suit exactly like the ones Jane used to wear to client meetings. That suit meant money. The tweed, academia.

"Ah, Professor Rifkin. Ms. Morrisette, please come in." Weststone made the introductions.

Jane silently congratulated herself.

"Ms. Frey has discovered some new Blake sketches and I believe the paintings and colored prints are new as well. We'll defer to your judgment, Professor."

"Of course, of course," Rifkin murmured. His attention had already been captured by the art displayed before him. He stood beside them for a moment, looking at each piece carefully. Next he took out a monocle—Jane bit her lip to keep from laughing—placed it carefully over his eye and approached the table. He bent over each sketch, making little clucking sounds and occasionally uttering a word or two that Jane couldn't hear. Weststone hovered next to him, answering his ejaculations in kind. After a while, they moved on to the pieces displayed on easels.

Morrisette took a cup of coffee from the assistant, then turned to Jane. "These were discovered in Winston-Salem, you say? In one of the tobacco or cotton family collections?"

"Actually, no. These were in Miss Essig's collection. She's just passed away."

"Essig?" Morrisette's eyes took on a vague look as she searched her memory, then shook her head. "I'm afraid I don't know the family. The name sounds English."

Jane hesitated. "Moravians are more often German or Czech."

"Moravians did you say?" Ms. Morrisette pursed her lips in thought. "Ah, does Miss Essig's family have ties to Fetter Lane, perhaps?"

"Fetter Lane?" Jane was surprised this woman knew the name.

"Wasn't there a Moravian congregation there? Isn't that where Wesley worshipped with them for a time?"

"Wesley? As in John Wesley, founder of the Methodists?"

"That's right. Wesley was very impressed with the depth of Moravian faith."

Jane decided she had to finish reading church history if this perfect stranger knew more about it than she did.

Ms. Morrisette continued. "William Blake's mother also attended church there. Her name was discovered a few years back in an archive."

"Please excuse my question," Jane said, "but how is it you know so much about this? Most people hardly realize Moravians exist."

"A book a few years back on Blake. Something about his 'sexual path'." She furnished air quotes. "Most people with a serious interest in eighteenth and nineteenth century art have read it by now."

"Of course," Jane said, "I've just recently discovered it."

Professor Rifkin turned to Morrisette. "I'm sure these are authentic, although we should do more tests before making an offer."

"An offer?" Jane asked.

"I help finance new purchases for the university and several museums," Morrisette explained.

"This art is owned by a family trust," Jane said. "I don't think they'll agree to sell." She didn't say that she'd brought the pieces without the trust's knowledge.

"We can meet and discuss it. If the family doesn't want to part with them, perhaps they'll agree to a loan? We can arrange a special exhibit. Borrow a few other Blake pieces. It would create quite a stir," Morrisette assured her.

The professor took out his monocle and looked at Jane. "Can we have a few more experts look at them? How long can we keep them?"

"I'm afraid I'll need to return them tomorrow."

"Tomorrow?" Both Professor Rifkin and Mr. Weststone exclaimed in union.

"We'd hoped to keep them for at least a week," Professor Rifkin explained.

"I'm sorry. If it were up to me alone . . ." Jane shrugged.

"Oh, dear. We'll have to get everyone over here this afternoon." Weststone bustled off to his desk calling for his assistant.

Professor Rifkin opened his mouth to object, but Morrisette intervened. "Of course we'll comply with the family's terms.

May we bring in our team for the rest of the day and let you pick the pieces up tomorrow, say noon?"

"I suppose I could fly back in the late afternoon. That would give you a little more time," Jane said.

"We'd be most appreciative." Morrisette turned to the professor. "Call your people. Get them over here as soon as possible."

"People have classes, you know. Schedules to meet."

"That's what grad students are for," Morrisette said.

Professor Rifkin pulled out his cell phone and walked away from them.

Morrisette turned back to Jane. "Is there something you'd like to do while you wait? I can arrange museum visits, tickets to shows . . ."

"Actually, I have plans," Jane said, "but thank you. Just email me the return flight information and when your car will pick me up. Mr. Weststone knows where I'm staying."

Morrisette accompanied Jane to the reception area where Weststone joined them. The assistant arrived behind him carrying her coat. "Our driver will take you wherever you need to go," he said.

"Thank you," Jane said. She took the dark wool coat and shrugged it on.

"It's the least we can do." He fluttered his hands and looked back toward the conference room. The chauffer arrived and held the office door open for her.

"I'll let you get to work," Jane said to Weststone. "I'm sorry I can't give you more time, but you can see them again in North Carolina."

The art dealer nodded, somewhat relieved.

Jane's appointment with Lois was late afternoon. Her stomach demanded attention first, so she asked the driver to drop her off in her old neighborhood. He gave her his cell phone number and drove off. She ate at her favorite Thai place—fish cakes and coconut soup. None of the wait staff recognized her. It had been several years, after all. After lunch, she called the driver. For the rest of the afternoon, she divided her time between the Morgan Library & Museum and the

Blake archives at the New York Public Library, getting to know Blake's work better. She searched the library's holdings on the OGMS, but found nothing new.

Around four, she headed for Lois's office. The car crawled through heavy traffic, Jane remembering how she'd been shocked by the obscenities truck drivers and cabbies hurled on a regular basis. Now they barely registered. She called to say she'd be late and the office assistant took her message. Jane arrived in the glass, chrome and leather decorated office just in time to find Lois ushering out another client.

When they left, Jane waggled her eyebrows. "Personal attention. Must be important."

Lois chuckled and took her arm. "Come with me." She walked Jane down the hallway, their footsteps muted by the plush grey carpet. Once inside Lois's corner office, she gave Jane the once over. "You look good. Haven't run to fat yet."

"It's good to see you, too." Jane plopped down in one of the deep plum chairs in the seating area away from Lois's desk and kicked off her low heels. "I can't even wear these all day anymore."

"It's the cocktail hour." Lois looked over at her assistant, who hovered by the door. "My usual." She turned to Jane. "What would you like?"

Jane shook her head, but Lois made a face. "Bring her—" she snapped her fingers, trying to remember "—a Jack Rose. Isn't that what your favorite commentator made last?" She smiled triumphantly.

"Right you are," Jane said, "but you might not have all the ingredients."

"Please, we're better stocked than the Bull and Bear."

Jane snorted. "I doubt that."

Lois picked a few files off her desk and sat opposite Jane, spreading the paperwork on a table between them. "I'm still waiting to hear from my asset, but I can show you what I've got so far."

Asset. Jane smiled at the word. Lois loved to talk like the head of the CIA.

Lois glanced up. "I assume you've discovered the origin of this organization. It's easily available on the internet."

"I haven't forgotten how to use a computer yet," Jane said.

"The group has gone through several permutations in other places. There's some prayer group using the name."

"I saw that," Jane said.

"But in North Carolina, the group has remained stable. Same families and groups involved." Lois turned a list around so Jane could read it.

She saw the names of the people she'd met at the attorney's office and at the house. Her eyes ran further down the list. "Cherokee Nation? Why would they be involved?"

Lois shrugged, then turned to take the martini from her assistant. "Thank you, Cindy. Did you get the trial brief finished?"

"Yes, ma'am."

"Good. You can go, then."

"Thank you, Miss Williams. Your schedule has been updated. We're still waiting on the reports from Germany."

Lois nodded, then took a gulp of her martini and sat back in the chair with a sigh.

"Long day?" Jane asked.

"Aren't they all?"

"Ever want to give up the fast life, retire, move to some tropical island?"

"I'd die of boredom in one week. I'm surprised you've lasted this long."

Jane shrugged. "I've taken up music again. Been practicing a lot."

Lois studied her for a minute. "Well, whatever flips your switch." Then she turned back to the files. "Now, here's a report on their monetary holdings. Not much to speak of, except the real estate.

"Known associates." She handed a multi-page list to Jane. "Mostly clergy and heads of spiritual groups—Rosicrucians, Masons, that sort of thing. Some politicians and attorneys. A few wealthy individuals who fancy mysticism."

Jane perused the list, but no other names jumped out at her. She wondered about the metaphysical types. What was their connection?

"We're running background checks, but nothing unusual has turned up so far," Lois continued. "There's another group in Alsace that seems to be related. Another in Saxony. I'm still waiting on those reports."

Jane tasted her drink, set it down, and turned the pages of the list, willing her brain to make some connection, but nothing came. She told Lois what she'd discovered. "A Ms. Morrisette—she's an art broker."

"Good reputation," Lois said.

"She mentioned a connection to Fetter Lane. Said Miss Essig's family may have come from there. There was a Moravian church in that neighborhood."

Lois shook her head. "Don't know anything about it, but I'll put somebody on it."

They sat sipping their drinks for a minute, Jane enjoying the luxury of a well-appointed office, realizing how much she missed this part of her old life.

"How's your portfolio?" Lois asked.

"Struggling. If I stay in this house, I'll be all right."

"Not comfortable, though. Not truly independent?"

"Or enough to afford you?" Jane quipped.

Lois favored her with a sour look. "You and I go too far back for that silliness."

"Still," Jane started to object.

"Please, I've done quite well handling some of your deals. Too bad yours got hit so heavily." A gleam lit Lois's eye. "Thing is, one of your old clients has insisted on seeing you."

"What, that leggy ding-bat not good enough for him?"

Lois chortled. "Aren't they the worst, though?"

Jane rolled her eyes. Few people understood this irritation, but Lois was definitely one of them. "I've been gone almost a month now. I'm out of the loop."

"He insists. I've made an appointment for you. He sent a ticket."

"What?" Jane sat forward, "but the art gallery is sending me home tomorrow afternoon."

Lois waived a hand to dismiss this, her ruby and diamond rings flashing. "We'll see that they're reimbursed."

"I'm supposed to take the Blake sketches back. I don't want to trust them to just any courier."

"I'll see to it. Your old client was quite insistent."

"Who?"

"Valentin Knight. Remember him?"

Jane stared at the ceiling, trying to pull up a face from her memory. Nothing. She looked back at Lois. "Who is he?"

"Lives in D.C. Family goes back a long way. American aristocrat, if you will. You helped him years ago with some oil and gas investments."

"Oh, that guy." Jane remembered the situation. She'd been hip deep in negotiations between British Isle Petroleum and a group of Saudi representatives. He'd been an oasis of sanity who dropped in unexpectedly, bringing U.S. government influence to bear and saving a bit of the environment in the process. They'd had dinner. Very pleasant, but she couldn't remember any details now. "That was years ago."

"He won't see anyone but you. Davis has been about to split a gut. Says Knight is moving his money. That you're not returning calls." Lois smiled wickedly. "I see you've still got some of the old spark."

"Bastard." Her chuckle didn't match the word. "Serves him right."

Lois plopped down a plane ticket. "You leave in three hours."

"What? But I told the gallery—"

"After this meeting you won't have to worry about money anymore."

"What do you mean?"

"He's paying quite a pretty penny for the privilege of having you handle the deal."

"Really?" This news stopped Jane's objections. "What's the deal?"

"I've prepared a report for you." She handed Jane a leather message bag. "Just moving funds. Simple."

"Then why the big fee?"

Lois turned her palms up. "You got me there, girl. Must be a crush or something."

Jane snorted. "Not likely."

"He checks out."

"What about the gallery?"

"Just call them and tell them something unexpected has come up. That I'll handle it."

"Okay, but I really need those sketches back. The OGMS doesn't even know I took them."

"Well, we can't have you arrested for art theft, now can we?"

"How long is this meeting in D.C. likely to take?"

"Just the one day. He says he's made arrangements for your return flight."

"Make sure the art arrives just after I do. Then maybe nobody will notice."

Lois shook her head, trying to keep a scowl on her face. But she burst out laughing. "Still up to your old tricks, I see."

"They weren't straight with me. I thought I was inheriting this house. I didn't know there were strings attached."

Lois pointed a finger at her. "You shouldn't have let that happen."

"I never imagined my old music teacher would be involved in anything clandestine."

"Uh-huh." Lois's look was jaded. "It's always the ones who look the most innocent." She stood, now all business. "Is the driver from the gallery waiting?"

"He should be."

"You've just enough time to check out of the hotel and get to the airport."

Jane walked to the door of her old friend's office. "I don't know how to thank you."

"Take me to Monte Carlo for the race next year. I've always wanted to see it. Now you'll be able to afford it."

"Deal."

★ ★ ★

That evening while Jane checked into her hotel room in D.C., David attended his regular lodge meeting in Winston-Salem. After the announcements and formal talk, the grand master, Ed Leigh, asked to speak with him privately. David waited in the hallway, wondering what this was about. The other brothers milled around, talking jovially. That was the reason he'd joined after college—for business contacts mostly, but he'd made many friends over the years.

His Scottish pal, James, had urged him to take the higher degrees. "That's where you'll learn the real secrets," he'd whispered. But David hadn't been interested in secrets. He'd been busy enough trying to find a full time job in music, working in middle management at Hanes, and watching his baby girl grow up way too fast. Then his son had come along, and he hadn't even thought about it again until this evening. Maybe he should talk to James now that he had time on his hands, but his mind drifted to Jane instead. He wondered what she was doing.

Soon the grand master appeared and led David into his office. Furnished with a long credenza and rectangle of a desk, both in a dark veneer, the room looked like it hadn't been redecorated since the 1950s. Ed gestured for him to take a seat, then settled behind his desk. "Thank you for staying behind to chat."

"Sure," David said, wondering again what this was all about.

Ed opened a file, put on a pair of wire framed reading glasses and perused the few pages, then looked back up. "Mr. Spach—"

"David is fine."

"Of course, David." Ed smiled to put him at ease, which made him nervous. "You've been a member in good standing for some time. Went through to the thirteenth degree I see."

"That's right. I've thought of continuing now that I have more time."

"We don't put any pressure on our members. It's up to each person to guide their own development." He paused again, took a breath as if to speak, but let it out without saying anything more.

"So, what did you want to see me about, sir?"

"Oh, please call me Ed."

"Okay, Ed."

The man looked down at his desk again, seemed to set his shoulders before he met David's eyes. "I suppose you know that many Moravians have been members of our lodge. Here, in Pennsylvania, D.C., and in Europe."

"Yes, I'd heard that before." David thought this an odd comment.

"I've received some information that concerns me. Do you know Jane Frey?"

Small town, David thought. *One date and everybody knows.*

He sat back in his chair. "I do. We were in school together."

"I suppose you know she's taken over Miss Essig's old house?"

"So I've been told."

"She might not even know what I'm about to tell you—" David assumed by the elevated eyebrow that Ed would prefer it stay that way "—but individuals in her family have been members over the years. Some rather deeply involved."

"That right?" This conversation was not going in the direction he'd imagined.

"It seems that a couple of hundred years ago, the Frey family might have come into the possession of certain . . ." Ed looked up at the ceiling while he searched for the right word, "artifacts. Spiritual antiques."

"Such as?"

Ed ignored the question. "Our national headquarters thinks some people may be searching for them."

"National?" David's shoulders tensed.

"They're concerned that this group has learned of Miss Essig's death and might take advantage of the situation."

"How so?" David was glad she had that bulldog.

"I don't know. I just wanted to let you know, ask you to keep an eye out for anything unusual. Be sure Miss Frey is safe." He paused. "You are friends, aren't you?"

David didn't really hear this question. "Is she in any danger?"

"I wouldn't think they'd go that far, but it's worth watching for strangers in the neighborhood. Any little odd thing." He paused, watching David thoughtfully. "We let the Szeges's know, too."

"That's good," David said, although he didn't know how a minister and his civic-minded wife could help. "Do you know what these people are looking for?"

"I'm afraid I don't have specifics."

"That might help," David suggested. "Moravians don't usually go in for artifacts, you know."

"Certain valuables have been known to pass through the Masons, especially in the past. This seems to be one of those instances where the Masons and Moravians intersected. I'll see if I can find out anything more." Ed stood up, indicating the meeting was at an end. "In the meantime, just let us know if you notice anything. And if you don't mind, let us know if she finds anything or leaves the house unattended so we can help keep the place safe." He handed David his card. "My cell is on the back."

David took the card and nodded. "Err, thanks. You'll let me know if you learn anything more?"

"Will do."

☆ ☆ ☆

About two in the morning, Philip Martin jiggled the door handle of the English Tudor house to see if the bulldog was inside. No bark. He'd watched the old, fat lady take him over to the other house shortly after Jane left. Dreher's so-called security had been easy to elude.

Good. The coast was clear. He'd disabled the electronic security system for the whole complex, turned off the cameras and replaced the feed with a loop of the previous hours. Philip retrieved a small screw driver from his backpack and removed the lock, opened the door and slipped inside.

He took the carpeted steps two at a time, then walked down the hall to the closet he'd seen Jane disappear into that night. Tapping on the wall, his luck held when the back panel clicked open. The flashlight showed a narrow stairway, which he took. Ending in the basement, he tapped along a wall in the identical paneling until one moved slightly. He reached into his pocket and pulled out a lock pick. He had the panel open in thirty seconds.

Amateurs.

A noise startled him. He shone his light behind him. It was reflected back by cat eyes. He grunted and walked through the panel. Secured it behind him. Didn't want that damn animal giving him away.

He flashed his light down one side. The floor seemed to slope down, then drop off. Steps probably. Along the other wall he saw a few doors. He went that way. Door number one opened into a long room with alcoves off the sides. He shone the light around. An altar stood at the far end and above it hung a large painting. Deciding to risk it, he switched on the light and walked on silent feet to the other side of the room.

Luck was with him. The painting matched the description Coche had given him. Philip gave the room a quick once over, checking the alcoves for cameras or any independently wired security device. Nothing. Only straight-back chairs and beds in a couple of rooms. What was this, some kind of a dormitory?

He walked back to the altar where he saw the phallic-shaped stone and cup on either side of the long table. The painting showed a couple fucking, one reaching toward a bleeding Jesus. These Christian types were twisted. Must be some kind of sex club, a room for hanky panky, maybe wife swapping. At least that's what he figured. No fancy equipment, though. Most people who had sex in dungeons did so with a full array of bondage toys. Not these guys. Just an altar with your typical symbols of male and female. Then private rooms, for couples he imagined. Small towns were so boring.

He stood on the altar in his stocking feet and checked to see how the large painting was secured. Two hooks on the back. This treasure hung only by a wire that ran through them. He tested its weight. A bit heavy, the gilded frame accounting for most of it, but the size would be the real challenge. It came off the wall easily. He pried it loose from its frame, working slowly so as not to damage the painting.

Once he had it free, he shoved his feet back into his shoes, then pulled out a roll of plastic bubble material and wrapped the painting, taping it closed when he was done. With painstaking care, Philip carried the burden across the room. The bulk clanged against something above him, the sound muffled by the plastic. He looked up to see a metal star hanging down. He moved back, and the star light fixture came loose from the plastic, swaying a bit, then coming to rest. Philip moved slightly to the right and continued toward the door. His shoulders started to burn from the awkward angle. A few steps more to the end of the room.

Setting the painting down, he propped it against his shoulder and opened the door that led to the hallway. The top just fit under the door, but bumped again the opposite wall in the hall. Philip spent a few minutes angling the painting, jiggling it back and forth until it finally slid out of the room. He leaned it against the wall and closed the door. From there it was relatively easy to maneuver down the hallway. The panel opening created a bit of a challenge, but this was nothing compared to getting the large canvas through the cellar door and outside. Sweating even in the cold early December night, at last he secured the painting in the back of the small van he'd rented for this night's work. He started to close the door, when he noticed the cat had jumped inside. He scooped her up by the scruff of her neck, ignoring her protest, and unceremoniously dumped her back inside the cellar, securing the door. He climbed up the back stairs, closed the hidden panel in the closet, and ran lightly down to the main level. He replaced the door handle, then locked it. The dark night had greyed. Dawn was close.

He climbed into the front of the van, started it up and drove out the other side of the horseshoe-shaped driveway. No cars. No pedestrians. The windows of the surrounding houses were still dark. He parked on the street and slipped into the antebellum house, put the security system back on normal. Then he drove to a facility near the Greensboro airport and parked beside a large shipping crate. He unloaded the painting and strapped it tight for transport, then drove the van back to his hotel where he caught a few hours' sleep.

The next day on his afternoon flight, Philip stretched out in his first class seat back to D.C. and ordered another scotch. Coche had confirmed the painting was already on its way. He told Philip he could have a few days off. Finally he could escape this suffocating small town. He hoped the old man would have a more interesting assignment for him next time.

Maybe he'd do some poking around on his own. Figure out what this was really all about.

CHAPTER THIRTEEN

Jane stifled a yawn. The six o'clock wake-up call felt more like four. She was standing in front of the St. Regis, where her mysterious host had put her up for the night. Not only one of the most expensive hotels in D.C., but he'd sprung for a suite. She'd thought the flowers a bit over the top. A dozen red roses. Maybe Lois was right. Maybe he did have a crush on her. David might have some competition. Trouble was, she couldn't really remember Knight's face.

She hummed in time with the steps of a jogger as he ran past. A black stretch limo pulled up and the driver got out. His glaze skimmed over two men waiting for a cab before landing on her. He approached. "Ms. Frey?"

"Yes," she said.

"Mr. Knight sent me for you." The driver opened the back door and she slid across the rich leather seat. The car nosed its way through already building traffic, although Jane still spotted a lot of people going about their early morning activities—dog walkers taking their pets out before they headed off to work, more joggers, some power walkers. She hummed the tune again, then realized it was the same one from her dream. Continuing to hum, Jane slowly pulled out a piece of paper, making no noise, as if she were sneaking up on prey. She turned it over and then hummed again, noting down a few bars before she ran up against a blank. She closed her eyes to listen, but heard only the ambient sounds of the city.

Her head jerked up in surprise when the car entered the parking garage of a white concrete office building. They'd only gone a few blocks. Was Knight trying to impress her, treating her like some visiting oil sheik? She didn't need tight security. The driver pulled into a loading area, got out and opened the back door for her. He pointed out the elevators. "Eleventh floor, madam. Mr. Knight is expecting you."

"Thank you." Jane hummed the tune again on the elevator, but couldn't move past the beginning.

The doors opened onto a formal greeting area with low couches and side chairs on either side. The receptionist stood, a pert young woman probably in her early twenties. "Ms. Frey?" At Jane's nod, she came out from behind the desk. "Right this way, please."

Jane followed the woman down yet another long hall carpeted in deep blue. The receptionist opened a door, revealing a large, comfortable office with a stunning view of the White House, the Capitol Building, the National Mall and the river beyond. A movement on the right pulled Jane's attention back to the room. A tall, silver-haired man in a richly tailored navy suit was rising to his feet.

"Ms. Frey. I'm glad you were able to come on such short notice." He held out a well-manicured hand, his snow white shirt set off by gold cuff links.

"Mr. Knight." Jane shook his hand. "It's a pleasure to see you again. What has it been, ten years?"

"Longer, I think." Knight's smile suggested they both knew this.

Last night she'd looked through her computer files, finally coming across his name. She hadn't looked for pictures, though. He was handsome. "We met in Riyadh?"

"That's right."

"I must say your assistance was invaluable," Jane said, "if surprising."

Knight did not answer this unstated question, but turned to a table against the wall laden with pastries, fruit and urns. "We got you here very early. The least we could do is offer you breakfast."

"I'm fine, really," Jane said.

"I'll have a croissant and coffee, please." Knight addressed the assistant, who picked up the tongs and chose a pastry for him. "Are you sure you won't have something? I understand you enjoy *pain au chocolat?*"

Jane's eyebrows shot up. "How—"

"Lois and I go way back." Knight smiled conspiratorially.

"Since you went to such trouble," Jane said.

Knight nodded to his assistant, then gestured to the collection of chairs. "Please, have a seat. I know you are curious why I insisted on working with you."

"I must admit I am." Jane took the arm chair, and Knight resumed his seat on the small sofa adjacent to it.

He waited for the young woman to place their food on the coffee table, picked up his cup and took a sip. Once she'd closed the door, leaving them alone, he set the cup down again. "Since the change at your old firm, we've decided to move some of our investments."

"I see." She didn't, but thought she'd figure it out as soon as she studied the paperwork.

"You'll probably recognize some of the deals. You were involved with many of them."

Jane picked up her own coffee, waiting to see what he'd add.

"I only intervene directly when there's a need—as there was with the BIP/Saudi deal."

"That was a tough one. I was beside myself. There would have been a major spill in the Arctic," Jane said, studying Knight's face. "You saved a bunch of polar bears, to mention only one species."

He accepted the acknowledgment with a smile. "It was my pleasure. And duty." Knight kept his answers concise, like most CEOs Jane had worked with, used to keeping his cards close to his chest. He was all business. No overtones of romance or anything more personal.

She continued, "I was impressed. It's rare to find anyone in that business who's concerned with the environment."

"Unfortunate, but true," Knight agreed.

Jane waited to see if he'd say more, but he didn't. She drank down her coffee, hoping it would finish waking her up.

"So, about our business today," Knight deftly steered the conversation away from the past. "This is another circumstance in which I felt compelled to intervene. I did not appreciate your being dismissed and an inexperienced person—" his mouth pursed up as if he'd bitten into a sour plum "—assigned in your place."

"Thank you, Mr. Knight." Jane bit her lip to stop the smile that was forming.

"In fact, our board has decided to cease our association with your old company. Now," again the strictly business tone, "we've set aside this office for your use."

Jane tried to contain her surprise at being given such a luxurious space.

"All the relevant information is on the desk. I've given you a temporary employee ID and computer." He turned to a phone next to him and pushed the intercom.

"Yes, Mr. Knight?"

"Send Chase back, please."

"Yes, sir."

Knight turned to Jane again. "Betsy Chase has been assigned to you for the morning. Once you've finished with the transfers, I hope you can join me for a little tour I've arranged."

"I look forward to it," she said. Jane had seen D.C. a number of times, but accompanying her benefactor on yet another trip through the nation's capital was the least she could do. Maybe then she could ferret out if he had intentions other than business.

"Excellent." Knight tapped his forefinger against his lips trying in vain to hide his faint smile.

There was a soft knock on the door, then it opened and a woman, this one probably in her late twenties, walked in. She was dressed in the corporate uniform—black skirt, white blouse, black jacket, her dark hair pulled back in a bun. A few tight curls had already escaped, framing her face in a halo of softness. Probably not the effect the young professional was hoping for, Jane thought, but she preferred it.

"Ah, Ms. Chase. As we discussed, you'll be working with Jane Frey this morning. Please give her your full cooperation."

"Of course, Mr. Knight." The woman came close to clicking her heels.

He stood and addressed himself to Jane. "My own office is two floors up should you need me. I'll leave you to it."

Jane spent the morning doing absolutely routine financial transfers that, as it turned out, a junior assistant could have handled. She scanned each account, running her eyes through the various sources of the income, occasionally pulling up relevant files on the deals involved. Some were connected to oil and gas transactions she'd been involved with in some way. A few carried Mr. Davis's signature. Others she or her firm had nothing to do with. She noted the parts of the world where the wells had been drilled, the subcontractors involved, the types of platforms, the environmental damage incurred, the legal teams managing the deals, the banks involved, but could find no consistent pattern. Whatever this was about was not immediately obvious. The only trend seemed to be that Knight was investing more in green energy.

Jane had thought she'd puzzle it out as soon as she studied the files, but the pattern eluded her. Lois hadn't told her enough, that much was clear. She'd been in a hurry though, and Jane trusted her attorney. Knight's staff had done a lot of backup work to prepare for these transfers. One thing was sure. Moving this much money would not go unnoticed by the bankers, not to mention the oil and gas industry. Perhaps he was trying to make some kind of political impact. But why involve her? Maybe he was trying to send Davis a message about Jane's own firing or his choice of a new assistant, but this seemed a rather extravagant way to do that. It was probably political, Jane thought, glancing out the window at the array of federal buildings.

Chase sat across the room at a smaller desk reviewing account numbers and verifying transfers once they'd been made. Maybe Jane could pick up something through office gossip. She went to the credenza and poured herself another cup of coffee and piled pineapple, strawberries, kiwi slices along with two fruit kabobs on a plate. "Can I get you anything, Betsy?" Jane asked.

The woman blushed. "You shouldn't be getting me coffee."

"Why not?" Jane asked. "I'm right here. How do you take it?"

"Uh," Betsy frowned slightly.

"Black? Cream and sugar?"

"Skinny, no sugar."

"Coming right up." Jane poured Betsy a cup and took it to her, then brought her mid-morning snack to the adjacent chair. Betsy thanked her profusely. "Have you been with this firm long?"

Betsy picked up her cup and took a sip, then set it down and darted her eyes toward Jane, then back to her computer screen. "Mr. Knight hired me right after I got my MBA. It's the only firm I've worked for." Betsy lifted her chin and squared her shoulders.

"I take it you're more than content here."

Betsy's face lit up. "He's the best. Kind, considerate. But mostly he has such high standards—I mean in terms of the deals he does." Her dusky skin flushed. "The people too, of course, but he always tries to do something for the environment or set up some percentage to go toward a civic project. Like the school we built in Chad." Her eyes shone.

Maybe this is the crush, Jane thought, but she asked, "Were you involved in that?"

Betsy nodded. "It was my first trip to Africa. I knew about the poverty in some areas, but seeing it firsthand . . ."

"I know what you mean," Jane said. "It's shocking, but you must feel satisfied to work for a powerful firm that tries to do some good. I used to wrestle with my conscience after many a deal." Jane ate pieces of melon off a long wooden stick one at a time.

Betsy pointed to the computer, indicating the contracts they were dealing with. "I can imagine."

"Especially after starting off in the sixties, with civil rights and the feminist movement. We had such high hopes." Jane smiled to take any sting out of these words. "It's good to know Mr. Knight has kept true to those values."

"You remember the civil rights movement?" Betsy's tone was deferential.

"Yes," Jane said with a smile. "I grew up listening to King's speeches. The first news I remember as a child was Little Rock. And my hometown is thirty miles west of Greensboro, where the lunch counter protests were."

Betsy turned to face her fully. "My mother always talks about those days. She was one of the Freedom Riders."

"Wow." Jane's eyes widened. "A brave woman."

"You all were."

"Well, some more than others," Jane said. "It took an incredible amount of nerve to get on those buses. Your mother faced real violence."

"She was lucky, though. Nothing terrible happened." Pride filled Betsy's face, then a wisp of yearning. "I wish I'd been able to listen to Dr. King speak. Live, that is. Did you hear him here in Washington?"

"I did." Jane's gaze went to the window, but she saw the past, the crowds of people marching, laughing and singing. Felt the heat of bodies pressed into the National Mall waiting for King. "It was glorious. The thing is, when you're young you think that's the way the world is." She looked at Betsy's earnest brown eyes, her clear brow. "You think it will stay that way. When it turns back to cynicism and corruption, it comes as a shock."

Tears filled Jane's eyes, the surge of nostalgia surprising her. Retirement was making her soft. She looked down at the carpet until it passed, then smiled up at Betsy. "As I said, you're lucky to have a boss who believes in those old values. And a hero for a mother."

"Thank you." Betsy took another sip of coffee, then turned back to her work.

"I have to admit to being a bit . . ." Jane searched for a word "bemused by all this." She waved a hand at the folders piled on both desks. "These accounts seemed to be in good hands, so why the change? And why insist I handle this? You could have done it without my help. You're quite competent."

Betsy flushed under Jane's praise, but also hunched her shoulders uncomfortably. "I'm sure Mr. Knight has a good reason. I've come to trust his judgment."

"Of course." So Betsy wasn't the gossipy type. Jane speared another strawberry. Returning to her desk, she spent the rest of the morning reviewing deals, opening new accounts and transferring funds. The last file held orders to transfer money to a Swiss account in the name of Jane Frey. She read the amount and gasped: $13,131,313.13. She put on her reading glasses, but the amount stayed the same.

"Oh, my God," she whispered.

"Excuse me?" Betsy lifted her head and looked over at Jane.

"Oh, nothing." Jane looked down at the figure again. Lois hadn't been kidding. But why? Why would Knight pay her so very much for one morning's work? A series of the number 13. There was something strange going on here, no doubt about it. She punched up the account on her computer, but hesitated before making the transfer. Surely there was a catch, but Lois had vetted the deal. She should have asked Lois about Miss Essig's house sooner.

Bracing herself, Jane hit return. Her financial worries were over. She just hoped there wasn't a hidden cost that would amount to more than she'd just deposited.

The door rattled again and the young receptionist pushed in a serving cart topped with covered dishes. She cleared the breakfast trays and laid out a large bowl of green salad, sandwich wedges, and a pitcher of iced tea. Jane and Betsy helped themselves and ate while reviewing all the transfers, dotting i's, crossing t's and reading out every account number as the other watched carefully. They finished up just after half past one.

Jane buzzed the receptionist. "Mr. Knight asked to be notified when we finished."

"Yes, ma'am. I'll let him know right away."

Betsy piled the files on another cart and rolled it toward the door. "Thank you, Ms. Frey. It was a pleasure working with you."

"The pleasure was all mine."

Betsy pushed the cart over the door jam, the wheels rattling, and disappeared down the hall. Jane turned to the window, looking off toward the stretch of green that was the National Mall, remembering that hot August day long ago, the trees heavy with leaves, when it seemed the world had changed forever. King's dream filled the hearts of every listener. Now, she could just make out the bare branches of the trees lining the streets next to the mall, some brown leaves still clinging to them. The trees would bud again, but the world? Some things had changed, though, she reminded herself. Betsy would have worked here as a maid and not an accountant before they'd marched. Now she had a fair shot to be promoted to a high position.

Behind her someone cleared his throat. She jumped and, looking around, found Knight standing in the doorway. "Ready for that tour?" he asked.

She stood. "I am. But first, I wanted to thank you for your generosity. It will make all the difference to me."

Mr. Knight inclined his head. "You deserve it. Do you know how many millions you've helped my company make over the years?"

"Not me personally. I must say I'm still a bit bemused by it all."

"As I said, I didn't like how you were treated." He gestured toward the door. "The sights await us."

She shrugged on her wool coat and followed Knight down the hall. Jane knew there was more to it than that. His answer hadn't really been an answer at all. Yes, she'd been treated shabbily, but not thirteen million dollars' worth of shabby. If she had to guess, Knight had just thrown down the gauntlet to the oil and gas world, moving money to greener pastures. Literally. The last time she had failed to look a gift horse in the mouth, she'd regretted it. Lois had checked it out, but once more, she'd taken the gift, consequences be damned.

At the front door of his office building, Valentin Knight paused. "You don't mind if this is a walking tour, do you?"

"Sounds good." Jane pulled her wool scarf closely around her neck. Still accustomed to Denver's dry weather, the humidity drove the cold deep into her bones. The late lunch crowd jostled against each other on the sidewalk. Jane and Knight walked down a few blocks, skirted the White House, then reached the National Mall and turned west.

Knight looked over at her. "I didn't think we had time for the White House tour today. I would have liked to show you a few interesting little details. Have you ever been inside?"

"I've attended a few state dinners," Jane answered.

"Of course," Knight said, "but there are certain advantages to being a simple tourist. One gets to study the paintings and architecture more closely."

"That's true. While I was there all I could study was the political subtext of polite conversation."

Knight guffawed, which didn't fit her image of him at all, and she relaxed a bit, lengthening her stride, the small gravel crunching beneath her feet. People filled the benches in the park south of the White House, even in the tepid sun. One ate a sandwich. A woman lay with her head in her lover's lap. A mother with a toddler sat watching her child chase the pigeons. They walked down to the reflecting pool and headed toward the Lincoln Memorial.

Jane was glad she'd kept up her running. Knight strode by her side, his breath even, fit for a man his age. If he had romantic intentions, he'd broach them on this walk. She looked down at his hands and confirmed what she'd seen before. A wedding ring. But men of power seldom confined themselves to one woman.

They walked past the Viet Nam War Memorial, Knight barely slowing. Jane glanced over at the long lists of names, growing exponentially as the panels representing the years in the war progressed. She'd come after it had been completed, leaving carnations beneath names of boys she'd known in school who had died in the war.

They reached the Lincoln Memorial, white marble, the fluted columns adding a sense of grace and expansion. It looked like a Greek temple, somehow appropriate amidst the neoclassical architecture of the other buildings. Knight climbed the steps, but instead of going in, he turned and looked down the green expanse, catching his breath. Jane explored inside, remembering again that day when King stood in the entrance and invited the country to dream of equality and justice, to become what it was meant to be. She paused before the statue, then went back to Knight.

He pointed down the Mall. "Architecture is one of my hobbies. And how buildings blend with the land." He hesitated.

Here we go, Jane thought.

He took another breath, then said, "You know that many of our Founding Fathers belonged to the Masons."

Jane contained her surprise, but the snicker escaped. "I've heard that, but surely you don't go in for conspiracy theories."

Knight frowned down at her. "Oh, all that. *Novus Ordo Seclorum.* That Masons are out for world domination." He paused, as if at a loss what to say. "People really do believe the most extraordinary things." His lips pressed into a tight line.

Jane stumbled, trying to find a way to smooth over her gaffe. "The Moravians, too, if the websites are to be believed."

"Indeed?"

"Something about the 24/7 prayer movement. Tell me what you were going to say."

"I suppose it was along the same lines." He chuckled. "I was reminded of the urban legend that the National Mall was built to represent the Tree of Life, so prevalent in Masonic lore."

Jane stared at him, entirely unprepared for this turn in the conversation. So it wasn't romance. She shook herself. After all, this man had just changed her life in exchange for a morning's work. She could humor his eccentricities. "The Tree of Life? Like in the Bible?"

"Eve plucked the apple from the Tree of the Knowledge of Good and Evil. The Tree of Life is a metaphor. A meditation tool, if you like, representing the creation process. But the Mall was not completed during L'Enfant's time, so of course its resemblance to the tree is just a myth."

Regretting her *faux pas*, Jane sought for a way to put Knight at ease again. "I have a weakness for urban legends. My college professor chided me for believing alligators lived in the New York sewers."

Knight stiffened beside her.

Not the right note.

She tried again. "I guess people attach spiritual meaning to things that are important to them."

This remark was better received. "If you are interested in legends . . ." he waited for her nod, "this place is considered to be the head of the Tree, the pure light of God, the source. Perhaps the Great Emancipator is well placed?"

"I would say so," she answered, curious now. Businessmen didn't usually go in for metaphysics.

Knight walked back down the steps and they headed east up the other side of the reflecting pool. The paths were empty now. Some invisible bell seemed to have rung, calling all workers back to their desks. Or maybe they were underground in those infamous tunnels of the Library of Congress and basement cubby holes of the Congressional Office Buildings.

Knight did not walk closer to her or ask her to take his arm. He continued to treat her like a colleague. He paused at the path to the Jefferson Memorial. "I hope you'll excuse me if we don't walk all the way around the lake.

"That's fine," Jane said. "I've been there, too."

"As a young man, I would take the whole route each day before heading to the office." He pointed across the lake to the beautiful white domed building, a circle dotted with columns resembling another temple. "Franklin Roosevelt laid the cornerstone himself, another Mason."

"Really?" Jane asked, searching his face for some clue about why he was sharing all this Masonic lore with her. She took the bait to see where it would lead. "So, what does the legend say about it?"

Knight's eyes lit, pleased by the question. "The Jefferson Memorial and the White House balance each other on this imaginary tree. Jefferson represents justice, and next time you visit, read the panels. They do reflect the theme."

"I've always admired Jefferson, but he's gotten a bad reputation of late."

"Ah, yes. Sally Hemings. Jefferson freed his slaves in his will, but his children didn't honor it."

"Handy to wait until you die," Jane quipped.

"They were men of their time," Knight said. "We're still trying to accomplish what James Madison wrote in the Preamble, trying to form 'a more perfect union'."

"And the White House? Built by slaves," Jane said, but took the sting out with a smile.

Knight looked pleased to be spared an argument. "The White House represents mercy, benevolent leadership."

Jane burst out laughing, "Well, that's definitely a stretch."

"An ideal," Knight suggested. "In fact, many of the statues at either side of the government buildings represent these same principles—justice and mercy in balance. I suppose the Founders hoped we'd be guided by these two principles."

"One can always hope," Jane said.

They walked on. Jane noticed a man close by in a dark raincoat whom she thought she'd seen before, but they all dressed alike here. She turned to her host. "I must say I'm surprised by your interest in these things."

"As I said, architecture is a hobby, especially colonial. The builders were guided by their Masonic beliefs to reflect the ideals of the country in their plans."

Jane pointed to the tall, white obelisk dominating the center of the Mall. "Don't the Masons claim to come from Egypt? Does this explain the shape of the Washington Monument?"

"They do make that claim. I believe that they also trace themselves back to the builders of the Temple of Solomon. That they've kept the secrets of mathematics and proportion in architecture."

"My cousin is an architect." She winced inwardly at this lame contribution to the conversation. Was this just polite conversation? She felt out of her depth.

Knight nodded politely and continued to walk in silence.

"Okay, you must keep up our game," Jane objected.

"Game?"

"What does this legend claim about the Washington Memorial?"

"Oh, yes." Knight perked up. "The obelisk is the heart of the Mall and the heart of the Tree of Life, the station of beauty."

Jane paused to crane her neck upward. "It is."

"What?"

"Beautiful."

Knight laughed. "The Egyptians called the obelisk *Ib Ra,* the heart of Ra. It is said to bring the energy of the sun to the earth."

"And the rest of the Mall?"

"Oh, here it gets a bit more imaginative. The art museums are on our left where the Tree places Venus. Beauty of a more diverse and sensual nature. The Art Museum, the Sculpture Garden, the Archives. Perhaps that is a match."

Jane smiled, enjoying the game now, if that's what it was. "Don't forget the chocolate cake in the café next to the ice skating rink."

"So you are a devotee of chocolate," Knight said. "Lois was right again. And on the right side is Mars, more intellectual. The Air and Space Museum."

Jane wrinkled her nose. "That one doesn't seem to work."

Knight pointed. "The Pentagon is over there, across the water."

"That's cheating," Jane objected. "It's not even close to the Mall."

Knight's laugh was good natured.

They had reached the now empty fountain in front of the Capitol Building. "Here we have the Moon," he said, "the living waters of life."

Jane was distracted by the man in the raincoat standing at the far end of the block, also waiting to cross the street.

Knight turned to her again. "Tell me more about yourself, Ms. Frey."

"Jane," she said.

"Please call me Valentin."

Jane pronounced it carefully, thinking he was an old-fashioned gentleman. It took him the whole walk to be on a first name basis.

"I was named for an old scholar who lived in England," Knight explained, "and then moved to Germany. An affectation of my father's."

"I see," Jane said politely. One more thing among many that she did not really see, but this was trivial compared to the rest.

"I was born and raised in this area," he continued. "And you?"

Apparently their game had ended. "In North Carolina. Winston-Salem, but I moved soon after college. I've lived all over."

"And you said that your family is Moravian, is that right?"

"Did I say that?" she asked.

"Perhaps it was something about a conspiracy website." Knight looked amused.

"That's right." Jane shot a look at him, but now he was watching for traffic. "It's common in that part of North Carolina. We settled the area." Being a Moravian seemed to be coming up in conversation quite a bit. A wild thought crossed her mind that now he was going to start asking her about Blake paintings.

Knight motioned for them to cross, then stopped on the sidewalk on the other side of the street and pointed to the white dome in front of them. "Did you know that one of the architects of the Capitol Building was a Moravian?"

"Not a Mason?" Jane joked.

"That, too." His smile was triumphant.

Jane stopped short. "You're kidding."

"Certainly not. Benjamin Henry Boneval Latrobe was his name. Born in England." Knight cocked his head. "Some place that starts with an 'F'. Can't recall exactly."

"It wasn't Fetter Lane, was it?" she asked.

A ghost of a smile passed over Knight's face. "No, I'd remember that."

He knows about Fetter Lane? What the heck?

The spot between Jane's shoulder blades prickled and she looked around, suddenly feeling exposed. The man in the raincoat had paused.

"Excuse me, Valentin. Do you know that man?"

Knight looked around, his eyes sliding over the one she'd spotted.

"He's standing on the curb over there." She indicated the direction with a jerk of her head.

"Sharp eyes. He's part of my security."

"You have a security team?" she asked.

"People who deal in oil and gas need them, you know," Knight explained.

"I see." Jane had never felt the need for one, but she'd never been a CEO.

"At any rate," Knight picked up his narrative, "LaTrobe's mother was born in Pennsylvania.""Bethlehem?" Jane tried to focus back on the conversation.

"I'm not sure, but her father sent her to England to go to school and she married there. Her stories of the colonies ignited curiosity in the mind of her son, so he moved here. Some people call him the father of American architecture." He stopped in front of the Capitol steps and gazed up at the building as if to illustrate his point.

This white dome out did them all, the two wings of the building stretching out, a magnificent sight on the crown of the hill.

"We'll have to go around to the east to get in. A nuisance sometimes, all these security measures. Our tour is scheduled for half past two."

They walked up the sidewalk, then down the side of the Capitol Building, past the bare dogwoods but still green lawn. "So, what does your urban legend say about the Capitol?"

"Excuse me?" Knight frowned for a second. "Oh, the Tree of Life. The Capitol Building represents the foot of the tree, the place where Divine Law is made manifest."

Jane shook her head. "It would seem the opposite has happened."

Knight stopped and regarded her quite seriously for a few seconds. "You have hit the nail on the head."

Once they reached the tour entrance, Knight's arrival created a bit of a stir. The attendant went for her supervisor, who called in his supervisor, who welcomed them like visiting royalty, even in these halls of democracy.

"Valentin," the portly lead supervisor held his arms wide and they greeted each other with a hug.

"May I present Jane Frey," Knight turned to her. "My special guest today. Meet John Taylor, an old friend and caretaker of this national treasure."

"He is too kind," John demurred, but his pleased expression said otherwise. The man stretched his hand out and Jane shook it. A quiet strength flowed from him.

John turned back to Knight. "I've arranged a private tour with my most experienced guide."

"Excellent." Knight clapped John on the shoulder.

A man in his late-thirties hovered a few steps behind their group, dressed in the requisite blue suit, white shirt and now blue tie to match the party holding power in the Senate. "Here he is now." John motioned the young man forward. "He'll take good care of you. Come by my office later?"

"I'm afraid I have another engagement, but let's have lunch soon," Knight said.

John's shoulders drooped, but he nodded. "Then I'll leave you in Ben's capable hands."

Knight's face lit up as he turned to the guide. "Is your name Benjamin?"

"Yes, sir."

"How serendipitous. I was just telling Jane about Benjamin LaTrobe. She's from a colonial Moravian family."

"Is that so?" Ben smiled politely. "Shall we begin over here?"

"Lead on, my good man," Knight said.

Ben walked them over to a statue dominating the lobby. "Here we have a replica of the Liberty Statue that adorns the top of the Capitol Dome. Not the same as the one in New York Harbor, of course." He allowed them to study the statue, adding a comment here and there. Jane stepped back. She was beginning to get her fill of white marble.

Ben turned toward an auditorium, gesturing for them to follow. "Do you wish to attend the video presentation?"

"I think we can rely on Jane's excellent grasp of American history." Knight raised an eyebrow in question and Jane nodded.

They climbed the stairs. "LaTrobe was first hired to supervise the construction of the Capitol," Ben said, playing to his guests' interest, "but he had to follow William Thornton's plans. He chafed at this restriction. But when the Capitol was destroyed in the War of 1812, LaTrobe became head architect."

"I see," Jane said, realizing how many times she'd been repeating this phrase in the last two days.

"LaTrobe also designed the White House porticos, as well as several churches, houses, bridges and the Washington Canal."

They arrived in the Capitol Dome and Jane stopped in the middle, staring up at the impressive expanse above her. Ben explicated the *Apotheosis of Washington,* in which the father of their country was raised into heaven by Liberty and Victory. "He is attended by thirteen maidens, who represent . . ." Ben paused and looked to Knight, who frowned, "the states, of course." Then he talked about the various paintings running along the border.

"Uh, huh," Jane repeated at appropriate intervals, but her attention was on what Ben had been about to say before Knight steered him away from it. What was going on here? She asked a question to see what the response would be. "So was Dan Brown right? There's a statue depicting Washington as a god to match the painting?"

Ben's eyes shot to Knight, "Yes, that's right." He hesitated and Knight jumped in.

"Remember this was the early days of the democracy. People wanted to make Washington the president for life. They portrayed him as a god." He looked up at the painting. "You know what Washington said, of course." It was a challenge.

"That we didn't get rid of one King George so we could appoint another one."

"Excellent." Knight nodded his approval.

Jane followed Ben and Knight through the hallways and old rooms, passing LaTrobe's smaller dome, the Supreme Court's original headquarters, and the first Senate meeting rooms, where Ben illustrated the acoustics and how difficult it had been to keep secrets even in the early days. Various Greek figures oversaw the proceedings in the form of white statues looking down from high spots. Ben explained them all, but Jane's attention was waning.

The tour ended in what Ben called the Crypt. "The dome is supported by these forty Doric columns." He rattled off how much the dome weighed and the mathematics of the space. Jane let it wash over her like water. All the early mornings seemed to be catching up to her.

Then he moved to the middle of the circle of columns. "This piece marks the exact center of the city, dividing it into four quadrants. Each has a different zip code, depending on which side of the star your office falls on." He smiled at this bit of trivia. "Before it was placed, an eternal flame burned here. But the fire left soot on the white marble, so it was filled in."

Jane looked down at the marker. Something about the design tickled her memory. The music that she kept hearing had begun again at the back of her mind. She yawned, putting up a hand to hide it.

"This has always reminded me of your star," Knight said in a subdued tone.

Jane blinked. "Star?"

"The Moravian star you hang at Christmas."

"Oh, yes." She smiled. "The Advent Star. I loved that as a child."

"LaTrobe studied at Niesky, the Moravian school." Knight added. "Did you know it?"

Jane shook her head, widening her eyes, trying to wake up.

"That is where your famous Moravian star was first created."

"Oh, right. In a boy's geometry class."

"Correct. And look here." Knight pointed to the design on the floor in the center of the room. "Another star, yes?"

Jane leaned down to look more closely. Four white rays shot out to the directions with four smaller rays between each of the main ones. "It does look like a star. Maybe that's what it reminded me of."

"Your star forms the very center of our nation's capital." Knight spoke quietly in her ear.

Music surged in Jane's mind, the same tune, but more of it this time. She listened intently, hoping to catch the main melody, but it faded. She looked up at Knight and blinked as if she were coming up from deep water. Glanced around. Ben leaned against one of the columns a few steps away from them, an almost reverent look on his face.

"I hope you've enjoyed our little tour," Knight said in a normal tone. "Thank you for indulging me in one of my hobbies."

Jane shook her head, remembering her manners. "The pleasure was all mine," she mumbled.

Knight followed Ben back to the main tourist desk, Jane walking along beside him. Her sleepiness fled as they came up to the ground floor.

Knight thanked their tour guide, then led Jane to a waiting limo. The man in the black rain coat she'd noticed on the Mall opened the back door for them and slipped into the front.

After a couple of blocks, Knight turned to her. "The driver will drop me off at the office, then take you to the airport. Your flight leaves in two hours."

With this, Jane surfaced fully into ordinary life. "But my luggage. I didn't check out this morning."

"I took the liberty of having Betsy pack your things and check you out. I hope you don't feel this is an invasion of your privacy."

"No, not at all," Jane said, but she did feel a bit squeamish about getting her luggage packed by assistants. Still, it had been Betsy. Reliable, honest Betsy. Too close to a maid's duties for comfort, though.

The limo pulled into the same parking garage she'd arrived at early this morning. The man in the black raincoat opened Knight's door.

Jane spoke quickly before he got out. "I can't thank you enough for everything you've done for me."

Knight beamed at her. "It was an honor and a pleasure to assist you."

Jane nodded. "Goodbye, then."

Knight got out of the car. "Perhaps I will see you again sometime."

CHAPTER FOURTEEN

Jane's plane landed in Greensboro just after nine that evening. She pulled her carry-on from the overhead bin and made her way to the parking lot, glancing around from time to time to see if anyone was following. Just standard caution for a woman alone at night. She started up the rental, thinking it was about time she bought something new. Maybe she'd put some solar panels on the English Tudor, get a plug-in car, stick it to the oil companies. Like they'd notice.

As she paid for parking, a silver sedan pulled up behind her. Nothing unusual in that, but it kept pace with her to the freeway and stayed a few car-lengths back for several miles. She slowed, hoping it would pass her and she could catch a glimpse of the driver, but the car matched her pace. It stuck with her the whole way to Winston-Salem. She got off before her usual exit, watching in her rear view mirror. No headlights.

Just as she relaxed, the sedan showed up again. She took side streets toward home, trying to shake them, but the silver sedan found her and followed her down the rolling hills of Broad Street. Jane drove past her street and another one, then turned right on Gloria Avenue heading east, away from her house. The sedan continued down Broad. Jane stopped, rolled down the window and leaned out, trying to see the driver, but all she could make out was a shadow. Male, probably.

She turned her car around and drove to the house. She pulled into her garage, turned off the engine and listened.

Nothing. She got out, peeking around the door. No headlights out front. She glanced around the side of the garage and peered through the thick bushes at the side street. A street light, but no headlights. No engine sounds.

Jane made her way through her backyard, then walked in shadows to the Sisters' House. She knocked on the back door. A light illuminated the window in an upstairs bedroom. Snuffling sounds came from the kitchen, then a bark and the sound of scrabbling toenails on linoleum. The porch light switched on and Dorothea's face appeared between the parted curtains.

"Oh, Jane. You gave me a turn." Dorothea opened the door and moved out of the way of the bulldog who barreled through.

"Winston." Jane bent down to receive a bath of dog kisses. Winston curled himself into a circle, his rear end wiggling more than his stump of a tail. "It's good to see you, too."

Dorothea smiled benevolently at the scene. "So you're back."

"Thanks for taking care of everything. Again." Jane emphasized this last. She hugged the round woman, whose return hug seemed a bit subdued. She must be sleepy. Dorothea always seemed to be up at the crack of dawn. "I'm sorry to come late, but I wanted him with me tonight."

"It's no trouble at all," Dorothea said.

Jane waited, but the normally loquacious woman didn't add anything else. "I'll see you tomorrow, then?" Jane asked.

Dorothea only nodded.

Jane walked back, feeling a little better with the solid bulldog by her side. Inside, the cats deigned to notice her presence when she finally found them curled up in the living room, but they dropped their aloof act once she filled their bowl. She retrieved her carry-on and purse from the car, still watching the shadows, Winston in tow. Back inside, she locked the door behind her and walked back down the hall, dropping her luggage at the bottom of the steps. Better check the messages. She made her way to the library. Exhaustion washed over her and she leaned against the wall. To think she used to be able to keep this kind of schedule—up before dawn, working until midnight, jetting through time zones. The blinking red light of the answering machine caught her eye. She walked over to the desk and pushed the play button.

"Jane, this is Lois. You're not going to believe what I've found. Call me. On the land line."

"Tomorrow," she said to the machine. She carried her luggage up the stairs and got ready for bed. Once she pulled back the covers, the cats arrived to claim the choice spots and Winston lay down on the rug. She listened in the dark, but heard nothing. No car lights flashed across the ceiling of the room. At last, Winston's snores lulled her to sleep.

☆ ☆ ☆

Next morning, Jane pushed back the curtains to the front bedroom to look for the silver sedan that had followed her from the airport. The street in front of the house was empty. She went up into the attic and pressed her face against each of the windows, looking all around the neighborhood, but found no trace of the car. After a shower and a cup of French roast, she shrugged off her nervousness and turned on her computer. Lois had sent her an email giving her the number for the company transporting the Blake art. About twenty minutes before they were scheduled to arrive, Jane took up watch at her dining room window. She walked back to the library and looked out the back to be sure Dorothea wasn't wandering up the garden path for a visit. She returned to the front window and there it was—the silver sedan, parked on the next block over, but clearly visible. And empty.

"Shit."

She moved to the living room window and scanned the front yard. Empty as well. "Winston, come boy."

Winston galumphed down the steps and arrived in front of her, ears perked. "Come," she repeated, slapping her palm against her thigh. She headed across the living room for the screened-in porch, bulldog right beside her. The bare branches allowed her to see all the way down to the rose garden, but the evergreens blocked the side yard.

Winston pushed at the screen door and she let him out first. He sat in the drive waiting, showing no signs of alarm, just impatience for her to follow. Together they checked the yard, making a circuit through the apple trees on the side, past the well-mulched vegetable garden, then checked the compost pile, the bare grass where the old chicken coop had stood, and finally the bushes behind the garage. Winston found no strangers lurking about nor did he catch any new scents. His ears drooped when he realized they weren't going for their run.

The grinding of brakes in front of the house sent Jane running up the driveway just in time to direct the delivery truck. She waved for them to pull around to the side. Better not advertise to the whole neighborhood. Under Winston's close supervision, the two men who'd packed the paintings and prints for New York made short work of carrying in the small crate. She asked them to take it up the stairs and leave it on the landing. They handed her the portfolio of sketches. She signed for everything, and they drove the truck around the drive and out the other side. Jane locked the side door behind them, then checked all the others. The sedan still sat empty just down the street.

Hammer in hand, Jane pried open the crate, lifting each piece out carefully, going over each one with the feather duster, and returning it to its place in the Blake room. She knocked the crate into several pieces and carried it to the basement, hammer stuck in her pocket in case she needed it. Then she headed for the library. She needed to call Lois.

Just as she picked up the phone, the doorbell rang. Winston stood in front of the door, ears perked, rear wagging. Friend rather than foe, then. She opened the door.

Anna and John Szeges stood on the step.

"Hi," Jane said, trying to cover her surprise. "How nice to see you."

"We need to talk," Anna said, her voice stern.

"Uh, sure." Jane's stomach knotted. She felt like she'd just been called to the principal's office. She led them into the living room and stood back, letting them decide where to sit. They remained standing. "Can I get you anything?"

"Sit down, Jane."

Surprised by her commanding tone, Jane sat in the arm chair next to the bookcase, then realized there were no other seats around her. She jumped up and moved to the fireplace, perching on the edge of the love seat. Anna sat across from her, but John stood behind his wife, looming like a crow in his black suit.

"When we knew Sister Emma was passing, we tried and tried to find the right person to oversee this house," Anna began. "I thought it should be Dorothea, the purest and sweetest soul in our group."

Jane tried to interject, but Anna pressed on. Apparently this was a prepared speech. "The Lord had other plans. After Emma insisted we add your name, we drew the lot three times, against my husband's advice." He stirred behind her. "The lot is rarely used in modern times and it's against tradition to draw more than once, but I insisted. You had left the church, left all spiritual ways, and I couldn't imagine how you would be a suitable successor. And now you have proven me right."

They know about the New York trip, Jane thought.

"What are you talking about?" she asked.

Anna ignored her and pressed on. "And yet the lot did fall to you. There must be something I do not see."

"Where is it?" John asked.

"Where is what?" Jane looked up at him, frowning.

"The painting."

"Uh, how did you—"

"You think we're that stupid? That we wouldn't notice that you stole one of our most loved and valuable pieces?" he fumed.

"But I returned the paintings this morning," Jane said, straining forward. "I just put them all back."

"All?" Anna's gaze sharpened.

"That's impossible," John said. "Now all the entrances have new locks, thanks to you. You could never have gotten in without this." He held up a shiny new key.

"But . . ." Jane pointed toward the stairs, "I just . . . . Wait! That painting? Oh, fuck."

"Keep your filthy language out of this house," Anna scolded.

John hesitated, studying her, then asked, "What painting are you talking about?"

"The ones upstairs in the Blake room. I took photos and sent them to an art dealer. He said they might be originals and asked to see them." The words tumbled out. "I shipped them to New York—"

"You what?" Anna shouted.

Suzie B burst out from beneath the couch and ran up the stairs.

"But they're back now." Jane held out her hands to forestall them. "They were delivered this morning. I know I should have asked, but . . ."

The two stared at her, incredulous.

Jane flushed a furious red, anger replacing embarrassment. "You weren't honest with me, either. I thought I was inheriting this house. You never explained I was just a caretaker. You lied about what the OGMS was. There are strange things going on around here."

"What strange things?" Anna asked, "What is she talking about, John?"

"I don't know," he said.

Anna and John stared at each other, their faces confused. Then both turned their eyes on Jane. There was a moment of silence.

John took a long breath, struggling to master himself. "Show me these paintings you're talking about," he said in a calmer voice.

His quiet tone took some of the wind out of Jane's sails. She blinked, then stood. "Follow me."

She led the two up the stairs, opened the door to the small bedroom and stood back. "After you . . . please," she managed.

The three crowded into the room. Jane pointed to the painting of a series of angels circling a man who held his hands in his head, distraught and disheveled. "The art dealer said this one is new. At least none of the Blake experts had seen it before." She kneeled down and thumbed through the sketches. "And these." She showed them the Garden of Eden sketch, then the one so like the painting in the tantric room.

"That must be it." John leaned down to examine this last one. "Someone must have seen this study and realized we had the finished work."

"You mean that big one down in the . . ." Jane struggled to find the right word, but failed. She pointed down.

"Yes, Jane, that one. It's been stolen," he said.

Jane's eyes rounded. "You're kidding."

"Do we look like we're kidding?" Anna snapped.

"So, you're telling us you didn't take it?" John asked.

Jane gaped like a fish. "Take it? I would never— How could I even get it down? Much less carry it out? It's huge. "

John studied her a moment longer, then said, "We saw you enter that room on the security cameras, but they were disabled the night of the theft."

Jane shook her head in disbelief. Could this really be happening? Then she looked back at the two accusing faces. "Do I look like I know how to disable a security camera?"

"Clearly we don't know what you're capable of," Anna said primly.

"When did this happen?" Jane asked.

"We're not sure exactly. None of us had been downstairs for a few days," John answered.

"Oh, my God." Jane's hand flew up. "I'll bet it was that Phillip and his Southern Belle cousin."

"Who?" John asked.

Jane told them about Phillip LeBelle's visit and his interest in the art work. "In fact, he's the one who got me investigating this. I never would have imagined any of these were originals if he hadn't suggested it."

John's eye lit up. "Would you recognize them?"

"I think so."

"Could you describe them clearly enough to produce a sketch?" he continued.

"Maybe."

"Good." He turned to Anna. "I'll call Dreher." He pulled his cell phone out of his pocket and walked out of the room.

Anna and Jane stood regarding each other like two bristling cats. Finally, Jane broke the silence. "I'm sorry about that painting. I really am, but I didn't take it. I wasn't even here."

"We still don't know exactly when it was stolen," Anna pointed out. "But we'll get to the bottom of it. In the meantime, we don't think it's safe for you here. Not after the theft. And now this news."

"What do you mean?"

"Talk to Dreher." Anna showed herself out, leaving Jane wondering what she'd meant.

The first thing Jane did after they left was call Lois. The phone rang through to her voice mail, unusual for a work day. Where was her assistant? "Lois, you have to call me. Something's happened."

She looked out the dining room window. The silver sedan was gone. She paced the length of the living room, Winston watching with a concerned look on his mug. Jane found herself sitting in front of the piano. She opened it and started playing random chords, searching for something calming, but her fingers never found the right sounds. She closed the lid and went into the library to call Lois again. This time there was no answer at all.

The doorbell rang again and she found the mysterious Mr. Dreher standing on the front porch.

"Ms. Frey." He inclined his head slightly.

"Please come in."

He was accompanied by a woman carrying a sketch pad, who he introduced as Salali Waterdown. "She's a member of the Order of the Grain of the Mustard Seed."

"You mean the Omega Grant Management Systems?" Jane snipped.

Winston growled, but Dreher studiously ignored the bulldog. "We were not straightforward with you from the very beginning because we do not advertise our existence."

"It seems like you should tell a person who is asked to live in one of your houses." Jane turned on her heel, not giving him time to respond, and ushered them into the living room. "Can I get you anything?" she asked, her ingrained southern hospitality overtaking her anger.

"Coffee would be most appreciated," Salali said. Her melodious voice matched her soft skin. Her hair, two streams of silky black, framed her angular face.

Jane went into the kitchen, Winston close on her heels, and filled the basket with fresh grounds, poured in water and waited, leaning against the counter, head in hands. What had Anna meant when she'd said Jane wasn't safe here anymore? Why wasn't Lois calling back? Winston leaned against her leg and whined. She stroked his head, but his soulful eyes still emanated concern. The coffee machine's light indicated the cycle was finished. Jane poured the whole pot into a carafe, grabbed mugs, cream and sugar, and carried it all back into the living room, almost tripping over the solicitous bulldog.

She found her cousin Frank in deep conversation with Dreher. Jane came up short. "What are you doing here? Don't you have to work?"

"I heard about the theft. You said you were in New York?"

"Yes, I took some of the sketches up to an art gallery."

"Jane," Frank shook his head, "you should have asked."

Frank's admonishment penetrated her defenses. She could hear her grandmother's voice telling her why her actions were wrong. Childish shame flooded her, washing the anger away. She looked down at the floor, fighting the feeling. Jane knew she should have asked to borrow the art pieces and had used their deception to excuse her own duplicity.

"I'll get another cup," she mumbled, her face beet red, and escaped once more into the kitchen. Tears blurred her vision and she tried to wipe them away, still reaching for her self-righteous anger. But it didn't come. Instead, the soft weight of a bulldog leaning against her leg let the tears escape. After a minute, she washed off her face, squared her shoulders, and went back to face the music.

Frank broke off his conversation with Dreher, taking in her red eyes, and opened his arms to hug her. Willing herself not to cry more, Jane returned the hug. "Thanks," she whispered.

"Any time." He pitched his voice for her alone.

Winston let out a long sigh.

Jane pulled back and cleared her throat. "So, who wants coffee?"

"I'll take some." Salali's smile was kind.

Frank shook his head. Jane poured cups for Salali and herself, then took hers to the couch, sitting across from Salali, just as she had sat across from Anna earlier. Dreher sat across from Jane.

Salali started. "Let's begin with you describing this man. Then we'll sketch the woman."

"I'll try, but it's been several days."

"If you can't remember enough detail, we can put you into a light hypnotic trance," Dreher suggested.

Jane's eyebrows shot up.

"Frank will be here," Dreher hurried to add.

"We might not be able to get a good picture without that," Salali intervened. "Now, let's start with the man. Would you say his face was round, oval, one of these shapes?" She held up a sheet of paper with a series of circles and ovals in dark black lines.

"Uh, that one," Jane pointed to one of the shapes, "but with a square jaw." Then she answered a few simple questions and a picture began to form. This stimulated her memory further and soon Philip looked at her from the sketchbook. Jane wondered if Salali did this kind of thing professionally.

"I do," she answered the unvoiced thought.

"Oh." Jane's mouth mirrored the sound.

"I sometimes work for the police as a psychic investigator."

"Really? I didn't know people actually did that."

"Oh, they don't advertise it, let me tell you."

"Seems like a lot of things aren't advertised," Jane said, this time without rancor.

Salali tore out the sketch and handed it to Dreher, then started fresh, asking questions about the woman who'd accompanied Philip. Jane had more trouble remembering her.

"Would you give me your permission to put you in a more relaxed state? It might help you remember," Salali said.

"Uh," Jane glanced nervously at Dreher, "You mean hypnotize me?"

"Only if you're comfortable, of course."

"I suppose that would be all right. If you do it."

Frank came and sat next to her on the couch while Salali led Jane through a relaxation process. Jane resisted at first, but the heavy weight of a bulldog lying down on her feet finally allowed her to relax. The room slipped away.

". . . steal that painting?" A rough voice asked.

Jane's body jerked. Her eyes flew open.

Dreher leaned toward her eagerly.

Jane whipped her head around, scowling at Frank, then fixed Dreher with a glare. "What in hell did you just ask me?"

Dreher sat back with a huff.

"How dare you try to invade my mind?"

"What are you trying to hide?" he countered.

"Nothing, you're the ones who were hiding things. Maybe still are."

A ripping sound captured her attention. Salali held up a sketch that caught Margaret exactly.

"Wow," Jane exclaimed despite her anger.

"I'm sorry," Salali mouthed, then pitched her voice for all to hear. "Jane is an excellent hypnotic subject. We should be grateful that she's given us such good information."

"Thank you, Salali," Dreher said, "Would you and Frank take these sketches to my office? I'll be right over."

Salali's eyes cut back and forth between Dreher and Jane, but she rose and collected her things.

"We'll talk later," Frank squeezed Jane's hand.

Jane followed them to the door. On the front porch, she whispered to Frank, "Why did you let him do that?"

"He just jumped in." Frank shook his head in frustration. "I thought it would be more disturbing to you if I tried to stop him."

Jane frowned. "You don't think I did it, do you?"

"No, I don't." Frank said. He hesitated before adding, "Remember you're family. You're always welcome at our house." With that, he followed Salali down the front walk.

Jane took a deep breath and walked back to face Dreher. "You seem to have a lot to learn about respecting other people's boundaries."

He laughed. "That's ironic coming from you."

Jane flushed. "Ya'll started the lying. I was wrong to borrow the paintings. I admit it, but I didn't steal anything."

Dreher shook his head, then squared his shoulders. "Your innocence or guilt," he emphasized this last, "is yet to be determined. But either way, I can no longer guarantee your safety in this house. We'll give you forty-eight hours to find other arrangements. You are hereby evicted."

"What?" Jane yelled. "You can't—"

He turned on his heel and walked toward the front door, Jane following, Winston right behind her.

"You can't do this," she shouted.

"I think you'll find that we can," he barked at her. "Read your contract." Dreher slammed the door behind him.

Winston charged the door, barking. Jane yelled in frustration. She grabbed her star pendant. Damn it, she belonged here.

The phone rang. She ran into the library. Maybe Lois was finally calling her back. Lois would find a way to fix this.

"Jane Frey?" a male voice asked.

"This is Jane. Who am I speaking with?"

"This is Gregory Titlebaum, the lead partner at Titlebaum, Smyth and Williams."

"Oh, good. I was just about to call Lois."

A heavy sigh pulled Jane up short. "I'm sorry to have to inform you that Lois Williams was involved in a car accident late last night."

"Oh, my God. Is she all right?"

"I'm afraid I have bad news." His throat seemed to be closing around the words. "Lois died of her injuries just a few hours ago."

Jane's mouth worked, but no words came out.

"We found a file on her desk with a note. Apparently she'd tried to call you."

"Uh, yes, last night, I think. But Lois can't be dead." An image of Lois laughing, her rings sparkling as she made some gesture, flashed across Jane's inner eye. "Are you sure?"

"It's a shock." His voice was thick. "Would you like us to appoint someone else to represent you?"

"Someone else? Lois and I . . ." Jane squeezed her eyes tight. A sob escaped. Then she said in a rush. "Please send all my files. She has my current address." Then Jane realized she wouldn't be staying in this house. "Can you overnight it?"

"The thing is," he hesitated, "the NSA has seized her computer and cell phone. They were in the car. They're coming here to take all the files tomorrow."

"The NSA?"

"That's correct."

Jane couldn't imagine why they'd be involved. "Lois left me a message about the case we've been working on."

"We'll see if we can find out."

"When is the—" Jane couldn't say the word. She still couldn't believe it. "When are the services?"

"We'll let you know."

"Thank you." Jane hung up and slumped into the chair. She stared at the phone. Winston laid his head in her lap and she stroked him, tears rolling down her face. The two cats sat in the doorway, watching. The bulldog tried to push himself into her lap. Jane slipped out of the chair and buried her head in the dog's neck. He whimpered and tried to turn around to lick her face.

Jane wept for her lost friend, for her wicked sense of humor, for her camaraderie over the years, for that shared knowledge of what it had been like as women to break the glass ceiling, for being the one person who'd known her so long. She wept for her lost childhood dream of living in this house, of playing music, even teaching, continuing Miss Essig's tradition.

Then it hit her. Lois's death might not have been an accident. Maybe something about this whole business had alerted the wrong people. What had Lois said in her last message?

You're not going to believe what I've found.

Could the car wreck have something to do with the theft of the Blake painting? With the money transfers? Knight had said anyone dealing in oil and gas needed a security team. Maybe Lois had been murdered.

Jane reached for the phone and dialed the only person alive that she still trusted.

CHAPTER FIFTEEN

David pulled up in front of the old English Tudor with a squeal of tires. He jumped out of his old Chevy, slamming the door behind him with an ominous squeak. One day it would fall apart completely, but he didn't have time to worry about that now. He ran up the sidewalk. He'd thought about Ed Leigh's warning all the way over. About halfway to the door, a man stepped out of the trees on the side of the house. David stopped short and reached for his phone before recognizing him from the lodge. He couldn't remember his name. The man waved David on and stepped back into cover.

David ran to the porch and rang the doorbell. Jane had sounded frantic on the phone. He'd gotten her message late, after his last student of the day. He returned her call as soon as he could, but she didn't want to go into detail on the phone. Not when someone might be listening, she'd said. That had scared him. Now it seemed Ed had posted a guard. He wondered if Jane knew she was being watched over.

Jane opened the door, then stepped out and looked up and down the street. "You didn't see any other cars, did you? A silver sedan?"

He took in her puffy eyes, her tangled hair. "Jane, you're scaring me. What's going on?"

She pulled him inside and stood in the foyer, hugging herself. She shivered. Winston ran up to him, then circled around and sat next to Jane, his eyes on David's face. David gently took Jane by the arm and led her to the loveseat in the living room, then wrapped a chenille throw around her. "I'm here now. Tell me what's happened."

"They're kicking me out. And Lois. She's dead."

Tears flowed down her face and she swiped at them with her sleeve.

"Who's Lois?"

"My attorney."

"Oh." David frowned. "I'm sorry. It's just . . . I've never seen anyone get so upset over their lawyer dying."

Jane laughed in spite of her tears. "She was my best friend. She looked out for me." She squeezed her eyes shut. "Damn it. I'd stopped crying and now—" a shudder ran through her.

David put his arms around her. Jane buried her head in the safety of his shoulder and wept. He stroked her hair and made soothing noises, waiting for the storm of tears to pass. Winston laid down next to them, his head on Jane's foot, and the cats jumped on the other loveseat. After a few minutes, her sobs slowed. She lifted her head, took a napkin from a coffee tray that sat on the table and wiped her eyes.

"Tell me," he said.

Jane sat staring at the carpet, shaking her head from time to time. "I don't know where to start."

"The beginning."

"But I don't know where the beginning is, not really."

"What happened to your lawyer?"

Jane abstractly pointed toward the library. "Her boss called and said there was a bad car wreck. She died this morning." Jane shook her head. "Before that, Dreher told me I have to get out."

"Out of where?" He looked around at the living room and grand piano in the corner. "Here?"

Jane nodded.

"But, I thought . . . . Wait, who's Dreher?"

"Head of security for the OGMS."

"What's that?"

Jane looked at him. "The Order of the Grain of the Mustard Seed."

"The what?"

"You don't know about it?"

David shook his head.

Jane squared her shoulders and explained the origins of the OGMS, how the organization had survived in the Carolinas, and perhaps elsewhere, that her family had given the land in trust to the organization, which had built the houses and the church.

"So when Miss Essig died, your family said you could have the house?"

"No, they pulled my name by lot."

"Lot? Somebody's still using the lot?Jane nodded. "You know about it?"

"I've heard of it, but the practice was discouraged."

Jane sat silent for a minute, staring out the window. David touched her hand and she turned to him again. "So why are they making you leave? Can they even do that?"

"Yes, they can. I checked the contract."

"But why?"

"Because they think I stole the painting."

"Painting?" He was having trouble keeping up.

"The Blake original down in the—" Jane stopped short and stared at him. "David, you're not going to believe what I found in the basement."

David sat back and peered at Jane, worried at this sudden turn in her story. Had the shock affected her mind?

"The basement?" he asked quietly. "Jane, you're not making sense."

"No, I swear."

"What? You swear what?"

"Come with me." Jane grabbed David's hand and pulled him off the sofa. She led him down the steps to the cellar and through the laundry room. He thought they'd reached the back wall, but she turned sideways and squeezed through a hidden opening into a back room.

He followed close behind, then rammed his shin into something in the dark and muffled a curse. "Jane, what are we doing down here?"

"It's right here." Jane let go of his hand, leaned down and picked something up. A beam of light appeared, illuminating the wall. She walked to the pine paneling and pushed a couple of times until something clicked. The panel opened.

"Oh, my God." David stepped back in surprise.

"Just wait until you see." Jane reached for the door handle and tried to turn it. "Oh, shit. I forgot. John said they put in new locks." She shined the flashlight beam all around. "This is a whole new door."

David stepped up to the metal security door and jiggled the handle with the same result. "Jane, what are you doing with a secret panel in your house that has a locked metal door behind it?"

"I'm trying to tell you. There's a secret underground room down here. And more. There's a hallway and more rooms that I didn't even see."

"What's in the room?"

"That's the part you wouldn't believe. It's a tantric room."

"A what?"

"You know, a place for sacred sex."

David stood stock still. Then he looked at her carefully. Her hair was still mussed, but her eyes were steady. At least as far as he could make out in the dim light.

"I know that sounds nuts, but I'm not making it up," she said. "There was a big painting in there. A William Blake painting."

David couldn't remember who Blake was, but now wasn't the time for minor details.

"Somebody broke in and stole it," Jane said. "After I discovered it. So they think I took it. Or that I'm in cahoots with the thief. Especially after I took the other originals to New York to get them appraised."

David shook his head. "How long have you been here? A month? How'd you manage to get yourself into so much trouble in such a short time?"

Jane stared at him for a second, surprised, then started to laugh. "I guess I have a talent for it."

"Come upstairs." He walked back toward the passage in the concrete wall and held his hand out for her. "You need to tell me the whole story from the start."

And she did. David made tea—chamomile—and they settled in the living room. She told him everything, from the first call from Miss Essig, Davis firing her, to her getting the house, the meeting with the lawyers, and the night she'd been awakened by the chanting and found the tantric room.

David shook his head. "Moravians are doing this?"

"I've been reading about it," Jane explained. "They called it the 'sifting times'. Zinzendorf preached the religion of the heart, that Christ's crucifixion had purified us if we believed. He saw the human body and all its parts as free of shame."

"Zinzendorf preached this?"

"Yes, and that intimacy between married couples was a form of liturgy or something."

"What?" David asked.

"Zinzendorf was way ahead of his time," Jane said. "He taught that the Holy Spirit was our mother, so the Trinity was Father, Mother and Son. That husband and wife could participate in the sacred marriage, their joining representing coming into unity with Christ. He said that sex didn't need to be for procreation only." Jane blushed, a small smile on her lips.

David felt a fierce desire to kiss those lips, but he pulled back from her. Now was not the time.

"They venerated the wounds of Christ as the source of our salvation. They talked about 'hiding in the side wounds'."

David made a face. "That's disgusting."

Jane jumped up and went to the piano. She opened the lid and played a few chords, then started a hymn. "Rock of Ages, cleft for me. Let me hide myself in thee."

"Oh, my God. I never realized what that was about."

"Practically the Baptist national anthem," she said. "But Zinzendorf's son, Christian Renatus, I think his name was, had a group in Marienborn who took it too far. At least they thought so at the time. Christian declared that all humans were female, spiritually that is, and Christ was the husband. Some say he claimed the gender of lovers didn't matter. Some even think they had orgies."

"You're kidding?" David said. "Orgies in the eighteenth century?"

"Well, Christian was an aristocrat. And a teenager. You know how rich people behave. Papa Zinzendorf heard about it, though. He was in London and went back to Germany to put a stop to it. Then word got out and leaders of other religious groups condemned the Moravians as sinners and adulterers."

"Marienborn, did you say?"

"That's right. Zinzendorf closed the settlement and dispersed the congregation."

"So, they must have come here," David said, pointing to the east.

"Huh?"

"The New Marienborn Moravian Church," he said.

"You're right." Jane played a dramatic chord on the piano, then stood up. "Just think, here we kids were taking lessons from the impeccable Miss Essig, and all the while we were sitting on top of a *Kabinet*. That's what they called the rooms where husband and wife would meet." She sat next to him on the couch.

David shook his head. "I wonder what my grandparents would say if they knew."

Jane leaned back with a sigh. "I wish that was the only mystery. That room seems tame now after Lois has been killed."

"You really think she was murdered?"

Jane shook her head. "I can't be sure. But it's possible. I may have gotten my best friend killed." She looked up at David, lost, sad, scared.

He yearned to take her in his arms, to comfort her, protect her. He contented himself with taking her hand. "Oh, come on now. You didn't kill her. And it could have been an accident."

Jane shook her head. "I still can't believe it. Dreher said he can't keep me safe here. Not after the robbery."

"So he's just throwing you to the wolves?" He couldn't believe they'd treat her like this. And that she might disappear again.

"It must have been a group decision. Frank knew before Dreher even told me. He said I could stay with him." A spark of anger flared in her eyes, but died quickly. "I just got here.

What will I do with the animals?" Fresh tears flowed down her cheeks.

"They belonged to Miss Essig. I'm sure someone here will care for them."

"I don't want them to. Not after the way they've treated me."

David thought for a minute. "My son can keep them. He has a lot of acreage. Bought an old farm, but he doesn't work the land. There's plenty of room and my grandkid loves animals."

"You're a granddaddy?" Jane's smile was wistful.

"I am," he said. For the first time since he'd gotten there, she started to look a bit hopeful.

"Thank you." She squeezed his hand.

David struggled with himself. He had to tell her about his meeting with Ed Leigh, but keeping lodge secrets was deeply engrained. "So, how do you think original art work got here?"

"You know William Blake?"

David shook his head. "I can't remember."

"An English painter, print maker and poet. Turns out his mother was a Moravian. Back when the family lived in Fetter Lane. Miss Essig's family might have come from there."

"Now, I have heard about Fetter Lane in Sunday school. Various Protestants had congregations there. I looked it up once. Some of the craftsmen in that area did work for the Templars."

"As in Knights Templar?" she asked.

"If I remember right."

"I guess our ancestors were more colorful than I ever imagined." She leaned down and stroked the bulldog, who leaned heavily against David's knee.

David watched her for a while. She seemed calmer. "So, you said there were other mysteries." He picked up a clean mug and poured himself some tea.

Jane wrinkled her forehead, thinking. "Oh, yeah. I got the Masonic tour of Washington, D.C."

David almost spit out the cold chamomile. "You what?"

"The head of a big company insisted I help him transfer some funds. Lois said he didn't like how I'd been treated, that he insisted I do the job, but the whole situation was odd. A junior associate could have taken care of it. And he paid me an enormous sum of money."

"Um, that's nice." David thought of his measly pension and adjunct's salary at the two colleges.

Jane nodded. "When I first got here, I was grateful for a place to live. Now, I could buy this house five times over."

David sank into the corner of the couch. She was definitely out of his league. But she'd called him. Because he was a friend, he told himself. He'd help his friend. It was the right thing to do.

He steered the conversation in what he hoped was a more comfortable direction. "So this was the same guy who gave you the Masonic tour?"

"Yeah, he took me on a walk on the National Mall. He kept talking about what he called an urban legend."

"What was the legend?"

"That some people think the National Mall is modeled after the Tree of Life. Not like in Genesis, but the Jewish—is it Kabbalah?"

David paused. This was one of the deeper secrets of the Masons. "Who was this man?"

"His name is Valentin Knight."

All David could do at first was stare. Finally he asked, "Did you say Valentin Knight?"

"Do you know him?"

"Know of him. He's only one of the most powerful mystics in the world."

"Mystics? He's a business—wait, how do you know this?"

"I joined the Masons after college." At her look, he hurried to defend himself. "It was a good way to meet people, especially in business. I was looking to feed my family, get a better job. Plus, I've always been interested in spiritual teachings."

"You?" A small frown crossed her face.

His chances were getting worse and worse. They were just friends, he reminded himself firmly.

"Here I always thought they were just a social club," she said.

"They are that, but the degrees teach you meditation, philosophy, sacred mathematics, that sort of thing. Like I said, for me it was more for business contacts."

"So, you're a Mason?"

"Yeah, but I haven't taken all the degrees. My friend James knows more than me."

"I thought Moravians didn't go in for that sort of thing."

"Actually, that's not true. Over the years, lots of Moravians have been Masons."

"That's what Knight said."

The time had come. David cleared his throat. "Funny thing, the leader of my own lodge said the same thing to me just the other night." He studied his hands.

"What did he say?" Jane asked, her voice sharp.

He looked up to find her scrutinizing him, her eyes hooded. "I'm not supposed to divulge lodge secrets, Jane, but given the circumstances, I have to tell you."

"Tell me what?" She scooted down to the next cushion on the sofa.

David told her about his conversation with Ed, how he thought her family might have some artifact that had been passed through the Masons. "He's worried some group is trying to get their hands on it."

"But—" Jane jumped up and started to pace. "Now you're telling me Blake was a Mason?"

"I don't think this is about Blake," he said, afraid her next steps would be to show him the door. How had he gotten so attached to her in such a short time? "But I think Blake was a Rosicrucian."

"What's the difference?" Jane asked.

David shook his head. "They're both metaphysical orders. There's some cross-over." He waved his hand. "That's not important right now. I asked Ed if he could find out more details about this artifact, but I don't think I've taken enough degrees for him to tell me."

"Enough degrees?" she frowned.

"That thing Knight told you about the National Mall? That's a big Masonic secret."

"It's true?"

"Yes."

"So you learned that in one of your . . ." she snapped her fingers, trying to remember the right word, "degrees?"

"No, I had to get James drunk to get it out of him."

"James?"

"Yeah, he was hinting around after he took some advanced class."

"Not so good at keeping secrets, is he?"

"He's a musician. Scottish. They're way into the Masons over there. We're good buds."

Jane sat down on the loveseat across from him. "So, somebody or worse, some group is after an artifact they think my family has?"

"That's what Ed said."

"What's it got to do with this house?"

"Ed said that with Miss Essig gone, they might try to take advantage of the confusion. They seem to think it's hidden here."

"There are more rooms down there. I wouldn't put it past that Dreher. But my family's just ordinary, garden variety Moravians."

David raised an eyebrow. "Maybe not so ordinary as you thought. Not if they gave land to the OGMS."

Jane looked at David thoughtfully. "What do you think it is? What artifacts are the Masons supposed to have?"

David snorted. "The question is what don't they have. The legends are amazing. Plus there's Fetter Lane and the Templar link. The Knights spent years digging at the Temple Mount in Jerusalem, and they were hip deep with the Rosicrucians, so the possibilities are endless."

Jane sat forward, a keen look in her eyes. "Tell me."

"Oh, geez. Well, besides your run of the mill gold, silver and precious gems?"

"That's a good start."

"You've also got the Head of John the Baptist, the Holy Grail, the Arc of the Covenant," he ticked them off on his fingers, "the Spear of Destiny—"

"No, wait." Jane held up her hand. "I thought Hitler stole that from some museum in Austria, and it was returned after the war."

"There are alternative versions of that story."

"But do they have any credence?"

David gave her a surprised look. "People who hunt for treasure aren't always the most logical."

Jane started laughing. "Okay, so the Arc of the Covenant could be down there in some room?"

David smiled, glad to see the Jane he knew start to reemerge. "Or it could be the Garter of the Winter King or John Dee's missing manuscript."

Jane shook her head. "I don't even know what you're talking about."

"Those are just the treasures I can think of off the top of my head."

"But people don't take this sh— stuff seriously, do they?" She smiled self-consciously. "My language has really cleaned up since moving into this house."

David looked around the room. "I know what you mean."

"But David, surely in this day and age nobody believes some ancient relic that will make them—" she waved her arms "—invincible is hidden in the basement, do they?"

"I'm afraid so," he said. "Some people take these legends dead serious."

Jane flinched away from his wording. "So how do we know what they're looking for?"

David shrugged. "I could talk to Ed again. Maybe James would have a clue."

"I guess I should just pack up and leave. It's this house they're interested in, not me."

David pursed his lips together.

"Right? Jane asked, her voice almost shrill. "Don't tell me they think I have the Arc of the Covenant stashed away somewhere? That they're after me?"

"Ed did seem concerned about you personally, not just the house."

"Damn it all to hell," Jane shouted.

Winston woke up barking, looking around for the intruder.

Jane put her hand over her mouth. "If Miss Essig could hear me now."

David started laughing, because he'd been thinking the same thing.

"What am I going to do?"

"We. What are we going to do?" David put his arms around her. She leaned her head against him.

"You don't have to—" she started to say.

"Shush. I don't have to, but I'm gonna."

He felt her smile against his shoulder. "I'm not going to let anything happen to you. I know Ed's got a guard on the house, so you'll be safe tonight." He started to pull away, but she tightened her grip.

"Please don't leave me alone tonight."

He stood stock still.

"So much has happened . . . with Lois and all. There are plenty of extra bedrooms."

He tried not to let his shoulders droop.

"It's not that I don't . . . I mean." She lifted her head and stepped back. "I just don't want to be alone."

David forced his voice to sound normal. "I understand. I'd be happy to stay."

"God, I hate feeling like this," she said, fists clinched.

"Crying over the death of an old friend doesn't make you weak. Besides, you've just lost your house and you just moved in."

Her hands unclenched.

He looked at his cell phone. It was early yet. "Have you eaten?"

Jane shook her head.

"We could order a pizza."

"Right, and the delivery man pulls an AK47 out of the box."

"It would be an XM8 more likely."

"What?" Jane's eyes had taken on that wild look again.

"Want me to cook you something? I make a mean omelet."

"You cook?"

"For other people."

Jane ushered David into the kitchen. "How can I help?"

"Sit." He pointed to a bar stool and opened the refrigerator. He pulled out a carton of eggs—from pasture-raised chickens, he noticed. Goat cheese, organic. He wished he could afford these kinds of ingredients. Scallions, peppers, garlic, onion. Found a jar of capers. Took down a big pan hanging above the stove.

"Wow. You're serious about this."

"I watch the cooking channel," he said.

Jane opened a bottle of wine and poured them both a glass. David took a swig, then slowed down and savored the next sip. "That's good."

"I know wines," she said.

"I'm a beer man, myself, but I'd drink this any day."

They ate in the dining room on the fancy china. After they finished their meal, Jane opened another bottle of wine, this one better than the first.

David talked about his kids, telling funny stories, and watched Jane relax. They ended the evening at the piano, playing various childhood favorites, reminiscing about Miss Essig and their musical careers. David tried not to press against her side or stretch over flirtatiously to reach a key.

"You know, I've been dreaming about a piece of music," Jane said.

"What piece is it?""Something new. I wanted to be a composer when I was little, but I bombed in theory."

"Naw, you were always the smart one."

"Not in that class, believe me."

"Play it for me."

"I've only got the first few phrases." She closed her eyes, hands poised above the keys.

David admired the curve of her cheek, her elegant brow.

Her hands came down. The phrase began softly, like the first stirring of a spring breeze, then began to open, the gossamer wings of a dragonfly. She stopped and looked at the far wall, focused inward. "I can hear violins and a flute."

"Nothing for us horn players?"

She turned her head toward him, a faint smile forming. "I think I may find a part for you, David Spach."

Desire coursed through him, but he held still, not wanting her to know how strongly his body was responding to her. She leaned over and kissed him, her lips smooth and soft. He returned the kiss, trying to keep it light, holding himself back.

She gave a little smack with her lips and sat back. "Thank you," she breathed.

"It's my pleasure." His voice was husky.

Winston scratched at the side door, then turned and gave an impatient groan.

They both burst out laughing. Jane jumped up and ran to the door.

"Wait, I'll come out with you," David said.

They walked outside and stood shoulder to shoulder under a gibbous moon while Winston headed to the bushes. After he did his business, he came back out to the drive where he nosed around. The bulldog suddenly inhaled deeply and trotted over to the other side of the house. They followed.

He growled at a clump of trees.

"It's just me," a Scottish brogue came from the dark.

"James? What are you doing here?"

"Ed asked me to keep an eye out." He stepped from the trees and held his hand out for Winston to smell.

They walked closer. "This is my friend I was telling you about. James, meet Jane Frey."

She shook his hand. "Nice to meet you. I don't want you to go to any trouble on my account."

"It's my pleasure, ma'am." He made a bit of a bow. "We heard about the theft."

"And apparently the painting isn't the only thing they're after," Jane said.

James's breath blew out in a puff of surprise. "David," he said, his voice like a disapproving parent.

"She deserves to know," David said. "Do you know more about what they might be after?"

"We'll talk later."

"Come on, James. How can we keep her safe, keep the artifact from being stolen, if we don't know?"

"I really don't know." James said. "Ask the higher-ups. I'm on until midnight, then somebody else is coming."

"Thank you for helping," Jane said. "I can't tell you how much I appreciate you being here." She walked toward the house.

David waited until Jane was out of earshot. "I'm staying the night."

"Lucky you," James pitched his voice so only David would hear.

"Coming?" Jane called.

"Not in her bed," David said in an undertone.

"So you say," James whispered.

David ran over to Jane and they went back inside, Winston leading the way. She went into the kitchen and checked the water bowls. "I'm leaving the cat door open."

"I think that's safe." David hesitated, then asked, "Where should I sleep?"

They climbed the stairs together. Jane opened the door of a bedroom. "I'm in there." She pointed to a door kitty-corner to his. "Or you could sleep in the master bedroom."

"In Miss Essig's bed?" he asked, eyes wide.

Jane giggled, sounding a bit tipsy. "I haven't been able to move in there yet either."

He opened the door and found two twin beds. "This will be fine." He turned back to her, then yawned prodigiously. "Call me if you need anything."

"I'll put a new toothbrush out after I wash up." She stood on her tiptoes and pecked him on the cheek.

He patted her shoulder, trying to be reassuring. He worried his touch would telegraph his state of desire.

"I'll cook breakfast." She went into her room. Winston followed her.

"Lucky dog," he whispered.

CHAPTER SIXTEEN

Jane's eggs were runny and her grits lumpy, but David ate them with a smile. "I've just been having protein shakes in the morning" she explained. "Well, mostly coffee and toast."

"This is good," David soaked up yoke with a piece of multi-grain toast.

She didn't believe him. They cleaned up together, Jane comforted by the occasional bump against him as they loaded the dishwasher.

The doorbell rang and Jane peeped through the window to find a man in a crisp blue uniform standing at the door. She opened the door expecting an identifying badge of some company logo, but his uniform was blank. She asked for identification. He handed her his driver's license. "I'm a private courier. Titlebaum, Smyth & Williams sent me." He checked her ID, then gave her a box.

"Let me grab a pen." She turned to go into the library, but the courier shook his head.

"No signatures."

"Oh." Jane turned back, surprised. "Thank you, then."

David leaned in the dining room doorway, arms on either side. "I guess they don't want this traced." He carried the box into the library. "I should probably swing by home and change," David said. "I've only got two music lessons this afternoon."

Jane brushed her hands off on the sides of her jeans. "I'll go through all this. See if I can figure out what had Lois so excited."

David pointed an index finger at the box. "And what somebody doesn't want you to find."

"Thanks for all your help yesterday." Jane walked him to the door and kissed him on the cheek.

"Should I drop by afterward?"

"Please," Jane said, "We're in this together, right?"

"Right." He seemed relieved. "I'll be done with my last student at three. You be careful." He punctuated the last word with a tap on her shoulder.

After he left, Jane went back to the library and cut through the tape holding the box together. On top she found a typed note:

Attached you will find all records related to this case, plus old files. The group mentioned to you took all the attorney's records, but someone took these home the night before the accident.

The attorney contacted an informant, Jeff Spencer, who worked for the CIA, then later corporate security. Also the attorney was in touch with a Herr Leinbach in Herrnhut, Germany. No idea what this was about. Contact information for both is attached.

Be careful!

Herrnhut. The first Moravian settlement almost a hundred years after the Thirty Years War. The first link.

No names had been used in the note other than the two contacts. There wasn't even a signature. She supposed it could be traced to a particular printer, although this seemed unlikely given the sheer number in the world. Not like Perry Mason's day. Jane looked beneath the note and found two files, one on Spencer and a thin one containing Leinbach's address and phone number. Beneath that was a big stack of various documents all related to Jane.

She laid a few logs in the fireplace, wadded up the note along with some newspaper, and lit it. No sense leaving evidence for someone else to find. Then she grabbed another cup of coffee and started working her way through the files.

The cats settled on either side of her. The box contained mostly old deals Lois had helped with, all the real estate contracts from houses Jane had owned, employment contracts, then oil and gas deals that spanned a couple of decades. Nothing about the current investigation except the two names.

Jane took everything out of the box and Marvin promptly jumped in it. She closed the lid and after a few seconds, Marvin burst out. He jumped back in and she obliged by closing the lid again. He leapt out again, ran along the top of the sofa, then dived back into the box. She closed the lid.

Jane went back through each file, carefully turning every page looking for anything written in the margins, a new piece of paper stuck in the middle of an old contract, any internet addresses, bold-face type. Nothing turned up. Except Marvin, sticking his head up wondering why she'd stopped playing.

She went to the desk to turn on the computer, but her finger stopped almost of its own accord over the start button. What if her computer was being monitored? That seemed more likely than the printer being traced. The fire had died down enough for her to leave it.

She let Winston out for a bathroom break, but he charged the trees, dislodging another of Ed's guards. At least she hoped that's who he was. The man stood holding up his arms as if Winston were the police.

Jane tried not to laugh. "Winston," she called, but the dog ignored her. "He's all right. He won't bite."

"If you say so," the man said, his arms still in the air.

Jane introduced herself.

"Howdy. Ed sent me over to keep an eye out."

"Would you ask Ed to let me know who's coming? Otherwise, how can I tell friend from foe?"

"Yes, ma'am."

"I'm going out for a while. Just thought I'd let you know."

"I'll keep watch. Someone else is coming at noon."

Jane tried to haul Winston away from the man, who kept his hands in the air. "Put your hands down and let him get your scent," Jane said.

The man complied. Winston took a good, long smell, then stuck his head between the man's legs, sniffing again.

"Winston," Jane said sharply.

Satisfied, the bulldog went over to an area covered in pine needles and peed, then he pushed dirt over it with his hind legs, all the while eyeing Ed's new guard. Jane covered her mouth to keep from laughing. Then she bent down, slapping her leg. "All right, come on now."

Winston ran to her and wagged his whole rear.

"Inside, you." She pointed to the house and they ran up the back steps together.

Jane grabbed her keys and drove her rental to the library, watching to see if the silver sedan showed up or any car stuck with her. She didn't spot anything unusual. Inside, Jane accessed the internet, then got into a secure site from her old job—apparently Tami was too green to have found Jane's backdoor in. From here, she could surf the web without leaving footprints. She searched for evidence of who Spencer had worked for. A few pages deep, Jane began to find traces of him. After he left the CIA, Lois's contact worked for politicians, a congressman and a governor, until a couple of years ago. Then he started working for World Energy Corp.

She muffled a curse. How had Lois missed this? Jane knew this company. It was headed up by Henry Coche, a billionaire business magnate and international political player. Coche had recently spent millions hiring out-of-work rednecks to ride around on buses protesting legislation intended to help them out. Coche's people had designed a deviously brilliant plan to turn ordinary Americans against their own best interests. Most people were too badly educated to recognize this and they were trained to mistrust what his news organization called the 'intellectual elite', who were trying to explain things. Now he was getting these same people to protest the President's new energy bill. Coche's business practices were no better. His company had wrecked a large part of the Arctic and refused to clean up oil spills in Africa and the Gulf of Mexico.

The question was whether Spencer was loyal to Lois or Coche? Or only himself? She closed her eyes and thought back through the transfers she made for Valentin Knight. She was certain at least two had involved World Energy Corp. Had these transfers alerted Coche? Or had it been the thing Lois discovered, but hadn't had the chance to tell her about?

She looked at the time on the computer screen. She had a few hours before David was finished with work. She would look up websites about Masonic and Templar treasure. Then she realized there was a faster way to get all this information. But it involved a certain amount of deception, plus swallowing her pride. She got back in her rental and pointed it toward Uncle Pat's house. He was a devotee of all things smacking of conspiracy theories and Freemasons. She hoped he wouldn't be too angry about the beagles.

☆ ☆ ☆

Misty gave her a sour look. "I had to chase them dogs all over creation last time you was here."

"I'm sorry." Jane tried to look contrite. "I guess he pissed me off."

"Yeah, well," Misty fought a smile, "he'll do that."

"Who's there?" Uncle Pat's yell was followed by a spat of coughing.

"I reckon you can come in." Misty held the door open. "It's Miss High-Falutin'," she yelled over her shoulder.

"Who?"

"Your niece, Jane."

"Well, don't just stand there jawin'. Close the door afore you let all the flies in."

"Ain't no flies in December," she yelled, then whispered to Jane, "I didn't tell him about the dogs."

"Thanks," Jane said. She took a deep breath, preparing herself, then pasted a contrite look on her face and walked in the door.

His bird-thin chest rose and fell, laboring for each breath. A thin sheet of sweat covered his forehead. His skin had a grayish tint, but his eyes were fever bright. "I see you come crawlin' back," he wheezed.

"Uncle Pat," Jane tried not to show her shock at how his condition had deteriorated since her last visit. "You were right. I've come to apologize."

"Right about what?"

"The Moravians. They're not real Christians, just like you said." She winced, feeling guilty lying to a man on his deathbed.

"I knew it. What'd ya find out?" He leaned forward eagerly.

Misty appeared with more of her miraculous sweet tea. Uncle Pat's hand shook badly as he reached for it. Misty helped him take a sip, then put a straw in his.

"I don't need no cotton-pickin' straw," he objected, but drank from it anyway.

"Thanks," Jane whispered when she handed her a glass.

Misty shot her a mistrustful look.

Jane had thought through the recent revelations on the way over, searching for one that would set Uncle Pat off the most. "They think the Holy Spirit is a woman."

"Heathens. Idolaters," he shouted, then fell into another spat of coughing.

"And some of them are Masons," she added.

"Devil-worshipers—every last one of them. Did you know that the Statue of Liberty was given to us by the Freemasons of France? The preacher said her real name is Libertas. She's a demon. Harlot worship right there in New York harbor. Must be why the place is so full of filth and preversion." He paused to catch his breath.

Jane smiled at his pronunciation, but his string of expletives was often quite literary. Must be the King James Bible that he preferred. They both sipped their tea.

"First thing people see when they come into our country." He shook his head. "The Whore of Babylon is worshipped all over now. It's the end times, I tell you."

"What about the Freemasons? They're putting together some New World Order? Is that right?"

"Got that devil pyramid and the eye right on the dollar bill, but nobody thinks a thing of it." The tendons in his neck stood out. "They got that Egypt thing right there in the middle of our nation's capital."

"Egypt thing?"

"You know," he stretched his arm up, indicating something tall. "What's it called?"

"The Washington Monument?"

"That's it. The good Lord sent an earthquake to take it down." He hollered for Misty.

"What you want?" Misty stood in the door, one hand on her hip, insolent. The television played low in the background.

"Bring me that box of tapes I got in the garage."

"Which box? You got a bunch of 'em."

Uncle Pat shook his head and waved her away. "You can go see after we talk. Them Masons brung a whole bunch of pagan idols over here. Tried to trick our Christian Founders."

Jane didn't mention they were pretty much the same people. "What did they bring?"

"Supposed to have stolen the Arc of the Covenant from Jerusalem. Gold and precious jewels." Uncle Pat leaned back on his pillows and tried to catch his breath. "You'll see. I got it all catalogued in there. But we're in a new apostolic age. Them terrorists brung it on. We're going to capture the Seven Mountains. Clear these heathens out. Make way for the Rapture."

Jane didn't even ask what that meant. "Will you pray for me, Uncle Pat?"

His eyes filled up with tears. Guilt stabbed Jane's heart. "Girl, I'm glad you've come to your senses. Close your eyes."

Jane took his thin hand and did as he asked.

"Lord, I pray for my niece here who's just seen her way to you. Bless her and keep her away from these devil worshipping heathens. Chastise her and keep her steps on the straight and narrow. Bring your lash on her if she strays."

Jane cringed. This man must torture himself in the same way. She prayed that his suffering would be eased. Her first prayer in years.

He ended his prayer and opened his eyes, gasping for breath. "You got to move out of that demon-cursed house."

"Yes, sir." At least this was true. The part about moving at least.

"Now, you go on and let me rest. Misty'll show you where to look. You can ask me questions later." He leaned against the pillow, whiter than the old pillow case. It took him a longer time to catch his breath. When he did, he yelled for Misty, then fell back against the pillow.

"What?" she asked from the doorway.

Uncle Pat lifted his hand and pointed at Jane, but couldn't get enough breath to talk.

"He wants you to show me his research."

"Research?" Misty's tone went up along with her eyebrows. "All that conspiracy junk he's got in the garage?"

"That's right," Jane said.

"You watch your mouth, Misty" Uncle Pat wheezed. He closed his eyes and whispered, "Thank you, Jesus. I've brung my sister's child to you."

Jane followed Misty out to the garage.

Once they reached it, Misty turned on her. "What you playin' at? It's a sin to fool a dyin' man, you know."

"Just show me where he keeps the stuff on the Masons."

"You can find it yourself." Misty pointed to a row of file cabinets along the wall.

Jane stepped over and found boxes of video and audio tapes piled beside the file cabinets. Opening drawers at random, she realized to her surprise they were alphabetical by topic. She checked 'M' but didn't find Masons, but found them under 'F'. The files took up a whole drawer. There were notes on various rituals, a whole file titled 'The Whore of Babylon' on goddess worship, an even more fanciful one on the murder of infants, another on plans for world domination. Then she hit the jackpot. 'Stolen treasure', the file read. She took it out and then looked at her watch. David would be back soon. She stuck the file in her purse, then tiptoed to the front door.

"You ain't saying goodbye?" Misty asked.

Jane whirled around. "I thought he'd be asleep."

"I see you're helpin' yourself," Misty pointed to the manila file sticking out from Jane's purse. "Him not even dead yet."

"I'm just borrowing it. I'll bring it back." Jane turned bright red, remembering her borrowing of the Blake paintings might have led to this whole mess.

"Right." Misty snorted. "Just leave them dogs in their cages this time."

"They need to be walked, you know."

"You do it, then. You a new Christian and all." Misty turned on her heel and went back to her soap operas.

☆ ☆ ☆

Jane got back to Miss Essig's house and let Winston out to supervise the new security man who met his approval by scratching behind his ears. She went to the library in the back of the house and took Uncle Pat's file out of her purse. It contained some articles and a lot of transcriptions of shows from various radio ministers and some guy named Arthur Beale. She read through everything quickly. The file confirmed the list David had given her the night before, but added a whole lot more. These people Uncle Pat followed didn't distinguish between the Freemasons, the Templars or the Rosicrucians. They even threw in a few other groups Jane was less familiar with. According to the commentary, they were all devil worshippers set on world domination, secretly doing blood sacrifices to maintain control of all the governments in the world. Jane shook her head. As usual with such material, it was a mixture of ignorance, paranoia and the occasional gem of information.

The list of treasure started with gold and gemstones which seemed to come from Jerusalem via the Templars. They'd escaped King Philip the Fair, the French king who arrested and tortured Jacques de Molay among other knights, the note read.

Holy shit! Philip LeBelle. Jane slapped her palm against her forehead, remembering the visit from Philip and Margaret. *Could he be more obvious? I wonder what his real name is.*

According to this, de Molay had sacrificed himself so others could escape with the treasure. Where they took it was at question. The options mentioned were Scotland, an old Templar fort in the Mediterranean, Oak Island near Nova Scotia, Massachusetts, Rhode Island, and Washington, D.C. Nothing about North Carolina. But the articles all agreed that besides the Arc of the Covenant and the Grail, other treasure included gold, jewels and statuary from Egypt and Babylon. One contained a whole list of relics stolen from cathedrals in Europe—the hand of Saint Sebastian, the skull and finger bones of various saints, part of the true cross, the crown of thorns, the real shroud, and Longinus's spear, more popularly called the Spear of Destiny.

According to this list, the spear had come from a cathedral in Europe. No note on which one. Also listed was a jeweled skull worshipped by the Templars, the sword of King Arthur and the golden girdle of Saint Veronica. Jane had never heard of that saint, not that she was all that familiar with Catholic lore. It looked like Masonic treasure could include pretty much anything and it all sounded like urban legend to her. Herrnhut was the only solid lead. And Spencer, who was connected to Henry Coche.

Someone knocked on the door, a heavy, masculine hand, and Jane's heart lifted at the sound. She ran to the door, Winston right behind her, and opened it.

Dreher stood on the porch, hands on his hips. "I came by to check on your plans."

A thousand things to say came crowding up in Jane's throat, but none of them would help, so she swallowed them all down. "When do you need to know?"

"I gave you two days. One has passed."

"I'll be gone soon," she spit out and slammed the door in his face.

Hot tears filled her eyes. Damn the man. She walked through the living room, sat at the piano and played at random. This place was her true home, her heart's dwelling place. It had come from her family. How dare he exile her? The tears fell and she played, letting the music say what she couldn't. Soon the tears stopped, but she kept playing, remembering her many lessons with Miss Essig, her overnights with friends, climbing the tall pines and swinging with the wind.

Her fingers found music that raised her out of her memories, music that spoke of something fresh, of a promise. Jane closed her eyes and listened, letting her fingers take their own course. It was the piece she'd been dreaming. She let herself play and another phrase emerged, this one opening up a ground of sound, strong enough to support something big to come. Then she ran out of notes.

You can't take away my music, Jane thought.

The doorbell rang again.

Bastard, Jane thought. *Come back for more. Now I'll really give you a piece of my mind.*

She ran to the door and opened it. "What the hell do you . . ."

David stood there holding an overnight bag. He looked down at it, a flush spreading up his neck to his cheeks. "I didn't know if you'd want to stay in this big house all alone," he started to explain.

"I'm sorry. I thought you were—" She shook her head against fresh tears.

After a surprised grunt, he dropped the bag and pulled her close, nestling his nose into the hair behind her ear. "Damn, you smell good."

Jane pulled away, the storm of emotion gone as quickly as it had come. She brought David inside, locking the door behind them. "That asshole Dreher came by wanting to know when I'd be out."

"What'd you tell him?"

"I slammed the door in his face."

"What are you going to do?"

"I have an idea." Jane led him into the library, wiping her eyes with her sleeve. Files and papers littered the floor.

"Looks like you've been busy."

"I have, but I haven't learned all that much." She told him about Lois's two contacts, about Jeff Spencer's employers, and what she'd picked up from Uncle Pat.

"He sounds like a character."

"Listen, here's what I think we should do. I have to leave. Let's go see this Herr Leinbach. Find out what he told Lois."

"Go see? Isn't an overseas call cheaper than two plane tickets? Hell, we could Skype him for free."

"Yeah, and who else would be listening?" Jane pointed out. "Come with me. Let's go to London. Check out Fetter Lane."

"Actually, I talked to James. He said the place was bombed into oblivion during World War II. It's all been rebuilt. Says there's nothing left to see."

"Oh," Jane paused. "Then Herrnhut and Prague. We'll investigate these stories first hand."

"I don't have enough money to go gallivanting around Europe looking for clues that lead to Masonic treasure."

"I do," Jane said. At his frown, she added, "have enough money."

"I can't let you—"

"I need somebody to travel with me."

He looked down at her. "You don't strike me as needing anybody."

She smiled. "That's sweet, but I do. You know about the Masons. You're the perfect research assistant."

His eyes clouded.

"Among other things," she added.

"I have music students."

"Can't you find someone to take them for a few weeks?"

He tilted his head, considering. "But these people are dangerous."

"They'll be dangerous here or there."

David opened his mouth, then closed it. "Where do you get that kind of courage? I would never imagine doing that."

Jane shrugged. "I don't know. Dealing with rich assholes for twenty years?" She plopped down on the couch. "Come on. Don't tell me you haven't wanted to see Herrnhut all your life. Go to Prague?"

David stood in the middle of the paper-strewn floor studying her. "You're going to go whether I come or not, aren't you?"

She nodded. "But it would be so much more fun with you. Besides, my German is terrible."

Something shifted in David's eyes, then he smiled. "Mine is pretty good."

"See?"

He ran his hand through his hair. "We've got a lot of work to do, then."

☆ ☆ ☆

"We want to see if anyone follows you," Valentin Knight explained. "We think the real action is on this side of the Atlantic, but just in case our team will keep you under surveillance. If this guy is as good as I think, he'll spot us if we stay too close."

Jane paused to gather his full attention. "What are the chances I'll end up like Lois?"

Knight's shoulders fell. "I can't tell you how sorry I am. I never thought things would develop so quickly."

Knight had asked Jane to stop by D.C. before flying on to Lois's funeral. She'd left David to tie up loose ends. They would meet at JFK right after the service. She hadn't wanted David to be noticed there. Irrational, since he'd become a blip on their radar as soon as she'd bought their plane tickets.

The same chauffer who'd taken her to Knight's office picked her up at Reagan National Airport, but this time the drive took close to an hour. He left the city behind and headed to Knight's country home in Fairfax County. Blond stubbled fields were filled with horses and the occasional herd of dairy cows. Tall trees lined the road in places, and Jane relaxed. Finally, the car pulled through iron gates and meandered past several acres of pasture with blanketed thoroughbreds.

A stone mansion complete with turrets, gables and mullioned windows stood at the crest of the hill. The driver stopped in front of massive double doors. One of the doors opened and a man in the quintessential suit, vest and tie of an English butler strode out and opened her door. He'd showed her through the foyer, up a large staircase to Knight's capacious personal library where she now sat with her host.

A fire burned in the stone fireplace. Two leather chairs and attendant hassocks sat at angles to it. Knight occupied one, she the other. Floor to ceiling white-edged bookcases filled three of the walls. Across the room, the fourth was floor to ceiling windows overlooking flower beds tucked in for the winter and the edge of woods.

"I thought I was the one who had gotten her killed." Jane's eyes filled with hot tears.

"We thought there might be some reaction to moving all that money," Knight said. "My security team was watching you, but we thought Lois would be safe and only sent one person to protect her."

Jane gritted her teeth to keep herself from cursing.

"His body washed up in the Hudson this morning."

A pine log in the fire popped and Jane jumped. She waited until she could trust her voice. "So what is this all about?"

Knight shifted in his chair.

"I expect the truth this time."

Knight watched her, his eyes sad. He rubbed his temples, then straightened. "The balance of power in our world is changing. Members of the elite who share an altruistic view are making moves to loosen the stranglehold certain negative powers have on the economy and governments."

"The oil and gas conglomerate?" Jane asked.

"Among others."

"Good luck with that," she said.

Knight's mouth tightened. "Indeed, Ms. Frey, cynicism has been the tone of the last decade, but we can no longer sit back and tell ourselves their control is unshakeable. Global conditions are dire. We've passed the seven billion mark in population, and most people live without clean water or sufficient food, not to mention lacking even a modicum of education. Climate change is upon us already. All this is well known. But I wanted to let you know about one other indicator. The prophecy."

"What prophecy? You don't strike me as someone who believes in such nonsense."

Knight eyed her for a minute, then seemed to come to a decision. "I've been a member of a spiritual lodge for a number of years."

Jane remembered what David had said about this man, his awe when she'd mentioned her walk with him.

He continued, "Our training helps us distinguish true psychic vision from chicanery. A young man has surfaced who seems to be a pure seer."

"What does he predict?" She'd see where this led.

"That those who serve the light will regain power. A new era of peace and an uplifting of consciousness."

Jane snorted, then blushed at Knight's chilly expression. "I'm sorry, but I'm shocked that you would go in for this sort of thing. It's just like that guy who predicted Armageddon on—what was the date? He was wrong, of course, and all those people sold their property, spent their life savings."

"This is quite different."

"You got Lois killed over some crackpot prediction."

Knight regarded her for a minute. "I hope you'll excuse me for saying that you are hardly qualified to make such a judgment."

"And you are?"

"Yes, Ms. Frey, I am."

His use of her surname, the certainty in his voice, stopped her.

"Pardon me for stating my credentials. It's not seemly, but under the circumstances . . ." He spread his hands.

"Please enlighten me," Jane said.

He cocked his head at her as if surprised, the ghost of a smile on his lips, then said, "I am the head of the oldest spiritual organization in the Americas, begun by several of the founding fathers. Some of your church's members as well." He sat forward in his chair, clearly animated by the subject. "They sought to create a safe haven for the true spiritual teachings the Church of Peter had tried to wipe out over the centuries. Teachings that can be traced back into antiquity."

"So you're a Mason," Jane said.

Knight made a dismissive noise. "Our group lies beneath all the visible lodges. Always has."

He eyed her before continuing. "Not only do I carry this spiritual responsibility, I own a global, multi-billion dollar enterprise that wields a great deal of power. I am an advisor to heads of state, religious leaders and wealthy families who tend to exert more power than is commonly known." He blushed at this recitation.

"I guess I didn't realize you also held spiritual authority," Jane said in a softer voice. She'd known the rest.

Knight continued. "The prophecy speaks of a lost treasure. We need to recover it."

Jane frowned. "But I'm not an archeologist—" Knight raised a finger to forestall her. "At first we thought it might be the Blake painting you discovered in the *Kabinet* Room beneath your home."

"You know about that?"

"Of course. Now we realize the prophecy refers to something else. Something much older and more powerful."

"Powerful?""Ancient cultures knew ways to imbue spiritual energy into material objects. Egyptian lore, for example, speaks of the Opening of the Mouth ritual which tied the statues to the God or Goddess it represented."

Jane sat back, shaking her head. "But that's just—"

"Myth?" he finished for her. "Perhaps, but this idea is found around the world. Many strange stories exist about ancient artifacts that defy the material explanations of science."

Jane started to object, but he pressed on. "Nevertheless, it is not necessary for you to become a believer in any of this lore."

"Then how can I help you? I would like to see power come into the hands of more wise leaders."

His smile was genuinely warm. "Excellent. There is an old story that someone in your church, most particularly in your family, brought an artifact with them to the colonies which people in medieval days thought to have great power."

Now Jane did roll her eyes. "They believed in all kinds of silliness back then. If a monastery or cathedral needed funds, they discovered a relic. The pilgrims came for blessings. And spent money." She said this last with emphasis. "Besides, Moravians didn't approve of relics. They thought they became substitutes for a direct relationship with God."

"But someone thinks they have one," he said. "More importantly, this someone believes in it."

"So, let them. What's the harm in—" She stopped, thinking of Lois, remembering the thermos of tea laced with barbiturates.

"We are not asking you to authenticate these claims of spiritual power," Knight said. "We're asking you to use your trip to explore stories of any artifacts that might have been transported or stored by your family or those in association with them."

"But you know I've been kicked out of the house. I don't have much access to my family right now. Or the OGMS." This was not strictly true. Frank had offered her a room.

Knight raised an eyebrow. "You see? You've discovered some things already."

"True." Jane took a bit of satisfaction at that. "If you know about the OGMS, why don't you ask them?"

"They do not know what the thieves might be looking for besides the Blake painting. But we have other means to search those premises."

Jane regarded him for a minute.

"You may stay in my corporate suite in Prague. I'll put a security team on you."

She raised an eyebrow.

"At a sufficient level of alert. If you need funds—"

She smiled at this. "You've already taken care of me in that regard. I suppose I can't complain that giving me thirteen million also made me a target."

"You were already a target," he said, not elaborating.

Jane wondered how that had happened.

"Take your trip. Search out these connections. Let me know if I can provide resources or access." He stopped and held her eyes. "I'd appreciate it if you kept me informed of your discoveries."

CHAPTER SEVENTEEN

The towers of Prague shone in the December sunlight. David leaned against the balcony door, taking it all in, his breath misting in the cold. All his life he'd imagined making this trip, seeing Hus's statue, visiting Bethlehem Chapel where it had all begun, and now here he was.

But Jane wanted to leave already—rent a car and drive to Herrnhut. The place where it had started all over again three hundred years later, another village he'd always wanted to visit, but not in such a rush. He wanted to wait a day, adjust to the time zone and the idea of being here. He'd never left the United States before. He thought that Herrnhut should be approached slowly, savored.

Jane walked out onto the balcony of their suite looking annoyingly fresh. "Ready?"

"Why not stay here for a day?"

"Because these thieves are way ahead of us," she said, avoiding his eyes. "We need to find out what Leinbach knows."

He couldn't argue with that. He had argued that a suite was too expensive, but she told him the suite was leased by Knight's company, that he'd insisted they stay here for security reasons. Overlooking the river and the Charles Bridge, the whole of Prague laid out at his feet with the castle crowning the hill, he felt like the rich one today. He hadn't mentioned his disappointment that their suite had two bedrooms. Did she want to stay just friends or was intimacy the only thing she wanted to approach slowly?

It had taken them two days to leave. Dreher had relented once he knew her plans were solid. His son had readily agreed to take the animals, setting the two cats up in the large barn where they could chase mice to their hearts content. The bulldog attached himself at the hip to his grandson, peeling himself away only to see if the cats were still around. Satisfied, David gave his son Jane's international cell number.

"So you're serious about this lady?" His son tilted his head toward Jane who sat in the front seat.

David stood there, digging a small trench in the dirt with the heel of his shoe. "I'm helping her out. She's had some rough times."

"Yeah, Prague sounds real rough."

David reached out and mussed his hair. "Watch it, kid."

"Listen Dad, we all want you to be happy. Mom wouldn't mind."

David just shook his head. "You got the phone number?"

"Right here." His son patted his shirt pocket.

David got in the car and started it up.

"Have fun," his son shouted out, waving as they drove away.

From there, he dropped Jane off and went home to pack. Not really knowing what to take, he dumped in a week's worth of shirts and jeans. He wanted to bring his horn, to play in front of Hus's statue, but it was just too bulky. He tightened all the faucets, set the thermostat low, turned off all the lights except in the bathroom and locked up. His daughter said she'd come by and check on things every few days. Then he drove over to the English Tudor and found Jane in the library finishing up the reservations.

He argued against booking first class.

"You'll never get any sleep in coach," she answered.

"Why are you doing this on your computer? I thought you were worried it was bugged."

"Our passports will pop up on the grid as soon as we check in anyway. They'll probably notice this reservation in . . ." She looked at her watch ". . . say two more minutes."

She'd been right. He had slept on the plane. First time ever. But he hadn't slept much last night all alone in his own room. Not that he wanted to make love with her right away. Well, yeah he did, but he understood her wanting to get to know him better, be sure of him. Was that it? Or was she distracted by Lois's death? He wondered if something had happened at the memorial service. She'd gone to it, then met him at JFK, but hadn't said anything about the service.

He squinted at her face now, lit by Prague's morning sun flooding the balcony.

"Come on." Jane grabbed his arm and pulled. "It's at least a two hour drive and we've got an appointment to talk to Herr Leinbach at half past ten. We need to leave now."

David took one last look around at the spires, the castle on the hill, the birds soaring from tower to tower. Then he followed her. Seemed like he did a lot of that.

In the rental office in the lobby downstairs Jane rented a black Fiat 500 Abarth, brand new. David didn't argue about that. He just slid into the leather seat and nosed it into the rush hour traffic, now in full swing.

Just as he was getting used to the Fiat's quick responses, Jane pointed. "Here's the ramp."

David eased the sports car around a truck parked halfway up a curb, then took the turn and merged onto the highway. The gears shifted like butter.

"We take this road all the way into Poland." Jane sat back and looked around as they passed through the old city.

But David had to pay attention to the traffic. European cars were small and fast. Up ahead a sign flashed red bars, then a couple of miles later another one did the same. After the third, he figured out it was warning him that he was speeding, like the signs that flashed numbers at home. He pulled into the middle lane and slowed down.

Jane rode in silence. He let her be. Whatever it was, it would work itself to the surface eventually. That's how it was for him anyway.

The highway narrowed as it wound out of town, settling into a modern separated road, two lanes on each side. Brown fields replaced buildings with some patches of white under the trees.

He was grateful there was no snow on the roads. Jane said she could drive in it, but he couldn't. He'd lived in the south all his life. Snow meant build a fire, make hot chocolate and stay home.

David glanced over at her from time to time, but her head was turned toward the passenger window watching the scenery. Once in a while, she pulled down the visor and looked in the make-up mirror. He knew she was checking to see if anyone was following them. He wondered if she was regretting her decision to bring him.

David settled in, determined not to let her mood ruin his. He enjoyed the scenery, took a sip of the coffee Jane had bought back at the hotel. It was cold, but he drank it anyway.

The road climbed a bit, then the GPS announced in a clipped, British accent that their exit was ahead. They drove off onto a two-lane road, moving through the remnants of primeval forests.

Jane pulled down the visor again. "Looks like nobody's following us. At least as far as I can tell."

"Good," he said. "By the way, what did Knight say?"

"That he'd have someone watch out for us. I can't see them, either."

Jane stretched out her legs and David resisted the urge to put his hand on her knee. Then she looked out the passenger window again.

She hadn't really answered his question. Surely Knight had given her more information, but she wasn't ready to talk. David suppressed a spike of envy. He wondered what it would be like to meet Knight, to sit in the presence of a living legend. Stories of Knight's magical feats abounded, and his esoteric knowledge was said to be encyclopedic. What would it be like to visit him? Yet Jane hadn't mentioned a thing.

He glanced at her again. She stared out the window, her head resting on her hand. She'd never said anything about doing spiritual studies. Perhaps she wasn't finely tuned enough to pick up Knight's energy. Why would these people who were supposed to be following her think she would know what to do with a spiritual artifact, anyway? David shook his head against these thoughts. He was just annoyed with her aloofness, he told himself. He turned his attention back to driving.

The car molded itself to the road, handling the curves easily. Stories of the old magical forests of Europe filled his head, replacing his earlier doubts. Most of those forests were gone now, but these young trees shared roots from the old ones and still whispered their memories. The road ducked through Poland, and before he realized it, they were in Germany. No more guards and security checks at the borders. Windmills atop green, rolling hills replaced the trees, whispering of power and cities and the buzz of electricity.

The British lady inside the GPS announced that they had arrived at their destination. Jane sat forward, looking around. He paused at the stop sign, searching for any sign of the old settlement. The village here looked the same as the ones they'd been passing through. Then David spotted the shop on their right. Moravian stars hung, the red and white points crisp and clean.

Jane grabbed his arm and pointed. "We're here. We're really here."

"Sure looks like it." He grinned, turning left and steering the Fiat down the street.

Jane was now animated. "But where's the village?"

He spotted a gas station and a bank up ahead. That didn't look promising, so he turned right down a side street, passed an art museum, then drove into a parking lot and stopped. They both spotted it at the same time, across a yellowed field, rows of gravestones, these darker, more weathered than the white marble of Old Salem. At the back rose a white tower.

"There it is." David pointed.

Jane pounded on his arm. "Oh, my God. I can't believe it."

David whipped the Fiat around and drove back toward the main road, but he turned left a block before reaching it—and stopped dead. "Jane, look."

At the end of the street stood the church, a large, white almost barn-like building with rows of windows topped by an orange roof. A white clock tower sat atop that, and from the tiptop rose a golden weathervane. The Saal, the first church the

Bohemian Brethren had built freely and openly after their long exile.

David parked and they got out, standing on the sidewalk, mouths open, amazed that, like salmon, they had swum all the way back to the place that had spawned them.

Jane's hand found his. "Come on."

They strolled down the sidewalk passing more white buildings, large and blousy, big enough to accommodate the refugees of the past. Cables stretched across the street. Moravian stars hung from them in profusion. Stars for Advent.

"I can't wait to see this place lit up," Jane said.

"The sun should go down fairly early this time of year," David answered. "We're pretty far north. At least compared to home."

They walked another half-block and a driveway opened into a kind of courtyard. David squinted to read the signs posted in the window. Something about 24-hour prayer and where to take a shift. On the opposite wall a plaque announced this was the Single Brethren's House. Room rates were posted below.

"We could stay here."

"You could," Jane quipped.

"Where's Leinbach's office?"

Jane pointed at the church. "He said he'd meet us there." She took out her phone and pushed a button. "It's quarter after. We've got about fifteen minutes to check out the sanctuary before our meeting."

They hurried down the sidewalk and crossed the street. A few steps led up to the door of the church. David paused, his hand on the door handle. "This is all happening so fast." She watched him, her blue eyes lit with a flame of excitement. "I've always imagined coming here. And now, here we are."

"Aren't you excited to see it?" Jane shifted her weight from one foot to the other.

"It's like a pilgrimage or something. I don't feel prepared."

"You should crawl here on your knees like the Tibetans?" she teased.

"I guess." He laughed. "Well, not that extreme."

She leaned in and kissed him, then pulled back before he could respond to those soft lips. "I deem you worthy. Now, open the door."

He did, mostly to cover his surprise at her kiss, and stepped aside to let Jane go first. He took a deep breath and followed her into a huge, open room filled with simple, white benches.

At first it was hard to figure out where the pulpit was. Perhaps they didn't have one, following their rebellion against the officiousness of the Catholic Church that far. Then way at the end of the room in front of a bank of tall windows he saw a raised platform. A table stood there, draped in green. A white chair with a cushion in matching green fabric sat behind it. Simple, but elegant candelabras hung from the ceiling at regular intervals, but the candles had been replaced by tall, white cylinders topped with electric bulbs in the shape of a flame.

David sank onto one of the benches about halfway up the aisle. To his right, a balcony hung above the windows. An organ dominated the center, three panels of silver pipes filling the wall, a fourth set as a panel in the balcony's front. Jane settled next to him. She picked up a hymnal and leafed through it.

David closed his eyes and started the breathing exercises he'd learned in his Masonic lessons, calming himself, trying to capture the reverence he thought he should be feeling. After a couple of minutes, some measure of peace stole over him and he sent up a prayer of thanks for the tenacity and faith of his ancestors, for the morality and strength of character that he hoped had been passed on to him. He prayed for protection while they searched for the treasure some men were willing to kill for. And for guidance about what to do about this woman who sat next to him, her leg pressing warm against his.

Footsteps sounded toward the front of the church and David opened his eyes. A man stood in the doorway on the left of the pulpit—if that's what they called such a simple platform.

"I apologize for interrupting your prayers," the man said, his German accent strong. Then he looked at Jane. "Are you Miss Frey?"

Jane stood. "Yes, I'm Jane Frey. Herr Leinbach?"

He gave a clipped bow, then held out his hand in invitation. "Please, my office is upstairs."

They climbed a set of stairs, then on the landing David stopped to read a plague hanging on the wall. *Von Herrnhut in Deit Welt* it announced. A history of the Moravian church was painted in sepia on the wall with dates and events. It started in 1458 with the settlement in Kunvald, Moravia, and ended announcing the number of members the church had on five continents in 2008.

Jane climbed the rest of the stairs to join Herr Leinbach who waited on the second floor landing, his hands folded in front of him, the picture of patience.

"I never thought I'd be able to come here in my lifetime," David said.

Herr Leinbach smiled. "Many of our brethren make the trip now. They say the same."

David climbed the rest of the steps. Leinbach walked across the wood floor to a white door, but before he opened it, he turned to Jane. "It is an honor to meet a member of one of our oldest and most distinguished families." He bowed over her hand.

David tried to cover his surprise, but Jane didn't miss a beat. "Thank you," she said. She sent a questioning look to David before Leinbach straightened.

Oldest and most distinguished? He frowned. Moravians didn't hold much stock in worldly position. But then he thought of Zinzendorf. They had recognized his worldly station. Was Jane related to Count Zinzendorf somehow?

Their host invited them into a modestly appointed office with a window looking out on a garden. Leinbach motioned to two straight-back chairs in front of a desk piled with books and papers, uncharacteristically messy for the well groomed and proper man who took a seat behind it.

He folded his hands on top of a well-marked manuscript and said, "How may I help you?"

Jane leaned forward. "We found your name in the papers of my attorney, Lois Williams."

"Yes, Fraulein Williams."

"Perhaps you didn't know. She died last week in a car accident."

Leinbach straightened with a jerk. "But this is terrible."

"Did you know her well?" Jane asked in a kind tone.

"*Nein*, I only made her acquaintance through our correspondence."

Jane handed Leinbach a copy of her obituary from the *New York Times*. She gave him a moment to read it, then continued. "Her firm sent me copies of my records related to our business together. I found your name and address in them, but nothing else. May I ask what this correspondence was about?"

Leinbach studied her for a minute. "You've come all this way to ask this question?"

"We are on holiday," Jane said. "We wanted to see Herrnhut anyway."

Leinbach nodded his head, then opened a drawer on one side of the desk, took out a file and leafed through it.

David restrained himself from leaning forward to get a better look. Jane remained sitting, her spine straight as the weathervane on top of the church.

Leinbach looked up at them, his winter-blue eyes piercing. "Fraulein Williams emailed me about your discovery of the Blake paintings. I wrote back to her through the regular mail." He spread his hand. "I don't trust the security of this internet. I verified Blake's connection to the Brethren." Leinbach looked down at the file again and turned over a piece of paper. "She called me as soon as she received my letter asking about the house you were living in."

David noted his use of the past tense. How much did this man really know?

"I had to speak with Reverend Szeges first. After he explained the situation, I called Fraulein Williams back. We discussed the spiritual dimensions of the settlement in Salem, especially the New Marienborn complex." He folded his hands again, as if they should understand the implications of this.

"I hope you'll excuse me. I haven't been in the church since I was a child and am just now learning more about our history."

Leinbach's eyes widened in surprise.

"Would you please share with me what you told her?"

"What you have most likely discovered for yourself. That a core group kept to the choir system and made their homes in these four houses. Worshipped at the church."

Jane let the silence stretch, but Leinbach did not elaborate. "And the Order of the Grain of the Mustard Seed?" she asked.

Leinbach steepled his fingers and his eyes took on a faraway look. "Zinzendorf began this group while at university, then revived it when he began his missionary trips. Count Zinzendorf was one of the first who worked toward interdenominational cooperation. A pioneer. Several distinguished men joined, as perhaps you are aware." This last had the hint of a question in it.

"And the 24-hour prayer movement? If I remember correctly, the Unity held a prayer vigil that lasted for several years."

Leinbach pursed his lips in slight disapproval. "Actually, it lasted for a hundred years. It is called the Lord's Watch. In fact, it is still happening."

"I see," Jane said apologetically.

After a pause, she continued. "Information has reached us," Jane inclined her head toward David, "that a clandestine group believes my family is in possession of something quite valuable. More so than the Blake paintings."

Leinbach looked from Jane to David. "Indeed?"

"Perhaps some spiritual artifacts brought to the Americas either by the Brethren or the—" she paused, watching Leinbach carefully "—Freemasons."

Leinbach nodded, waiting for her to say more.

David took the lead. "This doesn't seem to surprise you."

"Of course not. Many Moravians have been members of the European lodges. Frederick V himself was a Rosicrucian."

Jane frowned, obviously not following this last, but David sat up straighter. "So it's true that the Moravians had deep connections with the Rosicrucian and Masonic lodges."

Leinbach glanced at Jane before focusing back on David. "But surely this is not new to either of you, especially given Jane's family background."

"As I said," Jane explained, "I've lived away from my family most of my life."

"The Rosicrucians were enemies of the Habsburgs. The Winter King was our last attempt to win Prague."

"The Thirty Years War," Jane said.

"Precisely." Leinbach looked like a beleaguered school master. "And Comenius himself attended university with Andrea in Heidelberg."

This knocked David back in his seat. "Johann Valentin Andrea?"

"The same." Leinbach pressed his lips into a tight line. "Heidelberg was a seat of metaphysical teachings. Anyone who attended classes there would have been versed in the mysteries. At least the rudimentaries."

"And this would not have been considered contrary to our church's teachings?" David asked.

"In the late fourteenth century, the Catholic Church forbade commoners to study metaphysics. The aristocracy was allowed to continue." He glanced at Jane. "Of course, those in rebellion against the Catholics continued their connections with the mystery schools. Now, we have abandoned such practices."

David stretched his senses to detect any deception. He had an uncommon ability to tell when people were lying, and he thought Leinbach had at least stretched the truth.

"So you see, Fraulein Frey," Leinbach said, "it is entirely possible that your ancestors may have come into contact with some ancient artifact."

"But the Moravians don't approve of relics, that kind of thing," Jane said.

Leinbach puzzled out her idiom. "Relics, no, not as an object of worship. Not as a substitute for a direct relationship with Christ." He paused and regarded her, perhaps wondering what her relationship with their Chief Elder was. He must have formed some conclusion before he continued. "But we were closer to the Rosicrucians and Masons in earlier times. Perhaps someone in your family did a favor for a friend and that person never returned to collect his property."

"I suppose that's possible," Jane said.

"As to the exact nature of this artifact, I suggest you consult with your own family. This is beyond my knowledge."

"I see," she said.

David could tell by the look on Jane's face that she didn't see at all. Her cheeks were flushed and she twisted a tissue in her hands. He hadn't expected the officials in Herrnhut to be in such close contact with the church in Winston-Salem, but then in the past Herrnhut had called the shots in the colonies. Now that the iron curtain had fallen and several decades passed, perhaps they had picked up where they left off. Perhaps they still thought of America as the colonies.

Leinbach pushed back his chair and stood. "I'm sorry to say that I have another appointment, but I will turn you over to Herr Kinne who has kindly agreed to show you through the museum and grounds. Later this afternoon Fraulein Pfeifer, our archivist, will meet with you."

"Thank you," David said when Jane didn't answer him.

"Please do let me know if I can be of any further service while you are in our village."

Jane stood and gave a stiff bow. "Thank you for this information, Herr Leinbach. I am sorry that I have not kept up with my studies."

Their host flushed, but returned her acknowledgment with a slight nod of his head, so different from his earlier effusion when they first arrived. He walked to the door and opened it. A small man with graying hair stood near the top of the stairs, hat in his hands, his cheeks apple-red from the cold.

☆ ☆ ☆

Jane greeted Herr Kinne with her professional smile and shook his work-worn hand. She'd actually been hoping for some time alone with David. He seemed to understand what Leinbach had said more than she had. She was still puzzled by his intimation that her family was so important. But her old job had trained her how to put her own questions on hold and play the charmed guest. And indeed, she was anxious to see Herrnhut. Perhaps she could slip in some questions that would shed light on their search.

They followed their guide down the stairs and through a hallway next to the sanctuary. Jane spotted the restrooms and excused herself. Just to have a moment alone. In the stall, she took out her Blackberry and started to text David, but then remembered his phone didn't work in Europe. Instead she pulled up the list of Masonic treasure to refresh her memory. Then she accessed a map of Herrnhut, trying to imagine where old artifacts might have been kept.

"Jane?" David's voice reached her through the door. "You okay in there?"

She flushed the toilet and opened the stall door. "I'm fine. Be right out." She washed her hands, then gave her hair a quick brush. Pushing her brush and phone back in her purse, she pasted on her smile again and joined the men in the hallway.

"I thought perhaps to start in the museum, if this is agreeable?" Kinne asked.

"Please, lead on." Jane said.

The museum reminded her of Old Salem, except the displays were less rustic. This had not been a colony in the New World, but a new village in Saxony. She looked over old farming tools, dishes, antique books. In the third room, Jane found yet another bust of Comenius. There had been a portrait in the last room, a bust in the first. He seemed much more important to the German community than to the Americans. At least she didn't remember hearing much about him in Sunday school.

"Herr Kinne?" Jane pointed to a bust inside the glass case they were standing next to. "I keep seeing Comenius. Can you tell us more about him?"

"He was one of the Unity's most important bishops. An innovator in education. He insisted that all students be treated with respect. Not mistreated by their teachers as he was when he was in school." The man beamed at her. He laced German with his English, which was passable, but soon he lapsed into German. She understood most of it, but David could translate if she needed help.

"So, he's best known for his writings about education?" she asked.

"Not just that." Kinne grew more animated. "Comenius ushered our church through difficult times. Because of religious persecution, he lost his home twice. After he fled the first time, his wife and two children died of the plague." The man paused to let this sink in. "He was exiled in Poland, then had to leave that country. But he never lost his faith."

"I'll have to read up on him again. In Salem, we didn't hear so much about him." She turned to David, who stood near the door, his gaze taking a quick inventory of the room. "Did you?"

David focused back on her. "I learned a bit about him in my lodge." So he had been following the conversation.

"Our bookstore is named after him," Kinne said, "since he lost his library twice in the fires. In his life, he thought the Unity would fail. His last book is a missive to the future in hopes the teachings would be taken up again. He even recorded his prophecies."

Jane took a breath to ask about this, until she saw David's expression.

"Are all his works translated into English?" David asked, drawing Kinne's attention.

"*Nein*, we only have them in German."

"I read German," David said.

The man's round face lit up. "*Gut.*"

David reached his hand out to her. "Perhaps we should go to the bookstore and pick some up."

"But first, I have a surprise for you," Kinne said.

Jane was glad their host didn't see David's scowl. He seemed to have discovered something and wanted to speak with her in private.

They followed Kinne to the front room of the museum. He exchanged a few words with the woman at the front, then produced a long skeleton key on a chain. "Follow me."

Kinne walked outside and crossed the street to a green triangle of grass with a street sign above it reading *Comeniusstrake*.

Jane pointed. "He's everywhere."

"Yes." Kinne acknowledged her comment with a clipped nod of his head. "Now, shall we go to *Gottesacker*?"

He led them up the hill between close trimmed trees, their large branches ending in large knobs, reminding Jane of gnomes. Two columns held up a white arch that read *Christus ist Auferstanden von Den Toten.*

"Christ is risen from the dead," David translated softly.

She flashed on the Easter sunrise service. The first words, "The Lord is risen," uttered in the predawn chill of early spring.

They walked under the arch. Before them, graves stretched in both directions in neat rows, the marble headstones weathered, but bleaching out at the edge of the cemetery where the more recent interments were. Jane bent down to one. The marker was old and difficult to read. She rose and followed Kinne up the path.

Their guide narrated as they walked. He pointed to a little placard next to the gravestone. "Here is Christian David, the carpenter from Moravia who got permission to begin this settlement here on Count Zinzendorf's estate."

David translated the stone haltingly. "Felled the first tree for the building of Herrnhut the 17th of June 1722."

Kinne continued reading another placard, but the names flowed past Jane. She strolled ahead, listening to the birds, remembering the funerals in her own God's Acre, the trombone band. Unbidden, the music that had been haunting her played again in her head. It continued past where it had stopped last time, two more phrases sounding. She walked farther up the path and sang it softly, willing herself to remember.

"Jane," David called, "come here. This is amazing."

Jane rejoined them, tucking her arm in David's. He gave a little start of surprise, then pulled her close.

Kinne turned to the women's side of the cemetery. He pointed to another ancient tombstone. "Eva Maria Spangenberg, the Eldress of the church in Bethlehem. Her husband, August, supervised the churches in the Americas. He went on the scouting trip to find Salem."

The names tickled Jane's memory, but David nodded, obviously keeping pace with Kinne's broad grasp of Moravian history. His eyes shone. Whatever had caught his attention in the museum seemed forgotten. She'd have plenty of time to pick his brain over lunch.

Kinne pointed up the slope to what looked like sarcophagi in the middle of the path. "And here we have the Count and his family." They made their way to the large graves covered in grey, engraved stone.

"They aren't with the others." Jane pointed across the flat graveyard. "Isn't this against our tradition?"

Kinne shrugged. "The Zinzendorf's are specially honored. Without them, we would not exist."

David bent down and translated the inscription. "Here rest the bones of the unforgettable man of God Nicolai Ludwig count and lord of Zinzendorf and Pottendorf." His family lay next to him on either side. David read each stone silently.

Jane watched him, glad she'd been able to give him this gift.

Kinne stood slightly away from them, his hands folded in front of his body. His grey eyes held a look of approval.

At least one of us meets their standards, Jane thought.

When David stood back up, Kinne pointed up the hill. "Do you know the story of Zinzendorf's tower?"

"I don't," Jane said before David could answer. She moved to his side and took his arm again.

"Some say his first wife reported seeing a rainbow that ended on this spot. It was one of the couple's favorite walks. Others tell the story that the tower was built to shelter the Lord's Watch, those who keep the continual prayer."

They reached the bottom of the white structure. Kinne pulled out the skeleton key and opened the door. "Please, you go first," he said with a sweep of his hand.

Jane let David climb the spiral staircase ahead of her. They emerged on a circular walkway. Wind turbines dotted the crest of the hill toward Rennersdorf.

"Amazing," David breathed. He reached for her hand.

Kinne hung back by the door, finally giving them some privacy. But whatever it was David had wanted to tell her was forgotten. He moved around the walkway, Jane at his side. The city of Herrnhut lay before them, its orange roofs nestled amongst the evergreens and bare branches of trees. The fields stretched brown under the winter sun. The soft blue of mountains rose in the distance.

David shook his head and turned to her, his eyes brimming with tears. "Thank you."

"But I needed you to come."

"No, it's not just that." He pulled her to him, a tear escaping. "I can't tell you what it means for me to be here."

Jane nestled against him. His sides shook. She snuggled deeper into his embrace. Footsteps approached, then stopped and retreated. She heard Kinne climb back down the steps.

"I didn't realize it meant this much to you," she whispered.

He laughed, released her and searched his pockets for a handkerchief. He pulled out a blue bandana and wiped his eyes, then blew his nose with a honk. "I didn't either. It's just so moving—to see what I've heard about all my life."

She turned back to the view. "It's beautiful."

"To think this little town sent out missionaries all over the world."

"And now their descendants are coming back. I'm afraid I'm a disappointment, though."

David just squeezed her hand. They continued around the walkway until they reached the door again.

"Where did Kinne go?" David asked.

"He left us alone. I think we'll find him downstairs."

David started through the door, then stopped and gathered her up in his arms again. Gently, as if he were handling china. She turned her face up to him and their lips met. She started to pull back, but David followed her. Warmth flushed up her torso, and she leaned into him, kissing him deeply. Just as this town had welcomed their bedraggled ancestors, his arms were a safe refuge for her. Finally they pulled apart. Jane blinked, taken aback by her reaction.

David pushed a strand of her hair behind her ear. "Think we can shed our chaperone?"

She chuckled. "I'll think of something."

They walked down the steps, Jane tucked under David's arm, the narrow space pressing them together. At the bottom, Kinne greeted them. He locked the door.

She wondered how much he guessed. "We'd like to explore the headstones. Look for our family names. Then get some lunch before my meeting with Fraulein . . ."

"Pfeifer." Kinne supplied her name. "I will be working in the labyrinth behind the museum if you have need of me."

"Thank you," Jane said.

"I can't tell you how much I appreciate your help," David called to his retreating back.

Kinne turned around and regarded him with serious eyes. "Please understand my meaning. It is my pleasure to welcome the pigeons who find their way home."

David threw back his head and laughed.

Kinne smiled, then walked toward the town.

"Well, my dear, dear Jane. What shall we do now?"

They wandered the rows, reading the dates, finding more than a few names from their family trees. Even a few from David's late wife. He told her about his own family coming from here to Pennsylvania, then south to the Carolinas. So much like her own family's story. They stayed close to each other, Jane's arm in his, but didn't speak of it. If they pretended not to notice, they could enjoy the closeness. Jane pushed thoughts of her homelessness, of Lois's death, away. They could make believe this was really just a holiday.

A loud growl from Jane's stomach broke into their exploration of *Gottesacker*. They were standing on the far end of the men's side of the cemetery. Jane looked over toward the parking lot where they'd first spotted the old settlement. A silver BMW was parked by the side and a man in a long black coat stood by it. Her hand tightened on David's arm.

"What?"

"Over there," she whispered.

Just as David turned to look, the man raised his hand and made the "V" sign with his fingers, then touched his chest.

Jane slumped against David. "Oh, thank God."

"What?

"He's one of Knight's security team. He told me he'd use that sign so we could recognize them."

"Is that wise? Some spy might notice and use it, too."

"Well, I'm glad to know who he is."

"Let's go eat."

CHAPTER EIGHTEEN

Jane and David made their way to *Löbauer Straße* and walked arm in arm under the strings of Advent stars. Heavy clouds hung over the swelling mountain to the east. Halfway down the street, they found a restaurant that also advertised itself as a beer garden. Inside, dark paneled walls and sturdy tables greeted them. Both ordered the fish. Jane decided to try the strawberry blond ale, joking that it was close enough to her own shade.

Just as the waitress brought their beer, the man she'd seen across the field walked in. At least she thought it was him. Broad in the shoulders, heavy set, but moving like a boxer, the man glanced around. Finding no other customers, he walked to their table. "I thought to introduce myself. I am Ivar. I work for Mr. Knight." His smile revealed rather sharp canine teeth.

David perked his head up in interest, but Jane hesitated.

The man fished in his pocket and came out with a business card, which he handed to Jane. It was identical to the one Knight had given her when she'd done work for him in D.C. She turned it over and found an eye of Horus drawn on the back with the initials VK signed in an old fashioned script. Jane recognized his handwriting from the documents he'd signed while she watched.

Satisfied, Jane held out her hand. "Nice to meet you, Ivar. This is David."

Ivar acknowledged him with a nod. "There is a chance of snow. When do you plan to return to Prague?"

"We need to meet with the archivist, then we'll see." At David's questioning look, Jane explained. "Knight advised me to spend nights in the Prague suite if at all possible. Said it was safer."

"You must be careful, yes?" Ivar asked. A quick smile made this silver wolf a touch more friendly.

"We will." She held the card out to him, but he shook his head.

"For you."

The kitchen door opened and the waitress came through laden with two big plates. Ivar sat at his table studying the menu, acting the perfect stranger. How had he moved so quickly? The waitress put plates of steaming fish with tomatoes and rice in front of them. Jane's stomach growled approval. They ate in silence for a few minutes.

Once the intensity of her initial hunger subsided, Jane sat back, fork in hand. "So, what did we learn?"

"Right. Back to business." David picked up his beer, his eyes narrowing in thought.

Jane felt a pang of regret. Would the magic that had fallen over them be lost now? "Yeah, what do we know?" she repeated more softly.

"For one thing, Leinbach knows you've been kicked out of the house."

"No way." She slammed the fork down on the table. "How do you figure?"

"He used the past tense. Said Lois asked about the house you *were* living in. It wasn't a translation error. His English is excellent."

"Damn," she said, suddenly embarrassed.

"And he wasn't surprised about the Masonic connections.""Not at all," Jane agreed.

"Even Zinzendorf seemed to have ties to them."

"Really?"

"Sure, at Fetter Lane if not at university."

"I remember. That book on Blake said that Fetter Lane gave refuge to a network of ecumenical missionaries who worked with—" she tried to remember exactly "—Kabbalism, Eastern mysticism, alchemy—maybe more."

"Swedenborg was there for a while, too." David added.

"Who's he?"

"You're the Blake expert."

The waitress came and offered them dessert. Jane shook her head no. "I'm no Blake expert. I worked in oil and gas finance and associated politics most of my life."

"Oh, is that all?" David said.

Jane made a face at him as if she were in elementary school.

He smiled. "Blake followed Swedenborg's teachings for a while. He was a Swedish mystic."

"I remember reading about him, too. Mason?"

"Maybe Rosicrucian."

"So they were also at Fetter Lane?"

"The Rosicrucians and Freemasons have always been intertwined. The Masons kept the secrets of building, but the spiritual teachings of the two groups are pretty much the same. And the Templars have interconnections with both groups. They had a smithy there for armor and weapons repair."

"The Templars were the ones who protected pilgrims to the Holy Land, right?"

"Supposedly. They went to Jerusalem to excavate under King Solomon's Temple."

"Great, so they could have a whole ton of artifacts."

"Right."

"And the Moravians had ties to all these groups."

David took a long drink of his beer. "They did."

"I guess I never realized how esoteric many of the colonists were. Somehow I imagined they were like the Puritans—rigid and unimaginative. Sure you'd go to hell if you strayed from the straight and narrow."

"Lots of the founders were involved in mysticism." He paused for a minute, then snapped his fingers. "I just remembered. Ephrata was right next to Bethlehem."

"Okay, Mr. Encyclopedia."

"Sorry," David said. "Ephrata was a Rosicrucian settlement. Zinzendorf studied with them for a while, but ultimately they couldn't agree on some of the essentials of belief."

"So Zinzendorf associated with the Rosicrucians and Masons, if he wasn't one himself. The Knights Templar had a smithy at Fetter Lane. Any artifact Zinzendorf might have had could be anywhere. He sent missionaries all over and travelled a good deal himself."

"Zinzendorf could have brought it to Fetter Lane. Or gotten it there. Taken it to Bethlehem when he visited. Or gotten it from the Ephrata settlement."

"And from Bethlehem, it could have easily ended up in Salem." A heaviness settled into Jane's chest. "There are just too many options."

"Then there's Comenius. I never realized he knew Andrea," David said.

"I didn't understand any of that."

David sat back and stretched out his long legs. "Johann Valentin Andrea was one of the—well, you could say founders of the modern Rosicrucian movement."

"Great, one more link to investigate." Jane finished her ale.

"They claim that their organizations can be traced all the way back to Egypt. The Masons say the same."

"We might as well give up if we have to cover that much history," Jane sputtered. She studied her empty beer mug. How much of this was true? The Moravian connection to the mysteries seemed irrefutable, but Egypt? That sounded more like myth.

She voiced this doubt out loud. "Can they really trace their lineage all that far back?"

"That's what academics always say, but the same teachings can be found in Greece and Egypt, also Mesopotamia. Not to mention the sacred geometry."

"Sacred what?"

"Ge-o-me-try." David said it syllable by syllable.

"Miss Essig had some books on that, but I haven't read any yet. How can math be sacred?"

"A musician can ask such a question?"

"What do you mean?"

"Music is math. It's all about using the harmonies of nature, like the Golden Mean. When we build using these proportions, it creates a sense of peace. Certain chords and tones change people's brain waves."

"If you say so," Jane smirked.

He seemed genuinely affronted. "Never underestimate the power of music. They've done studies."

"Can you show me some of this research?" Jane poked his leg with her foot.

"I could show you, but it's a Masonic secret, so I'd have to kill you."

The joke fell flat. His words tore at the sore spot in her heart.

Lois. Why did they go after you?

What would she do without Lois's brilliance and sense of humor? Who really understood her better? They'd had similar lives. They'd helped each other through so much, then laughed about it years later. A tear ran down Jane's cheek. She shook her head against more.

"Sorry," David said quietly.

Jane fished for a tissue from her purse and blew her nose. "It still sneaks up on me."

"It's been less than a week." David reached over and put his hand on her forearm.

The warmth and steadiness helped. "Thanks."

"My pleasure."

Jane ignored the huskiness in his voice. His casual masculinity, his broad shoulders and lake blue eyes moved her. She'd steeled herself to being alone for a long time. If she let herself sink into him like she had on top of the tower, she wouldn't want to surface for a long time. They had work to do.

She made herself focus. "Tell me about Andrea."

"Johann Valentine Andrea claimed authorship of *Fama Fraternitatis RC* and *The Chymical Wedding of Christian Rosenkreutz*. Maybe *The Confessio*, too."

"The chemical what?"

David chuckled. "It really means alchemical. It's a spiritual allegory, the story of a pilgrim who is invited to a castle that is full of miracles. There he attends the wedding of the king and queen. It's the last of the three manifestos that brought the Rosicrucians into the public eye again."

Jane thought about this for a minute. "Leinbach said Frederick V was a Rosicrucian. I remember the Thirty Years

War was between the Czechs and Germans against the Catholic ruling class."

"The Habsburgs. They talk about this history in Masonic Lodge. Frederick came from the Palatine in what is now Germany. He married Elizabeth. Not Queen Elizabeth, of course, but the daughter of her successor—James I. The Protestants of Europe joined together to bring down the power of the Spanish throne and the Church. They failed because England didn't join in. James must have still harbored Catholic leanings."

"So our ancestors had to flee to escape death."

"Right. The Rosicrucians were very involved in these politics. The Catholics have always tried to suppress the metaphysical teachings of the Gnostics. The Rosicrucians felt the Catholics kept the true teachings from the people. They call the church their 'ancient enemy'."

"So you think the Rosicrucians go back that far?"

"Sure. Like I said, it's the same teachings. That humans can achieve awareness of God. Even unity with the divine."

"As in the Unity?"

David snorted. "If they were Gnostics, they've turned from that teaching now."

"Maybe in public."

David looked at her sharply. "You think there's a secret group within the church?"

"Like the OGMS?"

"Yeah, but . . ." He trailed off, lost in thought.

"Okay." Jane tucked a fly-away strand of hair behind her ear. "Here's what we know. The Rosicrucians were involved in the Thirty Years War. For now, we'll assume the Freemasons are practically the same people. Comenius was friends with one of the founders of the Rosicrucian Order, so can we assume he was influenced by the teachings?"

David nodded. "Zinzendorf also."

"Either of them might have received secret artifacts. Hidden them with someone."

"I do remember that after Heidelberg, Comenius served as pastor in Fulnek. He probably lived there the longest before he was forced into exile. If he had an artifact, perhaps it was left there."

"Or he might have taken it to Poland with him."

"Let's hope this archivist can help you narrow down the options," David said.

"Odd she only wanted to talk to me."

"I'll go check out Zinzendorf's house and the other buildings while you talk to her. Drop by the bookstore."

Jane said goodbye to David and stopped in front of the Saal, trying to collect her thoughts. Where should she start with the archivist and, more mysterious, why had she insisted on seeing only her? Did it have something to do with Leinbach's comment about her family being old and distinguished? Jane glanced at her phone again and read the archivist's name: Penelope Pfeifer. Could she be British? But the surname was German. Perhaps she'd married someone from here. Maybe she was from the Fetter Lane congregation or some other Moravian settlement in the British Isles.

Jane shook off this round of thoughts and walked to the archives, the large, white building matching the surroundings. Inside, a round woman with straw-blond hair and dressed in a blue pants suit greeted her in English that buzzed with the guttural consonants of German.

Not British then, Jane thought.

After the introductions, Fraulein Pfeifer led Jane up the stairs to her cramped office. Jane sat in a wooden, straight-backed chair perfect for any Puritan and glanced out the window at the bare winter branches. On second look, the room turned out to be an adequate size, but every nook and cranny was stuffed with piles of books and manuscripts. Framed photographs covered every inch of the walls depicting Moravian settlements in various parts of the world, Moravian churches, large group shots of Sunday Schools, and some portraits of famous Moravians—two of Anna Nitschmann. No less than five were of Comenius.

Of course, Jane thought.

"I'm sorry that I haven't had the time to do a family report for you and your . . ."

"Friend," Jane supplied, feeling suddenly self-conscious.

Fraulein Pfeifer gave an apologetic look. "I promise to send one if you'll give me an address."

"That's very kind of you, Fraulein—"

"Please call me Penelope. It's a joy to me to help people connect with their origins."

Jane smiled. "Did Herr Leinbach speak with you about our visit with him this morning?"

A shadow passed over her clear brown eyes. "He did. I apologize if we have broken any confidences."

"No, actually that makes things simpler, although I'd recommend that you keep our business quiet. There's been one death associated with this . . . " Jane rejected the word 'quest'. It sounded too much like searching for the Holy Grail.

"I'm sorry to hear that." Penelope's voice was full of compassion.

"Then you know that some group of fanatics thinks I have some kind of ancient artifact in my possession." Jane made a deprecating gesture.

Penelope sat back in her chair listening intently, so Jane marched on. "Herr Leinbach confirmed the long standing connections between the Freemasons and Rosicrucians. The Knights Templar had headquarters in Fetter Lane, so the possibilities for what this artifact might be are somewhat overwhelming."

Penelope's open, joyful face clouded over as Jane spoke, but she still remained silent.

"We're sorry to bring these questions to you, but I've been asked to find this artifact before it falls into the wrong hands." She sat back and waited.

Penelope looked thoughtful and sat silent for so long that Jane shifted uncomfortably in her chair. Then Penelope seemed to come to a decision. She leaned forward, placing her palms flat on her desk. "Anna Szeges asked me as head of the Sisters' House here in Herrnhut—"

Jane gasped and started to push herself out of her chair.

Penelope held up a forestalling hand. "—to convey to you her apologies for not beginning your instruction as soon as you arrived in the Choir House. None of us realized how quickly things would develop. Perhaps the time is upon us."

Jane realized her mouth was hanging open, so she closed it. She had no idea what Penelope meant by the time being upon us.

"Anna asked me to explain more about what happened in the church after the Count's death. To give you some idea how our group came into being."

"Um, I had no idea—"

"Only the people involved are aware the choirs are still functioning," she said. Before launching into her story, Penelope plugged in a British-style tea kettle and added tea leaves to a flowered teapot. She leaned down and pulled up a tray with two cups, sugar and a white creamer. At Jane's surprised look, she smiled and said somewhat conspiratorially, "I thought we should be comfortable."

Maybe she's British after all. Jane ran her hand through her hair, entirely out of her depth. Apparently the choirs were still functioning here in Herrnhut, but it was not something everyone knew. So a secret church did exist.

While the water heated, Penelope began to talk about Zinzendorf's death. "He passed into the more immediate presence of our Lord right here in Herrnhut, which was a blessing.""We saw his tomb," Jane said.

"The Count was a charismatic leader with a sweeping vision. Our church flourished under his guidance, but—" she lifted her shoulders "—as is often the case with such men, his death left us rudderless. The Unity grieved deeply, but needed to redefine itself in order to continue. Many of Zinzendorf's more unusual teachings were suppressed. Unfortunate in my view."

The tea kettle whistled and she poured water in the pot, a thoughtful look on her face before continuing. "Many did not want to relinquish the way of life we'd developed under his leadership. But the new church leaders were anxious to redeem our reputation among the other Protestants. A few stalwart followers of Zinzendorf and his son acted to save them.

"As you may have read, the activities in Marienborn and Herrnhaag came to the attention of other religious leaders of the time and their reactions were not favorable." Suddenly she looked up at Jane. "You do know about the *Sichtungszeit*, don't you dear?"

Jane shook her head.

"The Sifting Times?"

"Only a little."

Penelope poured out tea, sat back and took a sip, then studied Jane for a moment. Her expression was kindly, but thoughtful. She acted as if she had all the time in the world. "Anna told me you'd read some, but she wasn't sure how much. Zinzendorf was ahead of his time. He taught there was no shame in sex, that the savior had redeemed our bodies. Sexual union could lead to joining with the divine. The husband, of course, served as the Bridegroom for the wife during their time in the blue *kabinet*. There was a liturgy."

"So I've gathered," Jane said.

"While the Count traveled to missionary sites, he left Herrnhaag in the hands of his son, Christian Renatus, who perhaps took things too far. Christian and a fellow elder, Joachim Rubusch, were not content to wait for death to become the wives of Christ and experience the soul's feminine nature. They created a ceremony for single men in the Unity that declared them to be women. The two traveled to several villages and performed ceremonies."

Jane raised her eyebrows. "So that's what all the fuss was about."

"In part. They also intimated that physical gender didn't matter, that anyone could be . . . well, serve as the wife of Christ. Rumors of wild practices spread. Some were scandalized. Scathing articles were written on the Moravians, accusing the people in these two settlements of orgies and perversions."

"Perversions, as in homosexuality?"

Penelope nodded. "It is my belief that Christian Renatus was homosexual and this was his way of coming to terms with his desires."

"A challenge for his father."

She gave Jane a surprised smile. "Yes, our Count was ahead of his time, but not enough in the case of his son. They reconciled in the end, though."

"I'd like to read more about it."

"One of our historians in Bethlehem is writing a book on this period." She took another sip of tea before continuing the story. "Zinzendorf had been exiled from Saxony during this period because of his ecumenical stance. He wanted all Christians united, even met with Jews and Catholics. It was this last, plus his blood and wounds teachings, that made many suspicious. Some other Protestants thought members of the Unity were Catholic spies."

Jane snorted. "After all we'd been through?"

"Indeed," Penelope exclaimed. "During his exile, Zinzendorf lived in Ronneburg Castle and granted asylum to religious refugees of various stripes. Herrnhaag was built during this time. Marienborn also. But with the scandal, the settlement was broken up, the people sent elsewhere. After the Count's death, the church leaders pushed his more controversial teachings aside. We became more conventional Christians. But some of us did not abandon the way of life or practices he taught."

"So we have the OGMS?" Jane asked.

Penelope wagged her head back and forth. "Yes and no. It's more complicated than that, but for our purposes here, yes. Since we have kept the more mystical side of the *Unitas Fratrum* alive, it makes sense that someone connected to other metaphysical lodges might have taken an artifact into safe keeping."

Jane's head came up.

"I've spoken with Brother Frank."

Jane's eyes went wide. "My cousin?"

"Yes," Penelope said, "and he says there is no tradition of an artifact in your family."

Jane threw up her hands. She traced the rim of her now empty tea cup thoughtfully. "On the plane over, I read a novel by H.D."

"Yes, Hilda Doolittle. Famous poet, friend of Ezra Pound. Another Moravian. Which book did you read?"

"The Mystery."

Penelope smiled. "Apropos. She writes about the Sifting Times in that one and hints at them in *The Gift*."

Jane didn't know about this last novel. "H.D. claims that Goethe came to Herrnhut looking for esoteric writings. Is there any truth to that?"

Penelope nodded slowly. "Goethe did come to Herrnhut, but the archivist at the time did not share any materials from the OGMS's private library with him."

Jane leaned forward eagerly. "Which means you do have secret esoteric writings."

Penelope's smile was as enigmatic as the Sphinx and she was just as silent.

"Is there anything in them that would shed light on this quest?" Jane realized the word had popped out with no hesitation this time.

"We kept some of Zinzendorf's writings safe, what are called the Green Books. They contain accounts of his mystical experiences, his visions and prophecies."

"Prophecies?" Jane sat forward. "Comenius, too, from what I've heard."

Penelope raised a rather scholarly finger. "Comenius recorded the prophecies of other people. Now back to the Green Books. I can go through them and look for clues to our current dilemma. I'll let you know what I find."

"Thank you," Jane said. She slumped against the hard back of her chair, her head whirling. She could hardly keep up with it all.

"Zinzendorf worked on them a good deal while he was at Ronneburg. There he was surrounded by people from many places. A variety of religious refugees. Today it is a tourist attraction. It is unlikely anything is left hidden there, but—" she shrugged.

"I see," Jane said.

"Perhaps you would like to travel to the other Moravian settlements close by. Marienborn has been absorbed by modern development, but you might find Herrnhaag of interest. It was built using sacred geometry."

"David said something about sacred geometry at lunch."

"Reuter, who was an architect and a devotee of Christian Renatus, wanted to lay Salem out using the same plan as Herrnhaag, but his vision was not followed. I believe they used an eight-sided design instead."

A cold chill ran through Jane, pebbling her flesh. She sat forward. "Did you say eight-sided?"

"Uh, yes." Penelope forehead wrinkled. "Originally the church in Salem was to be in the middle with eight streets coming off it like spokes on a wheel. The choir houses would surround the Saal. But the site was too hilly. The design wasn't used."

"Not used?"

"No."

Jane's shoulders slumped.

"But Herrnhaag was built as a twelve-sided figure with the spring in the middle representing the Well of Life." Penelope offered this bit hopefully, studying Jane's face. "It is in ruins today, but the well is still there. Also the energy of the site is quite active, if one can attune to such things."

Jane smiled weakly.

Penelope seemed encouraged by this. "Herrnhaag is close to Ronneburg Castle if you feel you can travel safely."

"A friend from the corporate world—" Jane didn't want to reveal her connection to Valentin Knight just yet "—has lent me a body guard."

"Good. Visit these sites while I study the Count's words. When you return, I may have news."

☆ ☆ ☆

While Jane talked with Penelope, David went into the bookstore and looked first for Comenius. His books took up a whole section. He perused the titles, thumbing through the books on education, but quickly put them aside and settled on his theological works. The bookseller helped him decide on the most famous *Labyrinth of the World and Paradise of the Heart*, beautifully illustrated, and his last work *Bequest of the Dying Mother*.

"That one was written when he thought the church was dying," the bookseller said. "He wanted to leave his thoughts for whoever might stumble upon them in the future."

After she wandered back to her desk, David picked up a couple more. His German would definitely get a work out. When he reached the front desk, he realized he didn't have the cash to pay for these. His credit card wasn't in the best shape either. He shoved his wallet in his pocket and walked back toward the Comenius section.

Blast it, they needed these for their research. Knight was funding this escapade, wasn't he? Knight had created some make-work for Jane so he could pay her some ungodly sum of money. That's the way she'd explained it to him. He didn't know how much she had, but based on the way she casually doled out hundreds, he was beginning to imagine it was quite a bit. He decided to let Jane buy them. He turned back to the front and left the pile with the owner, telling her he didn't want to cart them all over.

"Of course, sir." She wrote his name on a slip of paper and waved as he left the store.

Just don't get used to all this luxury, he admonished himself.

Jane hadn't shown up yet, so he wandered back to the museum, wanting to confirm something he'd noticed that morning. The woman at the front desk nodded him through. He sought out the display on the Advent Star. The case had a piece of paper inside giving the history, that the star had first been put together by a geometry class in Niesky in the 1830s. Just as he'd always been taught.

He walked into the next room and found a display about aristocratic families who'd taken the risk of sheltering the Bohemian Brethren, keeping the church alive. Amidst the family crests he found one with a motif almost identical to the Advent Star. He bent low to check the date. 1525.

"There you are."

He turned to find Jane behind him, a little breathless, her cheeks flushed. "How'd it go?"

"Interesting." She looked toward the window. "It's getting dark. Let's check in. We can talk over dinner."

Outside, Jane looked at his empty hands. "I thought you were getting books."

He flushed a furious red. "I left a stack with the bookseller. There were a lot of them."

"Good," she said. "Let's get them first."

The bell on the door of the bookstore rang as they entered and the woman behind the desk looked up. "Ah, there you are," she said in German. She brought out David's stack. "I was getting ready to close."

"Do you have any in English?" Jane asked.

The woman guided them to a section and Jane quickly chose a few histories of the church and two about Zinzendorf. Toward the front, she picked up knickknacks for presents. She paid without hesitation.

David studied the bare wood flooring.

They left the bookstore and went in search of their hotel, which turned out to be on the same street in what was called the "Old Moravian House." The clerk handed them two keys with a smile.

"Let's get our bags," Jane said after signing for the rooms.

David tried to shift all the books into one hand.

"You can leave those here, sir," the clerk said.

"*Danke*."

They walked up the street. By the time they reached the car, snowflakes had started to fall. David stopped. "Let's just leave the car here."

Jane held out her hand for the keys. She drove to *Comeniusstrake* and took the corner too fast. The rear slid sideways.

David gasped.

"Southerners," she said.

"Like you're not one."

She parked near the hotel, more careful of the slick cobblestones. They dropped their bags in their rooms, which turned out to be adjacent.

"Should we just go back to the same restaurant? I'm too tired to go searching all over," Jane said.

"Yeah, let's walk rather than drive," David said.

Jane shook her head, but she was smiling.

While David ate sausages, Jane filled him in on what she'd learned.

"So Salem was not built on the eight-sided design, then," he said between bites.

"No."

"Too bad. That might have solved half the mystery."

"True." Jane smoothed the edge of the table cloth.

"But she said the OGMS exists here," David confirmed.

"This proves there's a secret group in the church."

He nodded, enjoying the rich food.

"She suggested we check out the other Moravian settlements while we're up here. Ronneburg Castle, Marienborn, and Herrnhaag." Jane took out her phone and poked some buttons, then handed it to him. A map to Herrnhaag glowed in greens and browns.

"It's almost 600 kilometers. Why not go to the castle first? It's closer."

"She said it was a tourist attraction now. I thought we could see Herrnhaag, then maybe go to the Castle later. Stay until after they close. Do a little poking around."

"Sneaky." David reached for his beer. "But that's a long way in this snow. It would mean an early morning."

"We can take more than one day doing it."

"What about Ivar?"

Jane waved a hand in dismissal. "He said he'd watch out for us."

David set down his beer and sat back, replete. Jane fished in her purse. She piled enough money on the table to cover their bill and more. He pushed away another twinge of guilt.

"Come on," Jane said. "I think we've done enough damage for one day."

"Damage?" David asked, his eyes flitting to the pile of Euros.

Jane pointed to the array of mugs on their table.

The muted light of the restaurant had erased the years, the fine wrinkles around her eyes and mouth. Her silver hair looked blond again. He yearned to kiss those lips as he had this afternoon. Yeah, he was drunk, but he was pretty sure he'd feel the same way in the morning. He should talk to her about the money thing. Instead, he said, "I wonder what your Uncle Pat would say if we told him what we learned today."

Jane burst out laughing. "'I told you so'. That's what he'd say."

David reached out his hand and pulled her to her feet. She was a bit tipsy herself. Outside, the Advent stars had all been lit. They shone brightly against the dark night, casting all under their golden, red-tinged magic. David pulled Jane close and she snuggled against his side. They headed for the hotel, walking back through time.

☆ ☆ ☆

Philip leaned into the shadows of the alley watching the two besotted lovers stroll beneath the stars hung above the road. The black matte finish on the motorcycle he'd rented did not reflect the lights. He was sure Jane hadn't seen him. It was proving to be a little tricky to stay hidden from Knight's man, but he'd managed so far.

Spencer, his contact with Henry Coche, had asked him only to observe and report. He secured his helmet and straddled his bike. His afternoon meeting with the Herrnhut archivist had been productive, though. He'd searched Jane and David's rooms while they ate, but found nothing of interest. He'd put a tracking device on the Fiat. He'd be thorough, but he was beginning to suspect Jane didn't know a damn thing.

CHAPTER NINETEEN

Jane stumbled down to breakfast just as the birds began to stir to find a brisk and cheerful woman whose voice was just a hair too loud for this early hour. Jane downed her first cup of hot, black coffee and a bit of the fog lifted. David arrived, his eyes red, his shirt a bit rumpled. Without a word, she poured him a cup of coffee and pushed it toward him. Perhaps all that beer had snuck up on them.

"Thanks." He added a rounded spoonful of sugar, then enough cream to turn the fortifying black liquid almost white.

She made a face.

"What?"

"Nothing." She picked up a wedge of toast and cautiously bit into it. Her stomach behaved, but when she eyed the piles of meat and cheese, bowls of granola and berries, and round slices of cucumber and tomato on the side board, she turned back to her dry toast. David showed no such hesitancy about breakfast. At the buffet, he loaded his plate with piles of sausage, cheese and black bread. He plopped two plates down and sat. He forked a sausage and took a big bite.

"You'd eat sausage morning, noon and night if you could," Jane said in a mild tone.

David stopped chewing, looking at her carefully. He swallowed. "I suppose."

Jane tried some marmalade on her toast and her stomach accepted this addition with no trouble. David shoveled more sausage into his mouth and chewed noisily. Jane's stomach gave a lurch.

"What's the matter?" David asked, his mouth still full.

Jane stood. "Too much beer, I guess. I need some air."

"I'll meet you outside," David nodded.

The snow lay piled on either side of the street. Jane recognized Kinne bent low with a snow shovel busily clearing the sidewalk. He straightened and called *guten morgen* to her, the words issuing out in a cloud of condensation. She waved back. The crisp air held a promise of more moisture.

David arrived and stomped his feet. He blew on his hands, creating a small cloud. "Cold."

Jane pulled up the weather report. "Clear skies in the morning, with—" she looked at David "—an 80 percent chance of snow in the afternoon."

"I'm going back to bed." He turned around. "Except we checked out."

"The roads will be clear." Jane tugged on his arm. "You'll see."

David let himself be pulled along to the car. "We could go back to Prague. There's probably less snow in the south," he suggested.

"I'll bet the roads will be clear," she repeated.

"It is a long drive to Herrnhaag. We might get stuck there overnight."

Jane got into the driver's seat and opened the guidebook they'd bought yesterday of sites associated with the Unity. "'Herrnhaag—the name means Lord's Grove'," she read aloud. "'Designed to express the Moravian ideal. Planned as the House of God. The end times were expected soon and Zinzendorf declared Herrnhaag would then be the residence of Christ'."

"Optimistic," David said.

"'In the center of the town stood a well representing the water of life. Twelve gates were planned to echo the New Jerusalem in Revelations'." She looked up. "Uncle Pat would love this."

David laughed. "And some Moravians thought the hippies were extreme."

Jane kept reading. "'Construction began in 1738 and it quickly became the fastest growing Moravian settlement. Seventeen buildings had been erected around the square by 1750. Christian Renatus became the leader of Herrnhaag, but his father objected to his interpretations of his teachings and called him to London where he was living at the time.

"'While many think the scandals of the Sifting Times were the cause of Herrnhaag's demise, the real reason was the new governor of the region, Gustav Friedrich Count of Ysenburg-Büdingen, who demanded the Moravians reject their beloved Count Zinzendorf and swear allegiance to him. They refused, and people began to leave the settlement even before Herrnhaag was finished'."

"I guess it was a different kind of end times than they expected," David said.

"'By 1945 only Zinzendorf's *Lichtendorf*—that's 'Castle of Light'—and the Brethren's and Sisters' House still stood. Today, most of Herrnhaag is gone, but the original *Licht Saal*'—that means Light hall—"

"I still speak German this morning," David quipped.

Jane raised her voice, ignoring him. "'—is still there, but in disrepair. The original well still sits in the middle of the square. For a while the settlement served as an artist community. Now a Moravian pastor lives in one house and runs a summer youth camp. The Austrian army used the stones from the God's Acre to pave a road'."

David wrinkled his nose. "Bummer."

She looked up from the book. "I'm not clear how long Zinzendorf lived in Herrnhaag. What are the chances that he left anything there?"

"Why did Penelope suggest you go?"

"She said something about the energy of the site still being active."

"Ah," David said.

"Tell me what you're thinking."

"Are you sensitive to earth energies?"

"To what?"

"That's what I thought."

Jane whacked him on the shoulder with the book.

"Certain places on earth are considered power spots, where the energies are strong and kind of —" he waved his hands in search of the right phrase "—enhance our own clarity."

She frowned at him.

"Like Stonehenge or the pyramids."

"They only had a well at Herrnhaag."

"It still could be a power spot. Lots of springs were considered sacred in the past."

"But we're looking for an artifact, not an earth . . . What did you say?"

"Power spot."

"Besides, that sounds too pagan for the Unity."

"Oh, they had a place in nature they used to worship in the Czech mountains called Chalice Rocks or Kalich. Big, round boulders. You can hike in and sit there."

"Elephant rocks."

David's face lit up. "Yeah, the pictures look like elephants."

"That's what they call those kinds of rocks in Colorado."

"Maybe we can go there," he said, his face wistful.

"So if there's a Moravian power spot, it would be there, not Herrnhaag."

"I suppose." David rubbed his hands together.

Jane started the engine and turned on the heater, but didn't put the car in gear. "I'm betting Zinzendorf didn't leave an artifact in Herrnhaag."

"If he ever had one to begin with."

"Penelope seemed to want me to see the sacred architecture, but it's twelve-sided, not eight," Jane said. "I didn't get the impression she knew about the prophecy. It was more like she was sending us off sightseeing while she reads the Green Books for clues."

"Let's go to the castle," David said, loosening his coat in the growing warmth. "It's closer. If the weather changes, we can drive on to Herrnhaag."

Jane punched directions to Ronneburg into the GPS and pulled out onto the road. David took a firm grip on the roll bar, but after a few kilometers, the roads shone black under the morning sun. His grip relaxed. They drove through rolling hills that turned from white to green as the sun grew warmer, chatting amiably, listening to the radio.

From what she could gather, the U.S. House of Representatives was gridlocked over the president's energy bill. Accusations, innuendo and hyperbole flew thick and fast. They found a BBC station. The reporter commented on some of the allegations in a dry, ironic tone. The president was a socialist, not an American, a terrible leader, getting secret kickbacks from the banks, from oil and gas, was responsible for the rising gas prices. Yada, yada, yada.

Jane was suddenly glad she wasn't in the States. She wouldn't have been able to resist calling a few old contacts trying to urge them to do the right thing for once in their miserable lives. Not that it would do any good. She knew she'd turn on the rounds of talk shows, get angry, depressed, then cynical in turn. In Europe, the debate was only one of many stories, not a twenty-four hour nonstop circus.

She noticed David glancing between the steering wheel and the road. "What?"

"I think I can drive now. Like you said, the roads are clear."

Jane let out a gusty laugh. "You're in love with this car."

"I do like it," he confessed.

Jane pulled over and they swapped places. She kept an eye out to see if any cars were following them and spotted a silver BMW twice. Probably Ivar tagging along. She glanced around at the peaceful countryside, finding it hard to imagine danger.

They passed the small town of Lagenselbold, then followed the directions through winter grasslands, the dark soil showing stark against the remaining snow. They reached Neuwiedermuss and saw Ronneburg Castle on the adjacent basalt hillside, white walls faded to grey in places with the ubiquitous red roofs of the area. A boxy, squared tower rose over the complex. David pulled into a parking area near the pedestrian entrance. Cars filled the lot and Christmas music spilled from the courtyard.

"Why's it so crowded?" Jane asked.

"It's Saturday."

"Really? I'm losing track of the days."

"Looks like they have a Christmas market," David said.

"Good. We can disappear into the crowd."

They locked the car and made their way past a sign for the Burg Restaurant and Café to the gate of the castle guarded by men dressed in Templar outfits.

"Fitting," Jane mumbled to David.

She bought tickets and they emerged into the stone courtyard with windows running up the sides of the buildings framed in ruddy brown wood. A tour had just started, so they tagged along toward the back, blending in. The first stop was a pedal-powered well. The guide rattled off how deep it was, when it had been dug, while Jane and David looked around, getting their bearings. Next came the kitchen with an enormous sixteenth century stove. Racks on the wall held wooden spoons and metal strainers. A long rough-hewn table sported an array of cooking implements that Jane thought resembled torture devices. Wooden wine barrels of descending sizes nestled one inside another sat against one wall. A woman dressed in a period costume demonstrated cooking techniques, but her apron was suspiciously white.

"It's a living museum," David said, "just like Old Salem."

"That might make it more difficult to check the place out," Jane murmured.

"Unless we get in costume."

Jane shot him a look. "Don't you think they'd notice new faces?"

"It's Christmas." David shrugged. "Probably lots of new faces."

The group headed off to see the apothecary.

"Come on." Jane headed up a set of spiraling steps, David on her heels. On the next floor, they slipped into what looked like an empty room. Jane opened her mouth to speak, then noticed a bunch of people standing against the window.

"The armory," David exclaimed in delight and walked over to a display of suits of armor. One shiny knight leaned against a long sword with a wavy blade. David pointed to the helmets. "Nobody would recognize us in these."

"Yeah, but we couldn't move, either. Does the brochure say anything about where Zinzendorf's family lived while he was here?"

David skimmed, then shook his head. "Who's to say he left it in their rooms. Could be in the dungeon."

"Or maybe he didn't have anything," the new voice had a trace of a Russian accent.

Jane jumped back. David grabbed for her hand. Together they crept out of the armory to find Ivar's bulk blocking the hallway.

"You want to explore, how about we do it together?" he said, a scowl on his face.

"Uh, sure," Jane said.

He pointed a beefy finger in her face. "You make my job hard."

"Sorry," she mumbled.

"You want to wander around a drafty castle now?"

David came to her rescue. "Count Zinzendorf lived here for a while when he was exiled from Saxony. We thought we'd look around. See if we find any clues about the artifact."

"Count Zinzendorf is important in this quest?" he asked.

Jane crooked a shoulder. "Maybe."

Ivar scowled, then stepped back and gestured for them to go ahead of him. "I will go with you."

Jane had to admit the addition of Ivar with his defensive linebacker physique did make her feel more secure. She led on, going through bedrooms decorated in various periods, but nothing caught her eye. They headed down another set of stairs to a long hallway with windows. Inside each pane hung a crocheted snowflake or a stained glass angel. They took the next set of stairs and emerged into a cellar with a stone floor. A few barrels sat around for effect. Silence reigned, except for faint Christmas carols. The crowds seemed to have been drawn outside to a reenactment in the field.

"Good," Jane said. "This is a likely spot to hide something. Look for any sign of Moravians or the Count."

Ivar scratched his black beard. "What would that look like?"

Jane heaved a sigh. "You guard the entrance."

She and David went to different corners of the expanse and poked their noses into the nooks and crannies. All Jane found were old, round stones, damp corners and around one corner, rows of wine racks, mostly empty.

"Jane." David's muffled voice called from across the room.
She followed the sound.

"Over here." His head emerged from a kind of closet. "Look at this." He pointed to a stone that seemed to have a design set in it.

Jane peered over his shoulder, but couldn't make it out. "Do you have a flashlight?"

David pulled out a matchbook.

"You smoke?"

"Have you seen me smoke?" He sounded exasperated. "I have a thing about collecting matchbooks from places I go."

She tried to light a match, but it flared, then died out. The second did the same. "Here, let's trade places."

Jane knelt in the dark closet. David succeeded in lighting a match and held it close to the wall. The white points of the Advent Star caught the light. She reached down and ran her finger over it. It had been set onto the stone. Four long rays and four shorter ones. Jane took a sharp breath and pulled out her pendant. The designs were identical.

"Do you see it?"

"Yes." The two tried to fit side by side in the small space and began pushing at the stones to see if anything shifted, but they mostly succeeded in bumping against each other.

"Okay, you come out and let me try," David said.

Jane backed out of the space and stood up. This time her match lit and she held it near him. David pushed at the stone with the star on it, then began systematically to work his way around the adjacent stones. A draft of wind blew out the flame. She opened the matchbook again.

"Great, we're out of matches."

"Use this." Ivar handed her a small flashlight. She switched it on and pointed it at the stones David was working on.

"Ah, let there be light," he said.

Ivar grunted and moved back to the cellar door.

"I think I found a latch."

"Where?"

"Here, under the first stone on the floor."

"Does it open?" David took out a Swiss army knife, inserted the long, thin blade between the wall and the bottom stone and worked it back and forth, his tongue caught between his teeth, his eyes focused inward. Jane heard a soft click. David gave out a satisfied sigh.

"What do you see?"

"Patience. I haven't even opened it yet."

Jane shone the beam down. David pulled on a small, rusted circle of iron. The stone resisted, then gave way with a loud, groaning noise.

"Shhh," Jane hissed in his ear.

He laughed. "It's the floor, not me."

The thin rectangle of stone pulled back to reveal a hollowed out space beneath floor level. David reached up for the flashlight and shone it all around the box. Smooth stone reflected the light dully. The space was empty.

"Damn," he whispered.

"Maybe there's another compartment," Jane said.

David leaned in. The rock in the empty space seemed harder, perhaps basalt. Nothing budged.

"Let me," Jane said, realizing it was irrational, but just as someone will push the elevator call button even if it's lit, she needed to check for herself. None of the stones shifted. The compartment was clean and neat, the sides smooth, the joints tight. She reached for her camera and took a few pictures.

"Have you got anything to measure it with?" David asked.

"No, maybe Ivar does." Just as she turned to call him, she heard a surprised grunt, then the heavy thud of a body falling to the ground.

They froze.

Jane could barely make out the sound of someone walking toward them.

David pushed the stone lid back in place and pulled Jane back toward the empty wine cellar. They hugged the shadows. Something skidded across stone. Something metal. They heard a muffled curse. Jane felt David searching his pockets, then a sharp exhale. He probably left his knife on the floor.

The two ran toward the back. Jane headed for the wine racks, but David pulled her toward the left. She shook her head. She didn't want to hide down here and get stuck, but he insisted. He groped on the wall, then pushed.

Sunlight blinded her for a moment. The smell of roast pork filled her nostrils. Christmas music and crowd noise sounded loud in her ear. They emerged into the midst of the festival, ran a few steps into the middle of a group of tourists. David pushed their way through the group, apologizing as they went. The courtyard opened up and they ran toward the gate.

"But what about Ivar?" Jane asked.

David stopped by one of the men dressed as a Templar Knight. "I think there's some guy in the wine cellar who's sick. He might need help."

The man pulled out a radio and began to issue orders.

David and Jane slipped out while he was focused, then ran to their car. David took the driver's seat and pulled out of the parking lot. He drove carefully until they were a few hundred yards away, then floored it, tires squealing as he navigated the curving country road.

"Oh, my God," Jane said, "What just happened?"

"I think that guy found us."

"Philip?"

"If that's his name. Where are we going?"

Think! Jane forced herself to take a few deep breaths. "Prague. We should head back to Knight's suite. From there we can find out if Ivar was . . ."

"Hurt?" David asked.

"Or worse."

David looked over at her. "A dead body would create too many questions. He probably just knocked him out."

"Yeah, and we just left him lying there."

"Better one down than three," David said softly. "Now, compute a route for us. We shouldn't take the first one or two that pop up. We should go a different way."

Jane busied herself with the GPS, willing her hands to stop shaking, trying not to imagine that a second person had died. David was right. Philip wouldn't kill if he didn't have to. At least, she'd believe that until proven wrong.

But why did they have to kill Lois?

After a while, Jane started to relax a little. No cars followed behind them on this winding back road. At this rate, they wouldn't make it to Prague until the early morning hours. At least the snow had held off.

She switched on her phone and started studying the pictures. "What do you think was inside this space?"

"Who knows. I can get a better idea when we can upload these to a bigger screen. But that was amazing. An Advent Star and a hidden compartment."

"Maybe Count Zinzendorf did have an artifact."

Then the first snowflake fell and David pulled the car over. "What now?"

Jane wiped the smile off her face and opened her door. "I'll drive," she said.

"But." He frowned as more flakes turned the windshield white. "You sure?"

"It's just a little snow. The roads are still clear." She got out and walked around the car, but David hadn't budged. She opened his door. "Come on. It's perfect. Feels like Christmas is really coming."

He climbed awkwardly over the stick shift and buckled up.

Jane drove in silence, listening to the slap of the windshield wipers. After a few miles, she glanced over at David, who sat slightly forward, one hand clinched on the roll bar, knuckles white.

"Relax," Jane said. "I learned how to drive in snow while I was living in Colorado."

He gestured toward the white swirling over the pavement. "This doesn't make you nervous?"

She laughed. "It isn't even sticking yet. It's nothing like when I got trapped on top of a mountain in New Mexico. Complete white out and I drove my Acura straight into a snow bank. I thought that was the end of me."

"What happened?"

"The trucks came along and pulled me out. Sent me on my way. Just laughed at how grateful I was. Believe me, this is easy."

David eased back in his seat.

"I bought a Pathfinder as soon as I got back to Denver."

He stiffened. "But this is just a sports car."

"And we're not in the Alps. Just gentle rolling hills. Besides, it has front wheel drive."

"I bow to your experience."

But she noticed that he was still holding on to the roll bar. The snow picked up, falling thick and fast. She pointed to the backseat where their pile of books still lay. "We can do some reading in the morning," she said. "See if we can learn anything more."

David slapped the side of his head. "I completely forgot. James got me connected to a Masonic friend of his. He's supposed to give us the metaphysical tour of Prague tomorrow."

"What time?"

"I planned for ten. I didn't think we'd go farther into Germany. We could meet him in the afternoon."

"Good, then we can do some research in the morning. You can read and I'll go online. We'll see what your friend knows."

She drove in silence for a while.

"I almost forgot." She poked David's arm, keeping her eyes on the road. "You saw something in the museum."

"Oh, yeah. There was a display case in the third room of the museum dedicated to the Advent star."

"The star again. I loved it as a kid." Jane fingered her pendant, then tucked it under her sweater. "First created in Niesky by a boy's geometry class, right?" She didn't want David to think she was entirely ignorant of Moravian history.

"That's what I'd always been told, but that was in the 1830s."

"Zinzendorf was before that, too. And he must have put that star in the stone. Or some Moravian."

"This case in the museum had a drawing of the Advent star, but the date was 1525."

"So it existed before, but didn't get produced for Advent until the nineteenth century?"

"Maybe, but there's more. In another room I saw a display of coats of arms from the aristocratic families who helped the Unity in Bohemia and Moravia."

"I missed that."

"One family crest used the Advent star. They were called the star family. The surname was Grubovsky."

Jane stared at David, who frantically pointed to the snowy road.

"That's my grandmother's maiden name," Jane said. "But that doesn't make sense. My father's family came from Alsace. We're Germans."

"That's the male side of the family. Have you tracked your grandmother's side?"

"No."

And I call myself a feminist. Jane shook her head.

"I did some research on my own ancestry a while back. Two women put together family trees for many Moravian families. They said most Moravians are at least distantly related since the population was relatively small then and we married inside the church when possible."

"So you're telling me some branch of my family were aristocrats somewhere in the Czech Republic? That they sheltered the Brethren on their estate?" The snow was falling fast and thick now. Jane splashed the windshield with some fluid and increased the speed of the wipers, hoping David didn't notice that the roads were covered.

Luckily, he was still focused on his discovery. "It's possible."

"Leinbach kept referring to my family. He seemed deferential. This might explain it."

"There's more."

"What?"

"I remember hearing somewhere a conspiracy theory about *die Sterne Familie*."

"Sterne family?" Jane asked.

"It means 'star family'."

"What's the story?"

"I can't really remember," David said. "Maybe it was James who told me."

"Great. I find out the church I grew up in was hip-deep with the Rosicrucians and Freemasons, maybe even the Templars. Zinzendorf had a secret compartment marked by a star. Now you're telling me my family was aristocratic in the past and now is the subject of some conspiracy theory. And you can't even remember what it is?"

"I can go online when we get back to the hotel." David leaned against the passenger door, away from her.

Jane started to hand him her cell so he could search the web now, but she stopped herself. Suddenly she'd had enough. Unknown Blake paintings, sacred sex, Freemasons, every variety of mystics, and ancient artifacts. The sound of Ivar's body falling onto the stone. What next? That her family secretly ruled the world? If that was true, she wished they'd mentioned it to her when she was younger.

They fell silent. The only sounds were the wipers thudding back and forth, the purr of the engine. "Let's take the easiest route back. With this weather, we should be on the highways."

"Suits me," David said. He started punching in new directions. Soon the GPS announced a turn and they merged onto the main highway back to Prague. The road gleamed wet and black under the streetlights, but was otherwise clear.

Jane rolled her shoulders back, willing herself to relax. David was just trying to help. He wasn't anything like Uncle Pat who took his conspiracy theories as gospel. David knew the difference between wild conjecture and facts. At least, she thought he did.

Jane looked over at him. He had his head propped on his right hand, his elbow on the arm rest, looking out at the snow. At least he wasn't holding on to the roll bar for dear life. Being aristocrats was one thing, but another conspiracy theory?

"Let's get some gas," she said and steered the Fiat into the next service station. She stopped at the pump and got out, then pulled the hood on her jacket over her head. She reached for the nozzle.

David opened his door and stood up, blinking against the falling snow. "I'll get something hot to drink. Want coffee or hot chocolate?"

Jane didn't answer.

✯ ✯ ✯

David ordered in German, but the woman behind the counter spoke back in Czech. So they'd already made it over the border. He pointed to the signs on the wall behind the cash

register. The woman nodded and busied herself with cups. He
peered out the window at Jane, trying to puzzle out her shifting
mood. They'd spent a magical afternoon starting with that kiss
at the top of Zinzendorf's tower. She'd been bright and happy
as they walked through the *Gottesacker* finding family names.
He still felt the outline of her body against his side. The taste of
her mouth lingered on his lips. They'd been a close-knit team
running out of the castle, getting on the road. She'd even
laughed darkly at the adventure. But now some invisible wall
had slammed down between them.

He paid for their gas and cocoa, squinting at the unfamiliar
money, and walked back to the car. She sat in the car waiting.

He put one drink on top of the roof and opened the door.
"Hot chocolate for the lady."

"Thanks." She smiled weakly.

David got in and buckled his seat belt one-handed. "It's
starting to look a lot like Christmas." He sang the phrase.

She pulled the sports car back onto the freeway without
answering. David studied her out of the corner of his eye. The
dashboard lights softened her face, easing the anger, the grief
and confusion away, revealing the girl he'd loved in high
school. "I'm sorry this is so hard on you."

Her mouth tightened as if to deny his observation, then she
shook her head. "I'm supposed to be tough, you know. Take
care of myself. I'm not used to . . ." Her voice strangled.

David reached out and patted her shoulder. "I'm here to
help, remember?" But she just shook her head. He withdrew
his hand and leaned back, watching the fields fill up with snow.
For some reason, he wasn't nervous about driving in it
anymore. They hadn't slid once.

Jane's phone rang and she grabbed it. "Yeah?"

She listened, then heaved a sigh of relief, her shoulders
falling. "It's Ivar. He's alive."

She listened for about a minute. "Okay. See you then." She
clicked the phone off.

"What did he say?"

"He said he was only out for a few seconds. That he stopped
Philip from following us." She looked at David. "Said Philip
will be laid up for a few days."

David felt a surge of satisfaction, then wondered at his response.

"He said we did the right thing. His words were 'I'm glad you left me. I'm a professional'."

The two burst out laughing.

"He told me to go back to the hotel and he'd check with us in the morning."

"Why did it take him so long to call?" "Said he had to shadow Philip for a while. Make sure where they took him." Jane chuckled, shaking her head. "He said these Templar Knights came running in and scooped up Philip."

"I wonder what he thought."

"Serves him right for posing as Philip LeBelle. The Templars finally got their revenge."

Relaxed now, David started to hum *Good King Wenceslas*. He sang the third line. "When the snow lay round about, deep and crisp and even." Jane joined him on the next line, taking the melody. He fell into harmony. They finished the carol, humming when they didn't know the words, which was more often than not.

"When is the Feast of Stephen?" Jane asked.

"Don't know," David said.

He started to sing *Hark the Herald Angels Sing*. Jane added a beautiful soprano descant at the end. They sang more carols, running through the more popular ones. David started on the lesser known Moravian Christmas hymns, Jane joining in when she remembered the words, humming harmony when she didn't.

Music healed all. The magic came back.

Jane made good time on the highway. Back in Prague, she turned in the Fiat. They ran up to their suite and dropped off the books and overnight bags, then decided that since Philip was out of commission, they could go out. They walked up the streets hand in hand to Old Town Square where they stood for the first time in front of the Jan Hus statue in the center. The tall form looked like it had been sprinkled with powdered sugar.

David squeezed her hand. "Thank you for this."

She smiled, snowflakes in her lashes. "I'm glad you came."

They found a restaurant on the square where he ate steak and drank the best beer he'd ever tasted. Across the flagstones, the Hus statue grew white and heavy with snow. They finished with chocolate fondant, feeding each other spoonfuls. No words. No need. The old flame had rekindled.

Back in their hotel suite, Jane dropped her purse next to the sofa and massaged her neck. "We had quite a day."

He reached out for her, but she gave him a chaste kiss on the cheek. "I'm beat. See you in the morning."

Disappointed, David sat in his room looking out at the river and the lights on the castle above. He could almost hear Brian's voice whisper, "Patience, old chap. Give her time."

CHAPTER TWENTY

The next afternoon, David and Jane met their guide, Václav Myska, in the hotel lobby. David recognized him from the picture James had forwarded. He made the introductions and Václav's hand swallowed his in a hearty handshake. The man had a face made of rough plains, like a granite mountainside. Size notwithstanding, he moved with the deftness and grace of a quarterback. But he drove like a grandmother in his rattletrap Škoda.

"For the metaphysical tour, there is much to see. But we start where it all began," he told them. Then only smiled mysteriously when they asked for more information.

They arrived at a park. The trio walked past three tall dolmens leaning against each other to form a rough triangle.

"The Devil's stones." Václav's voice boomed.

"Where does that name come from?" Jane asked.

"Anything that predates Christianity gets labeled like that," Václav explained. He took a few more steps, then waved his arm in a gesture that took in the cathedral, graveyard and gardens. "Vyšehrad, the birthplace of Praha." He used the Czech name of the city.

"This ancient hill was center of power of the Přemyslid dynasty," he continued. "King Krok had three daughters, *Kazi, Teta, and Libuse. Princess Libuse* had vision of the seven hills of Prague growing into a marvelous city. She married commoner, Přemysl. Their dynasty lasted four hundred years. We think her mother of Praha."

He led them into the gardens, the beds covered in last night's snow. The paths steamed in the afternoon sun. "We should walk around hilltop in silence. See what we pick up." He pointed to his forehead, suggesting inner sight.

They began to stroll around the promenade that overlooked the Vlatava River. David tried to be receptive to the environment, but his mind kept running through the research they'd done that morning over a lavish breakfast served to them in the room. He compared that meal to his usual—and found his usual severely lacking. He was going home spoiled.

They confirmed what they'd learned in the last two days, reviewing the lives of both Comenius and Zinzendorf. David's search through the internet about the Star Family turned up a multitude of claims. They were a cluster of billionaires who claimed to trace their lineage back through the centuries, some said to the time of Jesus, others to the early Egyptian pharaohs. These families passed on esoteric knowledge from the deep past. Others claimed the cabal secretly ruled the globe, choosing world leaders and giving them marching orders. The wilder contentions had them performing blood sacrifice to maintain their power. The most extreme maintained they had extraterrestrial origins.

Jane had laughed most of it off, comparing it to the crazy claims she'd discovered about the 24/7 prayer movement. "Honestly, David, these people are just kooks. They take the metaphysical teachings literally, just like the Bible." She'd gone back to reading, then looked up at him from her perch near the window. "Don't you think that if my family were that powerful I would have known about it? Especially when I was working in oil and gas finance. Now, those are the people who secretly run the world."

He looked over at her now. She walked slightly behind Václav, her gaze sweeping the vistas. That invisible shield was up again, keeping him just on the other side of complete spontaneity.

Then it hit him. His vision darkened, then narrowed. He stumbled and caught himself before he sprawled onto the path. Václav led him to a bench. As soon as he sat back and closed his eyes, he saw in his mind's eye a stooped, gnarled old woman dressed in black. Soot marked her face and hands. She couldn't be more than four and a half feet tall. The old crone gestured for him to take her hand. Her grasp sent a shiver of cold through him, the wintry damp of a cave. Flames danced on the walls and people surrounded the fire, hands linked. A foreign chant rose with the smoke.

The old woman pulled David forward to a figure sitting above the circle on an outcropping of rock. She sat in shadows and her hair was dark. He couldn't see her face. Her hand reached out from the nest of her black clothes and pulled out a large dagger. The jeweled hilt gleamed and winked in the firelight. She whispered something to him, her voice like the stirrings of dried leaves in a puff of wind. David couldn't understand her words, but her meaning rang clear in his mind.

Thank you for your sacrifice.

Before he could even wonder what she meant, she plunged the dagger into his heart.

David screamed in pain. His hand flew to his chest.

"What?" Jane's voice came from far away.

David shook his head.

"What did you see?" Václav asked.

"See?" Jane frowned at their guide.

David opened his eyes to the snow-covered hill of Vyšehrad, and the pain stopped abruptly. His fingers fumbled at his chest. There was no tear in his coat or the shirt beneath. He opened his shirt. A tiny red line ran over his heart. It had not been there this morning.

"Oh, my God," he mumbled.

"What happened?" Jane asked.

He relayed his vision to them.

"Excellent." Václav murmured. "Most excellent."

"Some old hag stabs him in the heart and you say 'most excellent'?" Jane's face flushed red.

"He has been marked by the ancient ways. The Celts did their ceremonies on this spot."

David pressed his chest again. They had looked like Celts.

"His sacrifice has been received. Your quest will be successful."

"Quest?" Jane asked. "Nobody said anything about a quest." Her eyes cut to David, then back to Václav.

"You may not know, but the guardians—" Václav held up a finger "—they know."

"Jane," David said, trying to capture her attention, "Václav knows a great deal about Prague. Perhaps—"

Jane reached down and hauled David to his feet, interrupting him. They walked a few steps away from Václav, who obliged by turning his back. "But it's dangerous. I don't want any more people getting hurt." David took a breath to speak, but she pushed on. "And how do we know we can trust him?"

"James recommended him. They're old friends. He would know if Václav had any questionable connections."

"How can you be so sure? Lois had ties to the CIA and other intelligence organizations. She thought she could trust her contacts, but obviously she missed something."

David cupped the back of her head. She started to pull away, but stopped. "He knows more about the metaphysical history of Prague than anyone. If there are secret artifacts our ancestors took out of here, he's our man."

She stared at him for a full minute. "Okay, but when did you start . . . you know, having visions?"

David chuckled. "My mom used to see things. I got it from her."

Jane shook her head.

"It's true." David released her. "Takes some getting used to, I imagine."

"No, it's not that. I believe you." She studied him for a moment. "That's what bothers me." She smiled and his heart gave a lurch.

He walked back to Václav. "We are on a bit of a quest, actually."

Václav nodded sagely. "The guardians know."

Jane walked up beside David and took his hand. He tipped his head toward her. "Jane has just discovered an old family story. Her ancestors may have taken some spiritual artifact with them when they sailed to America."

"From Praha?"

"Maybe," Jane said. "Both our families were Hussites."

Václav's face darkened before he caught himself. Then he pasted on a broad smile. "I see. Americans coming back. Searching for your roots."

"Something like that," Jane said. "Even though my father's family is from Alsace, my mother's line comes from south Moravia. But the artifact could have come from any member of the Bohemian Brethren."

Václav shook his head. "I'm not familiar with it."

"The church the Hussites formed after Jan Huss was martyred."

"Ah, called *Unitas Fratrum* now. Comenius."

"Yes, Comenius was a bishop," Jane said.

"He was great mystic," Václav declared.

Jane stared at him.

"So we've discovered," David said, squeezing Jane's hand.

"You know story of the Spear of Destiny?" Václav asked.

"Yes, the Hussites threw it into the river after they defaced the cathedral, right?" David answered.

Jane jerked her head around in surprise.

"So story goes. Let's go see tomb." Václav looked at David. "Perhaps you see something else."

They walked down the hill toward Přemysl's old castle that now housed the Basilica of Saint Peter and Saint Paul. On the way, Václav gave them some background so they could understand the story in context.

In the fourteenth century, Charles IV made Prague the center of the Holy Roman Empire when he became the emperor. Charles collected a large number of alchemists and mystics of all kinds. Even consulted with the Jewish Kabbalists, highly unusual in his time. He attracted intellectuals and built a university. Brought in architects and artisans and built a great city, grounding it in sacred geometry.

Jane squeezed David's hand at this.

"He also collected relics. He brought body of Longinus from Rome."

"Who was he?" Jane asked.

"The soldier who stabbed Christ in his side while he hung on cross."

"Talk about adding insult to injury," Jane said.

"On the contrary," David interjected. "It was a common practice. Meant to hasten the inevitable. Crucifixion alone was a torturously slow death. Although your standard Bible will claim Jesus was already dead by then and the rush of blood and water from the side wound—" he emphasized these words "—was a miracle."

Václav nodded his agreement. "Since then, many myths have sprung up about spear. The most well-known is the story Hitler believed. That whoever possesses it is invincible."

They arrived at the entrance to the cathedral. They paused before three sets of carved, black doors, topped by double stone arches. The west door was open for tourists.

"Hussites destroyed many beautiful windows and art work during their rampage." Václav glanced at their faces in case they were offended. "As you know, they opposed relics. At this cathedral, they tore the body of Longinus from his sarcophagus and threw it in Vlatava River. Along with Spear of Destiny." With a flourish, he invited them into the cathedral.

Jane paid their admittance and then joined them behind the last row of pews. The sun streamed through the stained glass windows on the western wall, lighting the dark interior in streaks of rose, blue and gold. Intricate murals covered the walls in rich, dark colors. Paintings of saints hung from the pillars on either side of the pews.

"It's beautiful," Jane breathed to David.

Václav led them toward a corner chapel.

"Look." David pointed to a lion holding a broken sword.

"This commemorates defeat of the Winter King," Václav said. At Jane's frown he said, "Frederick V and Elizabeth."

"Right." Jane paused in front of the statue. "Just think. This is where it all happened."

"And in this corner is where our story unfolded. The crowds threw tomb into river, but the sarcophagus floated. It was restored to church."

"And the Spear?" David asked.

"Many think it was lost in Vlatava. Others claim it was never in tomb. There are many stories about the location of famous Spear of Destiny." Václav paused to gather their attention. "My favorite is that it served as time pointer in the famous astrological clock built by Master Hanus."

"No kidding," David said. He smiled at Jane. "Well, I never."

"But it was stolen from there. There are many stories."

"How long was it?" Jane asked.

Václav thought for a minute. "I'd say just about a meter."

David looked at Jane. "About three feet."

"That sounds like a match."

"A match?" Václav asked.

"To a hidden compartment we found in Germany," David said.

"A place associated with the *Unitas Fratrum*," Jane added.

"Interesting," Václav said.

Jane walked toward the marble sarcophagus covered in equal armed crosses, out of ear shot. David stepped closer to Václav. "But what does the lodge say?"

"That Spear was taken out of Prague to protect it."

"Where?"

Václav's smile was enigmatic. Then he relented. "Somewhere in Germany."

"But it was in a museum in Austria when Hitler took it." This from Jane, who had returned and overheard the last bit.

"A common belief," Václav conceded. "But I ask you this. If Hitler possessed Spear of Destiny, how could he have been defeated?"

"What if the Hussites didn't throw it in the river at all? What if that was a cover story? Maybe they took the Spear to get it away from the Habsburgs and the Church. Perhaps they hid it on an estate somewhere." David's eyes found Jane's.

Václav nodded his head, enjoying their repartee. "Then why were they driven from Praha? Why was Winter King defeated?"

Jane jumped in. "But you're both assuming the legend is true."

Václav turned to her. "If your ancestors took Spear of Destiny to America, they must have come into its possession later."

"I guess that's possible," Jane said. "Except my ancestors rejected relics, as you pointed out."

"Some did, but others were trained in mysteries," Václav objected. "Let's not forget Comenius."

"So we've discovered," Jane repeated.

"And during Charles IV's rule, Prague was filled with sacred objects. Perhaps your ancestors took something else." He glanced at his wrist watch.

David noticed the cathedral had darkened. The sun was going down.

"Tomorrow we explore more possibilities. Tomorrow we go to Charles's castle."

Jane and David wandered up to the square and found a vegetarian restaurant across from Kafka's home where they ate a delicious meal. They stood in front of Hus, then wandered around the Christmas bazaar for a while, buying trinkets and handmade crafts for gifts. As the booths started to close up, they meandered back to the hotel, the Christmas lights of shops and booths lighting the dark night.

Up in their room, Jane checked the computer and found an email from Penelope Pfeifer. "David," she called. "I heard from the archivist in Herrnhut."

"What's she say?"

Jane clicked the link and read it out loud.

I hope your trip to Herrnhaag was enjoyable. Will you be able to travel to Castle Ronneberg? Please let me know what you think of these places.

I'm sorry to report that the Count's comments on his visions are inconclusive. He speaks of his certainty that Christ will come again and live among the Brethren, about his hope that He will choose to live among us in Herrnhaag, the city built for our Chief Elder.

There is another entry about a prayer and – he uses the term 'working' – done for the colonies where 'our vision will fully flower much later in time'. He talks about something he calls 'The Star Code' and how it will be used at that time to 'light the lamp'.

Again, my apologies that I couldn't find anything more concrete. Please let me know how your journey goes. I would like to keep in touch and am always here for you.

Sister Penelope

"Star Code. Star Family," David said. "They must be connected."

"But how?" Jane turned halfway round in the chair to look at him. "Do you think the time he's talking about is now?"

"Could be." David crooked a shoulder. "Who can say?"

"'Light the lamp'? What do you think that means? Is it just a metaphor for a better time?"

David covered his yawn with his hand.

Jane laughed. "I'm tired, too. We can look at all this again tomorrow. See if we can make any sense out of it."

☆ ☆ ☆

"I don't think we're going to learn anything following Jane Frey around the Czech Republic," Spencer had said during their phone call last night. "I need you here. The level of activity has spiked."

Relieved his boss had seen the light at last, Philip slipped out of the hospital in the early morning hours. He'd had worse injuries. His ribs were bruised, not broken. His ankle worried him the most. It would be a few weeks before he could run at top speed. He left the two amateur spies in Prague under the watchful eye of a colleague, Miloš, who was not an amateur, if not quite up to his own caliber, and only too glad for some easy money. He reminded him to retrieve the tracking device off the rental car so he wouldn't go on a wild goose chase.

After making sure Miloš had everything under control, Philip made his way to Zurich where he boarded one of Coche's company jets that had been in Switzerland on other business. He relaxed in the luxury of leather seats, fine wine and a five-star chef who knew how to cook a steak. Coche also kept a young assistant on board, as versatile as the chef in her own trade. Philip bedded her to test out her expertise. She handled his eccentric tastes like the pro she was.

After their tryst, Philip downed two more pain killers, then switched on his laptop and caught up on the recent activities of the people who had attended Coche's event with the prophet.

The D.C. lodges were like ant heaps overturned, scurrying this way and that, their leaders meeting regularly. Philip picked up the buzz easily in email exchanges and on the social networking sites of regular members.

Valentin Knight, however, remained ominously silent. Philip had a hunch he was the man to watch, but first Philip needed to secure an invitation to a meeting. Several heads of the various spiritual groups in D.C. planned to review their combined information and decide what needed to be done to support the unfolding of the prophecy, which many thought was imminent. Philip sent Spencer an encrypted message listing his needs, then got some sleep. The assistant had changed the sheets and made herself scarce.

Once his plane landed, Philip took the Metro to his apartment and found his invitation to the meeting waiting. He changed into a nondescript blue suit and drove to the Grand Lodge on Pennsylvania Avenue. At the door, Philip presented his invitation to a surprised underling. He didn't expect to learn much from the meeting. Actually he preferred gathering his intel through clandestine methods, but these people needed to get used to seeing his face. He might need to slip into a ceremony unremarked.

The head of the lodge got the meeting started with a short prayer. Philip lowered his lids, then looked around to match faces to names from his list, reinforcing his memory.

"So be it," George Remus intoned and there was a general rustle, scraping of chairs, a few coughs.

After a minute, he continued. "The prophecy states that this is the time of a great shift. It speaks of a grid laid down by our ancestors. We've all agreed this probably refers to the general layout of the national government, including the Capitol Building and White House predominantly, but encompassing the National Mall and certain outlying structures.

"We have several ideas about the eight-petaled figure, but have not settled this matter. As we all know, use of the octagon is common in sacred geometry and found in most of the buildings in the target area."

Paul Balford stirred, George's equal in influence amongst the Rosicrucian brethren, but didn't speak.

George seemed to take this as a cue to continue. "The lost treasure has created the most speculation. There are many options. The holdings of the various lodges and groups have been kept under the strictest secrecy. For good reason." He looked around at the gathered leaders.

"But what seems most urgent is the message about those in control who would—" He glanced down at his paper and read out, "'There are those who would control it to stop the feeding of the grid. This will block your leadership from the new guidance'."

Here he stopped and looked around at the small gathering. "While I do not particularly care what treasures we are all keeping for the use of our group and posterity, I think we can all agree our nation is in dire straits. Certain influences—" his eyes strayed toward Philip, but he caught himself and turned his head back toward the group "—have strangled our nation. The economy has been hijacked by thugs, if you will pardon me for being blunt. All efforts to correct this situation are resolutely resisted. We find ourselves at a complete stalemate nationally and losing our standing in the world. It is not so important that America lead the global community. But I think we can all agree that it is important to protect the knowledge this nation was founded to liberate. We must never again allow the suppression of the true teachings." His face flushed, betraying his emotion. "Thus this unprecedented sharing of secrets."

Paul picked up seamlessly, as if giving his long-time friend time to repair his dignity. "So the questions remaining are to identify the eight-petaled figure and to determine how to pull control of the grid from the negative forces. Is this correct?"

George nodded, appearing thankful for the moment to collect himself. "That's correct. I think we can all agree the treasure can wait. If an artifact is the key, identifying the lock is the first order of business."

Murmurs and nods rose as George finished his introduction.

The head of a lodge in Alexandria spoke up. "There are too many options. Octagons are found embedded in floor tiles throughout the buildings. In murals. Many domes are eight-sided at their base. Some of the monuments themselves are octagonal. The Washington Monument even has eight windows at the top."

One man tentatively raised his hand. George gave him the floor. "Perhaps we are looking for a larger structure. One in which a building lies in the center and there are eight streets running from it. Think of Notre Dame in Paris."

At this, general conversation broke out, people listing even more potential sites. "I just don't see how we're going to find it in time," one man said.

Paul held up his hand and the conversations fell away. "I think we can limit our options in two ways. First, do we all agree this grid was laid down early in our history and that the octagon would have been created before the nineteenth century?"

There was a pause as the men considered this idea. "This seems likely," someone said. Others nodded their agreement.

"Next, I propose that we each send our most accurate sensitives—" Philip remembered the Rosicrucians preferred the term 'sensitive' to 'psychic' "—to a list of the most likely places. We'll then compare their responses."

Heads bent and people sitting near each other discussed this idea briefly.

After a few minutes, Paul asked, "This seems like a good idea, then?"

Affirmations came from around the room.

"Now for the list. Each lodge should submit an inventory of octagonal structures—small to large—to George and me. We'll research the dates of construction and compile a final list. In the meantime, please select who your lodge will send out to investigate. Remember the timing is vital. Choose someone who can do this immediately, even if their abilities are not as great as another who has obligations that would cause a delay."

Chairs scraped back and the general murmur of conversation rose to a pitch as the men prepared to leave, gathering coats, clutching brief cases, exchanging ideas.

What a colossal waste of time, Philip thought. Except he did need to be seen. He forced himself to greet a few people and exchange clucks over how difficult it all was. Personally, he found it invigorating. But he wondered why they hadn't thought of all the tunnels gnawed out beneath the government buildings and the National Mall itself. The place was a rat's maze of hallways and offices improvised from closets or sheet-walled from empty space, many layers deep. Wires hung from the ceilings. People scurried to and fro. Even the subway stopped in the middle of it all. The average citizen didn't realize that most of Washington's business was conducted underground in this dark, moldy warren. If there had ever been an energy grid, why did these esteemed gentlemen think it hadn't already been destroyed?

Philip had already ordered a list of possible eight-sided figures and buildings that the prophet might be referring to. His psychics had started checking them out. Coche could provide access day or night. Better to do their spying in the dark. He headed off to check on their progress.

CHAPTER TWENTY-ONE

Jane watched David butter his scone, then spread strawberry jam all over it. He sank his teeth into his creation, closed his eyes, and abandoned himself to the luxury. He swallowed, opened his eyes and noticed her still watching him. "What?"

"Nothing." She took a sip of coffee, hot and dark. She was glad they were climbing the hill to the castle today. She'd been indulging.

David took another tentative bite, smaller this time. He chewed this one more slowly, eyes closed, savoring the taste.

She laughed.

"What?" This time he sounded exasperated.

"Nothing."

"Stop saying that."

"What?"

"Nothing."

"Okay." She took another sip of coffee, put down the cup and scrapped a wedge of wheat toast across her plate, soaking up the egg yolk.

"No, I meant stop saying 'nothing'. What are you thinking?"

"I thought women were supposed to ask that question."

"You're impossible," he huffed.

"When did you start having visions?"

"I told you. I got it from my mother. Not something to advertise, you know."

She polished off her toast, poured herself more coffee and sat back, cradling the cup. "Tell me."

"Tell you what?"

"About your visions. When did you first realize you could see things other people couldn't?"

His suspicious scowl softened. "So you believe me?"

"I told you I did."

Still he was hesitant.

Jane shrugged. "After all the other improbable things we've discovered, why not? Besides, I've seen some things in my life that make me—well, open to possibilities."

He toyed with the crumbs on his plate, then pushed it away. "We were accustomed to it because Mom used to tell us what she saw from time to time. Her predictions always came true, too. At least most of the time."

"Like what?"

"Once we were waiting for a bus and she told us we had to move down to the next stop. Sure enough, the bus turned the corner, ran over the curb and took out the street sign we'd been standing next to."

"Wow."

"So when I first saw something, she explained how it ran in our family and it wasn't anything to be scared of."

"What did you see?"

David shook his head. "You won't believe me."

"Come on."

"An angel in church."

"Really?" Jane sat forward. "What did it look like?"

"No wings. That's why I ran to Mom. She explained they're tall beings of light, like a candle flame. Asked me if it had given me a message."

"Did it?"

David shook his head. "No. Just sort of twinkled at me."

"How old were you?"

"About eight."

"So now you're used to it. It's old hat."

"I wouldn't say that. It's not like I have them every day. Or often, for that matter." He swirled the last of his coffee around in his cup.

Jane picked up the carafe and poured him another cup.

He nodded his thanks, added cream. "That's the real reason I joined the Masons. I was hoping they could teach me how to control it."

"You mean your mother didn't?"

"For her, it was a gift. Something God would send to help her out. Show her the way forward. She thought it was greedy to ask."

"But you wanted to know more."

"Right, but I guess I never got deep enough into the Masonic teachings. With the kids and work . . ." He looked out the window at Prague Castle. "I wasn't a diligent student."

"You were busy with your family," Jane said.

"So, occasionally I'll see something, but it's usually related to an important event or a warning."

"Do you think yesterday was a warning?"

"No." David looked back at Jane. "Yesterday was different from anything I've experienced before. I could smell the damp of the cave and the smoke from the fire." His eyes took on a faraway mist. "I could almost understand the chanting. And when she stabbed me, for a split second I thought I was dying."

"Why did she stab you?"

"The Celts used to do blood sacrifice." He set his cup down and leaned forward. "James argues about it. Says it's Christian propaganda, but I've heard different. That they'd kill an old king and crown a younger, more virile man if their fields or flocks were not fertile for a while."

Jane wrinkled her nose. "Gives a whole new meaning to *noblesse oblige.*"

"So maybe she was sacrificing me for the success of this mission."

"But you're not exactly dead."

David's hand went to his chest. "Thank heaven."

"What is the mission exactly? Knight told me about this prophecy."

"Tell me again."

Jane repeated the prophecy about the eight-sided figure, how it seemed to be the lock to control an energy grid. "They think maybe a cabal of people into dark magic control the grid now. That the artifact is the key to this lock. That if they regain control, they can shift the world power toward the good," she finished. "It seems ridiculous to me. Pollyannaish."

"So why are we helping them?"

"Because these lunatics think I have the artifact. Or at least know something about it." Agitated, she walked to the window and pulled the curtains aside. Artists were putting out their wares on Charles Bridge. Musicians in little clusters leaned toward each other, instruments in hand. "And they ran me out of my home," she finished.

The English Tudor was home, she realized, even if her family had come from here or Herrnhut or even Fulnek, Salem was her home.

David cleared his throat. She turned back to him. He looked like a school master trying to decide how best to correct a wayward student.

"Okay, so if I hadn't taken the paintings, if I'd gotten their permission, then maybe I'd still be welcome there," she burst out. "But they lied to me, too, David."

"Two wrongs—"

"Oh, for God's sake. Get real."

"Sorry, I still think it's true."

"Don't be so naïve." She turned on him, heat filling her chest. "It's because you've stayed in that small town all your life. If you'd seen what I've seen, you wouldn't say that."

She expected anger, hurt, but instead he sat calmly and said, "Tell me what you've seen."

The compassion in his voice stopped her tirade. Her eyes filled. She shook her head against them. She'd been crying too much lately. She wanted to be angry. It was easier.

Then she answered his question. "Oh, it's too much, David, just too much. In Bangkok, all over Southeast Asia and in Eastern Europe, the children being sold for sex. They're incredibly young. So beautiful and innocent. And there are so many of them that if you saved a few, even a few hundred, they'd be replaced the next day. The starving mothers holding their dead infants in Africa. People walking half a day to get clean water. Don't even get me started on how animals are treated."

She pointed a finger at him, not seeing his expression, just remembering ridicule, faces from the past. "I know, silly liberal. Cares more about animals than people, but David, it will break your heart. And all the while the princes party and their fathers bargain and they all rent out women—the most beautiful women—whom they throw away at the end of the year. Or kill. It's all the same to them." Tears blinded her and she closed her eyes, fighting for control.

Then he was there, his hands on her shoulders, his voice soothing. "Come on." He gathered her to him. "Let it out. Just let it all out."

And she did. She shouted and sobbed, letting the outrages, the shocks, the weight of so many trips and parties and visits to natural disasters and war zones unwind their grip around her heart and fall from her shaking shoulders. He crooned to her, some small, simple tune. Rocked her while she cried it all out.

Music always heals.

In her head, voices chided her. *Oh, don't be that way. Come on, Jane, grow up. This is the way of the world. Always has been. Always will be.*

That's what they'd said, with their dead eyes and quirked up mouths, telling themselves that if they didn't make these millions, someone else would. Until she believed them. Almost. The shock this small town girl had buried deep, the morals that had been chided and jeered out of her, came crawling back out from hiding, shook themselves off and moved back into her heart.

Finally her sobs subsided. She blew her nose on one of the napkins clutched in her hand, then pulled her head back. Found a clean one and dabbed at David's shirt, soaked with her tears. "I'm sorry."

He pulled her tighter. "Shhh."

"You'll have to change shirts," she said.

He leaned down and kissed her forehead, then her temple, her mouth, his lips soothing, then seeking. She put her arms around him and leaned into the kiss. He reached under her knees and lifted her.

"But you'll hurt your back—"

He shushed her and carried her to the bed.

It had been a long time. She let him undress her, holding out an arm, lifting her hips. He kissed and caressed each part as it emerged from hiding. He seemed to like what he found. By the time she lay naked before him, she'd lost all her shyness, all hesitation.

She reached up and unbuttoned his shirt, pushed it back, ran her hand through the light ruff of hair on his chest. He pulled off the rest of his clothes and laid his length next to hers, warm and firm. Took her in his arms and began to stroke her, explore at his leisure.

It had been a long time.

☆ ☆ ☆

The phone roused them from where they lay entangled on the bed, spent and happy. Jane mumbled a protest. Then the door to the suite buzzed, waking her fully from her drowsy bliss. David reached for the phone beside the bed.

Jane grabbed a thick, cotton robe hanging on the bathroom door and walked to the entryway of the suite. She peered through the peephole. It was Ivar.

"Ivar! You're back," she shouted through the door. "Let me get dressed."

Jane ran back into the bedroom. David sat on the side of the bed, buck naked, still talking. She tore her eyes away and pulled on her clothes, closed the bedroom door and let Knight's security man in.

He took a few steps into the suite, locked the door behind him, and stood almost at attention. His silver hair did nothing to diminish the sense of dangerous competence in his wide shoulders, his athletic stance. His gaze penetrated like a wolf's staring down an elk. One eye was puffy and black.

She reached out to touch his face, then pulled her hand back. "You okay?"

"You should see him," Ivar said with a wicked grin.

"Coffee? I think we have a scone left." Jane flipped the linen napkin back and found the basket empty. "Oh, sorry."

"That's all right. I've eaten. I just came to let you know that Philip has left. He's gone back to the States."

"You took him out, huh?"

Ivar brushed this comment aside. "He hired a local guy to watch you." He waved his hand to forestall alarm. "I know this new man. He will only follow you, report back." He reached inside his long coat and pulled out an envelope from an inside pocket. "Here's a picture, just so you'll know."

Jane took the envelope and started to open it, then asked, "What does this mean, then?"

"You're free to travel more widely. The trip up north was a risk, but you found something, yes?"

She nodded.

"Now you may go where you wish, even stay overnight somewhere else. Still it would be best to spend most nights here."

"Thank you."

He nodded his head, accepting her gratitude with his surprising grace. "I'll still be watching, along with my team."

Then Jane wondered if this suite had surveillance cameras. Most likely. Her cheeks flushed hot.

"You still have my cell number?"

"Yes." Jane pointed at the desk where her electronics were arrayed.

"Good. Let me know your plans, but you can relax a bit. Have a vacation."

Jane thanked him again and locked the door behind him. David opened the bedroom door. He also wore a robe, but his came only to mid-thigh. She was glad Ivar hadn't seen him, which was irrational. They were adults, after all.

"Who was that?" he asked.

"Ivar."

"He's okay?"

"Got quite a shiner." Jane told him what the security man had said. "Who was on the phone?"

"Václav. Said he was up all night with the stomach flu. He can't make it today. Now his kid has it."

Jane tapped her chin, an idea forming.

David continued, "I told him to take a few days if he needed them. Hope that's all right."

"Perfect," she said.

"Huh?" David frowned.

"Well, I'm sorry he's sick, but a lot of clues seem to point to Fulnek."

"Remind me."

"Comenius. One branch of my family. Let's drive down there. Spend a day or two."

"How far is it?"

"Let's see." Jane walked to the desk and tapped the keyboard of her computer. David came up and stood behind her, his body radiating warmth. She suppressed the thought of just staying here. In bed. "Three and a half hours."

"I could make it in two and a half, three tops."

Jane laughed. "Three and a half would be fine, too." She checked the time. "It's only ten now. We could find somewhere to stop for lunch."

"Can we get that little Fiat 500 Abarth again?" David asked with a rakish grin. "It handles so sweet."

Jane laughed. "Why not? Ivar said to have fun."

CHAPTER TWENTY-TWO

Philip waited at a mall just outside Starbucks for his contact to show. People fought for space in the throngs, each armed with bags and packages that some weren't hesitant to use as battering rams. He'd moved away from Santa Claus earlier. Too many cameras.

His cell vibrated its way across the table. He grabbed it before it fell off the edge and found an email from Miloš. The daily report on Jane Frey. He read it and smirked. Jane and David were driving east. Still didn't know what they were looking for. He closed the phone. Philip had secured the list of artifacts and treasure held by the local lodges. It had raised his eyebrows. Maybe he'd do some "shopping" himself after all this was over.

A chorale group dressed in Victorian outfits straight out of Dickens strolled by. The round soprano looked like she might pop a stay in her corset if she hit high C. Finally he spotted his psychic mincing his way through the crowd, his forehead furrowed in pain. Timons—and he insisted on being called Timons, not Tim, the pretentious little prick—hated crowds. Said they were undisciplined, chaotic, that they gave him a headache. He stood just on the other side of a display of Christmas cups looking everywhere else except where Philip was sitting in plain sight.

Psychic, huh? Philip thought, but the man had proven himself. He was just high maintenance. Coche had plenty of people on staff Philip could have used, but he always did a double-blind check when he was involved in an investigation. That way he was sure of his intel.

Philip stood up, stuffed his phone in his jacket pocket, and walked over to Timons, who jumped in surprised.

"There you are. I had to park way in back. These crowds . . ." Timons flapped his hand like some queen from the Castro District, although he was straight. Philip knew. He conducted exhaustive background checks.

"Can I buy you an eggnog latte?" Philip asked, his tone compassionate, soothing. "Chai?"

"That would be most kind," Timons said, his hand flitting around his plum woolen scarf, but leaving it wrapped tight. "Eggnog latte, please." He flounced down in an empty chair, accustomed to being waited on. "'Tis the season."

Philip obliged. As long as Timons delivered, he'd baby him. Philip returned with the drink, let Timons take a sip, then said, "You picked three spots that fit the description I sent. Said these were the most energetically active. Your report was thorough, but I would appreciate it if you reviewed your reasons again. Refresh my memory."

Timons took another sip of his latte—Philip's lip curled, ridiculously sweet, these eggnog drinks, too fatty—then began to speak, now animated. By the subject or the caffeine and sugar, Philip couldn't tell. "This area is packed with eight-petaled figures, macro and micro, simply packed. But you specified the National Mall—up to three blocks out." Timons seemed pleased with this phraseology. "Even then, there were loads to sift through."

"That's why I called in an expert." Philip forced a smile. He was lucky this man was no empath.

"Third on my list is the Jefferson Memorial. It's not obviously an octagon, but the dome has alternating panels and openings with Ionic columns. The statue stands in the middle. An eight-sided building. There's a museum below, but the active rooms are around the edges, leaving the center relatively clear."

Timons took another sip of his drink, dabbed his mouth with a napkin and said in a low voice, "I don't know what they buried under there, but let me tell you. It's quite powerful."

Philip matched his quiet tone, hoping to keep Timons talking more softly. "What did you experience?"

Timons closed his eyes. "There's a column of light that rises from the statue and extends—" he raised his hand up in an elegant gesture "—oh, way past the earth's atmosphere."

Two people next to them paused to watch Timons. Philip had hoped the Christmas bustle would give them sufficient cover, but this guy was far too theatrical. Timons opened his eyes and took a breath to continue, but Philip cut him off. "I can hardly wait to experience it myself. My car is just outside."

He stood up and headed toward the door, Timons scrambling to follow. Once in the car—borrowed from Coche's company, he'd never let anyone in his personal vehicle—he merged onto the freeway clogged with fools headed to Reagan National. This was going to take a while, but at least their conversation would be private.

"What about connecting to an energy grid at the Jefferson Memorial? Did you get any sense of that?"

Timons sniffed, still ruffled by being interrupted unceremoniously. "Certainly an energy column extending that far above connects to the earth's grid."

"But I specified a network in D.C. A planetary web seems too general. How could something that large have such a specific effect?"

"The prophecy talks about dark forces trying to choke off the energy feeding this network."

Philip looked over at Timons to find him looking rather smug.

Timons continued, "If this is an attempt to control global power, then tapping down the planet's life force would accomplish that."

"Why do you think this is such a grand conspiracy?" Philip asked.

"One hears rumors."

So much for my double-blind test, Philip thought.

"Rumors? Do tell." He matched Timons' inflection. Philip wondered for the first time if he'd have to kill this little popinjay. He'd hoped to avoid such complications, but he had to keep his employer protected.

A rich chuckle rose from the man, earthy and practical, sounding far different from the ethereal space case who'd flitted around at the mall. "The spiritual world is small, even in a place as rich with metaphysical groups as this one. Word has spread of a new prophet with tales of a tug of war amongst the powers that be over an eight-sided figure."

Philip looked sharply at him.

"I've taken precautions, Mr. Martin. Recorded our conversations. Saved a copy of your instructions. All tucked away in a safe deposit box. If I should disappear, certain people have been instructed to open it."

Not impossible to destroy, Philip thought. He could track down his contact fairly easily. Erase all evidence. He doubted Timons had alerted more than one person. Still, his esteem for this man rose several notches. "I see."

Philip took the exit and drove across the river. "So why is the Jefferson Memorial third and not your first choice?" He did a quick, illegal U-turn, and pulled the car into the parking lot of the place in question.

They got out and walked toward the monument, Timons continuing his commentary. "Because it was built in the early twentieth century. You did say the grid was laid down by our founders, but most of the subsequent building around the White House and Capitol Building has been conducted by initiates. They can easily connect to the original energy network. That's not the problem."

They climbed the steps and circled the rotunda, Timons pointing out the columns and panels. "See, eight."

Philip stopped at the view across the water to the White House, and let his ankle stop throbbing. Damn that Ivar. The White House looked small, even fragile, from this distance. "What's the problem then?"

"Although there's that nice column of energy going up, I don't feel it radiating out. Not much at all. But we could dowse it."

Philip glanced around. The place was empty except for the staff. Too close to Christmas and early in the week. Still, someone walking around with a stick would draw attention. He'd send someone over, disguise the stick as one of those metal detectors they sold on TV to bored old geysers. "What made second on your list?" he asked.

"The Potomac Atrium in the National Museum of the American Indian."

"You're kidding," Philip said. "That's brand new, isn't it?"

"The building. Not the site itself."

"You could say the same of this place."

"But the energy is different."

"Let's head over there. Take a look."

Timons fell silent the few blocks it took to drive down to the end of the mall, which suited Philip just fine. He struggled to find parking with Congress still in session, if that's what they called grandstanding and making ridiculous suggestions that everyone knew would never get passed in the other chamber. Someone pulled out about two blocks away from the mall, so Philip grabbed the spot and maxed out the meter.

"Tell me," Philip said as they walked at a sedate pace toward the museum.

"A three-story octagon, the space open and clear for the most part. Used for performance pieces. Sometimes exhibits." They entered the building and made their way to the atrium.

"Look." Timons pointed up to the dome. Twelve nested circles surrounded the glass top, itself divided into a perfect eight-petaled flower. "Hidden in plain sight. The energy runs clean down toward the Capitol, then hits some sort of nexus where it gets distributed."

"I see." Philip was calculating how to stake out this area. Then he looked up at Timons, still admiring the window. "And your number one?"

"The Capitol Dome."

"Dome?"

"Yeah. It makes the most sense. And the energy is absolutely off the charts."

Philip stepped to the side of the room—circular spaces carry sound—and pulled out his phone. He called Spencer's assistant. "We need to get into the Capitol."

"Go over to the Longworth House Office Building. I'll have an aide of Representative Foxington come down with passes. She's one of ours."

"We'll be there in about five minutes."

"I'm on it."

They headed out the door and strolled down to the representative's building. A harried young man waited on the steps. Philip stopped in front of him and showed him a company ID from one of Coche's firms. The man squinted at the ID, handed Philip two passes, and headed back inside without a question.

Philip waited a few minutes, then followed the man inside. They took the elevator down and emerged in one of the corridors that led to the Library of Congress on the right and straight ahead to the Capitol Building. Timons followed, somewhat agog at the maze. They took an elevator up and stepped out close to the amphitheater where tourists were indoctrinated before taking the tour of the nation's Capital Building, now little more than a museum.

He led the way to the rotunda. Timons followed, eyes darting around.

"Ever been in here?" Philip asked.

"When I was a kid."

"So how did you make your determination?"

Timons frowned a bit. "Several ways. I can work off pictures—sort of like remote viewing, but more precise. A few other tricks of the trade. But this place exudes vitality. The energy grids pulse with power. And it's simple to walk by. Anyone worth his salt can get close enough to read the flows."

They finished climbing the stairs and emerged under the dome. A group was just finishing up, the tour guide pointing out the paintings hanging around the room.

Timons closed his eyes and swayed. Philip steadied him with an arm to his shoulder and moved to block him from view. "Yes," Timons murmured, "I think this is the place."

"What are you experiencing?" Philip whispered.

"I see a—" he shook his head "—like a gryphon sort of. Black, powerful, teeth bared. Guarding something."

The guide led his group away. Philip took hold of Timons' shoulder and squeezed. "Open your eyes."

Timons gave himself a shake. "Sorry, it's just so—"

"What part of the dome?" Philip asked.

Timons raised his arm and pointed up. "Imagine the intensity before they moved that statue of Washington. Above is the Apotheosis. It's where the space opens to divine guidance."

Philip snorted.

"I'm not kidding," Timons said, somewhat piqued.

Philip looked around. "We've got a few minutes before another group comes. Let's see what you can pick up."

Timons took a shaky breath, then closed his eyes once more. After a few seconds he jerked. "It's still there."

"What?"

"A dark being—like an angel. No, there are more. All black." He shuddered. "The energy flows up from underground and gets channeled out to a wheel. And from there avenues of energy flow out, first in eight channels, then twelve." His eyes started to roll back in his head. His voice deepened, then he spoke in a deep, guttural voice, "*The Nehemoth still guard the ways. We are the whisperers, the hinderers. None shall pass us.*"

Voices sounded on the stairs.

"Okay, that's enough," Philip said, his voice gruff. He gave Timons a shake.

Another group of noisy tourists burst up the stairs.

"Come back now." Philip clapped his hands. The sound resonated like a gun shot.

Timons shook his head, leaned against the wall to steady himself. "Yeah, they'll want to dislodge these beings. Replace them with a higher frequency. Clean the place out."

"There's more than one?"

Timons nodded, his eyes haunted.

Philip had what he needed. "Okay, let's go." He guided Timons down the steps and back to the elevator. Once they'd emerged onto the street, the man seemed to have regained some control. But he was visibly shaken.

"I'll drive you back to your car. Payment will be deposited by tonight," Philip said. He stopped beside his car, leaned close as if to open the door, but instead he whispered, "If you discuss this assignment in any way, I will feed you to those dark angels. Do we understand each other?"

Timons nodded, his eyes wide.

It would be better to kill him, Philip thought, *cleaner.*

Instead, Philip dropped Timons off, reinforcing his warning with a dark look, then headed across to the Whole Foods and grabbed a Sonoma chicken wrap. He ate it while he drove. His next meeting was with Aleister, one of Coche's most talented wizards. That's what he called himself, Aleister. And wizard. Philip wondered if he'd taken the name or been given it by his parents. Based on what he'd seen the man do, he'd grant him the wizard title. He swallowed the last of the chicken wrap and washed it down with plum white tea.

Aleister had just started briefing his group. He nodded at Philip as he slipped into a back seat, then spent the next half hour explaining the energy grids set up by Washington, D.C.'s sacred geometry. Or maybe reviewing, because he moved through it at lightning speed. Philip tried to keep up as Aleister's fingers clicked through the images he'd set up—the angle of streets, the way buildings sat in relation to each other, forming the pentagram, the square and compass, the Tree of Life—until Philip just let it all wash over him.

"They were brilliant," Aleister summed up, clicking back to the first slide in his report. "The founders built an encyclopedia of esoteric knowledge in stone. Any questions?" He fielded a few from the team about the geometric figures and how they modulated energy. Then he reviewed assignments.

Philip gave himself a shake and paid close attention. Even though he wasn't assigned to protect them, he needed to know who was where. He noted that Aleister assigned a man and a woman to each node.

The group was dismissed and they left, talking quietly amongst themselves, most avoiding Philip's eyes. Once the small auditorium was cleared, Aleister waved him over. "Looks like that fluffy psychic of yours almost wet his pants," he quipped.

"You saw?"

"Of course. I'm always watching you, Mr. Martin." Aleister put the emphasis on the last syllable, revealing the French origins of his name.

"How?"

Aleister crooked a finger, beckoning Philip to him, reached up and flicked one of the snaps on his jacket. "I convinced dear Henry I needed a camera to check in with you from time to time. That you might need my help immediately, something I'd need to see."

Philip usually did an electronics sweep every week, but this had eluded him. Aleister loved showing him up if he could. This was the one time he'd succeeded in a year. Well, if you didn't count that time in Rome. He pointed his index finger at Aleister and whispered, "Bang!"

"That little brunette really whittled your pecker." Aleister waggled his eyebrows like a scamp.

"You—" Philip remembered hanging his jacket on a hook in the plane. The camera must have fallen just right. "I'll slit your throat one day, really."

"Don't be droll," Aleister said. "Now, down to business. I assume you followed all that?"

Philip shrugged. "Enough, but you'll be doing the magic, right? I'll just protect your precious ass."

Aleister's breath hissed in irritation. "Muscle. That's all you're good for. You're a goddamn muscle head. Tell me—" His tirade stopped when he caught Philip's grin. Now it was Aleister's turn to point his index finger at Philip. "One day."

For a second, Philip held his hands up as if it were a real gun, then dropped them with a chuckle. "So, how have we fucked with the ingenious energy system our enlightened forefathers set up?"

Aleister sat forward, eyes lit. "Simple, really. We just called up the Qliphoth demonic equivalents to take up their appropriate stations."

"The what?"

"Honestly, you are an ignoramus," Aleister said without any heat. "The Fallen Tree." He sat back, a look of satisfaction on his face. "Simple is always best."

"So these mamby, pamby servants of the light are going to replace them with the right guys?"

"Right? Who's to say they're right?"

"I mean the Tree of Life guys."

"Half of them are female."

Philip put his hands on his hips. "How many times have you told me angels are—what's the word—androgynous?"

"So you do listen."

"Occasionally."

"As to your question, we think so. If they realize what we've done."

"Where will you be stationed?"

Aleister pulled up his diagram and went through the personnel and where they'd be working. Philip sat beside him, noting the areas, calculating the risks, thinking how to pull reports and schedules for a dozen different agencies tasked with security. "Can you send me this map? And your report so I can review it?"

Aleister pushed a few buttons on his computer. "Done."

"Is the time set?"

"The old man isn't certain, but my money's on Winter Solstice."

Philip gave him a blank look.

"December 21st? Longest night? If it was a sports team, you'd know the statistics on the most insignificant player."

He grinned at Aleister. "I pay attention to what's important."

"They'll try to flip the tree before they do the ritual to unlock the eight-petaled key. We'll be on-site twenty-four hours in advance. We might have to move on a moment's notice."

Philip picked up his keys. "No problem. See you there."

Valentin Knight swirled Applewood Estates reserve brandy in the sniffer, a gift from a cousin, but did not drink. Instead he watched the light from the fire dance in the amber liquid. He set it down untouched.

Jane seemed to be adapting well. They were off somewhere, she and her David, visiting another Moravian site in the eastern side of the Czech Republic. Ivar reported her safe and happy, beginning a romance. Good for her. He wished her well. That she was safe was his only real concern. She'd uncovered the Blake painting, started the ball rolling. Found a star embedded in stone at Ronneburg Castle. She had more of a role to play in the escalating conflict.

And escalating it was. Coche had pulled his man from Prague and brought him here to D.C. where he was sticking his nose into the lodge meetings, conducting his own psychic tests.

Then there were George Remus and Paul Balford, the two strongest leaders of the various lodges. Honorable, capable men, doing their utmost to identify the grid, to find the key to unlock it. He was following all their efforts, but when it came to security, international politics, they were amateurs. Entirely ignorant of some angles that would need to be considered.

He'd sent Minerva, one of his group's best, over to help, but they'd kept their meetings men-only. He picked up his sniffer and took a sip. Traced the fire as it spread through his chest. Now was not the time to cling to time-worn traditions. But they had. So he'd been forced to send Ron, with half the talent and a tendency to gossip. The lodges thought they'd identified the proper grid, but when it came to the sensitive point to work the grid, they always looked up when they should consider other options.

Knight shifted in his seat as a log hissed out sap. He should go to help himself, but something told him to wait. To stay still, as the sun would in a few days when it reached Solstice. To allow the energy to build until it pulled him into action. Already the force was growing in the grids, like the tension before a thunderstorm. But he kept the brewing tempest contained. He would release it only when it grew into a maelstrom.

He knew the place. And the time.

CHAPTER TWENTY-THREE

Jane relaxed into the long, easy curves of the Bohemian countryside, humming to herself. She pushed thoughts of the future away. Just luxuriated in the present moment, her body pliant and happy in a way it hadn't been for—well, she preferred not to think about how long. They drove for miles through fields, trees, and villages.

David broke the long silence. "Sounds like you've figured out that piece of music."

"Huh?"

"That tune you keep humming. Sounds like the composition you've been working on."

She hadn't realized she'd been humming, much less her new piece. But now that David called her attention to it, the tune evaporated. Jane sat up, trying to remember it all. She had the first two phrases, which she hummed again. "Do you remember the rest?"

"Ah, performer's anxiety."

"No, it's just—"

"Seriously. Composing is right-brained. You can't think about it too much. Have to catch it out of the side of your eye—or ear, I guess."

"I suppose that makes sense." Jane remembered studying music theory and banging her head against the keys on a number of occasions. One of her professors had told her not to despair, to study until the rules became second nature, until she didn't have to think about them anymore. "I hated music theory. Made me give up on being a composer."

"I had trouble with it too, but you just have to study it until it becomes second nature."

Jane gave a surprised laugh. "You sound like Dr. Mueller."

"Dr. Mueller." David slapped the steering wheel. "I haven't thought of him in years. You studied with him, too?"

She pulled her chin in and spoke in a sonorous, yet deeply disapproving voice. "You may use that chord there if you wish, Ms. Frey. However, I do not recommend it."

David snorted. "Oh, he was something, all right. I didn't realize you played cello."

"I don't. He was my piano teacher when I was in high school. Miss Essig recommended I study with him for a while. Said a serious musician should take lessons from more than one teacher. Then I had him for theory in college—and some music history. I forget the period."

"I suppose they all taught piano. It's the most popular instrument."

"I used to get to the conservatory early so I could sneak down the hall and play the harpsichord."

"In the new building?"

"Yeah, but I remember the old one. I used to run up those stairs and wait out in the hallway. They tore that building down, right?"

"Yeah, it was too modern for Old Salem."

"I guess that's good, although I miss the old white house at the bottom of Main Street."

David frowned. "Don't remember that one. I don't think we realized how good Salem's music program was when we were young. It's still top of the line."

"You'd know."

"Just relax and forget about your piece. It will come back." He held up an index finger. "Then I'll pay close attention. We'll capture it together."

Her stomach rumbled and they both laughed.

"Ready for lunch?" he asked.

She leaned over to look at the car's clock, but David hid it with his hand. "We're on vacation. Let your stomach decide, not some timepiece."

Jane lolled her head on the head rest. "Vacation, huh? You think our part in this quest is over?"

He was quiet for a minute, then said, "Quests are like music. If you're meant to be on one, it will come to you. Let's just have fun. See what we can find out along the way."

"That suits me. *Carpe diem* and all that."

He reached over and stroked her thigh, gently squeezed her knee. Warmth spread with his touch. His hand moved back up her leg and found her stomach beneath her coat. She opened her eyes in alarm. "You are watching the road, aren't you?"

He pulled his hand back. "Maybe we should pull over. Check in somewhere."

The husk in his voice sent a shiver of desire through her. Only a couple of hours ago he'd taken his time, kissed and caressed her until she'd lay under his touch like a green field beneath the sun. Then he'd rebuilt another kind of tension, her flesh warming, awakening, finally quivering like a sprouted seed just breaking through the soil. But once Ivar had left, they'd jumped into the car, not back in bed. Somehow Ivar's visit had made her shy of him, but now she almost regretted their decision. Even though they were supposed to be looking for the artifact Philip's employer was after. It seemed even Philip had given up on it.

His hand came back to her leg. Warmth radiated from it and a small moan escaped her.

A chuckle, rich as dark chocolate sauce poured over dark chocolate cake, escaped David. "I can't drive if you do that."

"Sorry." Jane pushed David's hand away and sat up.

"Aw," he said, genuine disappointment in his voice.

She ignored it and poked the map on the GPS. "We're near Jihlava. Want to stop for lunch?"

"So it's lunch you be wanting, then?" he asked, imitating his friend James's Scottish brogue.

"We need fuel." Her voice was low, suggestive. She was a little surprised by what a wanton flirt she'd suddenly become, but she enjoyed the new role. Pushing thoughts of her family, of her troubles with the OGMS away, she reached out and stroked his shoulder, tucked her hand under his arm. "But maybe that town's too big. Let's wait until we see something."

David nodded. "Just tell me where to turn."

After a few kilometers, Jane spotted a spire and the flash of roofs on a hillside. The river snaked silver between the pencil lines of tree trunks. "This looks promising. Take the next exit."

David turned the Fiat off the D1 and followed a road beside the Jihlava River that lead to a village. A restaurant sat on the edge of town, right next to the water. They parked and went inside where they were escorted to a table with a neat, white cloth and wax covered Chianti bottle of all things. Their table overlooked the silver stream running amongst rounded boulders. Some ice clung in the shadows, but the sun shone warm.

They talked about his children, her travels, while Jane feasted on the local trout and David on sausages. Would he ever get his fill of them? They both ate potatoes and drank the local pilsner. After they'd eaten more than they should, they sat back and sipped their beer, feet intertwined beneath the table. The trickling stream lulled Jane almost to sleep. Her composition rose in the back of her mind to accompany the sound of water flowing over stones. She listened, not grasping for it as David had suggested. It played out to the last phrase she knew, then stopped.

David grabbed the keys just at that moment, as if he, too, could hear that the music had stopped for now. "Ready?"

She stood up. He deemed himself fit to drive, even after he'd polished off two tall glasses of Pilsner. Jane watched him for a few miles, judging for herself, but he managed the turns back up to the freeway easily. No weaving across the middle line, so she sat back and watched the scenery go by, forests dotted with villages, fields of stubble.

Soon she realized she was humming again. She let her mind go dark, forgetting what she sang, whether it was a part of her new composition or scraps of Christmas carols and old folk songs, some about romance. David joined in, adding his rich baritone to her phrases in counterpoint or harmony.

"No, that's not how it goes," she said when David hummed her new composition. "It should be this." And she sang what she heard in her mind.

David listened, then replicated the phrase perfectly the first time. A quick ear.

She started at the beginning, the first blush of dawn in the sky, the quickening of a bulb that had slumbered beneath the earth all winter. Then David joined in, a low whisper, repeating what had come first, then adding ground, something to rest the ethereal promise of the first phrase on.

Jane smiled and continued, David improvising, her correcting, suggesting, until they had discovered the first ten minutes of the piece.

"There's more," Jane said to him, face beaming. "I hear horns, French horns, and violins. Maybe a harp, but I can't hear that part yet."

"I play French horn," David said. "Passably."

"I'd love—"

"Look." He pointed to a sign.

Fulnek 40 km.

Jane sat forward, eager, her composition forgotten for the moment. "How many miles is that?"

"What? You haven't gotten used to the conversion yet?"

"After all my years traveling, I should have."

"It's about twenty-five miles."

"We're almost there." She pulled out her Blackberry and started looking for a hotel. After a minute, she asked, "Hotel or guesthouse?"

David shrugged. "You decide."

"There's a wellness guesthouse, where—and I quote, 'you are prepared closet with a view of the castle, TV, internet connection, bathroom. Salt cavern, wellness, massages, beauty salon, exercise room available. Pension Relaxko,'" she read out.

"Closet?"

"Probably a small room. Glitch in the translation software."

"Salt cavern? Like in a cave?"

"I don't know. Want to find out?"

"Let's just stick with the basics. We want to go out, see the Hussite sites, find your ancestral estate."

"Okay." Jane poked a few more buttons. "There's a picture of this one. Looks good. On the town square. Hotel Jelen." She hit the translation button. "Deer Hotel."

"Deer Hotel it is."

Jane punched the address into the GPS and the little British lady's voice said, "Calculating." For some reason they both burst out laughing.

By midafternoon, they'd checked into a nice room, somewhat Spartan compared to Knight's lavish suite, and were standing in front of the concierge asking for information on the Hussite sites in town. The concierge only knew a few English words, but he and David pieced enough together in German to get directions to the Church of *Unitas Fratrum*. They had a memorial room to Jan Amos Komenský.

"I'm learning Czech," Jane declared, tucking her hand under his arm.

David smiled. "We're coming back?"

The town also featured the *Suchdol nad Odrou*, a museum of Brethren missionary work. They'd get directions to that from the church. Maybe they'd learn something about Comenius, but Jane wasn't hopeful about the missionary museum.

David opened the car door for her.

"So you're my driver now?" she quipped.

He stopped, mild alarm on his face.

"I'm teasing." Jane slipped into the passenger seat. "I'll be chauffeured around, but let me know if you get tired."

He threw the keys in the air and caught them deftly. "I love this car."

The church had one room dedicated to Komenský, better known by the Latin Comenius, with busts reminiscent of Herrnhut, samples of his work, a nice timeline and biographical information, but the man who showed them through insisted that Comenius had taken nothing with him into exile. "His house was burned. His family died." David translated as he spoke. "Then again when he was older. This is his tragedy."

"Thank you for showing us around," Jane said. "It's wonderful to see something from our history."

David translated this, and the man's forehead wrinkled, somewhat bemused. Europeans took their history for granted. They lived surrounded by it. David talked with the man a while longer, so Jane gave the room another quick look searching for any clues of artifacts. But she knew she wouldn't find anything.

Looking around, she was again struck by how the Europeans accepted Comenius as a mystic and an educator. It seemed to be common knowledge. Not in North Carolina. Maybe Uncle Pat and his ilk had managed to repress this aspect of Moravian history with their fire-and-brimstone fundamentalism. Maybe their neighbors just grew tired of attracting wrath. Or maybe it came from the Moravian connection to Calvinism that had happened after Comenius. Either way, fundamentalism had been wide spread when she was a child, politely looked down upon as a bit backward by many in her church. Not something you'd say out loud, especially in front of children, but she'd picked up this attitude from her father. Her mother had been eager to escape her own family and those ideas.

Once back in the car, David announced, "I got directions to the Sterne family estate. He said the family is defunct. That they fled long ago, probably into Poland. Someone was living in it about two hundred years ago, but now the place is a ruin."

Jane sank back in the car seat suddenly as flat as three-day-old pop, the elation of discovery fizzing away. "So there's no one. Nobody to ask about an artifact. No chance of reconnecting to that branch of the family."

David patted her hand. "It would have been fun to meet living relatives. Hear the history from someone directly connected to it."

Jane tried to smile.

"He said the missionary museum would be closed by the time we got there today. That we should wait until tomorrow, but he didn't think we'd find anything about ancient artifacts."

"I don't either." Jane looked out at a darkening sky, rag-grey clouds low and hanging.

"What do you say we go back to the hotel and find somewhere to eat?"

Jane frowned.

"What?"

"It's just—"she shook her head "—I was hoping we'd discover something. I want to be able to go back to Miss Essig's house."

"They may let you still."

"Why would they?"

"Didn't your name come up in the lot? That means something to them. If you apologized, say that you regret your mistake, demonstrated you'll be honest with them in the future."

Jane felt a stab of irritation. "They lied to me, too."

"Somebody's got to be the first to offer reconciliation."

"Maybe." She shook her head. "Some Bohemian Brethren I am."

"What do you mean?"

"They lost their homes. Their families and friends were killed. They didn't sit in a fancy Italian sports car feeling sorry for themselves."

David chuckled. "I think you just need some borsch."

"We're not in Poland." Jane fought the smile threatening to break through.

"I'll bet they eat it here by the gallons."

"Liters," she corrected.

☆ ☆ ☆

The Sterne family castle looked intact from the road, an orange roof just like she'd seen on so many other Czech buildings, then a round tower of grey stone rising on the right side. But as they drove through the winding curves of the road, holes in the wall appeared, shaking off the illusion of a home still lived in. A lone wall rose clean and straight, one last assertion of order, but empty windows framed tree branches beyond it. Jane drove across a low stone bridge—"Oh my God, there's a moat." She pounded David's arm—that led to a flat courtyard, part flagstone, part weed patch. She parked here and leapt from the car. David followed close behind.

"Hello," Jane called out. They'd been told the place was abandoned, but just in case.

No one answered.

She called once more, then blindly groped behind her for David's hand, found it and pulled him beside her.

There was a nip in the air here in the foothills of the Hrubý Jeseník Mountains, but she didn't feel the chill, not after last night's heated evening and her long, satisfied sleep beside David. He was the warmest human she'd ever slept beside, toasty as a tile stove, but softer. She knew this giddiness wouldn't last, but that just helped her relish it more.

The main entrance hall rose, two stories of unbroken stone before it sheared off in a jagged peak to one side. Blocks from the wall lay scattered in front of the building, knee high, some broad enough for them to lie on top of side by side. Above the gap in the entrance where the massive doors would have stood, the Star Family crest gleamed from the darkened stone, inlaid white marble, eight points with an equal armed cross in the middle.

They crossed the threshold side by side and skirted around a square block of stone in the middle of the entryway, moving farther into the house. A staircase scaled the east wall, ending in a pile of rubble, but the roof was intact toward the back of the house. Jane ducked through a doorway and down the hall.

"Careful, now. We don't want the place falling in on our heads," David called after her.

She turned a corner into a flurry of wings and speckled bodies. She shouted in surprise, jumped back, hand over her face. Brown and white birds made short flights or ran, long tail feathers dragging across the stones, escaping through a ruined kitchen into the bushes.

"What?" David arrived breathless behind her.

"Pheasants, I think," she said, pointing toward the kitchen. "Do you hunt?"

"Used to with my uncle. I don't really care for it."

"We could have a good meal out here if you did."

They headed down a long, stone passageway that led toward the tower. The first room they came to was mostly intact, a round library by the looks of it. Shelves ran the length of the interior wall, the straightest one. Empty windows framed a garden, some beds still discernible. Jane went over to the shelves and picked up a book, leafed through mouse-nibbled pages. It looked like Latin. "Can you read any of this?"

David took it from her, reached into his pocket and settled reading glasses on his nose. Carefully turning the pages, he peered close, then sniffed and wrinkled his nose. "Musty."

"It's damp. I'm surprised they haven't molded away."

"Look." David pointed to a series of illustrations. "It's a book on herbs."

Jane picked up another book that fell into tatters in her hands. Pellets of mouse droppings littered the shelf and a wad of paper in the far corner suggested a nest. She left it undisturbed.

Toward the middle of the room stood a work table filled with odd instruments. A mortar and pestle, easily explained by what must have been an herb garden just outside. Several bowls of varying sizes rested to one side, two broken completely, one with just a chip. One glass bulb with a long, thin nozzle lay on its side next to a candle holder, a small hand mirror and—Jane sucked in her breath.

"A skull." David blew some dust away from the grim face.

"What do you make of all this?"

"Looks like an alchemist's lab to me," David said.

"Alchemist? Like turning lead into gold?"

"That's a common misunderstanding. It has more to do with the transformation of human consciousness, although they did experiment with transmuting metals. Did a good deal of healing, some of them."

"What's with the skull?"

"The Masons use it as a meditation tool."

"Meditation?" She gave a little theatrical shiver.

"Well, to contemplate death. That this life is temporary. You see skulls in portraits of alchemist's laboratories."

"Cheerful bunch." Jane smiled despite her wry tone.

"Yeah," he said, acknowledging this. "This proves one thing, though." His eyes gleamed.

"What's that?" Jane looked around at the jumble.

"Your ancestors were alchemists, trained in the mysteries."

She toed a loose stone on the floor, then squinted up at him. "Yeah?"

"Definitely."

"So they could've had an artifact."

"It's more than that. It shows again that the Brethren and metaphysics were not in opposition."

"Leinbach said that the aristocracy studied it—or patronized those who did."

David nodded his concession. "This is in their house—" He pointed back at the passageway to the main quarters "—or at least the tower attached to it. Perhaps this person was in their employ, but they were open to the mysteries if not students themselves."

Jane drifted out of the room and climbed a few steps. The next one shifted under her weight. She tested the next step and found it solid, but around the curve of the tower, the way forward was blocked with a pile of rubble. She turned and picked her way over the shifting flagstones until she reached solid ones. There she found David standing with one arm on each wall blocking her way, a rakish smile on his face.

"Isn't this just . . ." She shook her head. "I mean, my grandmother's family came from this very place."

He nodded.

Jane walked into his arms and kissed him. He wrapped his arms around her, pulling her flush to him. The kiss deepened and she felt his body respond. She started to pull away, but he groaned a complaint. In a flush of heat, she reached for his belt, unfastened it, stopped. Then his hand found the skin of her back.

"But where?" she whispered. The Fiat was too small. Too exposed. Although there was no one for miles.

In answer, he angled her against the wall, moving down another step.

"Oh," Jane's laugh was lustful. "This would work. But it's cold," she managed to say against his lips.

Her boot-cut cargo pants fell over her shoes, and he lifted her, wrapping them both in his great winter coat.

The cold turned out to be no problem. In fact, she emerged from this intimate cocoon sweating. She opened her blouse and fanned herself. David admired the view, then bent to kiss her nipples through her bra. He stirred again, but then with a grunt of disappointment, said, "I guess we're not teenagers anymore."

"Sex on the stairs once is adventure enough for me," she said, then lolled her head against the rough stone wall.

"You are so beautiful," he said.

She smiled, languid, content.

His eyes grew wide. "It is cold," and he bent to cover his bare bum.

She straightened her clothes, ran her fingers through her hair. "Now what?" she asked with a breathless laugh.

He tilted his head toward the bottom of the stairs. "I think the steps go down. Let's see if they're solid."

Jane felt her way around the curved stairs, testing each step, hands on the smooth stone walls. Around the next turn, it grew dark. David switched on the flashlight they'd brought, illuminating the steps below, which ended after one more turn. Jane moved into a rectangular room, her steps echoing back to her. She walked forward and David followed, shining the light on the walls.

"Oh, my God." Jane's hand flew to her mouth.

"Wow!" David shone the light along the wall.

They were covered in illustrations, like the temples in Egypt, but instead of hieroglyphs, these were drawn. Spirals, stars and other geometrical figures. In the middle of each wall an eight-pointed star shone out, each with an equal armed cross in the center. They moved closer. Jane touched one spiral, then looked at her finger in the beam of light. No smudge. "What do you think these are drawn in?" she whispered, for some reason reverential.

"Don't know." David matched her tone.

He shined the light into the middle of the room. A larger star, embedded in the floor, winked in the light. From the ceiling hung the remains of a rusty metal star with tiny pinprick holes.

"What do you think this place was?" Jane asked.

"Looks like a ritual room to me. Maybe a place to teach the mysteries during the persecutions."

They moved to the opposite wall. Next to the large star was a smaller one. The illustration that followed showed a row of thirteen points laid out in a line. In the next illustration another row, thirteen again, was laid out, until at the end of the wall they found a figure that looked very like a nautilus shell.

"This reminds me of something," Jane said, cocking her head, trying to remember.

David shone the flashlight on the opposite wall, where the illustrations were reversed, ending with another large Advent Star intact.

She snapped her fingers. "Blake. There was a pencil sketch in Miss Essig's Blake collection just like this."

David bent close. "There's something written here, but I can only make out a little of it."

Jane crouched close to him. "What language?"

"Latin, I think." He bent close, then grunted. "Would you hold the light?" She shone the beam on the script. "Okay, the first letter is 'L'. I can't read the next, but after that might be an 'X'." The next word is completely obliterated."

She shifted the light slightly.

"Next comes another 'L' two blank spaces, then "is." Then an 'in'. Means the same in English. Then a smudge and 'men'." He moved, still bending. "Something here. It's not decipherable. The last word looks like 'Deu-'. Probably 'God'."

"So, what do we have? Wait, let me find something to write on." She fished in her pocket, came out with a pen. "Paper?"

David pulled out a matchbook from the restaurant they'd eaten at last night. Jane took the cap off the pen, opened the matchbook and almost dropped the flashlight.

David reached out. "I'll manage the light." He read out the letters and spaces again.

"Got it."

A gun fired somewhere outside.

They both froze.

David switched off the light.

Jane stuffed the paper and pen in her pocket. Found David's hand.

Silence.

Jane took a breath to whisper, but heard the scrap of footsteps outside. Then voices. The language sounded like Czech.

David switched on the light inside his jacket, letting it shine down, just a pool of illumination at their feet. They crept to the stairs. Started to climb, careful to make no sound.

Another gunshot, this one closer.

They shrank against the wall.

A dog barked, moving away from the house.

David glided up the remaining stairs and reached the main floor. He stepped out into the ruins of the kitchen, Jane following. She blinked in the sudden sun.

In the bushes outside, a brown and white retriever pointed, body quivering. Two men moved branches aside. One bent and picked up the body of a pheasant. Held it up to the other. They started to head back toward the woods.

David stepped out from behind a stone. His foot scraped against loose pebbles.

The men turned. One held a hand over his eyes, then smiled. The other waved. The first man held up a brace of birds.

Jane pulled her phone out of her pocket and clicked a picture, then waved.

"Hunters," she murmured.

"Looks like it."

The men walked closer, speaking Czech.

"English?" Jane spread her hands.

"Deutsch?" David asked.

They shook their heads. The man with the birds held them up again and said something. The other touched the rim of his cap, and they followed their dog back into the woods.

"Whew!" Jane said.

"No kidding," David said. "For a minute I thought we were goners."

"I never thought to ask Ivar for a weapon. After Ronneburg, that was stupid." Jane slumped against a pile of stone.

"But he said Philip was gone."

"And another guy had taken his place."

"One who would just watch us," David said.

Jane just shook her head. "I don't even know how to shoot a gun."

"I do," David said, "although I'd prefer not to."

She looked at the picture on her phone, pushed a few icons. "Okay, I sent it to Ivar. He can check their faces. See if he recognizes them."

"Maybe we should get out of here."

"I completely forgot." Jane walked back through the house and out to their car. She opened the back and pulled out a picnic basket.

"The pheasant made you hungry?"

She laughed. "No, silly. The camera. Let's document that room. This is much better than my cell."

"And the alchemist's lab."

"We'll take pictures of the whole place. My family will be delighted." She stopped for a moment, thinking of Frank, wondering why he hadn't returned her calls. David was right. To them what she'd done had looked like attempted theft. What had she thought, moving eighteen century sketches? But they'd just been casually piled against a wall. She should have asked permission. They might have said no, but then maybe Lois would still be alive.

They spent what remained of the afternoon taking pictures, first in the ritual room as they came to call it, then the lab, finishing with all the other rooms and half-fallen walls, the family crest outside and long shots of the house and area. Satisfied, Jane put away her camera as the sun began to settle behind the rolling hills to the west. She threw the keys to David.

His eyes lit. "I get to drive?"

She chuckled. "Men and their toys."

"Hey, you seemed to enjoy the way she clung to the curves—" David heard what he'd said and blushed furiously.

"Like I said, boys and their toys." She smiled as she got into the passenger side.

Ivar called Jane while they were still driving toward Prague. They'd decided to check out of their hotel in Fulnek. "If someone's going to shoot me, I'd rather it be in a big city," Jane declared.

"Tell me what happened." Ivar's gravelly voice gave her confidence.

Jane recounted the story, then asked, "Did you identify them?"

"On the government computers. Found their drivers licenses. Ordinary citizens. Probably out hunting, just as you thought."

"Where's the guy who works for Coche?"

"Still in D.C."

"And our tail?"

"He's about a kilometer behind you."

Jane looked out the back window, but saw several sets of headlights. "Should we have a gun?"

"You know how to use one?" Ivar asked.

"David does."

Ivar grunted. "I'll leave a small one in the room for you when we get back."

"We?"

"You didn't think I'd let you leave Prague without cover, did you?"

"Of course." Jane tapped her head. She was a terrible spy. "Thanks," she mumbled.

Ivar's raspy laugh filled her ear for a second. "You are welcome."

Jane pulled out the matchbook cover and studied the Latin phrase they'd discovered on the diagram of the star. She found a Latin translation site and began typing in words to see what she could figure out.

"This first word looks like it's missing a vowel." She looked over at David. "I don't mean to sound illiterate, but are the Latin vowels the same."

David shrugged.

"Great. Here's where we could use a Catholic." She tried all the vowels. The words with 'a' added extra letters and did not match the wall. The next three vowels produced the same results. She added 'u' and came up with 'light'.

"The first word is 'light'," Jane said.

"Good," David said.

"The last word is obviously 'God'. The next word ends in 'men'. Probably a common syllable." She poked around on the site for a long time, trying various combinations. Frustrated, she pulled out the camera and studied the pictures of the wall, magnifying the image. The word started with what looked like a straight line. She looked for other lines at the top or bottom or even coming off the middle. There was a shadow at the bottom of the letter, but she couldn't tell if it was something written on the wall or a real shadow.

Deciding to go with 'L', she typed in vowels. The only one that produced a word was 'Lumen', meaning 'light' or 'lamp'. She told David.

He chewed on his lip. "Maybe one's a verb and one's a noun. Or we can go with lamp."

"Then it reads 'Light lamp in blank God'."

"Must be 'in God' or 'of God'."

"Probably, but we're missing one word."

"We've found four."

Jane switched off her phone and leaned her head back against the headrest. The lights of the city drove back the dark of the countryside. "We're almost back."

They drove in silence, deciding to turn in the car in the morning. In Knight's suite, a gun sat on the desk waiting for them. David told her what kind it was, a name that did not stick in her head, and showed her how to aim it and work the safety. This she remembered.

He took two steps toward the master bedroom, then stopped, an uncertain look on his face.

"You can sleep with me if you'd like" Jane said.

His blue eyes lit with his smile. "I would."

Jane felt a tug of desire, but sleep is exactly what they did.

CHAPTER TWENTY-FOUR

Václav had perfect timing, at least in David's opinion. He called right at ten thirty. They'd had enough time for a morning of dalliance—although David's low back had developed a dull ache. Room service delivered a sumptuous breakfast about half past nine.

"Václav says he'll be here in ten minutes," he called to Jane. She was in the living room uploading the pictures they'd taken yesterday to Knight. Apparently the computer automatically encrypted files, reducing security risks.

Jane pushed back from the desk. "What's on the agenda today?" She twisted her hair up and clipped it, then shrugged into her coat.

He pointed out the window. "The castle. St. Vitus Cathedral."

"What should we be looking for?"

He hesitated.

"What's the matter?"

"I'm getting this feeling—" he looked out the window, then made himself focus back on her. Might as well spit it out. "If there's an artifact, I think it's back in Winston-Salem with your cousin."

"You mean Frank?"

"Think about it. He's part of the Star Family. Plus he seems to be a full-fledged member of the OGMS."

"True, but he told Penelope there was no legend of an artifact in the family."

"Maybe it's not something the family divulges. He might even know the whole history of the Star Family—and the artifact, if there is one—"

"You don't even think it exists?"

David moved closer. "Who can say? But I think you just stumbled into this accidentally. I'm not sure you have any part in this prophecy."

She watched him from those lapis blue eyes, a little furrow in the space just between her eyebrows. He stopped himself from leaning in to kiss it. She chewed on her lower lip for a moment. "You could be right about Frank, the turkey. He could have told me."

"Could he? What would you have thought, your straight-laced, socially upstanding cousin a member of a metaphysical organization? They probably have oaths of secrecy, like the Masons. Religious persecution was no joke a couple hundred years ago. The Inquisition would wring the names of others out of you before they burnt you at the stake."

"But this is the twenty-first century. Things have changed."

"Yeah, now they use water boarding."

Jane's laugh turned to a puff of air, as if she'd been punched in the stomach.

David went on. "Frank probably promised to keep these things secret when he was first initiated. The Masons still have some pretty steep oaths. He must have felt he had to keep it all under wraps. Just like many of the Brethren kept their mysticism to themselves, even from other members of the Unity."

She held up a finger. "One thing, though. Why did the lot fall to me? Why did Miss Essig even suggest they put my name in?"

"Assuming the lot even works."

"You don't believe in the lot? David Spach, I'm shocked." Jane's look of mock scandal made him smile.

"Maybe she was just fond of you, remembered how much you loved the place. Hoped you'd come back to your home."

"But there would be some bigger reason I'm supposed to live in that house."

Satisfaction warmed him. It must have shown on his face.

"What?" she asked.

"I don't think you would have said something like that when you first moved back. You're turning into a mystic."

She rolled her eyes.

"Maybe that's the mystery we're supposed to solve." At her wrinkled brow, he added, "Why you're in that house."

She brightened, her look mischievous. "Maybe there is no artifact, but I have found something."

"Yeah, that room."

She leaned in and tapped his nose. "I found you again."

A flash of joy lit him up like a string of Christmas lights, but before he could grab her, she was off. At the door she tossed him a look over her shoulder that almost stopped his heart. "You coming?"

She was something, all right.

Downstairs Václav waited on the side of the lobby, his scuffed boots, ragged coat and stubble of beard making him stand out in this hotel of sleek glass tables and minimalist chairs in elegant nooks.

"Here we are." Jane tucked her arm under David's, missing Václav's knowing grin. David smiled back a bit guiltily, although he didn't know why he should feel that way.

"Today we walk," Václav announced.

They trailed down the sidewalk behind him like ducklings. He pointed out the statue of Charles IV in its own small courtyard just at the foot of the bridge that was his namesake. "Meet mastermind behind Praha—Charles IV, Emperor of the Holy Roman Empire."

Jane snapped a picture.

"The most important thing about him is we share same name— Václav or Wenceslaus."

"Congratulations, Your Imperial Majesty." Jane curtsied to Václav.

She's sure in a good mood, David thought, wondering how much credit he could take for that, still digesting what she said to him before they left the room. He felt the same. Their time here was like a beautiful Christmas ornament, nestled amongst green needles, gleaming in the light, but delicate, vulnerable. Would it stand up to the ordinary small town life he was used to? He pushed these worries aside and listened to Václav's running commentary.

"Charles IV was king of Bohemia before being appointed as Holy Roman Emperor in 1355," Václav continued, "and he moved his court to his birthplace, Praha. He was educated in France, so he brought many Parisian builders, alchemists and scholars here. He established university and planned a new Prague. Some say he modeled it on Paris, which is only partially true."

They moved past the guard tower—which Václav pointed to—"I'll show you its secrets on the way back"—and onto Charles Bridge where a host of tourists gathered around the booths of artists and clusters of musicians, making the walk slow. Perfect to keep Jane's arm tucked under his. Didn't want to get lost.

Statues lined the walls of the bridge, which for the most part Václav ignored. But Jane kept taking pictures. "The real metaphysical secret of Prague," Václav continued, not attempting to lower his voice, so it couldn't be much of a secret, David thought, "is he wanted to create a New Jerusalem."

Salem's original name, David noted. But a common name, so it didn't mean that much.

"And he did, at least in geometry. In St. Vitus Cathedral, I will show you his inner Jerusalem. The outer Jerusalem—" he held out both hands, indicating the two sides of the bridge, then waved his hands behind him, "—is bridge and town. We shall visit all the spots if you wish."

"We wish." Jane said, then danced over to a group of musicians and paused to listen. They played one of Bach's canons for a string trio. She tossed in a couple of Euros and glided back to David's side. They continued picking their way through the crowd, pausing to look at photographs for sale, watch artists sketch caricatures of tourists and laugh at their renditions of movie stars and even politicians. Jane oohed at jewelry, picked up earthenware cups, considered Christmas ornaments, took pictures of everything. The musicians had spaced themselves at enough distance from each other so their music would not interfere with other groups. Some played carols, others classical pieces, even jazz.

David shifted from foot to foot. He hated shopping, but Václav seemed resigned to it. Used to tourists, he supposed, which they'd obviously turned into. Maybe he shouldn't have said anything about there being no artifact. At least not here. After their sixth such stop, he asked, "Don't you want to see the cathedral?"

Jane came back and took his arm with a smile. "I guess I can come back later. We live right next to the bridge, after all."

Václav gave a clipped nod and led them deftly toward the other side of the river, his broad shoulders parting the crowd. Once off the white bricks of the bridge, he pointed up. "Now we get exercise."

"Oh, good." Jane said. "I haven't been running." And she took off.

David took a deep breath and followed. At least she was walking. Well, speed walking. They forged their way up a block or so with stone buildings belly-up to the sidewalk, the stores refurbished and quite modern, before coming to a square. He spotted a Starbucks. They waited for the trolley to pass, then crossed. Once off the square, the climb started in earnest, shops, restaurants and people crowding the steep hill.

Václav, God bless him, slowed Jane down with his history lesson, explaining the gradual building of the castle and cathedral, the rule of kings and emperors. "Rudolph II is my favorite, though. A true mystic. Some say crazy, but I think a visionary. He gathered illustrious group around him—talented alchemists and astrologers. Even the famous John Dee lived here for a while with his friend Kelley."

"That's right." David remembered something about this.

Václav pointed out the famous pissing stone as they passed. "Still used," he said, as if asking David if he needed to stop. Jane did not take a picture. Instead, she stalked off, her back up a bit, a reaction Václav seemed to have been trying for based on his boyish grin.

They caught up to her around the curve and halfway up to the castle where she stood against the stone wall looking out on the city, a breeze playing with that silver hair. She turned her head, a smug smile seeming to ask why they were so red in the face, but she reached out for David, the smile turning genuine and pointed out over the city. "Have you ever seen anything so beautiful?" She settled against him, content.

He tilted her chin up. "Yes, I have."

She ducked her head as if compliments made her shy. Václav went off for tickets, leaving them a minute to catch their breath. Or at least David. They stood for another minute, taking in the green domes and hundred spires of the city. She nestled against his side, trying to name the famous landmarks. Neither cared to look them up in the guide book. That would mean putting an inch of space between them. Two teenagers looked at the old lovers and made a face. David staunchly ignored them.

Jane leaned close to his ear, her breath warm. "So we let the quest find us? If there is one."

"I think so," David said.

They turned to find Václav making his way across the plaza toward them, tickets in hand. They moved to join him.

"Cathedral first?"

"Sure," Jane said.

"Energetic center of St. Vitus is natural cliff used for sacred ceremony for thousands of years, just like Vyšehrad." Václav recited the vital stats of the place and David let them fade into the background. The roof looked like a dragon's back with its points rising at regular intervals. Even the spires were edged with them. He was sure they had some proper name, but didn't know it. He couldn't shake the feeling he was walking into a dragon.

They handed over their tickets and entered the nave. As one, David and Jane stopped and gaped, their eyes lifted above the clerestory.

"Oh, my God." Jane stepped aside to let the other tourists pass.

They walked up the left aisle, marveling at the intricacies of design and colors in the stained glass windows, necks strained back. Figures in green, red, then blue all winding their way up to the pinnacle with a separate panel of Christ. In the next, angels lay on their sides or in odd postures flanking a panel with human figures, all yearning upward.

"These windows were designed by Mucha in 1920s," Václav said, then explained what they were seeing.

For some reason David didn't want to hear all the Biblical references. He just wanted to be in the place, to feel it, to let it seep into his pores. He hung back, letting Jane and Václav move ahead.

The next window featured elegant, almost pastel people with halos. In the window at the front of the cathedral stood a magnificent crowned Christ, and next to him the Madonna in radiant purple. On the opposite panel—was that Charles IV's sharp chin and his family adoring the holy family?

David caught up with them at the east end of the cathedral just as Václav waved a hand. "A cathedral was open book. Most of people weren't literate, so stone work, the windows, paintings—all taught basic principles and repeated stories they heard in sermons.

"But those who could read were also trained in mysteries. At least, for most part. They understood hidden references. This is Lady Chapel, place of the Chief Feminine Elder."

That caught David's attention.

Václav pointed behind him to the sanctuarium. "This area represents celestial sphere where soul resides, and tabernacle, the seat of God, 'world without end, Amen'." He intoned the familiar phrase solemnly.

Václav was talking Kabbalah now, something David had a bit of a flair for. Well, at least he remembered the basics. Cathedrals were laid out on a Tree of Life pattern. The middle of the tree, the pillar of consciousness, moved from the unmanifest all, or as Václav had just said 'world without end', to the manifest world we live in.

Václav pointed all the way down the long church filled with stone carvings, statues, and paintings, to the entrance at the Rose Window. "The Rosetta is set in wall so that sun never shines on it."

"Why? It's so beautiful," Jane asked.

"It represents process of enlightenment. The adept must maintain inner fire night and day for transmutation to occur."

Jane listened, her lips slightly parted, clearly fascinated. Václav's words stirred David's memory. He'd studied all this—a long time ago it seemed.

"Want to see Charles IV's Inner Jerusalem?"

"Sure," Jane said, eyes eager.

Václav walked down the southern isle, pointing out the tomb of St. Vitus, then Charles himself. "Wonderful, powerful, yes," he said in a low voice, "but here is real treasure."

Just at the triforium, he paused before the door to a luxurious chapel. A red velvet rope blocked the entrance. Jane stepped up eagerly and craned her neck to see into the recesses.

"St. Wenceslaus's Chapel, planned by Petr Parler who designed cathedral and built a great deal of it before his death. Charles had a big hand in it, of course. Built according to Saint John's vision of New Jerusalem." He gave David a questioning look to see if he remembered.

"A square?"

Václav nodded his approval. "All sides supposed to be equal, measured at twelve thousand stadi. The architect added another square outlined in tiles." He pointed.

"So the chapel is a double cube," David said, remembering that form so important in sacred geometry. "An altar in the cathedral."

"A church within a church. A Tree of Life within a Tree of Life. At one time the room held all gem stones mentioned in vision, all at proper corners. Much of it is gone now, but magic remains."

Jane stepped back, giving David room to take it all in. Murals filled the arched walls. A golden replica of the cathedral sat on an ornate wooden table. The altar and a low table made of deeply polished wood gleamed in the tepid winter sunlight filtering in from the high windows. Unlit white candles, pure as untouched snow, sat atop them. The chandelier began with a circle containing simple equal-armed cross, the symbol for Earth on the Tree of Life, and fell in two larger golden rings of lights. Gilded trim winked from every wall. The place was filled with gold.

"Every king of Bohemia came here alone and sat in silence to prepare for coronation. Presidents have followed this tradition. The power remains, even if some of the outer trappings have been lost through centuries. This is heart and soul of Praha."

David turned to Jane to explain some of the sacred geometry of the chapel, but she stood as if entranced, eyes closed, gently swaying.

"Jane," he whispered.

She held up a hand to forestall him. After a few seconds, she murmured something.

He leaned in closer. "What?"

"Do you hear it, David?" she whispered, awe lighting her face.

"Hear what?"

She smiled, beatific as the saints gazing down from their stained glass windows high above. "I hear it all now."

Then she crumpled.

"What the—" David grabbed her head just before it banged on the stone floor.

☆ ☆ ☆

"So the chapel is a double cube," she heard David say. "An altar in the cathedral."

"A church within a church. A Tree of Life within a Tree of Life." Václav sounded excited, like this fact was of great importance. "At one time the room held all gem stones mentioned in the vision . . ." His voice faded mid-sentence. Her vision narrowed. She stepped back from the velvet rope. Put a hand to her head. Someone was playing music faintly outside. Or was it the organ? She turned her head to look for the source.

She listened, intent, her body taut as a string tuned to the highest C. The piece had started as a whisper, a promise, wafting down from somewhere high above the cathedral. Then a bass note answered from deep within the rock beneath them, rising up and meeting the celestial strand. The two blended mid-air, wrapping around each other, a double helix. A pause, followed by a surge of sound that fled in the cardinal directions like rabbits let loose or birds flying out. Yes, a flock of brilliant blues, reds, yellows and even purple.

David was asking her something. She held up a hand to forestall him.

Her composition played on. Nothing could stop it now. It would play to the end. All she had to do was listen.

"Do you hear it, David?" she whispered.

"Hear what?"

"I hear it all now." She closed her eyes to listen and the world tipped.

She made her way down a hallway laid with scarlet carpeting soft beneath her feet. The floor dipped down in a ramp, but this time she did not fall. This time the piece played on, the flow from above delivered by flutes and violins, a stream of freshness and new life. The bass and French horns answered, the earth opening, receiving, then returning that stream of sound in a celebration of growth. The straight, vigorous force of a stem rising up from rich, brown earth, of vines spreading, green and vigorous. Next the violent burst of red flowers—tulips bloomed, the spiked edges of poinsettias opened. Roses unfurled and gave themselves to whoever came to their altar, wanton and sacred. Their scent filled the air, a perfume that made the heart ache.

She came to a door, ancient oak crowned with seven arches, each a new octave. She pushed it open. Emerged into a natural cavern. Water trickled down the rounded stone, adding its sound—nurturing, soothing, feeding life, which drank deep and redoubled its growth. The vegetation ran rampant and fertile, multiplying into an uncontrollable riot of sound and form. Of triumph.

Jane walked across the worn stone to the spring. Sank to her knees. Drank deep of the cold, iron-tinged liquid.

She sang the final note into the water.

And collapsed.

Jane floated in a golden sphere of perfect stillness, a new silence born from the riot of sound that had come before. Inside a pristine sphere of light. Rays spread in crystalline clarity, star-like.

Someone's face appeared above her. Leaned down. "You must take this music back," he said. "Play it in this place."

He put out his hand. His sleeve was brocade gold cloth, his beard dark. Round-edged crosses rose from the crown on his head. Gold arched from the cross across the top, the dome of heaven, but spiked like the cathedral roof.

"Charles?" she asked, her voice cracking with incredulity.

"Of course," the Emperor answered with a slight chuckle. "Who else?" He reached down to help her up.

She hesitated. He was royalty, after all.

"It must be at the darkest moment." He grasped her hand and pulled.

Jane grabbed his forearm in return, not wanting him to strain.

"Jane?" David's face swam into view.

"Charles?"

David frowned. "It's David." He pulled her to a sitting position.

She blinked and looked around. People crowded around. A man in a uniform pushed through, speaking in some other language. Czech. She was in Praha. She was in Charles's church.

She started laughing.

David snorted and rocked back on his heels.

Václav's bulk appeared by her side, blocking out the tourists crowded around.

"How in the world did you get the name Mouse?" She smiled up at him, drunk with success. "You're so big."

David and Václav exchanged a look.

"Isn't that what 'Myska' means?" she asked.

David leaned closer. Put a hand on her forehead. "Are you all right?"

"Never better."

Václav shook his big head back and forth with a bemused smile. "We're glad to hear it."

Jane grabbed David's shoulder and started to pull herself up.

"Best she stay seated," a heavily accented voice said in English.

Jane found the Czech official crouched beside Václav. "I'm okay, really."

"Does she need a doctor?"

Václav turned to her as if to repeat the question.

"I'm fine, really." Jane pulled herself up. "I must have fainted."

"I'll say," David exclaimed.

She stood, dusted off her pants. Looked into the officious face. "Got lightheaded. Shouldn't skip breakfast."

David blew his breath out heavily. They'd stuffed themselves full of eggs, sausage and toast only a little while ago.

The Czech official frowned.

She tried again. "Too much beer?"

The official shook his head and spoke under his breath. Mumbled something about Americans.

He fixed on David. "Your wife is not sick?"

David blanched. "She's not—" changed in mid-stream "—just got dizzy for a minute."

He took her arm. "I think we should call a cab and go back to the hotel. Let you lie down."

Václav spoke to the guard in Czech, then grabbed her other arm. Now she'd become a piece of luggage.

Jane leaned on David, lolled her head to take in the shafts of ruby, gold and emerald light from the windows. She could hear the music they made—the red a deep note, the emerald like rich earth. Should she be able to hear light? She tried to remember.

"He said to play it at the darkest moment," she said.

David made a strangled sound. "We need to get her back to the hotel. Can you get a cab, Václav?"

He ran ahead. David led her through the front door out into the square. The sun pierced Jane, running in a clash of symbols and the triumphant blare of a horn through the center of her body. "And the walls of Jericho fell."

"Oh, boy," David said.

Ivar appeared with Václav in tow. "The car is over here. Tell me what happened."

Jane listened to David's version, amazed she'd only been out for a few seconds. It had seemed much longer. In his voice, she heard fear, a hot, discordant sound. Fire, which was anger—at himself. Why did men think they should be able to forestall everything? All threaded through with the warm glow of love. And a stab of cold, which was how he thought he would feel if he lost her.

She snuggled against him, watching the city go by through the tinted windows of the limo. She briefly wondered why Ivar was driving such a big car.

Václav ran his large finger over the leather trim. Touched the flat screen in front of him. It sprang to life and he jerked back in his seat.

Ivar spread his hand between Václav and the computer. "Please don't touch anything, sir."

Jane leaned toward Václav and asked in a conspiratorial tone, "First time in a limo?"

The big man nodded.

"Check this out." Jane touched a button and a panel slid open.

Startled, Václav exhaled like a horse. The panel revealed a couple of bottles of liquor and glasses. She burst out laughing.

"Jane, would you be serious? What's gotten into you?" David asked.

"I'm glad you asked." She sat up straight. Really, she did feel a little inebriated. "I know what my part in the quest is."

This silenced them all.

"What?"

"But first, I need a piano."

David put his head in his hands and groaned.

"We'll run a blood panel. See if someone slipped something into the food," Ivar said.

"But we ate breakfast together," David said, "and I wasn't affected."

"Then a small needle. In that crowd . . ." Ivar waved his hand. "Knight is going to gut me if something happens to this one."

"Nobody slipped me anything," Jane said. "Would you all listen?"

The three men looked at her, worry and confusion marking their faces.

She addressed herself to David. "I heard the rest of the composition we've been working on. I know what I'm supposed to do with it."

He stared at her, clearly unsure.

"What?" Václav asked when David remained silent.

She started to speak, but Ivar held up his beefy hand. "Let's wait until we get back to the room."

"And I was serious about needing a piano. Think you can get us one?" She looked at the Russian security man.

"No problem."

Ivar was as good as his word. They hadn't been back five minutes before two bellhops in white jackets wheeled a Baldwin upright into the room and placed it in the corner with a bit of a flourish. Jane grabbed her purse and tipped them a bit lavishly, still filled with the abundance of the music. Ivar's security team poured over the instrument, checking for cameras, explosives—Jane couldn't imagine what all. The team had been in the suite giving it another examination when they arrived.

Ivar took a blood sample and swabbed out her cheek himself. "Just precautionary," he said. He did the same to David. Václav politely refused, which made Ivar eye him a bit.

After Ivar seemed satisfied that the suite and piano were secure, he turned to Jane. "I will report to Knight, but you'll need to tell him what you experienced." He pointed toward the computer.

Jane nodded, not really comfortable with this idea. She'd make her own decisions, but Ivar wasn't going to go away until she agreed. He promised to report the lab results as soon as he got them and left them in peace, giving Václav a long look before closing the door.

Surely he'd checked Václav out already, Jane thought.

David studied her a moment in the ensuing quiet. Finally he took in a long breath and asked, "Who's Charles?"

This sent Jane into gales of laughter. She grabbed a pillow off the couch and hugged it to her stomach, trying in vain to contain herself. Oh, life was grand.

"What's so funny?" he asked, clearly put out.

"I tell you I've figured out the music that's been haunting me since I moved into Miss Essig's house, that I know my part in this quest, and what do you want to know? Who Charles is." She cackled again, then pushed down her hilarity, which was threatening to set off her odd state of consciousness again. His jealousy sounded like discordant wind chimes.

"So what is your part in this quest?" Václav said, opening a bottle of Pivovarsky Dvur he'd found rummaging in the kitchen. He poured it carefully into a beer mug. "If I might ask, that is."

"He told me to play the piece at the darkest moment." She nodded as if this was self-explanatory, but they still frowned at her in confusion. "In this place I saw in my . . ." she searched for the right word.

"Vision?" David asked.

Was that what it had been? She hesitated to name it. It had been mostly sound. Much more than images. Surely a vision was seeing things, but she'd been inside the music, moving with it, or watching it move her, change her, grow through her and connect out into the world. The piece changed the world as it changed her, its vibration vital, bringing wholeness, balance, vigor. She stared at David for a moment. "I guess it was a vision. Do they make you dizzy? All giddy?"

"Not me."

She could see he wanted to ask something else. "What is it?"

"Who told you to play it?" he asked, cautious, his body leaning slightly away from her.

"Charles."

David wasn't going to ask.

Václav stepped up to the plate as pitch hitter. "So, if I might ask, who is Charles?"

"Charles IV," Jane answered, forcing back a silly grin. "You know, the Emperor of the Holy Roman Empire."

David just stared.

"Of course." Václav slapped his knee, suds spilling from his glass. He threw back his head and laughed. The whole earth laughed with him. At least it seemed that way to Jane. She joined in. David just stared at them.

Once the wave of laughter left them, David leaned back against the pillows on the sofa and said, "Why don't you take it from the top?"

So she did. She told them the whole story, trying to describe the music, but failing.

David waved his hands in dismissal. "You can play it for us later. Just tell us what happened."

She finished her story, then waited to see if it made any sense in the plain light of day.

"So, we need to learn this music, find where this place is," he ticked them off on his fingers, "and figure out what the darkest moment is. Right?"

"Simple, really," Václav said.

Jane moved to the piano and let her fingers play the now familiar beginning to her composition, then opened herself to the sound again. It moved from the golden sphere still glowing inside her, down her arms and spilled out onto the keys, lifting the room into a glory of harmony. Then she slowed, picking her way, humming to herself. A note that did not belong intruded. She frowned. Heard it again. Looked up.

"Sorry," David mouthed. His stomach growled again.

"Why don't you order us some lunch," she said.

"Here?" Václav asked.

"Sure, get whatever you like." She waved a hand in abandon, then turned back to the piano, took a breath and trusted. Her hands played until the end.

Jane let her head fall back. Quiet triumph filled her. Tears brimmed up like the spring and she let them flow over her cheeks, over worn stone, down into the earth. Tears were strength, moisture, nourishment.

David sat beside her on the piano bench, put an arm around her shoulders to comfort her, but there was no need. She leaned into him, shared the stream of life. Then opened her eyes. "We need paper. Music paper." She looked at Václav. "Can we get some?"

"We are right next to National Theatre. Near the Klementinum. So many concert halls. It is a simple thing."

She found her wallet and pulled out a fistful of Euros. "Is this enough?"

Václav choked back a laugh. "Do you want entire orchestra or just some music paper?"

She thrust out her hand. "Take what you need. Knight is loaded."

She felt something inside David relax. She frowned at him. "You've been worrying about paying your way. Didn't I tell you—"

His kiss silenced her.

By the time Václav returned, room service had delivered their lunch. Jane stayed at the piano, running through the composition once more, enjoying the certainty that it was here at last, that it would not retreat into the golden light and leave her in the ordinary browns and greys of the stones of Praha.

"You'd better come get something to eat before we devour it all," David said, still chewing.

"Yes, it's getting cold," Václav said. "You should eat after such a visitation."

That's when it hit her. She didn't want to be weighed down, to lose touch with the soaring freedom of the spiritual realm that had reached down and lifted her up into it. She was afraid the food would bring her all the way back and she never wanted to lose this feeling.

"Do not worry." Václav chuckled as if he were reading her mind. "The visions, they will come again."

Jane joined them around the coffee table where their feast was spread. Sandwich wedges of roast beef, pastrami and turkey sat on a platter. She took salad and a turkey sandwich wedge, but avoided the ever-present sausages.

After a few bites, she began to talk. "I hear violins and French horns. Trombones, of course," she smiled at David. "I need other instruments. I wish I could borrow one of those orchestras you mentioned," she said to Václav.

Václav chewed his pastrami sandwich, then took a long swallow of his second Pivovarsky Dvur. "Many of my friends are musicians. If you have score, they can play it."

Jane sat forward. "Really? When?"

"When will you have it ready?"

"Tonight?"

"Better make it tomorrow," David said. "I'll bet you're going to fall out early tonight."

Jane shook her head, still riding the golden light. She was sure she'd never be tired again.

"It will take at least a day, maybe two, to gather everyone," Václav said. He drained his beer and stood. "I'll be in touch."

CHAPTER TWENTY-FIVE

After Václav left, Jane and David got to work. They holed up in their hotel room, madly scoring the composition. She played the piano, sang, then went over each phrase repeatedly, trying to hear all the instruments at once. Even with David also playing and singing, they couldn't duplicate the piece. But she had it. She knew she had it. Very early the next morning, they declared it finished.

To celebrate, they walked out onto Charles Bridge. Their breath formed clouds in front of their faces. Mist shrouded the lamps. A crescent moon rose over the river, promising sunrise soon. The only sound was the gushing river washing her tension away. They walked back hand in hand, fell into bed and slept past noon.

Václav called around two o'clock to tell them he'd assembled a group of musicians. Jane was amazed when he told her who was coming and what instruments they played. "You've made me a veritable orchestra," she said.

His earthy laugh was reassuring. "Meet us tonight at 10:00 p.m. at Smetana Concert Hall. After the orchestra's rehearsal."

Jane consulted their guide book. "Ever heard of the Municipal House?"

David's eyes rounded. "Of course."

"He's got some members of their orchestra to help."

"Václav sure has connections," David said. "That's the home of the Czech National Symphony Orchestra."

"Oh, no," Jane said.

"What do you mean 'oh, no?'" David asked. "These musicians are top notch. They'll be able to play this right off the page."

"I know," she said, her nerves tightening like the violin strings she'd be conducting tonight.

"What?" David turned his hands over in question.

"It's my first piece. They'll know how bad it is."

"Oh, stop it." David sat at the piano bench and patted the space beside him. "Besides, it's a ritual piece. Meant to produce certain effects on consciousness."

"It is?"

"I'll bet every one of them is a trained mystic. This is Prague, after all. Now, let's go through it again."

David was a task master, and Jane's nerves loosened as they worked. She forgot about the waiting musicians and became absorbed by the piece once again. They went through it several more times. At last, David was satisfied.

"One more time," Jane urged. "I'm still not sure about this bridge."

David stood up. "We need to take a break. Forget it completely. Then you'll hear it fresh tonight."

"That's what I'm afraid of."

"Trust me. I'm an expert on performance anxiety." He smiled at her. Those eyes melted her heart. She moved into his arms. "What did you have in mind?"

He held her tight for a moment, and she felt his body begin to respond, but then his stomach growled. "I need to get outside again. Get something to eat. Come on."

They dropped the precious score with the front desk and ordered enough copies for their first run through. The concierge assured them that Mr. Knight was a frequent customer of the hotel's business center and he was used to handling this sort of thing. Maybe not music scores, but fast copies.

They walked to Old Town Square and stood before Hus, then made their way through the crowds to the astronomical clock and waited in the cold. The crowd grew even thicker. Jane welcomed the warmth. Finally the display began.

A man admired himself in a mirror.

"That's Vanity," David said to her, his breath warm in her ear.

The figure beside him was unfortunate, a stereotypical depiction of a Jew holding money bags.

"Should be an oil sheik," Jane mumbled.

On the other side of the clock face, skeletal death struck the hour, seeming to challenge a Turkish man beside him. "He's supposed to represent pleasure," David read from a brochure they'd picked up in the hotel lobby.

The doors toward the top of the clock opened and the apostles walked. Jane squinted up in the late afternoon light. Based on what she'd read, the figures had golden halos, but she couldn't make them out. The doors closed again and the crowd applauded, then milled about, deciding on their next destination. She and David walked up the square just a few steps and found a table next to the window in one of the many restaurants.

She let David order. It would be sausages of some kind, she knew, and Czech beer. Would she ever drink any other kind again? If they were lucky, they'd see the clock display again. But they'd be fed and relaxed for her debut as a conductor— with some of the best musicians in the world. She pushed these thoughts away.

After a somniferous meal, they waited for the clock display once again, which they enjoyed in the warmth of the restaurant. Jane could barely make it out over the heads of the crowd that had gathered, even in the dark. When the show was over, David stood up and shrugged on his coat. "Ready, maestro?"

Jane's stomach clinched. "What if the piece just doesn't work?" she asked.

David reached his hand out. She took it and he hauled her to her feet. "Only one way to find out."

The chill of winter woke them from the drowse of the beer and heated restaurant. They arrived in their suite with red noses, but wide awake.

"Good thing the concert hall is close by," Jane said, stomping her feet. "It's cold." She looked down at her cords and sweater. This was a special event, the first time her piece would be performed, so she went to the closet and rummaged around. She decided on a long sleeve, black dress, almost warm. Then threw on the Moravian wool wrap she'd bought at the Christmas market just in case. Checked herself out in the mirror. Better.

They gathered the scores from the concierge's desk and took their familiar route past Kafka's house toward the Hus Memorial, then walked the few blocks toward National Square. David pointed out Powder Gate on the way. "One of the thirteen entrances to Prague. Modeled on the Bridge Tower."

"Thirteen again."

"Right," David said. "Looking through one of those history books, I was reminded that both August and November 13th are holy days for the Moravians."

"I guess the clues have been around us all our lives."

David squeezed her hand.

Municipal House was touted as the best Art Nouveau building in Prague, but it was too dark to really get a good look at it. A dome rose in the dark night sky above their heads. The building offered French and Czech restaurants, both packed full, even at this late hour.

"We could live here for years and never get to all the places within blocks of our hotel," Jane said.

"Shall we move to Prague?" he joked, then pushed open the door to the concert hall.

The sight silenced them. Lights lined the frescos on ceilings and walls, lighting everything into a mellow gold from a distance. Above the hall, a round window featured milky panels, surrounded by rows of lights. Concert boxes lined the walls. Organ pipes filled the entire wall behind the stage. The orchestra was packing away instruments and chatting amongst themselves. She and David sank into seats halfway back until only a small cluster of musicians remained.

Václav arrived on stage, shaded his eyes and looked out into the audience. "Jane? David? Is that you?"

David stood and tugged her forward, something he'd been doing all day, she realized. Jane moved down the aisle, suddenly a school girl. She'd stood toe to toe with world leaders, Saudi princes and CEOs, gotten used to brokering deals in the billions, but having her precious composition judged by such top-notch musicians had turned her knees to jelly.

"Just one foot in front of the other. When the music starts, you'll forget all this," David whispered.

They climbed the stairs to the stage and Václav made the introductions, but Jane couldn't hold them in her memory. The leaves of the score shook as she handed them over to Václav, who took them from her as carefully as a new born baby. As he distributed them, he told the story of how the music had started as a dream, then been given to her whole at St. Wenceslas Chapel. By the time he finished, Jane wished the stage would open up and she could disappear like some visiting demon in an opera.

One of the musicians noted her red face and said, "My name is Kornel. Please, madam, we are friends of Václav's. We understand such things."

Another spoke and the first musician translated. "He says we are honored to explore this with you."

Her eyes disobeyed her and filled with tears. "I only hope it is worth your attention."

The first musician translated, and the others shook their heads or made dismissive noises, brushing aside her self-consciousness. They spread the score on their platforms and began to read through the piece. Their noises turned to little grunts and speculative oohs, which soon gave way to several picking up their instruments and making tentative runs through more difficult passages. Within a space of five minutes, they all had their instruments ready and were looking up at her—their conductor—ready to begin.

Jane took a deep breath and raised her hands, holding the baton that she'd found at the station of one of the most eminent conductors in the world. She counted four to herself, then began. And the sound that rose from them stilled her heart. So beautiful. How could it be so beautiful? The quiet breath of the violins gave such promise, the promise of light and knowledge and something wonderful ready to unfold. Then the French horns repeated part of the phrase, grounding it, testing out the idea in a denser form. The piece built, then backed away and picked up a new theme. The themes twined around each other, like strands of DNA, until they rose in a column of radiance and crescendoed, burst like a fountain, or perhaps fireworks, then fell in silent embers to the earth.

Jane lowered her hands. Unseeing, she stood, her body beating in soft rhythm to the afterglow of successful creation. The musicians murmured to each other and Václav walked up behind Jane to translate.

"It is most magnificent," a voice whispered.

"Truly a gift," someone else said. "How lucky to receive such music."

Jane's gaze shifted to those who spoke. "No, it's you. Your performance was—I can't tell you how marvelous you all are. You have fulfilled a life dream for me."

They handed the credit back to her, then began to talk amongst themselves with Václav and Kornel translating.

"Let's try it again. I missed a cue," the violinist said. "And here. This phrase. Perhaps it should be a little less *Adagio*. You have not marked it, you see." He smiled almost apologetically.

"Yes, please. I welcome your comments." Jane took out a pencil and began to take notes on her score.

They became a working group. David found a trombone and joined in next to the French horn. They played it again, each group making notes which she would add to the final score. After a third time through, the harpist sat back with a nod. "It is a fine piece of music. Very good for a first composition."

A tall, thin wisp of a man stepped forward, his violin still tucked under his chin. "There is something very familiar about it, though. Something teases me."

Another nodded. "I've been having the same feeling. The progression suggests something—almost architectural."

"There is a pattern beneath the themes. Let's break it down to the basics." He took out blank paper and spread it on a piano bench. The conversation became too incomprehensible for Jane, even with Václav's rapid-fire translation. They talked of dodecahedrons, pi, the golden mean, but as they drew, something quite familiar began to take shape on the page.

Jane moved closer, hovered over the man's shoulder. "David, come look at this."

He put down his horn and came to stand beside her. His sharp intake of breath confirmed it.

The man stopped drawing and looked up.

"No, please continue," she said.

Kornel translated, then asked Jane, "You know this pattern?"

"Perhaps."

The second man finished his sketch and stood back. There on the piano bench lay an exact duplicate of the diagram they'd found on in the ritual room of the Star Family house.

"David." Jane reached for his arm, trying to find an anchor, something firm that would hold her up. "How can this be?"

"Unbelievable," he breathed.

"This piece of music uses the ancient mathematical formula that creates the holy star," the violinist said, "and the finale lights the center, what has always been called the Eye of God."

"You said something about lighting the Eye of God?"

"Yes," Kornel answered for him. "This sequence is used in a ritual to light the lamp in the Eye of God."

"It is sacred geometry," the other said.

Jane shook her head, unable to speak. This matched the Latin phrase they'd found in the ritual room.

"You have studied the mysteries?"

"No," Jane whispered.

"But how can this be?" He turned to Václav.

"She comes from the old family," Václav said.

"What old family?" Kornel asked.

"The Star Family."

Jane touched her star pendant.

Some nodded. Others shook their heads in amazement. "The patterns of the universe remain the same," one commented. "Those who attune themselves find the same patterns."

"This image," she pointed "If you fold it up—"

"It is the Advent Star," Kornel said.

She looked up sharply. "You know about that?"

His smile was shy. "But of course. We are all initiates here. And you. You have obviously studied in a past life. The knowledge is making itself known to you again. What were you told about the purpose of this music?"

Jane stared for a minute. Past lives? What she'd been learning did seem familiar, but she thought it was because of what the other man had said. The basic patterns of the universe were the same. We were made up of those patterns, so we recognize them at some deep level of our subconscious.

"Jane?" David captured her attention.

"I'm supposed to play it in an underground cave. There's a spring there. He said to play it at the darkest moment."

Instead of the derision she still expected, even after all this, thoughtful looks filled the faces of these miraculous musicians. "This must be Solstice Night," the violinist said after a while.

"Most likely, unless he means some terrible event."

"It felt more physical than political," Jane said.

"Solstice, then," Václav concluded.

"And this cave. Do you know it?" Kornel asked.

"I've only dreamed about it."

"Tell us."

She described the dream of walking down the long hall with the red carpet, of going down a ramp, then into a natural cave with the spring at the back. "I've never seen such a place." Then it hit her. "Except the hallway. I did find a hallway with that color carpet and walls off the basement of the house I was living in."

"Zizi's Cave has a spring as well," Kornel said. "The sacred cave beneath the cathedral. Perhaps we are meant to play this in St. Vitus on Solstice."

"And who is this 'he' you keep referring to? Who told you these things?" another musician asked.

Jane blushed a furious red and studied her shoes.

"Come now," Kornel urged. "This is no time to be shy. We all receive such visitations at some point in our soul's history."

She looked up into Václav's kind eyes.

"It is for you to tell," he said gently.

She cleared her throat. "Charles. Charles IV."

"The architect of the city," the violinist said. "Of course."

"Yet you say this house is not in Prague?" Kornel asked.

"No, not in Prague" Jane said.

"Where is it?"

"Back home in North Carolina. A settlement the Moravians—uh, the *Unitas Fratrum*—they built a colony there."

David spoke up. "The house she speaks of is in a cluster of buildings—the church in the center."

Jane slapped her forehead. "With eight streets running off it."

"Of course," David said.

"Ah, more sacred geometry."

"And this hallway is beneath one of these houses?" Václav asked.

"Yes."

The group looked at each other for a moment, then Kornel said. "Perhaps we are to play this piece in both places."

"Yes," two people said at once.

He continued, "Here in Charles's New Jerusalem, and in Jane's home, the harmonic, the reflection, of Charles IV's Prague. They have taken his seed and it has germinated in another land. We shall connect them."

A shiver ran up Jane's spine and goose bumps spread down her arms. A deep resonant 'yes' sounded in the depth of her heart. "That's it."

"I can arrange access to St Wenceslaus's chapel," Václav said.

They all sat back, satisfied.

"But," Jane's voice was tentative, hesitant. "How am I supposed to get so many instruments into a cave?"

Kornel laughed. "Do not worry. We will reduce the piece to its essential tones."

"Or record parts of it. You can sing the rest."

"I can carry in a trombone."

"But I'm not even supposed to be in the house now. The door is locked," Jane objected.

"God will make a way." Václav said this with such conviction that Jane was certain it would be so. After all, she had found the music, discovered her part in this quest, against all odds it had been revealed to her.

She looked over at David. She'd been reunited with her true love, the man who matched her perfectly, against all odds, in spite of her resistance and striving to control her life as she saw fit, of her fear of following her dreams. But it had all led her back, back to her origins, back to the place she'd been born, back to his arms.

"We'd better hurry, though. Solstice is only three days away," David said.

CHAPTER TWENTY-SIX

Jane hummed through the musical distillation of her composition for probably the thousandth time, keeping her voice low so as not to disturb the other passengers on the airplane. She took out the one-page score and checked her memory. Perfect. Just like she knew it would be. She had the music down. The real problem would be getting into that hallway. She knew of two entrances. The one off the basement of Miss Essig's house—her house, blast it—and the one beneath the root cellar of the Sisters' House. The other two houses must have entrances, and the church, but they wouldn't have time to go fumbling around. The plan was to try to get back into the house, then go to the root cellar if that failed. Without alerting anyone.

Yeah, right.

David said to trust in providence, that if she'd been given this sound code—the Czech musicians had dubbed it the Star Code. They said it would light the Eye of God in the center of the star. It still gave her shivers. Anyway, everyone agreed that if she'd been given this Star Code, then the universe would clear her path.

The Czech group had made arrangements to play the full piece with all the instruments at the exact time the winter sun reached its most extreme point—they called it the southerly declination and knew the degree. She glanced at the corner of the score where she'd jotted it down, just in case for some wild reason they needed to know. -23.5 degrees. It would be about

three-thirty in the morning in Prague. One of them had joked
they'd wait until 3:33 a.m., and everyone had been impressed
by that number for some reason. It had been over her head, but
she believed David. He'd convinced her that she didn't have to
know every single Masonic secret to make this work. Maybe
she'd study it all after the fact. David said he belonged to a
lodge that accepted women. Geez, it was the twenty-first
century, wasn't it? She smiled, remembering how earnest he'd
been. She looked over at him.

He stirred from his half-nap. "What?"

"Nothing." She reached out and stroked his cheek. Felt the
rough edge of his evening stubble. He could shave later, just
like she could figure out later what they would do when they
reached Winston-Salem. But she trusted her gut, just like she
trusted him.

He captured her hand and brushed his lips against the back.
Turned it over and kissed her palm. A warm thrill ran through
her frame. If nothing else worked out, at least they had each
other.

David had contacted James, who said he would keep this
secret. James would try to get keys to the house and the new
steel door protecting the opening to the cave. Failing that, he
said he'd learn to pick locks.

"I told him Brian could help him, but he said Brian wasn't
an initiate."

"Neither am I," Jane said.

"Yeah, just keep telling yourself that," had been David's
answer.

Now on the plane, she leaned back against the headrest and
closed her eyes. She tried to imagine how the underground
cavern she'd seen in her vision could exist beneath the church.
New Marienborn was built on the highest point in that area,
and Washington Park did have a creek. She remembered as a
child playing near an overhang where water had seeped
through the stones. A natural grotto with moss covered rocks
and a few pools up to her child knees where, if you lifted a
large stone, crayfish scuttled out, looking for another hiding
place. When she'd gotten older, she picked them up and
watched their pinchers snap together.

Up the hill and across the street a natural ravine took up a whole block, never developed. If it turned out there was no natural cavern off the hallway with the scarlet carpet runners, then she'd sing the Star Code, as the Prague musicians had christened it, in whatever room she did find. Or in Washington Park where the spring flowed into a creek. That was the best she could do.

She laid the score out flat on her tray table to study it once more, but David reached out and put his palm down over it. "Get some sleep. This will be your last chance. Besides, you know it cold."

She started to protest, then realized he was right. She did know it cold. Jane reclined the seat back in her cocoon in first class, turned off the reading light and closed her eyes. In her dreams, the stars sang accompanied by the sound of tricking water.

☆ ☆ ☆

Philip stood with Coche's security team tucked in a hallway off the main dome of the Capitol Building. It was twenty-four hours before the exact degree of the Solstice. Aleister had been right. The various lodges were gathering. In his ear piece he heard the reports.

"A man is approaching the Lincoln Memorial. He's walking up the stairs."

Then, "He's unfolded a camp stool and appears to be reading the paper."

"Two women have entered the Washington Memorial. They're taking the elevator to the top. Please advise."

Single men and women walked casually across the green lawns, taking up their various stations at the spheres of the Tree of Life. Apparently the lodges had changed their men-only policy for this evening.

"The police are ignoring them. They seem to be patrolling in pairs, walking up and down the National Mall."

"I see a canine unit. They seem to be working with the lodges. Please advise."

In every case, the head of Coche's security team told them to stand their ground. "Do not engage. I repeat, do not engage."

At dusk, Coche's people, or really Aleister's, began to arrive, taking up their stations just around corners from the people from the area lodges, trying for now to stay out of sight. Philip received orders to start a patrol around the whole Mall, to look for anything unusual.

The whole fucking thing was unusual, so he didn't know what to look for. He'd just stop anyone who tried to interfere with Aleister's people. On his way around the south side of the Capitol, he saw Paul Balford getting out of a taxi. He was carrying a small gym bag, but security did not search him. Instead, they greeted him and ushered him inside the big, white dome. Philip walked a few steps down the sidewalk and reported what he'd witnessed.

"We see him," came the clipped reply. "Carry on."

Philip raised his collar against the chill wind that was blowing in off the bay and kept walking. He passed the next center. One man who he'd seen in the meetings caught his eye and nodded, mistaking the side Philip served. Philip nodded back and kept moving. He noticed the Metro station that disgorged into the middle of the Mall was closed. He reported this.

"Roger," was the only answer he got back. He hated being on the fringes of a mission.

After an hour, Philip began to get fidgety. He felt like his scalp had tightened, like electrical currents ran over his skin. They must have started their magic. He walked by the White House fence and heard low chanting from two men standing in an alcove. Across from them, two of Aleister's people stood. One raised his hand and drew flourishes in the air, his index finger circled by an enormous gold ring with a red gem stone. The people from the Lodge redoubled their chant.

"They've started," he said in a low voice into his radio.

"Just keep a look out for stray pedestrians. Ward them off," came his orders.

Fuck. Some underling could do this job. He walked the perimeter for another half hour, listening to the dueling chants, the half-voiced commands, his whole body tingling by now. A dull headache built. He could barely tolerate not being able to know what was happening, being powerless to help. For the thousandth time he wished he had a modicum of magical talent. The sidewalks were empty. It was just too fricking cold to be out. He wouldn't even get to vent his frustration on some unsuspecting tourist.

A familiar voice cut through his dismal thoughts, sounding in his ear piece. "Philip." It was Coche himself.

"Yes, sir." Pride and adrenaline surged through him.

"That bitch Jane is headed for Carolina. I need you to find her and stop her. There's a plane waiting for you at National. Aleister says that's the main attraction. This Tree of Life business is just a sideshow."

Finally some real action. Philip stepped to the curb and raised his hand. A company car pulled up. He jumped in the back and they roared around the Mall, through the tunnel and over to the airport. He just hoped he'd be in time.

☆ ☆ ☆

The bustle of preparing for landing woke Jane. She accepted the warm towel from the attendant gratefully, then filled out her declaration form and sipped her coffee, willing herself back from the dream. The music had filled St. Vitus, filled Old Salem, then flowed north. At the end she'd hovered in the stratosphere, watching the wave of music engulf the globe. The dream had soothed every part of her. She just hoped this peace lasted. They had to collect their bags and make a tight connection to Charlotte, then fly through to Greensboro. That would put them in Winston-Salem around seven in the evening. True solstice occurred at half past nine.

The door to the plane finally opened. She and David were first down the jet way.

If the exact line-up of the sun even matters, Jane thought, as she grabbed her bag and headed toward customs.

They waved her through after a few perfunctory questions. She tried to keep pace with David's long strides. But they'd agreed the maximum effect would be gotten from playing at the same time in alignment with the cosmological event. Both groups of musicians.

Kennedy Airport reminded her of her old life and the familiar cynicism threatened to rise. What was she doing signing some magical song inside an old cave hoping to affect the balance of power in the world? It was patently ridiculous. She'd gone soft in the head.

Still, the music was real. Her vision of Charles IV seemed to have been more than a dream. The musicians in Prague had done so much for her that she would make every effort to stick to the plan, if only to honor their sacrifices.

They ran onto the plane and sat catching their breath from the dash through the airport. But they'd made it this far.

Anna Szeges gathered the last of the coffee mugs and loaded them onto the tray, then grabbed a wet sponge and started wiping tables. A blizzard had shut down the last weekend of the Candle & Coffee Tour, wind howling, drifts up to two feet, nothing any southerner would brave, or tourist for that matter. They'd canceled the event for the day, the bakery assuring the organizers that they had sufficient mail orders of sugar cake so the confection would not go to waste, and decided to try the next weekend since their charities, not to mention the museums, depended so heavily on this event.

It had been the right decision. A few warm days of bright sun had melted the last vestiges of the snow tucked in shadowed northern corners, lighting the green of the fir garlands and deepening their red ribbons. Crowds of locals and tourists had tromped through, listening to the history of the church and settlement, hearing about how the Moravians kept Christmas, even if they could deliver the talk themselves, then sipping coffee and munching sugar cake, buying candles, Advent stars and souvenirs.

Anna wiped the last table, then tossed the rag into a laundry basket. Her back ached, but she was happily exhausted. She paused in the corner and watched the quiet buzz of activity. Soon the last cup was washed, the tables folded and put away, and the floor swept up. Anna said her goodbyes and drove home, hoping she had enough time to soak in the tub, maybe nap, before the next ceremony of the season.

The OGMS met monthly, with the theme of their service reflecting the season. With Christmas just around the corner, Anna always felt their Winter Solstice ritual marked the spiritual beginning of her celebration. It was her private time to meditate with her close spiritual family, tend to her own devotions before throwing herself once again into work for her outer community during their observation of the Savior's birth. The business of the Candle and Coffee event was usually well over by now, and her thoughts had already turned inward to contemplate the miracles of Bethlehem. Not her hometown, but its namesake. This year she'd have to make this transition in a couple of hours.

In the Sisters' House, she climbed the stairs, turning down a cup of cider from Dorothea. "I'm going to rest a bit before our evening."

"Blessings to you, Mother Anna," Dorothea whispered to her as she climbed the stairs.

Dear Dorothea. The best of us all, Anna thought.

"Blessings to you," she said in return. "You get some rest if you can."

Anna climbed the stairs and went to the window of her bedroom. She pulled back the muslin curtain. The shadows beneath the trees of Washington Park deepened as the sun sank, settling and darkening early on this night. Solstice called her to let down and sink into the fecund darkness, to wait for the sun to call her back from stillness and peace. In the last light, thin, low clouds misted across the winter sky. Then the first star sparkled in the deepening blue.

Anna turned back to her now dark room and lit a candle. She knelt, giving herself to that mystical depth, her mind quieting like a caterpillar waiting for wings. From that silence a prayer rose, feelings more than words—a simple prayer of gratitude for all her austere riches. Then she ran a hot bath and soaked until her back eased. She crawled into her narrow bed and slept.

☆ ☆ ☆

Jane could barely remember what her car looked like or where it was parked, so they wasted some precious time going through the parking lot clicking the unlock button, waiting for lights to flash. At last she found it parked toward the back of the lot, grimy from rains and wind.

David held up his hand for the keys. "I'm faster," he said, so she tossed them to him, stuffed the last of their luggage into the back and slammed the hatchback down. As soon as she closed the passenger door, David roared off.

"My phone's in the pocket of my coat. See if you can get James," he said.

She found it and pushed the unfamiliar buttons. A male voice answered, muffled. "James?"

"Yes?"

"This is Jane. With David. We've landed. We should—"

David took the phone mid-sentence. She didn't even blink at his rudeness. This was no time to stand on ceremony.

"So?" David asked. There was a long silence. "We'll meet you there at nine o'clock." He ended the call.

"Do we need an hour?" Jane asked. "If we can't get into the hallways through the two ways I know, we'll have to do some searching."

"We can't just rush in there," David said. "We're going to be doing a ceremony. We need to get in the right frame of mind."

Jane realized he was right. "Okay, but how about fifteen minutes earlier?"

David chuckled. "Okay."

"How do you propose we get into the right mindset?"

"We'll go to my house. Take a shower. Change clothes. Then meditate."

"Meditate?" Jane asked. "But—" That's when it hit her. They'd left Knight's protection behind them. Or had they? She turned around in the seat and scanned the cars around them.

"Yeah," David was saying. "I can teach you a few centering techniques."

"Take a few extra turns on the way to your house. Let's see if we've picked up a tail."

She felt David go still. Then he said, "You think that Coche's spy might be following us? What did they say his name was?"

"Philip. Anything's possible. He's probably still looking for the nonexistent artifact."

"But Ivar said he'd gone back to the states. Probably D.C., right?"

"That's what he said, but let's just see. I'll bet Coche is rich enough to hire more than one spy."

David pulled off I-421 and headed to Main. He turned onto Gloria Avenue and headed down to Washington Park, then went back up the hill on Vintage. They'd gotten a block and a half up the hill when Jane spotted a black Mercedes making the same turn.

David grunted and turned down Broad, then onto Shawnee. The Mercedes made the same turns, then sped up, trying to overtake them. "Oh, no," Jane said.

"Damn it." David floored it, but the Ford was no match for the Mercedes. The car pulled up behind them and flashed its lights, then pulled next to them. The driver raised his hand and made the "V" sign with his fingers, then touched his chest.

"Thank God." Jane slumped back in the car seat. "It's Knight's security."

"Unless Philip has learned his secret signal," David said.

"Oh, you." Jane punched him in the arm. "Honestly."

"Ouch." David rubbed his forearm, even though he had on a thick coat. "It could happen."

The Mercedes had fallen back a car's length behind them. David started laughing.

Jane looked at him askance.

"I must be jet lagged."

"Let's assume he wouldn't reveal himself if he wanted to steal the artifact."

"Good point." David pulled at the collar of his shirt. "Besides, I need a shave."

"We're terrible spies, you know," Jane said.

"That's for sure."

Once they reached David's little house on Sprague, the man got out of the car and approached them.

"Name's Butch."

Jane bit her lip to keep herself from laughing. The tension and time shifts were getting to her.

"I'll be your detail for tonight. Knight thinks the main focus of the ancient enemy—" Jane flinched at the phrase, but he seemed perfectly serious "—is still in D.C. I've got a couple of other people around the church and houses."

"Thanks." Jane said. "We'll be leaving in just under an hour."

Butch looked at his watch. "Don't cut it too close."

"We just need to prepare for the ceremony."

He nodded, seemingly familiar with such oddities. He worked for Knight, after all.

Jane hit the shower first, then found some clean black slacks, added an only slightly wrinkled rose colored top, and sat down in the living room to wait for David. He arrived just ten minutes later, freshly shaved wearing clean jeans and a fresh white shirt, and led her through a short relaxation session.

Afterwards, Jane had to admit that David's meditation had certainly calmed her. Or maybe it was Butch's presence or just relatively fresh clothes.

"Ready?" David asked.

She nodded, not wanting to speak and disturb the relative peace she felt.

☆ ☆ ☆

While Anna finished washing up the tables from the Candle Tea, Valentin Knight waited for the sun to set over his country house outside Washington, D.C. He ate a last full meal, his cook's eggplant parmesan with a big salad. Then took his aperitif in the library where he consulted a few books.

Once the sun was fully down, he showered and dressed in his ceremonial robe, taking a long sweater for warmth, and retired to his temple. He began his invocation, waking his temple slowly, quickening each level with the same careful attention he had eaten his meal and dressed himself. He savored the awakening of the space. His vision doubled for a moment as the higher frequencies roused and began to vibrate, fill with high, sweet light. Time floated away.

Knight laid out what looked like two golden coins, both antique. The first was an original, the first seal of the United States. The center eagle gleamed, resplendent. The shield had thirteen stripes that in a paper copy would be rendered in red and white. In one claw, the eagle clasped thirteen arrows. In the other, an olive branch with thirteen leaves. Above the head of the eagle, a cluster of thirteen stars lined up, forming a Star of David. The stars were surrounded by a glory, like those seen above the heads of saints. The seal reflected light from the candelabras set at various points in the room, making it seem alive.

Beside this Knight laid another gold coin. This reverse seal depicted an unfinished pyramid of thirteen rows of bricks. Above it hung the Eye of Horus inside a triangle. Above this the words *Annuit Coeptis* appeared in an arch, and below *Novus Ordo Seclorum*. 'God has Favored Our Undertakings' and 'New Order of the Ages', both lines from Virgil. He fervently hoped for both.

Knight settled down to meditate. He spread his consciousness up and out, asking for assistance from the highest realms.

✯ ✯ ✯

Noise on the stair woke her from a dreamless slumber. Anna glanced at the clock. She had an hour to prepare. She rose, but did not turn on the light. She could see by candlelight, as her ancestors had. She washed up again, then dressed in her ceremonial robe. As she fastened buttons of the heavy velvet, she felt the presence of a larger being just behind a veil somewhere, waiting. Downstairs the other women had gathered at the back of the kitchen. Anna took up her own tall taper from the wicker basket on the island counter, unlit for now, and followed Dorothea, their roles now reversed.

Dorothea led the way, first through territory familiar to her daily duties, the homely root cellar, where the potatoes slept in the cold, the fall apples from their few trees gleamed red like holly berries. Then she glided down more steps and into the hallway that led to their sanctuary. The women followed in silence, Anna last. She locked the root cellar door behind them and put the skeleton key in a deep pocket of her robe.

The red carpet stretched ahead, warm beneath her thin slippers, then was replaced by a worn wooden floor that sloped down to a tall oak door with seven rounded arches above it. Dorothea paused here and closed her eyes. Anna sent a prayer for guidance. She felt an answer, almost a flutter of wings. She heard the door open and opened her eyes, her feet stepping onto natural stone.

Water trickled from deep in the cavern, the sound calming and soothing. Two biers of candles lit the granite walls, catching the gleam of a quartz vein on one side. At the back of the cavern, a spring bubbled from the rock wall. Over the centuries the water had worn curves and hollows until it had formed a natural grotto hung with white stalactites and deep folds in the stone, softened and rounded, stained red in places from the iron deposits in the surrounding rock. A shelf of that rock jutted from the wall, which the flowing water had obligingly hollowed, forming a tranquil pool of liquid before it brimmed over in rivulets that ran in a channel back into the cavern. Someone in the long past, probably before her own ancestors, had brought their version of the divine to this land, had flatted a long shelf beneath the pool, stretching in both directions, where celebrants could set vessels or books or whatever they deemed important. To the side, little toad stools of rock had formed from drips on the ceiling.

Dorothea walked to meet Boehme, who had arrived from the other side of the cavern through a similar doorway. He was followed by his flock of men just as Dorothea brought the women in her wake. Anna fell back, grateful to be led this night, to rest and follow. John found her on the edge of the group of men and they stood as close as they could in companionable silence.

Salali Waterdown stepped forward, nodded to the priest and priestess of the ceremony, then dipped her hands in the spring. She washed her hands and face, then plunged her hands in again, bringing up clear, clean water, flush with life-giving minerals. She drank.

At last she turned back to face the group. "I welcome you here on behalf of my ancestors, the *Tsalagi*, who kept this sacred cavern before you joined us in this land. In this place, we honor Aktunowihio, the spirit of the earth, and Yowa, the Great Spirit, who you called God the Father when your ancestors came," she nodded to Anna and John especially, "and taught us to love his son, Christ Jesus, whose birthday we honor soon." She returned to her place on the women's side.

Dorothea stood by the pool as Boehme circled the room carrying a stick of incense, its smoke trailing in the air like a cold breath. He invoked the powers of air and fire to join them in their celebration. He returned to Dorothea's side.

She held her hands over the pool of water and spoke of the feminine side of God, dipped a pine sprig into it and followed in Boehme's footsteps, invoking the elements of earth and water.

Then the two stood before the spring, Boehme with an ancient oak wand pointed downward, Dorothea with an elaborate golden chalice held up. "Tonight is the darkest night," her soft voice somehow filled the furthest reaches of the cave. "We enter the Lodge through the Gate of Death."

☆ ☆ ☆

David drove the short distance to Miss Essig's house. They parked on Leonard Street, near her grandfather's old farmhouse, memories of chickens, apple trees and bees flooding her mind, then walked down to Dinmont, the road her father had tried to name Diamond, telling her mother he promised he'd give her a diamond one day.

Damn it, this is my home, Jane thought. *I'm getting it back tonight.*

They cut back toward Miss Essig's old Tudor. The windows were dark. Jane reached down to pet Winston, then realized with a stab the old, stolid bulldog was not with her. She missed his comforting presence. Smiled, remembering that night she'd heard the singing from the tantric room, their adventure that had led to all the rest. She brushed her hand across her forehead as if to wipe these extraneous thoughts away, but the images kept coming, accompanied she realized by the growing swell of music. The composition had begun to play in her mind.

They ducked into the evergreens lining the side of the property, avoiding the circular drive, and cozied up under one tree, letting the branches shield them and their eyes adjust. A sharp evergreen scent filled the air, clean and welcoming. A dark shape approached. Let out a soft whistle. David answered with the opening bars of a Christmas carol, plausible if anyone overheard.

James appeared in the gloom of the trees. "Nobody at this house. Lots of activity at the Sisters' and Brethren's' House. Something's up," he whispered.

"Good," David said. "Got the key?"

"I do, but Dreher's changed the locks to the house, too."

"I might know a way in." Jane pushed out from the cover of the trees and walked down the edge of the drive, avoiding the gravel. She ducked around to the side of the greenhouse, the two men following. Others probably watched that she couldn't see. She made her way to the back porch steps and bent down, pushing the panes of glass. Her fingers found the sharp edge of the broken one. "Here," she whispered.

David nudged her aside, took out a pocket knife he must have picked up at his house, and started working the rest of the pane loose. James pushed his way in next to her, wiggled on his leather motor cycle gloves, then took hold of the sharp edge, pulling it periodically until at last it gave way. He eyed the opening. "I'm not sure I'll fit."

"I can," Jane said, not really sure this was true. But she stuck her head and shoulders through, then stretched until her hands reached the ground. Once she felt secure, she angled her body and forced her hips through. It was a tight fit, but she kept wiggling until, with a painful scrape, she fell onto the greenhouse floor. Her upper thigh burned, but she had no time to inspect it. She ran to the basement door, hunched her shoulders in anticipation of some alarm going off, and opened it.

Silence.

David and James walked through.

"I cut the security wire," James said.

"That worked?" David asked.

He shrugged, then added, "And I brought a torch."

"We're not burning—" He switched on the flashlight just as she remembered he was from Edinburgh and spoke British instead of American English.

David took the flashlight and headed toward the laundry room, walked through to the back room and started pushing on the pine panel. Jane felt along the wall until she found the right spot, gave it a shove, and the wall clicked open, revealing the new steel door. James took a key from his shirt pocket with a flourish and handed it to Jane with a slight bow.

She smiled in the dark, then with a whispered prayer, inserted it into the shiny new lock. It opened with well-oiled precision. "Thank God," Jane breathed.

Philip watched Jane's group disappear through the basement door. He took out his Glock and waited a full minute before following. He found the door to the underground complex open and slipped through.

Jane stepped onto the red carpet, familiar to her more from the dream she'd had so many times than her one visit. The composition surged louder in her mind.

David followed, lighting the floor ahead with the beam of the flashlight, James bringing up the rear. They reached the turn. She paused, pushed the inner music aside to listen. A faint murmur came from the right side, so she turned in that direction, wondering if the hall would match her dream. And it did. Old, worn wood replaced the scarlet runner. Instead of steps, the floor sloped down. They inched their way forward, the composition playing in time with her breath. The murmurs they'd been hearing resolved into voices, the words still indistinct.

In front of them rose a tall oak door with seven rounded arches above it. Jane flattened her hand against the wood and found it unlatched. She pulled it open. The music swelled to a crescendo. The smell of damp earth flowed in on a faint breeze, the sound of water trickling, and voices, now distinct. The music quieted again.

"We enter the Lodge through the Gate of Death," a woman intoned.

With a start of surprised, Jane recognized the voice. Dorothea.

A semicircle of women separated Jane from the two people in front. Dorothea held a golden chalice, the man a wand. They were dressed like people in a Pre-Raphaelite painting. No one had noticed Jane's group yet.

Then the man in front proclaimed, "In the dark of the Winter Solstice, the Sun is reborn. In death as in the Lodge, we are reborn to the spirit."

It was Boehme, the man she'd first meet at the lawyers when they'd explained the trust to her. He'd come to the house when Anna had found out about the sedative. She could barely hear him through the music playing in her mind, growing louder. Jane stood blinking in surprise.

David came up to stand with her. James stood at her left side.

No one saw Philip enter.

★ ★ ★

The deep, winter silence of Knight's meditation began to vibrate. He heard voices beginning their own invocation accompanied by the trickle of water. The sweet strains of a violin sang through the aethers, answered by the mellow golden-bellied sound of a French horn. Images of a tall cathedral on top of a hill flashed in his inner vision. Then a song rose, a song he had memorized from a copy sent to him from Kornel in Prague. They must be in St. Vitus. He hummed along softly.

At the apex of the music, he bent and lit an old Chi Rho oil lamp in the middle of the altar. The scented oil wafted through the air. The universe hummed, one harmony of wholeness. A bud of new life formed, but remained sitting in the womb of this sound.

★ ★ ★

"This is the night the prophecy spoke of," Dorothea continued, "yet the key has not been discovered. Boehme will take us into prayer and meditation that it might be revealed to us."

"Let us close our eyes." Boehme sent up a prayer on the wings of his soft voice, asking the Mother to visit on her soft, dove wings. The Father to send his light.

Jane leaned heavily against David, the music building again, all the sounds of the orchestra playing through her. Her body tingled, her hearing faded. She clung to David's arm, her orientation threatening to slip away entirely.

Then Boehme's words came clear as a rung bell. "Let us listen in silence."

Jane's mouth opened as if of its own accord and she began to sing the simple chant the musicians in Prague had given her. David joined in with his part.

A startled murmur ran through the semi-circle of people.

The music rose like a freed dove, soared into the perfect acoustics of the cave, and hovered there, the perfect tones of a crystal bowl or chimes. White light fracturing into the beautiful garnets, emeralds and golds of stained glass windows. Those Prague windows. They must be playing.

She was led forward. Heard whispers, gasps of surprise.

"She cannot come here," a lone voice protested.

"It's all right, Dreher," Boehme whispered. "She belongs with us."

Then hands grasped her arm and guided her. Her eyes were open, but the music had blinded her. David sang the answering ground notes, and the two spirals joined, forming the double helix of life.

The tinkling, trickling song of the spring called to her. It sang of life, of moisture, of growth. Her composition reached its own song of growth and the two joined forces, surging, tingling with triumphant life. Verdant green spread in her mind's eye—the vigor of plants, the heat of the sun. And red— the scarlet of summer roses, the vermilion of blood, of ruby wine in a golden chalice held up in gratitude.

"She has the key," Dorothea whispered. "Oh, praise Jesus, she has the key."

✩ ✩ ✩

Philip had been biding his time, waiting for someone to produce the artifact. He hadn't believed that song and dance about not having the key for a minute. He stood watching everyone carefully while Boehme prayed in the front. It had to be a distraction. Someone would slip out the side door— probably the men's side—and bring in the artifact.

Nobody moved. He waited patiently, a coiled snake ready to strike. But when Jane started singing, his head started buzzing, filling up with static. His nerves frayed and jerked, like he was standing too close to high voltage electrical wires. He tried the breathing techniques he knew, but that only heightened the disorientation. The images before him blurred.

He pushed through the crowd and grabbed the fat woman in front. Put his gun to her head. "Nobody move."

Boehme made a move toward him.

"I said stop." He spit the words through clinched teeth.

The male leader of the ceremony captured his attention. "Please put the gun down. Nobody wants to hurt you."

Philip tightened his grip on the old lady's throat. Why wasn't she screaming? He tried to focus on the man, but his face swam. If that Jane would just stop singing. Nausea rose in his throat. He couldn't stand being in here any longer, but he had a job to do. He shook his head to clear it.

A symbol clashed and clanged from somewhere behind Jane. She glanced back and her vision cleared. A strange man—she knew it was Philip, Coche's spy—stood in the open door, pointing a gun at the crowd. Jane knew she should react somehow. Stop what she was doing. But somehow she wasn't afraid. He couldn't stop them now.

Philip had grabbed Dorothea.

Jane reached out her hand and felt the spring water flow through her fingers. She'd expected it to be cold, but it was tepid and smelled faintly of iron. She only had to reach the end of this next soaring phrase, duck her head into the fountain of life, and release the last aching note. Then this fountainhead of new life would be released. Would permeate the liquid silver that flowed from this sacred wound in the earth, moist cleft in the side, and it would spread through the earth, dripping grace, spreading the balm of forgiveness and new life, of salvation. Yes, her eyes moistened and tears flowed. She could use that word again.

All sound was magnified. She heard the gun cock.

Jane flinched.

She pushed her hand against her mouth, trying to staunch the flow of sound, to save Dorothea, but it was beyond her now. She was not the one singing. Not really.

Never mind, dear. It was Dorothea's voice in her mind. *I have lived a good life.*

Tears flooded. Dorothea's voice blended with Miss Essig's last question to her. *"Will you accept this house and all that it entails?"*

Jane nodded again. Her heart said yes.

Then Miss Essig's last words, *"You were always such a good girl."*

With a sob, an apology, yet still jubilation in her heart, Jane knelt and sang the last note.

The key entered the lock.

It turned.

☆ ☆ ☆

The blur of motion to Philip's right caught his attention. A man rushed at him. He aimed and fired. But that didn't stop the music, that grating, sickening music that fogged his mind and made his gut churn.

He threw the old lady on the ground and ran out of the cavern.

☆ ☆ ☆

The gun shot deafened her. A heavy thud told her Dorothea had joined Miss Essig.

Jane fell to her knees and wept into the spring.

The opened lock released the flood. The music hit home, swirling in the water, expanding and flowing out and down, gushing out to spread this freshness, this vigor, yet this soft absolution, this new chance to fulfill the old dream.

Still a part of her wondered how a mere song could change anything, but she knew it would. That it already had. She could feel it happening right now beneath her feet, inside her body, feel the earth thrumming, the heavens rejoicing, the stream of freshness flooding out.

Philip had been too late.

☆ ☆ ☆

Jane's voice filled every crevice in David's raw heart, whispering that yes, it was real, this promise of reconnection, the glory all teachings spoke of, this reuniting with God. It soothed away the pain of all separation, of death. He fancied he heard Marley's voice in his ear, *"I love you, darling. I'm so proud of you. It's okay to love again."*

In his mind, he heard the supporting bass, the horns rising up and singing their bold promise of life. It must be the Prague musicians.

"Nobody move."

David spun around to find Philip standing in the center of the opened door, a Glock in his hand. He motioned with the pistol for the women to part, to line up to his left. Dreher melted back behind two of them.

The coward, what was he doing? Then Dreher dropped to the ground and began to crawl toward the wall.

"No," David shouted, trying to stop Dreher from leaving.

The barrel of the gun swung directly at him, wavered. Philip moved toward Jane, but grabbed Dorothea, round and beatific in her white robe with the purple sash. Her eyes flew wide for a moment, then, unbelievably, she smiled, her grey eyes accepting.

"I said stop," Philip shouted.

Jane covered her mouth as a child trying to stop herself from talking out of turn, her eyes wide. Then she turned back to the spring and dropped to her knees, singing all the way.

David lurched toward her.

The gun fired.

Screams filled the cave, then the triumphant last note from Jane's music rose up, creating a golden moment of pure stillness before all hell broke loose.

The crowd parted and David saw Dreher stretched out on the cave, crimson blood pooling on the red dirt, Boehme on his knees trying to staunch the flow, his own white robes turning a deep scarlet.

Dorothea frowned, shook her head in denial, then lifted it and closed her eyes, listening. The cavern echoed back Jane's song.

David ran to Jane, still on her knees by the spring. Her eyes looked misted, as if they'd caught a glimpse of life behind the curtain that usually separated their mundane world from the celestial realms and were still dazzled by the light. He put his hands beneath her armpits and helped her to her feet, then steered her away from Dreher's body. She focused on David fully.

"Dorothea." She shook her head, her eyes crinkling. "Poor Dorothea."

It took him a second to understand, then he said, "It wasn't Dorothea."

"She's alive?" The look of relief was quickly replaced by a frown. "Then who?"

David hesitated.

"Anna?"

"No, Dreher. He jumped Philip and—"

"Is he— "

"I think so," David said.

He glanced over toward the knot of people around Dreher. Reverend Szeges now knelt beside the body. The small group joined hands, bowing their heads. Reverend Szeges began to pray softly.

Jane moved toward them, but David held her back. "There's a lot of blood. He got shot in the head."

She hesitated, then pulled him to the edge of the group.

Reverend Szeges had opened his eyes and was speaking in a rhythmic, formal way. "Our Lord has said: he that hears My word, and believes Him who sent me, has eternal life, and comes not into judgment, but has passed out of death, into life."

David recognized the Liturgy for the Dead.

A few in the group responded, "Thou Savior of the world, so teach us to number our days, that we may apply our hearts unto wisdom."

Anna took off her robe and draped it across Dreher's face and shoulders. Then they sang.

Of course, there's music, David thought. *They're Moravians.*

"It is not death to die,
To leave this weary road
And midst the brotherhood on high
To be at home with God."

☆ ☆ ☆

Knight sat watching the flame of the Chi Rho oil lamp, its red center lightening to orange, then yellow. He heard the song begin again, this time a woman's voice. Then a sharp crack broke through it. Knight flinched. But the ripped edge of the ritual's fabric was grasped by hands of light, familiar hands, and a newly born spirit from the Gate of Death stretched across the black, gaping void and grabbed the other side of the tapestry, then began to weave it all back together.

Knight helped his friend, singing the glory all over again, while tears flowed for the loss of this earthly companion. But loss? For here Dreher was. He and Knight sang, and their music wove the fabric back together.

Hours later, Knight made his way to a corner where his butler had prepared a cot for his vigil, and allowed his body to sleep. But his inner vision remained watchful. The ritual was not complete. Not yet.

The composition was repeated by a choir of angels somewhere high above even Knight's reach.

He turned over and slept deeper.

CHAPTER TWENTY-SEVEN

Jane and David pulled back from the group around Dreher's body and moved a few steps toward the door they'd come in through. Frank stood in conversation with Salali Waterdown.

". . . can't have the police down here," Salali was saying. "It just isn't allowed."

"But there's been a murder," Frank's voice matched her low whisper.

"This cave belongs to the tribe. It was excluded from the land grant. Legally, the Cherokee Nation has jurisdiction here."

Frank reached out to Jane as they drew closer. "Thank you. Now we know why the lot called you home."

"I'm sorry about Dreher," Jane said.

Frank put his arm around her and squeezed, then turned his attention back to Salali. "What should we do?"

"I'll call my cousin. He works for the tribe. They can remove—" she shook her head, a look of disbelief passing over her face "—Dreher's body. Take it to the coroner. They'll file a report."

"Where's Philip?" Jane asked.

Frank raised his shoulders in a shrug. "He ran. Nobody knows. We were too concerned with Dreher."

"We've got him," a gruff voice announced from the door.

They all started, surprised by this sudden arrival.

"Had some help from the locals," the massive man said.

Frank moved in front of the door. "Who are you?"

"This is Butch," Jane said, "one of Knight's security team."

Frank's eyebrows climbed up his forehead. "As in Valentin Knight? The head of the Lodge of Melchizedek?"

"That's correct, sir. I'm afraid Philip slipped by our perimeter." He stood at attention. "I take full responsibility."

Frank gave Jane an appraising look. "How do you know Valentin Knight?"

"We've done business together in the past. He gave me a tour of D.C.," Jane explained.

"A tour?" Frank's eyes bugged.

"Mr. Knight gave us strict instructions to guard her with our lives, but we didn't think it right to come into the—" Butch glanced through the doorway "—err, lodge itself."

"Certainly not," Frank said.

"Again, sir, my deepest condolences." He took in the trousered legs sticking out from the white robe covering the rest of the body. "One fatality?"

"That's right," Salali said.

"I'll report to Mr. Knight. He said he would handle any legalities in case—"" he pointed again toward Dreher's body.

"Uh, all right," Salali said, frowning at Frank.

He shrugged. "That solves one problem, at least."

"The house is secure, ma'am," Butch said to Jane before stepping back through the door.

Frank gave her a weak smile. "I think I can safely speak for the group. The house is yours, Jane."

Jane wiped a tear from her cheek. "Thank you." She took David's arm again and he led her back through the hallway.

Butch followed.

They took the stairs up to the kitchen and stood blinking in the light.

Jane thanked Butch again, then asked, "You said you had some help from the locals. What happened?"

He looked chagrinned. "Yes, ma'am. Apparently a couple cousins of yours had been watching the house. Their dogs tracked Philip when he ran and cornered him."

"Cousins?"

"They might still be outside."

Jane headed for the backdoor.

"Wait," David objected. "Is it safe?"

"Yes, sir," Butch said, but they both followed close on her heels.

Jane stopped in the circular drive and a pack of beagles engulfed her, their tails a blur. She stooped down and started stroking their ears, talking to them. Pink tongues washed her face. Two men in overalls and boots stood to the side watching. One leaned on a long hunting rifle. Jane extracted herself from the dogs and walked over to the men. The beagles followed.

David walked up to Jane and touched her elbow. He didn't want her out of arm's length.

"Oh, David," she gestured toward the two men, "Meet my cousins Leroy and Clyde."

They regarded him through narrow eyes. Under their scrutiny, he felt a sudden impulse to propose to Jane immediately.

"What happened? How were you even here?" Jane asked.

"Daddy had hisself a 'tuition.'"

"A what?" Jane asked.

"A feelin'. Had a strong feelin' we should come see about you. Thought you were in danger," Leroy said. "We come up here to the park and let the dogs a'loose. Figured they could nose out anybody fishy."

Clyde nodded. "They headed straight for the house. We heard gunshots, then some fella come running out like his britches was on fire. The dogs took off after him. Treed him just like a coon." Clyde guffawed, then flinched and looked around.

Nobody objected to his language. David didn't see the point.

"Anyway, this here fella—" Clyde pointed at Butch "—he had hisself a pistol and he got that other fella outta the tree and trussed him up like a wild turkey and threw him in the back of this fancy car. Then he told us what he was hired to take care of you." Clyde's voice went up at the end of this last statement, turning it into a question.

"That's right," Jane said. "We work for the same . . . firm."

Clyde and Leroy considered this for a minute, Clyde digging a trench with his boot. Leroy drew out a packet of chewing tobacco from his overall pocket. He frowned at Jane and stuffed it back into his pocket without taking a pinch.

David took a step forward, holding out his hand to shake. "I'm Jane's fiancé."

Jane made a chocking sound, which she quickly masked as a cough.

"I want to thank you all for catching this man," David continued. "He's a murderer, and he was out to hurt us."

"Murderer, huh?" Clyde said.

"Ya'll gonna call the sheriff?" Leroy asked.

"That won't be necessary," Butch said.

They both grinned rather maliciously.

"We need to interrogate him," Butch added.

"Gonna waterboard him?" Clyde's eyes lit with enthusiasm.

"If necessary." Butch's tone was almost prim.

Leroy took keys out of his pocket. At a gesture from him, the beagles all jumped into the back of an old, green pickup truck. "Well, I guess we better be goin'."

"Lessen you need some help with that fella," Clyde offered.

"We can handle him," Butch assured Clyde.

"How's Uncle Pat?" Jane asked rather belatedly.

"Getting' ready to meet his maker, I reckon," Leroy said.

"Tell him thank you," she said. "I'll come visit real soon."

Leroy nodded his head, made a little salute to Butch, then looked at David again. "You comin' too?"

"I reckon," David answered, matching their language.

The two got in the truck and it started with a sputter. The dogs began to bay. "Shut up, now," Clyde shouted out the window.

David, Jane and Butch waved as the truck lurched out of the driveway.

Butch turned to her. "Your cousins are quite resourceful."

Jane laughed. "They are, aren't they?"

Butch smiled in return. "The house is secure. I'll just be finishing up with the . . . uh—" he stopped there.

David flashed on Dreher's body, the blood pooling on the cavern floor.

Jane thanked Butch. "David's here. I'll be fine. I guess I'll hear from Knight in the morning?"

"Or Spencer," Butch said. "Mr. Knight's head of security. Mr. Knight is in seclusion at the present time." He bid them goodnight and headed off into the basement again.

Jane climbed the back stairs.

David followed, suddenly exhausted. "Should I make us some tea?" he asked.

Jane put her hand to her head. "I think I need something stronger."

"Brandy?"

"Sounds perfect."

David found the bottle and poured a finger each into two glasses. Handed her one.

"Let's go into the library," Jane said. "I wish Winston was here. And those crazy cats."

"I'll be right there," David called after her as she headed down the hall. He pulled out his cell phone and made a quick call, then went into the library.

Jane knelt before the hearth, absently wadding up newspapers. "I feel terrible, David. I never got the chance to . . . well, I was still pretty resentful over him kicking me out of the house."

David knelt beside her and placed a generous pile of kindling on top of her already too big mound of paper. Then he placed three logs on top of this in a pyramid. "That's understandable. Just send him your thoughts now. Or at the funeral. Pray about it."

"He was just doing his job," Jane said mournfully.

"I'm sure he forgives you, Jane. Why don't you go sit on the couch?" He took a long match from the container Jane kept by the screen and struck one. He lit the paper in several places, moved the screen to block the flames, then sat next to her. "Besides, he gave his life for a good cause, didn't he? It seems to me that we were successful."

Jane lifted her head. "Yes, we were."

David picked up his drink. The ritual seemed far away now. "Tell me."

Jane relayed the whole story to him, sorrow and guilt giving way to wonder as she told him about how the sound had taken her over, how she'd knelt and sung into the spring, how the energy had run through the water. "But what will happen now, David? What exactly did we do?"

Just then a knock sounded on the backdoor. Jane stopped. "Do you think that's Frank? I thought I heard them all leave."

"I'll check," David said, trying to hide his smile.

Sure enough, standing on the back step was his son. David opened the door and the bulldog shouldered by him and trotted straight for the library.

"Winston!" came Jane's joyous cry.

David's son put the two cat carriers down on the kitchen floor and opened them, then straightened up as two cats shot out and ran for cover.

David took his son into a bear hug.

He laughed in surprise, then patted his father's shoulder. "Welcome home, Dad."

"Thanks. I know it's late. I wouldn't have asked, but—"

"It's no trouble, really. You're well? The trip was good?"

"Yes."

"Listen, I'd love to hear more, but I've got work in the morning."

"It's all right. Let's get together soon."

"See you at the Lovefeast? Then come for Christmas dinner. Should we expect two?" He smiled at him expectantly.

"Yes, two." David saw his son out and returned to the library. Winston sat on Jane's lap still trying to lick every part of her face. The cats had taken up their positions, one on the back of the sofa, the other on the ottoman.

Jane looked up when David came in. "Thank you." She pushed the dog's face away and patted the seat cushion. "Sit."

David settled next to her and Marvin jumped up into his lap.

"Now the whole family is home," she said.

☆ ☆ ☆

Christmas Eve came with its usual parade of Candlelight Lovefeasts, three in many churches. All the Moravians came to church on Christmas Eve even if they didn't come any other times—well, except for Easter. And all the other people in town came, too—Protestant, Catholic, Jewish, pagan, agnostic and even atheist as far as she could tell. They all celebrated the return of the light, whatever language they used to explain it.

And they enjoyed the cultural festival of Moravian coffee, buns, beeswax and music as much as a proclamation of faith for many of them. The simple meal, music and candle lighting made everyone feel a warm glow.

Jane went to David's church and helped behind the scenes, filling up the baskets with Moravian buns, making sure the crepe paper trim on the beeswax candles was pushed down so it wouldn't catch on fire during the service. David played in the brass band before each service, served coffee with the men during the Lovefeast, then brought out candles. After their third service, she couldn't drink anymore coffee or eat another bun. She waited for him near the door, but his progress toward her was continually interrupted by people chatting amiably with him. When he finally reached her, he said something about her giving him a ride to his house as they were leaving. She agreed.

It was all for show, but surely even the people they were putting on the show for knew he was staying with her. She didn't think they really cared, but she'd do whatever helped him feel comfortable. She needed his even breathing in the night, his solid flesh to brush against, whenever Dreher's pooling red blood flashed before her inner eye.

Since she'd sung her composition to the spring on Solstice night, she read a few papers every day, watched various news channels, and went through the important financial blogs, waiting to see if anything would change. Hadn't the prophecy spoken of a shift? But the world seemed to be trudging along as usual—heading straight to hell, as Uncle Pat had put it when they'd visited him. She'd been surprised to find him still living. Misty even reported he was a bit better.

That evening they got home from church and switched on their tree. They'd found Miss Essig's Christmas decorations up in the attic and trimmed a tree, bringing over some of David's favorite ornaments from his house. The Advent star had already been hung. Not bad for a late effort. No presents though. Well, she had bought a few trinkets from the Christmas markets in Prague that now lay around the crèche under the tree. David had objected, saying he didn't have anything.

They poured themselves a taste of brandy, hoping to cut through all the coffee they'd drunk. She sat in front of the fireplace in the living room, the *Wall Street Journal* and *London Times* spread out on the floor in front of her. She asked David to repeat the prophecy to her.

He sighed rather dramatically, she thought, then closed his eyes and recited it for probably, she had to admit, the hundredth time in the last few days. "In the center of the grid laid down by your ancestors lies an eight-petaled figure, just as there is another where the lost treasure is kept. There are those who would control it to stop the feeding of the grid. This will block your leadership from the new guidance."

She shook her head. "That spring is definitely not an eight-petaled figure, but I suppose the church and surrounding choir houses could be called one. One thing I do know. That spring sure started a strong flow of some kind of energy."

David smiled, listening to her recitation once more.

"What we did was part of this prophecy," she insisted. "It just felt necessary. Like something I'd been fated to do."

"Václav says the Prague musicians felt the same. Maybe the eight-petaled figure is there in St. Wenceslaus Chapel. Maybe we just made the connection from there to here." He shrugged. "Who knows what it all means."

She folded up the papers, then on impulse tossed them on the fire. "I did finally compose music. I'd always wanted to do that."

"It's a beautiful piece," David said. "And I found my lost treasure."

She looked up at him.

"You. I found you again," he said.

Warmth flushed through her. Contentment. Peace. It was a night for peace, wasn't it?

But she couldn't resist saying, "Yeah, I found an old artifact myself."

He smiled, then reached for her.

She held out her hand and he pulled her to her feet. They made their way up to their makeshift bedroom where they'd pushed two single beds together. They still couldn't quite imagine sleeping together in Miss Essig's room. Maybe after they were married. They'd planned a simple service in early January. Frank didn't seem to mind David's being with her beforehand. Anna suggested the OGMS had some helpful teachings about marriage and a ceremony. Jane told her they'd like to do it in the spring. She now realized the extra ceremony her family had celebrated at her confirmation had been her initiation into the OGMS.

Uncle Pat was the only one who kept asking when the wedding was and where David was living. She laughed, remembering David's announcement to her cousins that he was her fiancée. What a proposal that had been.

She pushed open the bedroom door. The two cats lifted their heads, nestled amongst the covers. Marvin meowed softly, his red mouth a good match for the poinsettias she'd bought yesterday. Suzie B blinked an eye, then returned to her nap. Winston lay across the foot of the beds, taking up half the space.

"Would ya'll make some room, please?" Jane said.

★ ★ ★

That same night, Valentin Knight finally left his vigil. He dressed carefully in his ritual robes, gathered a few implements of magic, then carefully lifted the Chi Rho oil lamp, still burning from when he'd lit it on Winter Solstice night. He called his car, gave the driver directions and rode in silence, watching the silvered countryside give way to suburban shopping malls. They reached the National Mall, which lay quiet under the moon. The neoclassical white buildings lined it like large wedding cakes in a row at a baker's shop, their edges softened by the moonlight.

Knight's limo drove down into an underground parking garage. A man rushed out to open his door. Knight got out, careful with the lamp, and they walked silently into the building, and made their way through the passageway from this office building into the Capitol itself.

His group had already assembled. Several of them had also been in silence since the night of the solstice. He nodded to Minerva, his second in charge, who began the invocation.

The circle of power built quickly. The seed energy had been sent and been sitting here for three days, silent like the sun at the southernmost point in the sky. Solstice. When the sun stands still.

But in the morning, at dawn, which would be soon, the sun would begin to move northward again. Christmas Day. This was the true gateway. He'd been silent, preparing, letting the energy build inside him, waiting for this moment.

Knight stood in the middle of the group, eyes half closed, and savored the energy. The circle was complete.

He nodded and the group began to chant, one woman a high soprano, another matching her at a fifth, then the others with their lower tones down to his dear, old friend George Remus, who hummed a deep bass note. It was Jane's composition, or the skeleton of it sent to him by the Prague lodge.

Knight waited until the music filled him, began to vibrate and move within him. He felt the sun outside nudging toward the horizon. The music built to a crescendo. Then he knelt on the Capitol floor beneath the dome next to the eight-petaled star where someone had placed a pure, white candle. The eight-petaled star designed by La Trobe that had replaced the original eternal flame. Both with the same meaning. Marking the sensitive spot, the energy center of the entire nation, of the dream of a New Order of the Ages. Not control by the elite. No, that had been the old order. Rule by kings, popes and aristocratic bloodlines.

But the new dream. 'We the People'. The dream of liberty.

They would take the new order back from the dream of money, of oil, gas, diamonds, stocks and bonds—that had wrestled it away from them.

Knight sang the last notes of Jane's Star Code into La Trobe's star, the marker set by that Moravian and Mason so long ago.

Then Knight lit the white candle sitting in the very center from the Chi Rho oil lamp. The light in the Eye of God burned bright.

The energy seeded in the star vibrated, then began to fill like water behind a dam. At last it burst open, flooding the eight lines that moved off this center star, flowing out along those lines of power, built to a flood, a gush, pushing away debris, blockages, quenching the fire of beings set to guard and block and pervert. The tsunami swept it all clean.

The group gradually fell silent, swaying in their places, savoring their work.

Knight intoned the ending of the ritual, thanking those beings who watched over the rim of their world, who blessed their endeavors. Releasing them.

They all parted in silence, each making their way home in the predawn glow.

☆ ☆ ☆

Dreher's funeral was held the day after Christmas. They'd had to wait longer than the traditional three days, but it was impossible to hold a funeral on Christmas Day. David played trombone. Jane stood beside Frank, just as she had for Miss Essig's funeral.

John Szeges led the service. People came from all over. Knight even attended and brought along dignitaries whose names made James and David's eyes bulge. Apparently the elite of the metaphysical world. They all shook Jane's hand and thanked her in serious, sonorous tones. She nodded and murmured her thanks to them, bemused by it all.

When business started again after the holidays, the news began to change. Congress passed the president's sweeping energy bill mandating the country switch to solar, wind and other alternative methods within a few short years. Somehow the same voices mocking this goal, declaiming it as impossible, as efforts to sink the country, sounded off key, out of touch, hopelessly out dated. The stock of the companies that built green technology soared while oil and gas reported its first quarter of losses.

Behind the scenes, men that Jane knew had led cabals of bankers, investors and industrialists frantically fought for survival, but their claws no longer seemed to find purchase. Fortunes were lost overnight. Young heirs, used to fast jets, women and civil servants at their beck and call, stood like deer in headlights. Some committed suicide.

Mr. Davis, her former boss, kept leaving frantic messages for her to come back to work, to pull some of her old strings, to return files that had never existed. Then the papers reported he'd been arrested for fraud, along with Tami. Even the Saudis were ruffled. Jane wondered what they'd do now. Knight had thrown them a life line. It was still not too late to grab hold of it.

The next morning Jane read a report that Henry Coche had been arrested for art theft. "Coche had in his possession a large oil painting by William Blake said to belong to a colonial organization in the Carolinas."

Jane pushed the paper over to David when he came down for coffee. "Look, they found the big Blake painting."

"Of all his crimes, that's what they got him on?"

"Ironic, isn't it."

"I'll say."

The news seemed to become the news again. The hysterical voices, the histrionic accusations, the name calling, the dirt digging flared up for a while, but people changed the channel and it died down, like a bonfire that had consumed all its fuel.

Jane watched in amazement. Her own money was safe. She'd invested in the new companies while she'd moved Knight's money that autumn day that seemed long ago. In fact, her money had doubled. She'd have to start a charity or something, she joked with David.

"What do you think happened?" she asked.

He shrugged. "We did our part. Václav and the guys in Prague did theirs. We'll probably never know the whole story."

"But it was just music, David," she said for the hundredth time.

He smiled. "Yes, it was just pure sound that set it all right somehow."

"Anna wants us to take the OGMS class on the married couple's liturgy, as she calls it. Want to do it?"

He put the newspaper down on the couch and regarded her. "Sure. Think we'll learn something new?"

Jane stretched suggestively. "Who knows? Our ancestors were sure full of surprises. She says after our wedding in the church, they'll do a special ceremony just for us down in the cavern, then we can go into the tantric room."

David looked doubtful. "Alone, I hope."

"Of course. When I found that room, I would never have imagined being invited to use it."

"Well," David began, but Winston trotted into the library carrying his leash, saving him from further comment.

Jane burst out laughing. "Who taught you that trick?" she asked the bulldog.

"Probably my boy," David said. "Let's go for a walk."

Jane let Winston off his leash once they reached Washington Park. They swung around toward the grotto she'd played in as a child, the grotto she now knew was fed by the spring beneath the hill. The water trickled down from the cliff which was hung with a few icicles in the deep shade.

They passed it by, letting the magic be.

ACKNOWLEDGEMENTS PAGE

Thanks go first to Marsha Keith Schuchard for her book *William Blake's Sexual Path to Spiritual Vision*, which started me on this path. My greatest gratitude goes to Rev. Dr. Craig Atwood, Charles D. Couch Associate Professor of Moravian Theology and Ministry and Director of the Center for Moravian Studies, who had already done all the research I thought I'd have to do and published it in books that amazed me. Thank you for saying a simple, "Yes, Zinzendorf did teach those things" to this amazed Moravian.

Of course, not everything in this novel really happened, but I did start on firm historical ground before I leapt off a cliff into my imaginary world. I'll be blogging about what's real and what's imagined after the book is released at http://theresacrater.com.

Thank you to Dominick Carlucci for his help with sacred geometry, especially the Eye of God. Thanks to the Winston-Salem Writers manuscript group, and others who offered writing advice, including Thea Hutcheson, Lynda Hilburn, Jonna Turner, Cynthia Kuhn and John Jackman. Thanks to Dean Wesley Smith for his workshops, my editor Jenifer Butler and cover artist Su Kopil.

Thank you to my ancestors for persevering.

Last of all, great thanks go to Stephen Mehler for taking me to the event where I discovered Schuchard's book, for going with me to Prague and Herrnhut, and for his enormous heart.

ABOUT THE AUTHOR

Theresa Crater brings ancient temples, lost civilizations and secret societies back to life in her paranormal mysteries. The shadow government search for ancient Atlantean weapons in the fabled Hall of Records in *Under the Stone Paw* and fight to control ancient crystals sunk beneath the sea in *Beneath the Hallowed Hill.* Her short stories explore ancient myth brought into the present day. The most recent include "The Judgment of Osiris" and "White Moon" in *Ride the Moon.* Currently, she teaches writing and British lit in Denver.

Visit her at http://theresacrater.com

See more at www.crystalstarpublishing.com

READ MORE BY THERESA CRATER

Novels
Power Places Series
Under the Stone Paw
The Illuminati have opened a hole in time, and now one of them steps through
Beneath the Hallowed Hill
One shot at unlocking the secrets buried beneath the Sphinx
Short Stories
"Bringing the Waters"
The High Priestess of Hathor must discover if the change in the skies above Egypt spells out doom for their world.
"The Judgment of Osiris"
The ancient gods of Egypt reach through time and claim Owen as their next sacrifice.

Available at www.crystalstarpublishing.com

Made in the USA
San Bernardino, CA
09 May 2017